ELLEN, COUNTESS OF CASTLE HOWEL

ELLEN, COUNTESS OF CASTLE HOWEL

ANNA MARIA BENNETT

Edited and with an introduction by
Mary Chadwick

WELSH WOMEN'S CLASSICS

First published in 1794 by the Minerva Press, London
First published by Honno in 2024,
from the second Minerva Press edition of 1794.
Hugh Owen Building, Aberystwyth University,
Aberystwyth, Ceredigion. SY23 3DY

Introduction © Mary Chadwick, 2024

No part of the book may be reproduced, stored in a retrieval system, or transmitted in any form, or by any means, electronic, mechanical, photocopying, recording or otherwise without the prior permission of the copyright owner.

A catalogue record for this book is available from the British Library.

Published with the financial support of the Books Council of Wales.

ISBN 978-1-912905-99-7
ISBN 978-1-916821-05-7

Cover image: Julius Caesar Ibbotson,
Penillion Singing near Conway, 1792
Cover design: Liz Gordon
Text design: Elaine Sharples
Printed in the UK by 4edge Limited

Introduction

MARY CHADWICK

Anna Maria Bennett (*c*. 1745-1808) was one of the most popular novelists of the late eighteenth and early nineteenth centuries. She wrote six novels between 1785 and 1806: *Anna: or, Memoirs of a Welch Heiress* (1785), *Juvenile Indiscretions* (1786), *Agnes de-Courci: a Domestic Tale* (1789), *Ellen, Countess of Castle Howel* (1794), *The Beggar Girl and her Benefactors* (1797) and *Vicissitudes Abroad* (1806). Her first novel, *Anna*, sold out on the day of publication and, in 1794, *Ellen* saw a second edition just three months after the first. Bennett was praised highly by many reviewers including Walter Scott and Samuel Taylor Coleridge, who described *The Beggar Girl* as "the best novel ... since [Henry] Fielding". She was also compared very favourably to Samuel Richardson and Frances Burney, who are now part of the canon of eighteenth-century fiction, and her works were read by Jane Austen and her family, feeding into Austen's juvenilia and the development of her own writing.

Over the last few decades Bennett has received somewhat sporadic critical and readerly attention. Feminist scholars have explored her portrayals of women's work and socio-economic position in late eighteenth-century Britain, and researchers who consider British literary history with a focus on Wales have paid particular attention to Bennett's two Wales-related novels, *Anna* and *Ellen*. Bennett's works mark a transitional stage in British fiction writing. The pacing of her novels is often fast and lively. Her main characters are drawn to be largely engaging or repellent but they are rarely two-dimensional or lacking in nuance, and her supporting cast members are provided with personality and depth. Bennett's novels reflect the canonical texts of the eighteenth century; she looks back to the tropes and motifs used by Jonathan Swift and Henry Fielding, notably in her humour and satire, her comic characterisation, and her development of plots centred on orphans who navigate choppy courses through early adulthood before finding security through marriage or inheritance or both. At the same time, she foreshadows nineteenth-century novelistic developments. Her narrative voice sometimes takes on the ironic tone for which Austen would become known and her depictions of gender and class relations have been described by Miranda Burgess as a forerunner of Dickens' social novels. *Ellen* is marked by literary trends such as the Gothic, by the ongoing processes of the integration of Welsh culture and people into Great Britain, by contemporary ideas about female education, and by the experiences of Bennett and her daughter as mistresses of wealthy, high profile men. Writing at a time of great personal stress, Bennett spun these themes together to create a text which, while sometimes contradictory or ambiguous, has a gripping plot, engaging characters, and a wealth of detail regarding late eighteenth-century life in a society which was marked by both tradition and transition.

The details of Bennett's early life remain obscure. Even her name is sometimes given as Agnes, rather than Anna. She was born in Merthyr Tydfil, sometime in the 1740s (an informed guess based on the 1761 and 1781 birth dates of her daughters). Her father was probably a David Evans, who was a customs officer or a grocer or both. At some point in Bennett's childhood the family appear to have moved to Bristol. Following her early marriage to a Mr Bennett of Brecon, who may have been a tanner or a customs officer, Bennett found her way to London where she worked in a succession of jobs including in a workhouse, a slop shop and a chandlery. It was in the chandlery that she met Sir Thomas Pye (*c*. 1708-1785), a wealthy and well-connected admiral of the Royal Navy. Sometime in the late 1750s or very early 1760s Bennett became Pye's housekeeper and mistress, enjoying an improved degree of material and financial comfort. She had at least four children with Pye during their time together: Thomas, Harriet (*c*. 1761-1865), Nancy and Caroline (b. 1781). The couple's relationship broke down in the 1780s, apparently in part as a result of Pye sending Bennett a letter intended for another of his mistresses. Although Pye made good on his promise to leave Bennett an inheritance of his house in Tooting, she experienced financial and emotional distress in the decades after the end of their affair. She moved between London and Edinburgh – where she briefly managed the Theatre Royal – navigating fluctuating fortunes. She died in Brighton in 1808.

Reading an author's biography into their work can sometimes be a risky business but *Ellen* does seem to reflect Bennett's experiences, and those of her daughter Harriet, as women negotiating financial and sexual relationships with little training or security. Several of Bennett's novels, notably *Anna*, *Ellen* and *The Beggar Girl*, engage with the issue of women's position in British society, with a focus on women's economic dependence on men and the difficulties faced by those who lacked familial financial support. In Wales, Ellen is effectively sold into marriage with Lord Castle Howel in order to save her grandparents' estate from the clutches of their grasping neighbour, John Morgan. Another financial transaction – the payment of her gambling debt by a man who is not her husband – brings about suspicions of adultery and the loss of Ellen's good reputation in the eyes of "polite" London society, precipitating her separation from her husband and her flight to the north of England. There are distinct biographical parallels between Bennett's childhood in Wales, her move to London and her subjection to the judgemental gaze of metropolitan society.

Letters which Bennett wrote to Pye between 1781 and 1785 chart the shift in her status from loving mistress, pregnant with baby Caroline (who was born in the winter of 1781), to financially pressed former lover. The letters are novelistic both in the events they describe and in their tone as Bennett's distress and anger cause her writing to become more and more passionate. The intertwining of a woman's body with her financial worth bubbles beneath the surface of Bennett's novels *and* letters, becoming explicit when she describes her own heart as "Poor disappointed ... honest and I will say ... Valuable" (Westminster City Archives, 36/71, undated, 1785?). Pye adhered to his promise to leave Bennett a house in his will but she clearly feared poverty in his lifetime: "your will is Like to do vast things for a woman, who Living, you have obliged to take up her bed and Walk, who is sent from the ark to where no olive Branches Grow ... it is more irksome than any Earthly Gratification to me to be obliged to Stand in supplant of my own subsistence" (Westminster City Archives, 36/72, undated, 1785?). The phrasing and passion apparent in the later letters resemble the dialogue Bennett wrote for the character of Winifred, Ellen's Welsh maid.

Perhaps because Bennett felt her own lack of preparation for the world she entered, the theme of female education is particularly significant in *Ellen*. Raised in innocent and unsophisticated seclusion in Wales, Ellen goes to school in Bath, where she receives training in polite female accomplishments, but must then navigate the unforgiving London social scene with little understanding of its unwritten rules. The preparation of young women for the world was the subject of much discussion in the 1790s and *Ellen* takes its place in those debates. Some late eighteenth-century writings, notably Mary Wollstonecraft's *Vindication of the Rights of Woman* (1792), sought to reform society alongside, or through, a reformation of the ways that young women were taught. Other authors focused on the ways that the education of girls and young women might prepare them for the world as it was, and it is this latter approach which can be seen in *Ellen*. Moira Dearnley reads in the novel a significant element of anger on Bennett's part regarding the position of women in British society, notably her belief that young women were rarely truly equipped to be independent of men. Bennett appears to have done her best to counteract this dependency – she trained her daughter Harriet for the stage and hoped that another daughter, Nancy, might support herself through drawing. Bennett, Harriet and her fictional heroine Ellen all entered a kind of prostitution, bartering themselves or being bartered by men in attempts to gain financial security for their families, before being forced to deal almost alone with the implications of those transactions and the results of those relationships breaking down.

The preface, or 'Apology', which Bennett added to the second edition of *Ellen* makes clear that she was suffering acute distress as she wrote the novel, as a result of legal battles which saw her lose a significant amount of money. In the early 1790s, through the influence of her lover, Douglas, 8th Duke of Hamilton (1756-99), Harriet gained the lease of the Theatre Royal in Edinburgh, in a partnership with Stephen Kemble. When Harriet returned to the London stage in the winter of 1792-3, Bennett took her place as theatre manager in Edinburgh. Hamilton appears to have pushed Kemble out of the theatre, resulting in a legal battle which caused Bennett much stress. Kemble and his associate John Jackson sought to regain the lease at the same time that Harriet's husband sued the Duke of Hamilton for having "criminal intercourse" with his wife. In the preface, written as an apology for errors perceived in the first edition, Bennett makes clear that her experience of "the greatest Distress, both of Mind and Circumstances" was the result of a gendered imbalance of power, as Kemble and Jackson "forgot their Character and Manhood, to combine against the Laws… and the Sex they were born to protect" (p. 12).

While there is clear evidence of Bennett's precarious gendered experience, any biographical foundations for her portrayals of Welsh life and the sustainability or decline of Welsh culture are more obscure. At the end of the eighteenth century, as revolution and war made continental travel less appealing to wealthy Britons, attention turned to Wales, Scotland and Ireland. People rich enough to travel in comfort toured Wales, discovering for themselves the sublime views of Welsh mountains and the "unspoiled" nature of Wales's countryside and inhabitants. Alongside this surge in domestic tourism there arose a rage for novels set in Wales, Scotland, Ireland, and less well-travelled parts of England. Bennett's first novel,

Anna, capitalised on this literary trend. Nine years later, *Ellen* saw Bennett return to her literary, and biographical, origins.

Bennett did not deviate from the convention of Wales-related novels whereby an innocent, open, straightforward central character (usually female but sometimes male) is raised in Wales but then encouraged, or forced, to encounter corrupt metropolitan life, usually in London, where individuals concertedly seek to appear, rather than to be, honest. This common narrative trope enabled authors to draw comparisons between a virtuous life in Wales and the appealing but dangerous society of a large city. In these novels, lines are blurred between accurate portrayals of Welsh life and the reproduction of stereotypes (positive and negative) which readers expected. Bennett's depictions of mountainous, wild Welsh landscapes and an ancient great house are both accurate *and* informed by the fashion for Gothic literature which predated the trend for Wales-related novels. The home of Ellen's grandparents, Code Gwyn (probably a mis-spelling of the Welsh name 'Coed Gwyn', meaning 'White Wood'), is, at the beginning of the text, crumbling yet well-maintained, through the hard work of its female inhabitants. Exhibiting a widely recognised Welsh trait, the family offer generous hospitality to unexpected guests. When these guests first arrive, they interrupt a stereotypically Welsh scene in which the Code Gwyn family and their servants are gathered together in the great hall, singing and dancing to music provided by a harpist. The impact of an English presence upon this scene is significant. The butler hurries to shepherd the servants back to their quarters, in a capitulation to an English system centred on a much more stark differentiation between social classes. This contrast between English and Welsh ways of life runs throughout the novel although it is most pronounced in the first volume. The Welsh home of the "anglicised" Lord Castle Howel is much more comfortable than that of the proudly Welsh Meredith family. As Jane Aaron points out, social sophistication throughout the novel is aligned with adherence to English norms. When Ellen leaves Wales for an education in a school in Bath, Bennett describes the shame her Cambrian heroine feels as she recognises her unrefined accent and her lack of ladylike accomplishments. To be educated into the ways of a proper young lady, Ellen must move away from Wales and her Welsh family, adopting English manners and behaviours.

As well as their use of a set of oppositions centring on Wales/England, country/city and virtue/vice, authors of Wales-related novels often incorporate characters who hail from other parts of Britain, or who have travelled around the globe, particularly to the East or West Indies. *Ellen* is no exception. Bennett includes Scottish and Irish characters; her heroine travels from Wales to Bath, then to London, and then to the north of England; and she imports one of her villains, Lord Claverton, from a military career in the West Indies. One of the functions of these characters, and journeys, is the exploration of a developing sense of British unity and the consideration of Britain's geo-political status at a time of war on the continent and the ramping up of colonial exploitation. The Act of Union between Scotland and England (and Wales and Ireland) was brought into law in 1707, creating the state of Great Britain. The different cultures of the four nations had been interconnected for centuries before the Act of Union but the eighteenth century saw efforts on the parts of authors across many genres to chart and shape the development of particularly British identities. Simultaneously, the reassertion of the historical, linguistic and cultural specificity of Wales, Scotland and Ireland took on increased significance; it is no coincidence that the eighteenth century saw the creation of both the Honourable Society of Cymmrodorion, and the Gwyneddigion Society, designed to support Welsh culture, and the Welsh language, inside and outside of Wales. Bennett explores in both *Anna* and *Ellen* the nature of the relationship between Wales and Britain, and between Welsh culture and a developing British outlook.

Bennett's uses of Welsh settings and characters in her novels are more thoughtful than some of her fellow authors' deployment of details of Wales as simple splashes of "local colour". Critics who write about these particular texts often note the relationships between Bennett's depictions of women's experiences and her portrayals of Welsh life and culture. Francesca Rhydderch, for example, reads Bennett's young Welsh female characters as symbolic of the nation of Wales, to be scrutinised, "improved" according to English ideals, and exploited by English (or Anglicised Welsh) men. The treatment of the specifically Welsh ways of life which she outlines in the first volume of *Ellen* similarly suggest Bennett's reflections on the sustainability and value of Welsh culture in late eighteenth-century Great Britain. As Sarah Prescott observes, Bennett's first Wales-related novel, *Anna*, ends with a relatively positive and optimistic portrayal of Welsh life and of cultural difference from England, as the newly-wealthy heroine makes her life in Wales. At the close of *Ellen*, the heroine and her beloved new husband appear invested financially and emotionally in their (extremely substantial) Welsh estates, and in the communities which they support. But a sense of loss nevertheless haunts the text. Older characters have died or dramatically aged, the fabric of the

Merediths' house and the lands of the estate have declined, and there appears to be no question of Ellen and Percival, whose virtuous characters were so strongly formed by their Welsh upbringings, making their life together anywhere other than London. No doubt inflected by the stress of Bennett's experiences at the hands of men, and British law, it seems that the virtue, generosity and kindness exhibited by the proudly Welsh Meredith family will not be sustained.

REFERENCES:

Aaron, Jane, 'A national seduction: Wales in nineteenth-century women's writing', *New Welsh Review*, 7/3 [27] (1994), 31-8.

Burgess, Miranda, *British Fiction and the Production of Social Order, 1740-1830* (Cambridge: Cambridge University Press, 2000)

Dearnley, Moira, *Distant Fields: Eighteenth-century Fictions of Wales* (Cardiff: University of Wales Press, 2001)

Prescott, Sarah, *Eighteenth-century Writing from Wales: Bards and Britons* (Cardiff: University of Wales Press, 2008)

Rhydderch, Francesca, 'Dual nationality, divided identity: ambivalent narratives of Britishness in the Welsh novels of Anna Maria Bennett', *Welsh Writing in English*, 3 (1997), 1-17

Mary Chadwick has particular interests in eighteenth-century women's writing, gender and nationhood, and unpublished or neglected poetry, letters and journals. She has published on Jane Austen, Mary Wollstonecraft, Mary Barker, and the histories of "ordinary" British women, and would like to dedicate this edition of *Ellen, Countess of Castle Howel* to Alwyn, Bertie and Ted.

NOTES ON THE TEXT

This edition of *Ellen, Countess of Castle Howel* is set from the second 1794 Miranda Press edition of the novel which includes the 'Apology'. Its aim is to present a readable text that reproduces the original published source as closely as possible. With this balance in mind, a few archaic spellings (e.g. 'color', 'to-day') have been silently amended. Bennett's original spellings of personal and place names have been retained, however. A very few capital letters and full stops have been added or removed to aid readability. A more substantial number of commas have been removed, although copious quantities remain. There are also a few silent corrections to word order. Chapters were incorrectly numbered in volumes one, two and three of the 1794 edition; the numbering has been corrected in this edition, which also includes a few explanatory footnotes added by the Honno editor.

The reproduction of Welsh and other regional dialects was common in eighteenth-century fiction. Bennett's representation of the Welsh maid servant Winifred's mode of speech has been left as published. Letters transposed in her discourse include C for G ('Cot' for God), F for V ('fery' for very), P for B ('putter' for butter), V or F for W ('vat' for what, 'fith' for with), and T for D ('tairy mait' for dairy maid, 'tog' for dog).

Winifred is also the mouthpiece for Bennett's use of language and modes of thought now recognised as deeply racist and antisemitic. These expressions, including the words 'neger' and 'blacks' used in a derogatory way in volume one, and the words 'turk' and 'Jew' used similarly in volume three, have been reproduced as Bennett wrote them.

ELLEN, COUNTESS OF CASTLE HOWEL

ANNA MARIA BENNETT

"Others make men, I only report them." MONTAIGNE

VOLUME I

Apology

Although a Work sent into the World confessedly abounding in Error, will not allow a Defence, it is hoped it may admit an Apology.

The History of Ellen was composed at a Period, when the Writer was, in consequence of Engagements, entered into on laudable Motives, involved in the greatest Distress, both of Mind and Circumstances.

The few who know the Author's History, for the last Eighteen Months, know also, the little reason she had to apprehend the evil she has encountered. But it is to Him only, who fashioned the Mind of Man to the destined Trials, her *Sufferings* can be known.

Four Hundred Miles distant from Home, Family and Friends, a Stranger in a Country, where she was literally *taken in,* her Spirit broken, her Health impaired, her little Fortune sinking, the unoffending Victim of a Party, who forgot their Character and Manhood, to combine against the Laws they professed to Support, and the Sex they were born to protect, her Domestic Peace and *dearest pride* totally destroyed, what wonder Female Fortitude sunk under such accumulated Ills? and that as a Resource from Mental Derangement she sought, in the airy Regions of Fancy, any Subject which by diverting thought from "Self," might sometimes afford a temporary "oblivion of Sorrow."

At this Time, and under these circumstances, was Ellen conceived and brought to maturity. Thus, then, she is presented to the Public, as an alleviation of Grief and Misfortune; and as such, may her demerits meet indulgence from the Bosom of Sympathy, and her Errors escape the keen Edge of severe Criticism; may the Reader, happier than the Author was, and more capable than she ever will be, become at once both Judge and Protector.

LONDON, MARCH 12, 1794

Chapter I

On one of the dark stormy nights of December, when the wind and snow without, opposed to a cheerful circle round the blazing fire within, formed a striking contrast in favour of the latter, the family of an ancient Baronet, whose seat was embosomed in the brown mountains of North Wales, were suddenly disturbed by a noise which called forth its native guards.

Lion, Whitefoot, Bruin and Dulcet, quietly stretched at the feet of the domestics before a large kitchen fire, were instantly roused. Scarce had Edward Griffiths, the grey-headed butler and house steward, unbarred the folding doors which lead into the court-yard, than the aforesaid guards rushed out in full cry; and in a second, the report of a pistol was heard.

But before I proceed further, it may be proper to describe the family and mansion, thus unusually disturbed.

Code Gwyn, is a large Gothic mansion, built at a time, when imperfect laws and civil discord obliged the chiefs of the country to consult safety, more than pleasure and convenience, in the construction and situation of their houses; it stood at the foot of a very high mountain, on the top of which still remained the ruins of a fort, which was its defence to the north; it was surrounded by innumerable trees, planted time out of mind, and forming avenues in all directions, which, as the branches entwined, excluded the solar ray: at the end of one of the front avenues ran a rapid and, now, discoloured torrent, over which was an antient stone bridge, the scene of many a bloody fray, when the gallant ancestors of the present family maintained their right against the inroads of the mountaineers.

The building itself was in the form of a fortress; it was enveloped with high walls, and surrounded by court yards; the top of the middle building was crowned with turrets, and at the four corners stood towers, whose nodding ruins seemed to tremble at the ravage of all destroying time; the entrance was through a pair of large, heavy oak, folding doors, into a spacious hall, ornamented with rusty swords, shields, helmets, trophies, banners and bucks horns. On the opposite side were a pair of correspondent doors, which opened to the mountain; but, as a lawn intervened, free from the heavy plantations, which were carried in a serpentine form to the old fort, they admitted, what was excluded from every other part of the house, the uninterrupted light of heaven. The windows were large, heavy, and ill painted; the shutters and frames, oak, which the long labours of household damsels had converted into mirrors: the floors and grand staircase were of the same materials, and in the same order; the furniture, particularly of the best apartments, was grand, but antique; and, though every part of the house exhibited proofs of great female management, the damask hangings, in spite of neat darning, were in a ruinous state. The hall appeared to be the bond of union between the heads of the family and the domestics – there the harper had his seat, and there the avocations and labours of the day constantly closed with a dance, in which all the younger part of the inmates mingled, without a frown on the brow of pride, or presumption in the bosom of poverty.

Sir Arthur Meredith was, at the period this history opens, in his seventy-fifth year, tall, corpulent, and, apparently, robust; a profusion of white waving locks parted on his fair open forehead, and conveyed some idea of their hyacinthian beauty, before age had silvered them over; his large black eyes still retained the fire, which, when animated by sensibility, or inflamed with anger, was, in either degree, pleasing or awful; a Roman nose, florid cheeks, and teeth still perfectly sound and white, formed a face, that, from youth to age, could hardly be said to decay, since, in both, it was remarkably handsome; but time had been less lenient to his person; that had been so tortured by habitual gout, and chronic disease, as to render the use of a wheel-chair necessary, whenever he removed from one apartment to another, on which account, the room adjoining the great parlour, formerly a library, was his bed-chamber.

Lady Meredith, six years younger than Sir Arthur, was a tall thin woman, whose mild blue eyes, fair complexion, and a certain placidity of countenance and manners, invited confidence, and inspired respect; her heart was the seat of truth, and her tongue the law of kindness. She was the heiress of a noble Welch family, whose dignity far exceeded their wealth; her estate was exceedingly involved when she married Sir Arthur, who was of too thoughtless a turn to attend to payment of either principal or interest; the mortgage had been foreclosed, and the estate long passed into other hands.

This venerable pair had been blessed with a numerous offspring, four of whom were now living.

Edmund Meredith, who, as second son, was, according to the antient custom of the family, brought up to the church, in order to enjoy the living of Code Gwyn, into which he was inducted by his father; having lost his elder brother, was now heir to the estate and title. His character will be best told by his actions; his ostensible residence was at the rectory, but most of his time was passed at Code Gwyn.

Catherine, a virgin of thirty-two, had early in life imbibed a taste for reading. The old library abounded with romances, and she had been eighteen years dreaming of dwarfs, tournaments, distressed damsels and wounded knights. She read till daylight, slept till noon, wrote verses, took snuff and seldom wore whole stockings; but, with all her eccentricities, her heart was sensible to the finer feelings. Without a regular system of conduct, she was benevolence itself; she could seldom keep a shilling in her purse, and as it happened that there always were those, in or out of the family, who wanted some article of clothing, and as Catherine Meredith was sure to be the confidant of such wants, her wardrobe was very ill furnished.

Lewis was a lieutenant in the navy, who, on account of the eminent assistance of Sir Arthur at a strongly contested election, had been recommended to the patronage of a naval commander; but the party interest having coalesced, and Sir Arthur of no further use in that point of view, the young man had served ten years a lieutenant, and had been now absent on the West India station four years.

Agnes, a handsome woman of twenty-six, a great manager, who, in conjunction with Mrs. Martha Griffiths, housekeeper, and sister to the butler, made the best pastry, pickles and preserves in the kingdom; she was also famous for home-made wines, mead and vinegars; the brewer had his directions from her, and she had all the merit of the fine flavoured cyder; she inspected, with Mrs. Griffiths' assistance, both dairy and poultry, and if the female servants were disposed to be idle, they were sure of a lecture, for she exactly knew the quantity of knitting or spinning their other business would permit; and, as the profits were her own allowance, she was, comparatively, rich.

Mary, a very plain girl of twenty-two, had the rage of scribbling on her. She was so happy as to have a bosom friend in the next parish, subject to the same disease; and as their correspondence, which was carried on in fictitious names, was the mutual joy of their lives, it is not impossible, but the world may be one day favoured with the letters of LUCRETIA and AMANTHIS.

There was also in this family a petted grand-daughter, the posthumous child of their eldest son, who died in a decline, and was followed by a beautiful young woman, his wife, within one hour after the birth of her infant.

Sir Arthur Meredith succeeded his father in an estate of two thousand pounds a year, charged with a heavy mortgage, and younger children's portions.

The family lived precisely in the same style, from generation to generation; the same number of domestics, the same mode of living, and the same rental from their farms; and having neglected to raise their tenants, equivalent to the advance of every necessary of life, these had grown into opulence, as their generous landlord had, insensibly, become involved in difficulties.

Sir Arthur, therefore, so far from discharging the debts and old incumbrances, was every day adding new ones.

John Morgan, Esq. a rich neighbour, willingly advanced to Sir Arthur, on every emergency, and the ease wherewith money was obtained, so lulled the Baronet, and he was, besides, of so easy, hospitable and benevolent a disposition, that, while he saw the long familiar faces of his train of domestics, while his old coach held together, and the almost foundered coach horses could draw his Lady and family to church, while that family were tranquil and happy, he seldom burthened his thoughts with the state of his finances. As the rents came in, the steward paid them away; when money was wanting, Mr. Morgan provided it, without giving Sir Arthur any other trouble, than just signing a parchment, by way of security, in which, indeed, lately, it had been thought proper for Mr. Edmund Meredith to join.

On the evening the disturbance happened I began to relate, the family at Code Gwyn had, according to antient custom, been dancing out the old year, and the younger part had just left the great hall on a summons to supper, when the firing of a pistol called every being out, save Sir Arthur, who was lame, and his Lady, who, being subject to nervous affections, had not power to stir.

Sounds of different voices approaching the house, mingled with joyful exclamations, still more excited the wonder of Sir Arthur, when a sun-burnt young man, in blue uniform, entered and knelt before him, followed by the whole posse who had gone out, and two other strangers; one, a square built man in blue, the other, a tall, sickly looking person, enveloped in great coats.

Lewis Meredith had nearly fallen a martyr to the climate, rather than leave his ship, when the Colonel of a regiment on the station became, unexpectedly, by the death of his uncle and cousin, a Peer of the Realm of Great Britain; some wild excesses having rendered his absence from England convenient and necessary, he had exchanged a lieutenancy in the guards for a company in the West Indies, and after long residence was thought to be dying, when, by the opportune departure of his relation, he became a Peer, and a man of fortune. Mr. Macshean, surgeon of the man of war to which Lewis Meredith belonged, a Scotchman of great medical knowledge, had been persuaded by the lieutenant to give his attendance to Colonel Claverton, who wanted confidence in the Surgeon of his own company, and Meredith, out of *his little,* assisted the Colonel's very reduced purse.

The first thing Colonel Claverton did, on receiving the news of his good fortune, was to take his passage home, and as nothing was so dear to him as self, and as he believed Lieutenant Meredith one of the best sailors, and Macshean one of the best Doctors in the world, he prevailed on the Commander in chief to give each of these officers leave to return to England, on account of health, and generously engaged to pay their passage.

Meredith, as we have said, was an invalid; but Macshean's motives for accompanying his noble patient were too deep and manifold to be at this time delineated. They set sail in a Merchant-ship, which brought them, after a tempestuous voyage, off Anglesea, where they were obliged to put in, and, to the Lieutenant's great joy, he found himself, after a few hours travel, thirty miles only from his paternal home.

The weather was intensely cold; great quantities of snow had fallen, and, before the mails were established, every traveller knows how tedious and difficult a journey from those parts to London was; Lord Claverton was really too much indisposed to undertake it, and the inns being inconvenient and ill furnished, it was with great satisfaction he heard a chaise and four would carry them in the course of one day to a comfortable habitation.

At the rattling of the carriage over the stone bridge, the dogs, who were unused to the sound of any but the heavy old coach wheels, took the alarm, and the foremost having reached the chaise, just as the friends were assisting the invalid out, he, who was not remarkable for patience, fired his pistol and shot the animal dead.

Never was family more united than that of Code Gwyn: Sir Arthur wept aloud on his son's neck, while his daughters were dividing their attention between their almost fainting mother and the welcome brother. Mr. Meredith pressed the Lieutenant to his fraternal heart, the servants crowded in, and old Griffiths sobbed.

Those exquisite sensations in some degree subsided, in respect to the strangers, and the Lieutenant had no sooner introduced Lord Claverton by name, than Griffiths hurried the domestics out of the parlour.

Lady Catherine rose with dignity to welcome them; Miss Catherine figured to herself the idea of a sick knight, and advanced nearer, to take a full view of a person, whose arrival savoured much of the books she had studied. Miss Agnes retired immediately to consult Mrs. Griffiths on the new arrangement of the table; and Mary, having a Lord for her subject, was determined to begin a letter, that very night, to her friend, Miss Peggy Jones.

Sir Arthur and Mr. Meredith were inborn gentlemen; they respected, without being abashed at the presence of a nobleman, and the true politeness, inherent to the character they supported, rendered their compliments easy to their guests, and had the effect of composing the rest of the family: mutual introductions took place, an easy chair was drawn next to the fire for the invalid, Miss Agnes sent in a salver of cordials, and old Griffiths set about some additions to the table and sideboard, with the activity of twenty-five.

The company being thus comfortably seated, congratulating each other on the event of the night, were, a second time, alarmed by a voice of female distress. The folding doors were thrown open, and a young girl appeared, tears streaming from her eyes, her hands and face smeared with blood, and dragging in her arms the still bleeding carcass of poor Lion. A sight so new and unexpected, struck them with amazement, particularly the strangers.

"My dear girl," said Mr. Meredith, "where have you been, in the joyful confusion of the night I had quite forgot you."

"See," said she, sinking under the weight of the dead animal, "see what the strange men have done! O, my dear dear Lion," throwing herself by his side, "what harm had you done to them? You only took care of your own master and mistress, and they have killed you for being better than themselves."

Lion was a great favourite; joy at the arrival of their young master had licensed the intrusion of the servants, regret for the animal, again brought them to the door; an awkward girl, niece to the housekeeper, sometimes maid, sometimes champion, and, oftener, companion to the distressed damsel on the ground, pushed in, and taking the dog in her strong arms, desired the fair mourner to be comforted; for a very good reason, all the crying in the world would not bring Lion to life; and, for her part, she was sure the strangers were negers, for none others would hurt such a harmless creature; and, inteed, she thought "Master Lewis might a come to his own home, without bringing savage negers with him." At the end of this speech Winifred Griffiths thought proper to stalk out with the dead animal in her arms, without deigning to cast a look around.

"My dear child," said Lady Meredith, "we are all sorry for poor Lion, but you must not forget your uncle."

The Lieutenant, though very fond of this young relative,

could not help laughing at her appearance, which she observing, retreated behind Sir Arthur's chair, who advised her to go and compose herself. "In the morning," said he, smiling and looking at the blood, "you will not be quite so much in dishabille."

This gentle hint turned her attention to her own figure; "Gracious!" she exclaimed and happening to encounter the face of Macshean, distended into a broad grin, ran out of the room covered with confusion.

"A very extraordinary young lady this," said the Peer, smiling ironically.

"She is a very good girl, my Lord," answered Lady Meredith, "the accident to Lion wholly engrosses her; you will like her better, when you know her more."

"Every body likes Ellen," said Sir Arthur.

"Your grand-daughter, I presume?"

Lady Meredith bowed.

"Lion was the largest of his kind," continued his Lordship, "I ever knew to be a lady's favourite."

"His appearance, it must be confessed, was a little formidable," answered the Surgeon.

"I expected him at my throat," returned the Peer.

"I dare say, my Lord," said Miss Meredith, gravely advancing, "you took him for some miscreant Knight in disguise?"

"Madam!"

"I say, my Lord, I presume your prowess would not have been exerted against the poor dog, had you believed him to have been a dog; but, as Code Gwyn has certainly the air of an enchanted castle, and Lion was so uncourteous, it was natural for you to conclude he was some disguised enemy; I am extremely concerned your arms, which have, doubtless, been bright in conquest, should be disgraced by so ignoble a subject; I heartily rejoice, however, the deed was done with pistols, which are, indeed, weapons fit only for the canine race; your bright sword, my Lord, which I make no doubt you have often drawn in defence of virtuous damsels, and renowned knights, remains unsullied by a mean contest."

"Madam!" repeated his Lordship in astonishment.

Miss Meredith had made her speech, and retired to her seat.

When the reader knows how famous Lord Claverton was for rescuing "virtuous damsels," and what reason he had to admire "valorous Knights," they will account for the entire change of countenance Miss Meredith's absurd speech produced; he complained of indisposition, wished to retire, and, with a cold determined air declined partaking of the supper, which was setting on the table; the surgeon offered to attend him, but his services were rejected; the valet was summoned, and so *exit* my Lord.

Perhaps a happier set never met than the supper party this night at Code Gwyn: Lewis sat between Sir Arthur and my Lady; Catherine rested her arms on the table, while she defended her address to Lord Claverton against the good-natured attacks of Mr. Meredith, whose romantic turn, though he knew he could not cure, he wished to curb. Doctor Macshean was *now* listening to Miss Agnes's process of making distilled waters, *now* saying civil things to Mary, and *now* drinking bumper after bumper of Welch ale to Sir Arthur, and his messmate's health; and we must confess, the Baronet and his son pledged him until it was time for the ladies to retire.

Chapter II

Lord Claverton's ill humour was not lessened by the morning's reflections; he, very charitably, consigned Code Gwyn and its inhabitants to the devil; and cursing their outré civility, made two resolutions before he rose from the bed of down, which, for neatness and comfort, might repose a Prince. First then, he recollected several circumstances it was no longer agreeable to remember, such as acts, innumerable, of kindness from Lieutenant Meredith, and which, therefore, having no further use for, it would be convenient to bury in oblivion. To break, therefore, with the hospitable family, under whose roof he was at that moment enjoying comforts, to which he had long been a stranger, was resolution the first. And, secondly, to leave Code Gwyn, and all its horrid inhabitants, the most disgusting of whom was the awkward girl and her friend Lion, the instant a carriage could be procured. He had just arranged these important manoeuvres, when Mrs. Griffiths bounced into his chamber, and having discovered he was awake, withdrew the window curtains, opened the shutters, and asked if his Lordship was ready for breakfast, which, on account of his sickliness, Miss Agnes had ordered to be sent to his chamber.

"Sickliness!'" returned he.

"Oh, aye, to be sure, my Lord, you does look very deadly, but our clear air, and goats whey –"

"Curse your whey, you stupid old devil," interrupted his Lordship, in a kind of inward voice, which, as Mrs. Griffiths was a little hard of hearing, excited her attention, without making her acquainted with his invectives.

"Did your Lordship please to speak?"

"Where is my scoundrel?"

"Where's, what–" The valet at that instant entered. "Oh, Mr. Joseph, your Master wants you." He was followed by two rosy cheeked damsels, each carrying plates of different eatables; three sorts of rolls, buttered and dry toast, biscuits, cakes, eggs and home made sweetmeats; then came Edward Griffiths, with a massy tea equipage of the last century, and after him a straight-haired footman, with a large tea kettle.

"My Lord wants something, I cannot make out what, to be sure, poor gentleman, his lungs be infected."

"Are you laying in provisions for a siege?" cried Lord Claverton, in amaze, as he viewed the breakfast.

"Dear me! my Lord;" answered the old housekeeper, officiously arranging the teaboard, and smiling exultingly, "Peace and Plenty, that's our way at Code Gwyn."

"Are the whole family coming here to breakfast?"

"Here! oh dear, no, they be all in the great hall, as merry as grigs, God bless 'em, but here, lord 'tis new year's day; I wish your Lordship a happy new year, if please God to *restore* you."

Lord Claverton's looks testified disgust and impatience. Mrs. Griffiths saw something was the matter, and as she seldom was at the trouble of puzzling herself about causes, stumbled on the one most mortifying to our Peer.

"Well, well, don't despair; come, to be sure you do look mortal sad, and Miss Agnes thinks as how you have been poisoned by the blacks, and if so be –"

"Turn the beldam out of the room," said his Lordship, in a rage he no longer sought to repel.

Joseph was a shrewd fellow, who liked too well the entertainment at Code Gwyn to venture affronting, on his *own* account, a lady, whose authority in the servants-hall was entire; he saw his Lord was decidedly angry; but Mrs. Griffiths, who began to suspect the same thing, had not the most distant idea of the cause; her preceding the breakfast into his chamber, her remarks on his bad looks, and prayer for their amendment, were so many different means of paying her court to a Lord, and obeying Miss Agnes, who had particularly charged her to mind their mutual management in the morning repast, she had no apprehension *she* could have given offence, it was therefore *her* turn to look amazed. Joseph beckoned, nodded, and winked in vain. To be turned out of a room, or be spoken hastily to, was perfectly new to Mrs. Griffiths, who, with the garrulous propensity of old age, blended such an unaffected goodness of heart, such an eagerness to enter into the misfortunes of every being, for the sake of alleviating as well as talking of them; she had passed from Lady Meredith's pretty *young* waiting maid, to the deaf old housekeeper, in an unimpeached gradation of honesty and affection. In short, it was not more dangerous to rouse Lion than affront her. She ejaculated, "Deliver me, good Lord!"

"Get out of the room, you canting old hypocrite," roared Lord Claverton.

"*You* a *Lord*!" said the old lady, with bitter emphasis, and she stalked slowly out of the chamber, all her Cambrian blood mounting to her cheeks, without deigning to look one way or the other.

"This moment get me a carriage; let me get out of this infernal family."

We have said what were his Lordship's resolutions, but it

was not to be. The snow had fallen so heavy in the night, the road over the mountains was impassable; no carriage could be got nearer than ten miles, and it was not safe to venture even a horse, as the wind set, the snow drifting against the side of a declivity by which they must pass, on their way to England. So unaccountable was the aversion Lord Claverton had taken to Code Gwyn, that could the journey be undertaken with any thing less than *personal* danger, it would not have been delayed; but ill health, change of climate, the heat he had left, the cold he had to encounter, contributed to reconcile him to the warm room, which he resolved to leave as little as possible, while he was compelled to stay. He had just sent away half a dozen plates of provision, and set down to his coffee, when the Surgeon and Lieutenant paid him the compliments of the morning.

Notwithstanding the prudential resolves which an hour before were the result of his pillow cogitations, he did not think proper to commence his operations when it was uncertain how long he might remain under the roof he despised, but his invincible dislike to the whole family determined him to make his indisposition an excuse for avoiding their society – he had the head-ache, his nerves were shattered, he could not bear conversation. He had in *reality* been often attacked in this way before he embarked for England, it was therefore no unnatural conclusion that his complaints were returned, the Lieutenant very good humouredly offered to sit in his chamber, though he added that his mother made a great point of his accompanying her to church.

"To church!" cried Lord Claverton, staring.

"Just so, my Lord," answered Dr. Macshean, "though it is three miles off, and the snow two foot deep."

"Oh, pray go to church," said Lord Claverton, ironically, "I hope all the curious set will follow."

The Lieutenant, a little piqued, assured him that excepting those necessary to attend on his Lordship, and his father, the whole family *would follow*.

Lord Claverton knew what was right, though he seldom condescended to act up to that knowledge, and apologized; he, however, would not accept of the company of either of his fellow travellers, but insisted on their obeying orders. They had not been gone five minutes, when Joseph who had the gift of penetrating his Lordship's disposition, in a very superior degree, and consequently understood the Code Gwyn family were objects of his contempt, came in, with a satirical grin on his face, to beg his Lordship would go into the gallery, and see the old family cart take up its load.

"The gallery! where the devil's that?"

Joseph opened a door opposite to the one they entered from the staircase into a long gallery, furnished with a great number of old portraits, with a very large painted bow window at the further end, which served only to make "*darkness visible*".[1]

More for exercise than curiosity, Lord Claverton stalked down, but instead of troubling himself about the family cart, as Joseph so wittily termed the coach, was returning when, through the gloom at the further end, he saw a door open, and a form approach, which his warm imagination likened to the houries of Mahometan Paradise.

It was a slim elegant female, dressed in a calico jacket and coat, short enough to discover a beautiful turned ankle, open at the neck, and arms as white as snow, a profusion of light

---

[1] Quoting John Milton's *Paradise Lost* (1667).

brown hair in natural ringlets shaded her alabaster forehead, a pair of lovely brows and lashes, two shades darker, gave her clear blue eyes a hazel cast, her features were more beautiful than regular, her lips of the deepest rose pink, half open, displayed a set of small white teeth, her complexion pure and elegant, and her form a model of symmetry; she tripped along the gallery, tying on a straw hat, and was followed by a short thick black eyed girl, carrying a white dimity cloak and a pair of mittens.

Lord Claverton was struck – such a creature to be an inhabitant of that dark dungeon! His ardent gaze as she drew near raised a crimson glow over the most lovely face and fairest neck he had ever seen – she courtesied and went on.

"What a Hebe!" exclaimed the Peer.

"Her name is Ellen," quoth the waiting damsel, also courtesying, and passed on.

Lord Claverton having followed the fair vision, as he was half inclined to think her, with his eyes, hastily returned to the bow window to see if it made any part of the loading Joseph described. She was lifted up the step, light as a Gossamer, by Lewis Meredith, the carriage drove very slowly off, but Lord Claverton's eyes were rivetted to the spot. Joseph was at hand and as penetrating as ever.

"Shall I make any enquiries about that young lady, my Lord?"

"This moment."

Joseph descended to the servants hall, Lord Claverton returned to his chamber, the face, shape, complexion, and innocence, he met in the gallery, still before his eyes. Joseph soon returned with a meaning-face. It was the identical young lady whose warm embraces, though they might animate a statue, failed to recall the mastiff to life, and her maid, the same civil being, who had bestowed on his Lordship the epithet of neger.

Lord Claverton had lived some years abroad, his connexions were a *little* among the sallow beauties whom Plutus tempted to abandon their country and health together, and a *great deal* among their wretched slaves, the face of every young woman he had seen since his arrival in Britain, appeared therefore to advantage, but *this girl* was beyond any thing he remembered in his connexions even before he left England; very ignorant, and indeed foolish, the tears she shed for her dog evinced her, but no matter, he should have the less trouble in getting her, which if he liked her as well at the next interview, he was resolved upon. 'Tis true, beautiful as Ellen was, it was the beauty of a tall child; but neither did *that matter*, it was a fault every day would mend.

"Joe," said the noble Lord, "I'll have that girl." (Joe thought as much from the moment he met her in the gallery.) "Therefore (picking his teeth) do you contrive to know every thing about her."

"Her maid is so cursed ugly! my Lord.'

"That's your affair, I shall only keep the Mistress – Damn it, I wish I had not been so ill this morning."

"To be sure, my Lord, that is a pity because you cannot possibly leave your room today, and the family –"

"Oh, curse the family, don't talk of *them*, but, d'ye hear, you may get acquainted with the old beldame."

Joe promised to do his best and my Lord's impatience soon sent him on his honourable mission. Meanwhile his Lordship very deliberately began to lay the plan of his future establishment, in which, however, he considered it as *too* great an honour for a little country rustic to be included, and therefore intended to keep her for his hours of relaxation, in a small box, near the metropolis.

It was thus the noble Peer contrived to elude the enemy while the *simple* Knight, under whose hospitable roof he was entertained, not being able to go to church, read the lessons of the day to Mr. Griffiths, and while his as simple family were asking the blessing of the Being they served on the new year, a custom still adhered to in many parts of antient Britain.

The return from over-seas of the son of a beloved chief was news too interesting to his tenants and neighbours to be concealed; it had spread over the Parish with the addition that Master Lewis brought home with him a Lord, and another great man, who would unquestionably be at church with the family on so great a festival as New Year's Day. The folly of these ignorant people was pardonable, since it was impossible *they* could conceive how little respect the lords and great men of the world pay even to the Sabbath day.

But although the peasants waded through the snow, some to say their prayers, others to see the strangers, a lord was not the very strangest sight they had ever seen, for there actually was at that time a nobleman who resided from June till February every year, at his Castle, within three miles of Code Gwyn church, and though a lord is a Lord every where, they are not, we presume, all exactly alike; the Lord of Castle Howel for instance, was (as reported) a cross, proud, reserved, old man; whereas, him at Code Gwyn was, if not young, much younger, and moreover, had come from beyond sea with Sir Arthur's son, who was well remembered to be the best-hearted, best tempered youth in the world, and who, as they had been constant hearers of all his dangers, either from his own letters or the weekly papers, which Sir Arthur read to them, was expected, if he escaped the perils of the sea, to be a second Benbow, or Matthews at least, two of the greatest Admirals they had ever heard of.

Code Gwyn Church was crowded, and a general shuffle in the congregation, with whispers that hissed through the aisles, saluted the young officer as he led his mother to the pew, followed by Dr. Macshean, his sisters and niece. This had scarce subsided, and Mr. Meredith mounted the pulpit, before a second object of curiosity and wonder appeared, in the person of a lady of the *haut ton,* whose chariot wheels had rattled the few villagers who were *not* at church into consternation, and whose dress (the extremity of the fashion), free step, and undaunted manner had the same effect on those who were.

Lady Margaret Howel very rarely visited any place of worship, but being, to her infinite mortification, confined to the dull mansion of Castle Howel, and having heard of the arrival of the Lieutenant and his friends, came to Code Gwyn church, in hopes to see something human in the shape of man. Up then tripped Lady Margaret to Sir Arthur's pew, and astonished Macshean with the ease of her fashionable courtesy – "Who," said he, in a whisper to Catherine, "is that old lady?"

"Old Lady," replied Catherine, "she would deem you a very uncourteous knight to call her so; she is the spinster of great fashion, has read very little."

The service began, Macshean's observations were full of matter: Lady Margaret's rolling *grey* eyes often encountered his more penetrating black ones, and those she saw, did not indicate any of that cold reserve, which had frozen her sensibility in the parson, who, sometime back, she condescended to think tolerable.

Lady Margaret had an entire aversion to her family name, and finding her small fortune an insurmountable objection to any exchange, was taking great pains to remove it, by accumulations at her brother's expense, and had it already in her power, amply to reward the kindness of any gentleman who should assist her in converting Lady Margaret Howel into Lady Margaret any thing else.

Mr. Macshean was the younger son of a reduced Scotch family, poor, dependent, and excepting his patron the Peer (for whom, by the bye, he had not the most profound respect) friendless, he had been taught by many a bitter lesson of experience the art of accommodating himself to the whims and caprices, and even tyranny of *others,* when his own disposition, with power, would have qualified him to be as whimsical, capricious, and tyrannical, as the *best.* Lady Margaret came to church in an elegant carriage, with two footmen in splendid liveries, and as he perceived, notwithstanding an immoderate bloom on her cheek, she was an old lady with young inclinations, he concluded from her equipage she possessed the ne plus ultra of *his* wishes, in consequence, he certainly looked, and said, as many passionate things as the time and place would admit. Lady Margaret, in wonderful good humour, invited herself home with the Code Gwyn family, merely to congratulate Sir Arthur on the arrival of his son, whom she obliged to take a seat in her carriage, and although she had made a thousand protestations against ever venturing on the mountainous side of Castle Howel, *now* condescended to be dragged, step by step, after the old coach, in momentary danger of having her carriage broken, and herself thrown out.

When the great court bell rang, and Lord Claverton strided

across the gallery, to steal a glance at the beautiful rustic, he was not a little surprised at recognizing Lady Margaret Castle Howel, whose face had many years been a fixture at every public place of polite resort; he swore, the old hag had laid her fangs on the Lieutenant, and congratulated himself on his resolution not to stir out of his apartment; but a quick foot ascending the stair soon made him regret every moment passed in it.

Ellen, more beautiful from the glow which air and exercise left on her cheek, her hair disordered by the wind, the smile of content dimpling round her mouth, and her natural beauty increased by the happiness the arrival of the Lieutenant diffused in the family, gaily tripped to her apartment, followed by her faithful shadow Winifred, and again dropped a courtesy to his Lordship as she passed.

"Heavens! what an object for attention – for admiration – for ruin."

His eyes followed till she was lost at the farther extremity of the gloomy gallery, when he retired slowly to his room.

Chapter III

Good humour and conviviality now reigned in every part of Code Gwyn House, save that where his Lordship was honourably agitated by feelings not altogether new, though more violent than he had lately experienced. The ease with which he had a minute before settled the business vanished, difficulties innumerable presented themselves to his imagination, but it is the province of daring minds to overcome difficulties – by daring I do not mean bravery, no; there is a sort of resolution, more bold than bravery; more persevering than courage; more witty than wise; more pliant than good humour – of this sort was the daring of Lord Claverton. The girl he was resolved to have, but how that glorious point was to be accomplished; how a mind formed in the very bosom of purity was to be corrupted; how, after succeeding, to escape the sober dignified resentment of Mr. Meredith, or the passionate vengeance of the young officer, for the break of every law of hospitality, were points that began to puzzle him.

A boiled chicken, and white soup, which Mrs. Griffiths pronounced proper for a *sick body*, was served, and sent back untouched, on which, as loss of appetite was, in her opinion, the *greatest,* if not *only* sign of danger, she very gravely presented herself at the elbow of Lady Meredith, and assured her, the Lord, above stairs, was in a very bad way.

Lady Margaret's warm congratulations, her politeness to the Lieutenant, and her condescension to every body, had quite eclipsed Lord Claverton; and, as to Mr. Macshean, *he* was as deeply engaged in laying plans as his Lordship himself could possibly be, and with more probability of success; he by this time understood, Lady Margaret was the only sister of the Earl of Castle Howel; he saw, notwithstanding a vast deal of powder, she was grey; and a vast deal of rouge, she was ugly; but it was a desirable thing to be related to an old Earl, and a very undesirable one to be dependent on a profligate Peer, he therefore "sighed and looked." But deeply engaged as his externals were in besieging Lady Margaret, and as his internals were in arranging every advantage therefore, he did not forget the possibility of a disappointment. The instant Mrs. Griffiths mentioned his Lordship's illness, he arose from table with an apologizing bow, and hastened to his patron, followed by the Lieutenant.

Lord Claverton was in so profound a reverie that the Doctor began a florid apology before he perceived they were in the room. The sight of the Lieutenant, however, restored the invalid to his usual presence of mind, and "Ha! Lewis, how are you?" with a smile, that proved he had not taken offence, and an animation of countenance that also evidenced a nearer approach to convalescence than he had yet observed set the Doctor's mind at rest. In short, it was one part of his Lordship's present scheme to be wonderfully good humoured; he attributed his want of appetite to confinement, determined on a reform, and, being most cordially invited, actually condescended to join the happy party below.

Lady Margaret, whose tedious years had rolled insipidly on between London and Castle Howel, perfectly remembered Captain, now Lord Claverton, and, as I have before said, Lord Claverton knew her Ladyship, they were, or professed to be, very happy at so unexpected a rencontre; their mutual con-

Ellen, Countess of Castle Howel

gratulations kept the company standing, to the great edification of the domestics, who were fixed in open-mouthed admiration, till Sir Arthur from his wheel-chair interrupted the fine breeding of his quality guests.

"Set a chair here," said he, pointing to his right hand, "My Lord, you are welcome." The benevolent smile, the sincere look, and the cordial shake of the hand, dressed the welcome in nature's most attractive garb; truth, honesty, and inbred politeness, graced every action of Sir Arthur Meredith.

"Frankness in him was not the effect of familiarity, but the cause of it," he was a gentleman of *god's making*. Lord Claverton took the offered seat with more pleasure, as on part of the gouty stool at her grandfather's feet, her blue eyes raised to his, with a mixture of love and reverence, sat the blooming Ellen.

There were present, who annually dined at Code Gwyn, on New Year's day, besides the guests we have named, Mr. James, the Surgeon, Apothecary, Man-Midwife, and Physician of the village, Mr. Percival Evelyn, a youth of eighteen, an eleve[2] of the rector's, and John Morgan, Esq., Lord of the next manor, before introduced to the reader as the convenient money-lending friend of Sir Arthur Meredith, a gentleman who will make a conspicuous figure in the events of this history, and who will gradually unfold his own character, I shall therefore only say, few men addressed their superiors with more servility, or treated his equals with more apparent frankness and plausibility, which was indeed extended to such of his inferiors as were not dependent *on* or in debt *to* him; these sort of people he made in every sense feel *their own*

---

[2] I.e., pupil

littleness, and *his* consequence; he was a perfect adept in the whole art of bowing, and managed the bend of his body according to the rank or riches of those he addressed, with an exactitude that would have done honour to Sir Pertinax Mac Sycophant himself – to every branch of the Code Gwyn family Esquire Morgan bowed particularly low, to Lord Claverton and Lady Margaret Howel still lower.

His *Lordship's eyes* were fixed on Ellen, Esquire Morgan perceived she was grown tall, and prodigiously improved; he drank Sir Arthur's health, and a happy new year, in a glass of ale, which he declared he preferred to Champaigne.

"Who is this gentleman?" whispered Macshean to Miss Meredith.

"He is the demon of avarice!" replied she, "and owns the great house on the hill; he buys every body's estates, and lives in a corner of his own mansion."

Macshean knew enough of the world to be certain it was not worth his while to take a look from Lady Margaret to bestow on John Morgan, Esquire.

The good humour of the company was increased by the addition to their society, the Lieutenant rallied his sisters on their being old maids; Miss Meredith gloried in the title, rather than unite herself to any man who had not achieved some great adventure, and given proofs both of valour and love.

Squire Morgan called the young man to order, he declared the ladies were all too young to fall under that odium; he was warmly seconded by Mr. Macshean, who had his doubts whether a woman of twice Miss Meredith's age could be properly called an old maid; a woman, who could feel and inspire the tender passion was not surely of that description; there *were women,* one of whom he had the honour to *know,* who had passed the childhood of their days, but who were still objects of desire, and more worthy the attachment of rational beings than it was possible a mere girl could be.

Three persons, and three only of the company fully comprehended Mr. Macshean – these were Lady Margaret, Lord Claverton, and Squire Morgan, the latter bowing very low to her Ladyship, replied, "exce signum."

When the ladies retired, the noble invalid attended them, and the Rector's young eleve, who appeared to be quite at home, after helping Ellen to adjust Sir Arthur's cushion, followed her into the drawing room.

Percival Evelyn was too handsome and too attentive to Ellen, to escape Lord Claverton's notice; the plainness of his dress, his unobtrusive manners, the blush that crimsoned his naturally pale interesting face, when called on to give his sentiments by the Rector, the diffidence and bashfulness that accompanied all his actions, shewed him a very despicable rival, but a rival his Lordship feared he certainly was, and was therefore particularly watchful of both Ellen and him.

The night being very cold and dark, Lady Margaret was prevailed on to accept the second best room; cards and the gentlemen appeared together, but the harp in the hall was a more welcome summons to the younger part, and even Lord Claverton would dance if Ellen would be his partner.

Whether it was the disaster of her dead favourite, which Winifred did not fail to remind her of; whether his Lordship was a bad partner, or from what other cause, certainly this arrangement did not particularly please Ellen; she was, however, so fond of dancing, the gloom vanished by degrees, she chatted, sung, and laughed herself so completely into Lord Claverton's heart, that before they parted for the night it had struck him, a little polish would render her fit to grace his Peerage.

The education of Ellen had indeed been extraordinary; she had learnt to read of the Rector, to write of his Clerk, to dance of old Griffiths, to sing and play of the family Harper, and to ride of the Bailiff. In this exercise she was so expert, that it was common for her maid Winifred and herself to catch a horse on the mountain, no matter whose, and gallop two or three miles without bridle or saddle; she was very famous for discovering birds' nests, and minded not any height to get at them; ready to follow any body's hounds through thick and thin, and was even an excellent shot. With all these accomplishments she was now but in her fifteenth year, with the face of Venus, the form of Diana, and the greatest romp in the world; yet the natural sense she was blessed with, the example of Lady Meredith and her daughters, the sentiments she imbibed from them, and the constant practice of every virtue, even in her unpolished state of nature, rendered her artless conversation charming and entertaining.

To his Lordship's great joy she was evidently entertained by the glowing picture of London, he contrived to mixing his conversation; but he could not, with all his art, extort one wish from her to see or be seen there.

The Squire took his leave at a late hour, and the company separated, apparently delighted with each other.

Chapter IV

At breakfast, the three persons, bent on conquest, met with all possible advantage; Lady Margaret gave a formal invitation to all present to spend that day week at Castle Howel; Lord Claverton having found *prodigious benefit* from the *air,* no longer talked of a *sudden removal.*

Mr. Macshean and the Lieutenant attended Lady Margaret on horseback, and were introduced to the Earl of Castle Howel; when her Ladyship, with unusual volubility, descanted on the present happiness of the Code Gwyn family, explained the reasons she chose to assign for her visit there, protested they were the best creatures in the world, and that she was particularly indebted to the politeness of the two gentlemen who escorted her home.

The Earl bowed to each: Lady Margaret lamented living so long in the neighbourhood without having cultivated such agreeable society; she had engaged them to spend a day at Castle Howel.

The Earl bowed again, and Lady Margaret having opened her scheme, was silent, considering on the next step towards completing her conquest over the irresistible Macshean, for so he now appeared to her warm imagination.

Mr. Macshean, who was always upon the watch for any thing that might be eventually advantageous, attempted to enter into conversation; but a grave bow, or a single monosyllable, was all he could gain from the Earl, and perceiving his Lordship was totally indifferent to whatever subject was started, and that Lady Margaret looked restless and dissatisfied, while the Lieutenant was attentively examining some fine charts of the sea coast, which hung over the chimney, he arose, and casting a languishing look at her Ladyship, and most profoundly bowing to the Earl, asked the Lieutenant if he would go.

The sailor was on his hobby-horse, he loved his profession, and every thing appertaining to it interested him. The Earl was not so abstracted but he could see the young man was uncommonly pleased; he patronized the artist who published the charts, and gratified at so unequivocal a mark of approbation, from one who must be a professional judge of their merit, invited him to his dressing-room, where he had another set, by the same hand.

Here was a golden opportunity, which Macshean did not suffer to escape. The windows overlooked a rich prospect of land, wood and water; ease and affluence seemed the natural inhabitants of this magnificent castle; the ornaments and furniture were superb, there was even an air of contented grandeur in the livery of the servants; and Lady Margaret, the Medea who had the clue to this golden fleece: could a lover, a poor lover, and a Scotch lover! be less than eloquent? What Mr. Macshean said, or what he did, we leave our readers to imagine from their own feelings.

The Earl of Castle Howel was, at the period this history commences, in his fiftieth year; he had, in his youth, disobliged his father, by marrying the beautiful daughter of an obscure Attorney, in London, who he accidentally saw in the street, and following home, became so enamoured of her, that he considered all other blessings of life as mere trifles in comparison with the possession of her. It however frequently happens that the wisest of frail mortals are so little able to decide on the right road to happiness, that they take the exact opposite; of this the Honourable Mr. Howel was an instance. He offended his father, and all his noble relations, by marrying Miss Capus, of Spital-Fields, and after Miss Capus had been one month looked up to as the Honourable Mrs. Howel, he discovered he had mortally offended her, by raising her out of the reach of a smart young man, who officiated as clerk to her father, and who had indeed entirely forestalled Mr. Howel in the possession of his fair bride's person and affection.

The reader will expect the consequences: Mr. Howel was dependent on a stern obstinate father; Miss Capus would not be the Honourable Mrs. Howel for nothing; if she might not have the splendour of an Earl's daughter, she might as well have stayed in Spital-Fields, with her father's clerk.

Too charming to be without admiration, and too vain to be displeased at exciting it, her acquaintance became very general, and very suspected; for some little time Mrs. Howel could dress and show with the most expensive, without any visible fund to support her fine taste: Mr. Howel was the first who chose to make enquiries into so strange a matter, he was followed by the whole beau monde; these indeed were better and sooner informed, but a very little time returned the fair bride to Spital-Fields, and her father's clerk. Mr. Howel had proofs enough of her ill conduct to obtain a divorce, but he had taken a disgust to the sex, and resolved never to marry again, and as he became indolent and careless in the matter, it dropped off course.

A few years, however, rendered the legal divorce of importance; his two elder brothers died; the honours and estates of Castle Howel were entailed on the male heir, the next in succession after Mr. Howel was a person who had rendered himself particularly obnoxious to the family, and it was a very serious matter with the old Earl and two maiden sisters, Lady Frances, and Lady Gertrude Howel, to disappoint his expectations.

The Earl of Castle Howel's express found his son in a remote corner of Switzerland, studying Botany. He received the news with great philosophy, and returned to England by easy stages, within two months after he was expected.

The first business that engrossed the old Earl, and his two sisters, was that of settling the divorce, and fixing on a proper person to bring an heir into the family.

His son was, on his part, no less engaged in planning and laying out a piece of ground for botanical experiments.

The divorce could not be obtained; the time had elapsed; one witness was dead, another not to be found, and the lady-wife, by experience had become cautious; the Earl was grieved, the two noble spinsters outrageous, and Lord Howel pursued his botanical experiments.

Lord Howel succeeded his father in title and estate, but his aunts, who were rich, retired to an estate they had in the North of England; the Earl died intestate and insolvent; Lady Margaret, his only surviving daughter, received a cold invitation to accompany her aunts to the North, but she had sense enough to observe, that while her father, who played high, kept race horses, and was at the head of every fashionable expense, out-lived his income, her aunts were making the very *most* of his brotherly affection; from them she imbibed a laudable regard to the grand movement of all our actions, *self interest,* and wisely resolved to continue with a brother, whose situation was a security against his marrying, and abstracted turn of mind left her sovereign mistress of his house; she therefore declined, under the plea of sisterly regard, her aunts' invitation; the force of that plea they perfectly comprehended, and gave her prudence due credit.

The ladies departed on civil terms with their nephew and niece, having extorted a promise from the former, that as soon as it was possible to get legally rid of his wife, he would marry some young woman, and make them all happy in the long desired addition to the family, on their part engaging his male heir should be theirs also.

Lord Castle Howel had many antediluvian notions of honour about him; he inherited Castle Howel estate entail, no debt of his father's was binding on him, but he considered he had long lived with comfort to himself on £200 per annum, he was now in the receipt of £20000, the debts of the Earl, including those of honour, amounted to sixty thousand; these debts he considered as part of his inheritance, and appropriated one-third of his income to pay off principal and interest, which reduced his rent-roll to 14000. The apathy of his disposition was not removed by excess of fortune, but innate honesty of heart predominated so far, as to bring him to his closet once a week, for the first year, to arrange his expenses according to his ideas of filial honour, and having so arranged them, he resigned the command of his family to his sister, taking her vouchers, for the general disbursements, while he amused himself with botanical and philosophical experiments, and patronizing genius wherever he met it.

Mondays, during the season, the huntsmen, with a fine pack of dogs, were in the field, and usually collected a large company of plain country squires, for whose entertainment there was a public dinner; but as *their* general conversation neither suited Lord Castle Howel, nor Lord Castle Howel *theirs;* and as Lady Margaret was neither handsome nor rich, few visitors, except on hunting days, troubled Castle Howel.

Lady Margaret, though doomed nine months of the year to this insipid vegetation, passed the other three more to her taste; they had a house in Grosvenor-Street, and her Ladyship was among the leaders of the high ton, she was constantly in the circle, had a box at the opera, patronized the fashionable favourites of either theatre, was a subscriber to all the music meetings, had her Sunday concerts and assemblies; in short, as the old song says, "Wherever a fiddle was heard she was there," but year after year elapsing with equal sameness, without one offer of marriage, was a terrible drawback on her enjoyments; she had long persuaded herself it was want of fortune that deprived her of the attentions she saw paid to older ladies than herself, and as long had been endeavouring to remedy the evil.

The Earl's family were thus situated, when a certain honest peculiarity of manners, and a blunt freedom of address, added to an uncommon good-humoured set of features, interested his Lordship in favour of Lieutenant Meredith, and gave Doctor Macshean an opportunity to breathe his passion at the feet of Lady Margaret.

Dinner was announced before either of the tete-a-tete parties were up, and before the visitors made their bow, Lord Castle Howel joined Lady Margaret's invitation to be better acquainted.

Chapter V

Meanwhile the hours passed at Code Gwyn with little satisfaction to Lord Claverton, his affairs went on in rather a retrograde motion, though he had done so much violence to his polite nature, as to sacrifice two whole hours to the backgammon table with Sir Arthur, had listened to a favourite rhapsody from Clelia, by Miss Meredith, admired the economy of her sister, and read three long letters from Lucretia to Amanthis. Ellen and her maid Winifred, insensible to both cause and effect of such great humiliation, had strolled away to the parsonage, and it was dark before she returned; her absence, when he found she did not appear at the dinner table, took away the little appetite he had, and his chagrin got the better of even his consummate art; he asked, with feigned indifference, if Miss Ellen had accompanied Lady Margaret?

"Oh!" replied the old Baronet, "this is too fine a day for Ellen to be at home, she will return as blooming as a rose: Have you seen her?" addressing Mr. Meredith.

"No," answered he, "but I dare say Percival has; I suppose they are together."

Lord Claverton coloured, and removed from table really unwell; the facility with which he had planned to seduce the young beauty was no more; not that a single scruple as to the means necessary to be employed troubled him; no, it was his observations on Ellen herself, and a rising jealousy of the tall awkward youth, whom one moment he despised, and the next feared, that disturbed him.

A long series of ill health, the consequence of early irregularities and a hot climate, entirely pervaded the nervous system of Lord Claverton, the least opposition to his passions both irritated and weakened him, he was on the present occasion therefore, in a very unenviable state; he retired to his chamber, and was joined by Doctor Macshean, so much worse, that *he* talked of medicine, but was interrupted by his Lordship's impatient inquiry of, "who was below?"

"In troth" replied the Doctor, "my Lord, I was so alarmed at the account I heard — "

Lord Claverton turned pale, "Account! what has happened, is Ellen returned?"

Had his Lordship sent for Dr. Macshean on purpose to make him the full confidant of what passed in his mind; had he taken the utmost pains to elucidate every present sensation, and minutely explained every future intention, the wary Doctor could not have been let more fully into his patron's secrets, than by the voice and manner which accompanied the simple interrogation —

"Is Ellen yet returned?"

Dr. Macshean immediately seated himself, and improving on this unguarded lapse, was in five minutes invested with as much authority, as prime agent to Lord Claverton, as he himself chose to accept; that is to say, Lord Claverton did not propose, nor did Dr. Macshean hint at the seduction of the girl; each party understood the other too well, to be so much in either's power; but the friendship of his Lordship to the Meredith family, and his particular liking of the pretty Ellen, on account of her *innocence* and *vivacity* might certainly inspire a wish to serve and a blameless desire of knowing every thing that concerned *her,* and the Doctor might engage to gratify such his patron's wish and desire, without the least reflection on his own *moral* character.

Lord Claverton and his friend had yet the tea-cups before them, when Ellen's voice warbling a Welch air, as she passed the gallery, gave the welcome information of her return, and as the Peer's spirits were immediately above par, he proposed joining the family.

Squire Morgan, whose business at Code Gwyn became every day more frequent, was in the parlour, and Lieutenant Meredith having amused his father, and gratified his mother, with an account of Lord Castle Howel's particular goodness to *him;* the instant Lord Claverton entered, the Squire took occasion to congratulate the family on the acquisition of *two* such noble friends as the Earl, and (bowing very low) Lord Claverton.

As Ellen undesignedly drew her chair between her grandfather and the Peer, he was in high good humour, and appeared to listen so attentively to the long stories Sir Arthur loved to tell, she, for the first time looked at him with attention; the pale and languid, though handsome countenance of a Lord, who seemed to like her dear grandfather, and who, the Squire most humbly insinuated, might essentially serve her uncle, the Lieutenant, interested her; after a steadfast observance, which, though he affected to be wholly engrossed by the long story, did not escape his Lordship, she pleased and surprised him by an address, in which softness and sympathy were blended.

"How do you find yourself this evening, my Lord? Griffiths said you were worse."

In spite of all his art the blood mounted to his cheek; the Doctor's looks encountered his Patron's, and both concluded matters were en train.

Squire Morgan, without seeming to dare to raise his eyes to Lord Claverton, or to attend to any thing but the long story, which he had heard at least one hundred times before, had *his* observations too, but he concealed them in a low bow, and took his leave.

Winifred Griffiths was an ill made girl, not yet eighteen, with black hair, eyes, and eyebrows, short nose, wide mouth, strong white teeth, high cheek bones, and a very fresh colour, spoke very bad English, and worse Welch: Joseph Wilks, however, by his Lord's commands, fell desperately in love with Winifred's beauty, presented her with two handsome silk handkerchiefs, and a pair of silver buckles, and pressed very hard for a promise of marriage.

"Why, as Cot shall safe me, Mr. Joseph, your cifts are fery coot, and you are a fery well behafed footman, put my uncle Griffiths will not cive me a farthing of fortune if I don't ask his consent."

"Fortune! what did his charmer think he valued fortune? No, Joe Wilks would have Winifred Griffiths, if Winifred Griffiths would have Joe Wilks, in spite of her old cross uncle, or his fortune."

"Ay, Cot knows, cross indeed. But then Miss Ellen; oh, she would not leave Miss Ellen, no, not for all Code Gwyn was worth, and, to be sure, it was the finest, the best, and greatest place in all the world!"

This declaration led to a secret Mr. Joseph would tell his fair Winifred, under the *seal* of *secrecy,* which was, that as Lord Claverton was as much in love with her mistress, as he was with herself; she might safely promise to marry him, without leaving Miss Ellen.

This point being settled, Winifred very readily folded up the handkerchiefs, put the silver buckles in her shoes, and proudly anticipating the day when Ellen Meredith should be Lady Claverton, promised to marry his footman; the agreement being signed and sealed in the usual way such agreements are commonly signed and sealed between footmen and waiting maids, the parties separated; Winifred to shew her cifts and boast of her conquest, to the rest of the maids, keeping, however, her promise of secrecy in regard to her mistress; and Joseph to report to his Lord the progress of his passion.

The day fixed on for the visit to Castle Howel arrived, Ellen begged to stay at home with Sir Arthur, and Lord Claverton was immediately too much indisposed to attend; Lady Meredith could not press his Lordship, but her pride as well as that of her daughter's was too much gratified by the admiration Ellen always excited, to dispense with her; and Lord Claverton, to his great mortification, had another day to pass, either in his chamber, or at the back-gammon table, as, though he might be very suddenly and dangerously taken *indisposed,* he was too cautious to raise suspicion in the family by a too sudden *recovery.*

Lady Meredith dressed Ellen herself, Miss Catherine adjusted her fine hair, and, indeed, by the uncommon attention of all the ladies, one would be led to believe they had a presentiment of the consequence of that day's visit, to Castle Howel.

Doctor Macshean was also particularly attentive to *his* dress, and the ladies being ready, he handed them, with great ceremony, in to the coach, into which (as he declined riding on horseback in respect to the dressing of his very thin and, in many parts, grey hairs) he also stepped himself.

Edward Griffiths, who always attended Lady Meredith, and

two other grey headed servants, followed the old coach, in its sure though slow progress.

As they entered the fine Park, and approached the Castle, by roads kept in the nicest order, Ellen, whose longest journey had been to Code Gwyn church, was charmed with scenes so new; she had never once conceived there was in the world any thing superior to Code Gwyn, where, though the Parks, and all the walks and grounds, spoke too plainly the gradual decay both of the health and property of the venerable owner, there yet remained a superiority and grandeur, so much out of all comparison above what she had seen at the house of Squire Morgan, Mr. James, the Apothecary, or any of the opulent farmers in the neighbourhood, that she had not entertained a doubt but Code Gwyn was the finest seat, and Sir Arthur the first gentleman in the world, not excepting Lord Claverton, of whose importance she had, within the last twenty-four hours, by the help of Dr. Macshean and Winifred Griffith, formed a very high opinion.

Lady Meredith, who had, in her youth, been the companion and friend of the Ladies Gertrude and Frances Howel, while they resided at the Castle, was revolving as the carriage rumbled slowly on over the pleasant hours of juvenile hilarity: Miss Catherine could recollect many fine descriptions of Cassandra and Clelia, when the Oroondates and Alexanders had sighed under such shades as those they were passing: Miss Agnes lamented the pasture at Code Gwyn was much inferior to that at Castle Howel: Mary was studying fine sentences to adorn a descriptive letter to her friend, Miss Peggy Jones: and Doctor Macshean – but it is impossible to delineate the variety of thoughts that occupied his ideas; a marriage into the Earl's family had so many glittering appendages – one would be first, another would be first, and all would be first. What, however, was rather extraordinary, the fair lady who was the grand mover of all, was not thought of till the coach stopped, and he saw her significant smile from the bow window of the drawing-room, then indeed the Doctor saw Lady Margaret, and though he had handed the pretty Agnes, into the carriage, and pressed her hand with great gallantry, he now declined any civilities to the younger part of the family, and transferred all his care to Lady Meredith.

Mr. Meredith and the Lieutenant, who rode on horseback, were already with the Earl.

The grand staircase, the marble hall, gilded ornaments, fine figures, and rich vases, which filled a number of niches as they passed, astonished Ellen, she had not eyes enough to look round, and the rest of the party were introduced and seated, while she stood at the door, afraid either to advance or retreat, the Earl himself was the first to take notice of the young visitor.

Lord Castle Howel was an enthusiastic admirer of the beauties of nature, his heart had paid homage to one of the finest works of the creation, uncultivated by education and unblest by talent; from her he had retreated with disgust, and the vegetable world next attracted his attention. His misfortune, with respect to his wife, was a continual guard on his passions, his eyes were in subjection to his situation; and though the sublime and beautiful of all descriptions attracted him, he chose to live secluded from temptation, and it was seldom he allowed himself to contemplate the face of a beautiful woman; but one now presented itself, from which he apprehended no danger, where all the charms of modesty and innocence were blended with a something more than beauty.

Impelled by admiration he hastily advanced towards Ellen, took her hand, and led her blushing to Lady Margaret.

"Whose little angel is this?", said he, "How came you not to introduce her?"

Lady Margaret had been too long a sedulous observer of her brother, to mistake any of his actions, she directly saw Ellen would be a favourite, and from that moment she was a little divinity.

Dinner was served with all possible magnificence, and cards introduced but not attended to: Lady Margaret, with all that marked attention which fine-bred women *can* pay, to those on whom they condescend to form designs, won on the unsuspecting heart of Lady Meredith. She presented Miss Meredith with several old Romances out of the library; chatted with Agnes on the merit of domestic economy; and presented Mary with a handsome ebony ink stand, filled with crow pens and French paper. Mr. Meredith admired a fine pointer, Lady Margaret begged it of the Earl for him – In short, she was every thing to every body.

Doctor Macshean, who hitherto considered only the immediate advantage of his union with Lady Margaret, could not but be pleased with a woman, whose internal policy so exactly corresponded with his own, and whose easy manners and address, at her brother's table, gave his Scotch family pride a pleasing earnest of what she would be at her own, when his visionary castles should be realized, and, by her interest, he should be an established Physician, in the Metropolis, which was the goal of his ambition.

In the mean while Ellen and the Earl were seated on a sofa, at a distance from the rest of the company, the latter too much engaged with his new acquaintance, to attend the manoeuvres of his sister.

His heart (torpid as his early disappointment and disgust

had rendered it) insensibly warmed to a being, on whose countenance the finger of nature legibly displayed every amiable trait of the human mind – the face of Ellen was a wonder, yet her beauty ceased to attract where her natural bashfulness gave way to frankness and vivacity.

The result of the favourable sentiments she thus artlessly inspired, was an inquiry into her education, and it is difficult to say, whether Lord Castle Howel most regretted her deficiencies in modern accomplishments, or admired her native graces without them; he was far from fatigued when supper put an end to the tête-à-tête, and bid Ellen good night with paternal complacency.

Chapter VI

Lady Meredith was amused while undressing, by Ellen's rapturous praises of Lord Castle Howel, he was, she declared, almost as handsome as her grandfather, and quite different from Lord Claverton.

"He is so sweet tempered, Grandmamma, so like my uncle Edmund; and, do you know, he says so many sweet things."

"He is very good, but what does he say?"

"That my uncle Lewes was born to be an Admiral, and that you must have been very handsome when you was young; and indeed I told him, so you are now, and he said – now what do you think he said? He said, that *I* was like you, but many people have told me that, and when I have looked in the glass, I do think I am."

"Then, my dear, by that rule, you think yourself handsome?"

"Why, yes, Grandmamma, I *do* think my face is handsomer than many people's, there's Winifred's, you know, she has very pretty black eyes, and more colour in her cheek, and yet I think I like my own face best; but now, Grandmamma, only tell me what you think of Percival Evelyn's face, is not his a pretty one?"

"Prettier than your own, Ellen?"

"Oh, yes, a vast deal; his eyes are prettier than Winifred's, or any body's, except my Grandpapa's; and though he is pale, what a sweet colour be his sometimes; why did he not come with us? I dare say Lord Castle Howel would have liked him very well."

"Go to sleep, child, and dream of Lord Castle Howel."

"No, I don't think I shall dream of *him*, but I dare say I shall of Percival."

"Indeed!"

"Yes, indeed, I am always sure to dream of him; and, do you know, Grandmamma, though I am ashamed when he tells me so, he dreams of me too; he told me this morning he dreamed last night that he saw me carried over towers, and high buildings, he was afraid of my falling, and yet he could not get at me, and he said he cried so his pillow was wet. Wasn't it very shocking?"

"Oh, my dear, you must not mind dreams."

"No, I don't mind them, only I thought of Percival, when I saw the top of the Castle this morning."

While Ellen was thus portraying her feelings to her venerable parent, Lord Castle Howel was traversing his apartment, and ruminating on the lovely child, whose mind and person promised so much perfection. He was a man of nice honour and great generosity. I have no children, said he, I will adopt her, educate, and bring her into life; she will amuse my heavy hours, and adorn my festive ones; but the world! – the world! – Aye, well, if the censure of the world forbids me to indulge myself in her society, I will educate her *for* the world: and firmly resolving so to do, he went to rest, satisfied with his own intentions towards Ellen and all God's creation.

The morning shewed Lord Castle Howel his fair visitant by day light, for although the hour of dining at Castle Howel and London differed by at least two hours, yet lights must be introduced with the dinner. Ellen was still Ellen, the morning being frosty, she who hailed the rising sun at home, had now been rambling out, long before Lady Margaret left her room.

Lord Castle Howel and his young friend were again seated on the sofa, the tête-à-tête of the preceding night was renewed with increased approbation on both sides, and before the Meredith family took leave, the Earl asked Lady Meredith, half joking, if she would give him her grand-daughter, which she, in the same good-humour, promised.

From this period Doctor Macshean became a regular, though private, visitor, at Castle Howel.

Joseph apprised his Lord of the return of the carriage, who flew with avidity to the hall door to receive Ellen.

Ready for the same service, but too modest to keep his station when his Lordship appeared, stood Percival Evelyn; the proud Peer attempted to look him into contempt; it was, however, but an attempt; for Percival Evelyn, under his rustic bashfulness, had fine natural sense, and great personal courage, and although, by his own humility Lord Claverton got so far the advantage of him as to receive Ellen from the coach, he resolutely advanced to welcome her home; she extended her hand to him with an air of the most familiar friendship, asked a number of questions, which her vivacity did not give him time to answer, and entirely regardless of Lord Claverton's ill health, of which he complained, or of the intense cold, which she seemed not to feel, stood chatting away till reproved by Lady Meredith, when she suffered herself to be led in by the smiling, though inwardly enraged Lord Claverton.

Mr. Meredith, who did not sleep at Castle Howel, was indisposed; a disappointment of the heart in the early part of his life, had extremely injured his health; he was subject to nervous fevers, and bilious complaints, which often confined him, and filled his family with apprehensions for his life. He usually left the rectory on the first symptoms of an attack, but Lord Claverton's stay rendered Code Gwyn less desirable, and less convenient than his own house, and Percival was now come to fetch Miss Meredith, who, with all her romance, was his favourite sister.

The conversation of the preceding night dwelt on Lady Meredith's mind; Percival Evelyn, she, for the first time, discovered was too much in Ellen's thoughts; *his* expectations were moderate indeed! Ellen's no less so; together they must be wretched, separate each might be fortunate. These reflections occurred to Lady Meredith, during her ride home, and the impropriety of suffering two amiable young people, partial to each other, to be in the same house, with their feeling engrossed by the same object, also occurred, while Ellen pleaded, with great eloquence both of speech and look, the necessity of somebody's accompanying her aunt, in the care of her dear uncle; but a grave negative, from Lady Meredith, silenced and disconcerted her.

The next morning Lady Meredith went to visit her son alone; this was the second real sorrow Ellen had ever felt, and as it was an unusual deprivation of indulgence without a consciousness of offence, that sorrow was blended with some little resentment.

Winifred happened to be also in great trouble; she had unfortunately burnt a sheet of paper, wrote all over by Amanthis to Lucretia, giving a full and particular account of the visit to Castle Howel; and, in running out of the way of Mary, who was a little of the vixen, struck Sir Arthur's gouty foot in such a manner, as to excite anger in the bosom of meekness itself. Lady Meredith recommended it to Mrs. Griffiths to punish her for her carelessness, and forbid her to appear in her sight.

Winifred's sorrow was always boisterous, and, her disgrace happening while Mr. Joseph was present, was such an aggravation, that the servants' hall echoed with her injuries. Ellen went hastily to enquire what could occasion such violent exclamations of grief.

Winifred no sooner beheld her young mistress with tears in *her* eyes, than all her own cares vanished.

"As Cot shall pless me, Miss Ellen, you have been crying your eyes out, vat the tivil is the matter fith my lady?"

Ellen was sure she did not know, but she was very cross.

Winifred believed the tivil himself had got his cloven foot among them.

Mistress and maid being united in one cause, were proceeding to Ellen's room, to unbosom, when, in the gallery, they were met by Lord Claverton, who very anxiously enquired of Mr. Meredith's health.

This was the right key.

Ellen immediately entered into a history of his disorder, and lamented her grandmamma would not let her go to him.

Lady Meredith's conduct did not, it will be presumed, appear so very unreasonable to his Lordship; but it was not his business to dispute the point, he contented himself with soothing her vexation, and speaking well of the objects of her warmest affections, even Evelyn came in for some share in his compliments, and so, by degrees, lessened her agitation, and prevailed on her to walk up and down the gallery with him till she had recovered her spirits and temper.

When a man once takes it into his head, he will be very fond of a woman; or, when a woman feels the same disposition towards a man, it is amazing with what ingenuity they spin out every little thread of event till it forms a web of happiness or misery.

Lord Claverton considered Lady Meredith's ill humour as a most fortunate circumstance, for it procured him the company of Ellen two whole hours after she had ceased to remember her vexation, without forgetting the kindness of his consolation.

Chapter VII

Lady Meredith having found her son in no immediate danger, made her visit short, and returned, eager to impart to Sir Arthur her observations on Ellen's conversation with her, at Castle Howel. He agreed with her, that a permanent attachment to Percival, who was wholly dependent on their son, and (except as his eleve) totally unknown to them, would ruin their child, without bettering him; they were, therefore, designing proper means of separating them, when Lady Margaret Howel was announced.

In the same breath that she asked for the sweet Ellen, she congratulated Sir Arthur and Lady Meredith on their good fortune, and proceeded, with an apparent candid liberality, to inform them, her brother had taken an uncommon liking to the charming child, that he thought she promised to be one of the greatest beauties of the age, that he considered her want of education as a serious misfortune, which he would be happy to redress, by instantly sending her to Bath, at his own expense, and give her every advantage which the finest instructions could bestow.

Sir Arthur and Lady Meredith looked at each other, they thought of the benefit their darling would derive from this generous offer of Lord Castle Howel, and their bosoms swelled with gratitude; but they recollected they must part with her, and their eyes filled with tears.

Dr. Macshean entered, and neither one sensation nor the other was observed; Lady Margaret said, she would leave the

Baronet and his Lady to consider of the business, and left the room with the Doctor.

After a short silence,

"What good will a fine education do her?" said Sir Arthur, "without we could give her a suitable fortune?"

"Very true," answered Lady Meredith, "but she is so charming, that – and besides, Sir Arthur, we have so little in our power; I am thinking, in depriving her of so generous an offer, we really shall be guilty of an act of injustice; what can we do for her?"

Sir Arthur sighed. "What shall I do for a companion, when I am laid up with the gout?"

"And who will read and prattle away the long evenings with me?" said Lady Meredith. "But these regrets are selfish, we must *conquer them*, the dear child may make friends."

"*May*," answered Sir Arthur, "she *will;* her face is a recommendation of her heart from God himself, she will be in his protection, let her go."

This conversation had long and frequent interruptions from the feelings of Sir Arthur and his Lady, the determination was painful in the extreme, but as they were both convinced it was right, Lady Meredith followed Lady Margaret, and thankfully acquainted her with their acceptance of the Earl's generous offer.

Ellen was now summoned; she was still with Lord Claverton and her favourite Winifred.

"As Cot shall safe me'" cried Winifred, "my Lady has learnt to bear malicious, I am feart to co down."

Ellen, without speaking, obeyed the summons, her little heart again swelling with resentment; but when informed of the change that was soon to take place in her situation, that she was to leave her family, to be moved from the loved spot, where, till New Year's eve, she had not known a sad moment, all regret for her late disappointment vanished; she looked at her venerable parents, when told she was to leave them; bursting into a flood of anguish, she flew to the bosom of Sir Arthur, her arms round his neck, his involuntarily clasping her.

"My dear grandpapa, will you then part with your Ellen?"

The affecting question, followed by sobs and dumb expressions of grief, overcame Sir Arthur.

Lady Meredith, in whose placid mind meekness and fortitude were blended, led her to her chamber, and there explained to her the generous motive that dictated an offer of such advantage, but in vain was the good lady eloquent on every advantage that would result from the offered protection of Lord Castle Howel.

To be accomplished, elegant, and well informed, was fine; but to stay at Code Gwyn with Sir Arthur and Lady Meredith, to be instructed by her uncle and aunt, and share in the amusements of Percival Evelyn, was a thousand times finer.

Two hours passed in adducing solid reasons, on the part of Lady Meredith, why the Earl's offer should be accepted, and in hearing the innocent and no less feasible ones of Ellen, why it should be rejected. But hers was the voice of uninformed simplicity, warm in its natural attachments, and totally unacquainted with the world. Lady Meredith was herself a child in experience, yet she could argue as well on a point where the obvious interest of Ellen was concerned, as the best counsel in the world.

Strongly impressed with the idea, that a secret attachment was taking root in her heart to young Evelyn, the more she reflected the more earnest she was to remove her from so dangerous an attraction; and as all opposition to her wish was perfectly new to the child of her heart, she at length prevailed. Ellen consented to return to Castle Howel, with Lady Margaret, and thankfully accept the Earl's noble and disinterested offer.

By the time this conference was ended, the purport of Lady Margaret's visit was spread over the house. Winifred, notwithstanding Lady Meredith's commands not to appear in her sight, was seated on the ground at the door of the chamber, and it no sooner opened, than she set up a cry, and fell down at Lady Meredith's feet in strong hysterics.

Ellen, fondly attached to the humble friend of her youth, bathed her face with her tears, and was kneeling by her, when Lord Claverton, alarmed at the extraordinary noise, appeared in the gallery, and with an exclamation of surprise asked the cause of Winifred's sorrow. The answer he received was as great a blow to him as it had been to Winifred, and as unexpected too; he descended with hasty and perturbed steps to the parlour, where Lady Margaret sat, with undisturbed countenance, apparently hearing the fond regrets of the old Baronet, but really engrossed by the tender looks of Doctor Macshean.

Lord Claverton, too much interested to be on his guard, immediately asked the cause of a commotion that was visible in the countenance of every inhabitant of Code Gwyn, Doctor Macshean and Joseph Wilks only excepted.

Lady Meredith and her weeping child entered before he was answered, the latter with her straw bonnet tied over her flowing hair, ready to attend Lady Margaret, but her swollen eyes and dejected looks were to Lord Claverton a welcome proof of her reluctance.

The fond grandmother entreated Lady Margaret to allow for the caprice, which in youth, is often the result of unlimited indulgence. Lady Margaret embraced and encouraged the fair novice, and promising she should return to Code Gwyn in two days, took her in her carriage, which was followed by the tears and vociferous exclamations of poor Winifred. Her Ladyship, at her brother's request, invited the Lieutenant to accompany his niece, but as his guest, Lord Claverton, who professed an uncommon friendship for him, complained of sudden indisposition, he politely excused himself.

The feelings of his Lordship at this moment were rather troublesome. What could induce Lord Castle Howel to take a young girl under his protection but beauty? What was her want of accomplishments to a man, who did not mean her attainments should be sacrificed to his pleasures? Judging from himself, he had no doubt but the Earl meant to get possession of the young beauty for his own private amusement; but, as *he* was some years younger than Lord Castle Howel, and, as he rightly presumed, as superior in the art of intrigue as in person, the scheme of sending her to a school at Bath, which he found was proposed, did not, on recollection, appear so terrible. Ellen, in the bosom of her family, under the affectionate eye of Lady Meredith, and the piercing one of her son, in the habit of strolling about with Percival Evelyn, or listening to the heroic reading of Miss Meredith, was certainly a more difficult conquest, than Ellen at a public boarding school.

There were *governesses*, and some he *knew,* who were assailable; the medical quality of the Bath waters was a pretence for his openly going there; the Code Gwyn family could not suspect his motive for visiting a young lady, with whom his acquaintance commenced under their own roof, besides he might very naturally invite the Lieutenant to accompany him. These thoughts succeeded each other in rapid progression, while Sir Arthur's family were pursuing Lady Margaret's carriage till it was no longer visible.

Lord Claverton was indisposed – Sir Arthur's gout threatened him – the ladies had headaches – and the Doctor and Lieutenant being left to themselves, the latter proposed to walk to the Rectory to visit the Parson.

They found Mr. Meredith asleep, Percival by his bedside, and Miss Meredith reading in the study; rest and quiet being the usual specific in Mr. Meredith's disorder, after just looking at the sick man, tea was ordered and Percival summoned to join them.

The extraordinary whim, as Doctor Macshean chose to call it, of Lord Castle Howel, had been discussed over and over between him and the Lieutenant, and it recommenced at tea.

Miss Meredith, for her part, wished there was not a black design at the bottom, to spirit her niece away, and so keep her out of the knowledge of her friends, till some gallant youth achieved wonders in effecting her release; for, as to her education, she solemnly assured the Doctor, *that* was perfectly complete; she had herself heard her read through seven quarto volumes of Cassandra, the folios of Clelia, and Princess of Cleeves, and few people, she would say, could give more force to the greatness of Oroondates' soul, or more grace to the tenderness of Cassandra's, than Ellen Meredith.

Young Evelyn, too much used to Miss Meredith's rhapsodies to attend to her conversation was looking over an old newspaper, and sipping his tea, in a kind of absent listlessness, when the sound of a name most familiar and dear to his heart, and a confused recollection of the conversation, brought a crimson glow into his face, which retreated in one moment, and left it pale as ashes; his eyes, naturally full, swelled in their sockets; his eye-brows were distended, and every sense was converted to ear, when Miss Meredith proceeded in her eulogium on the finished education of her niece, her surmises of the causes of sending her away, her prognostics of the consequences, her dislike of a modern education, and her regret at parting with Ellen; the Lieutenant laughed at her romantic phrases and odd notions; the Doctor, who made it a rule to be all things to all men, though he spoke not, looked a coincidence with Miss Meredith, when suddenly Percival Evelyn fell back in his chair.

Miss Meredith shrieked, the maids, one of whom was old enough to be a grandmother, rushed in, and set up a lamentation in their own harmonious language, which very much resembled the Hibernian howl. Mr. Meredith waked out of the first natural repose since his indisposition, rang his bell, no regard was paid to it, he with great difficulty reached his morning gown and got to the door, but could distinguish nothing but a confusion of sounds, now moderated by the Doctor, now increased by the women, and feeling himself weak was returning to his bed, there to wait an explanation till some part of the family were at leisure to give it him, when a yell reached his ear, that quickly banished all attention to his own weakness; it was Martha, his old maid, who screamed, "Percival is dead." There was now no apparent want of health in Mr. Meredith, he rushed down and found his young eleve without any sign of life, a cold dew on his forehead, and Doctor Macshean in the act of letting him blood; Miss Meredith, in terror at the accident, appealed to her brother, without wondering at his presence, whether he should or should not be bled.

Mr. Meredith looked on the pallid face with speechless agony and astonishment; the incision was made but no blood followed the lancet; Doctor Macshean looked very serious; Mr. Meredith in sad, but solemn composure, ordered the door and windows to be opened, and, no longer weak, raised the boy in his arms, loosened his collar, and directed Martha to bring a tub of warm water; she obeyed, but in her hurry a trifling mistake occurred; as they were brewing, she substituted warm wort for water, but by the time she returned, the young man had opened his eyes, he bled freely, and the colour of life re-animated his face.

It was in vain he was urged to assign a cause for this sudden attack, in vain he was pressed to describe his present feelings; his eyes were fixed, and, to the surprise of every body, he continued silent; a tear strayed involuntary from either eye; they dropped on the hand of Mr. Meredith, and increased his astonishment. Miss Meredith now recollected her brother's situation.

"Good God! Brother," she exclaimed, "why did you come down? You will get your death."

Percival heard this and recovered his speech; lamented having exposed his friend to such hazard, intreated him to return to his chamber, and begged with such earnest sadness that he might accompany him, that they retired together, attended by Martha, who went to put her master to bed leaving the Lieutenant, Doctor Macshean, and Miss Meredith, to talk over and wonder at the strange event, till the moon arose, when the Doctor and Lieutenant walked home.

Chapter VIII

The Earl, delighted with Ellen's simplicity, and that frankness of heart, which mingled expressions of tender regret for the friends she was so soon to leave, with gratitude to him for the cause; and finding his attention much more pleasantly attracted by the beauty of a human than a field flower, undertook himself to begin the formation of a mind so open and naturally docile.

Lady Margaret had already sent measures and orders to Vigo-Lane, for a complete assortment of fine linen and cloaths, suitable to the age and appearance of a school girl.

The depression of Ellen's spirits was increased when shewn to her elegant apartment; she had hitherto slept in a small chamber adjoining her grandfather's, Winifred was her bed-fellow, and had, usually, some light hearted tale or other to amuse her with while undressing, when her venerable parents called out the salutations of the night.

She was now in a large room superbly hung, richly carpeted, furnished with gilt cabinets, and large mirrors, but with a loneliness of grandeur that recalled the comforts of her own little chamber, in such vivid colours, she burst into tears; the servant who attended her reported this to the Earl and his sister, the former immediately conjectured the cause, and begged Lady Margaret to invite her to take half her bed. Lady Margaret's rule, from which she never swerved, was, to be always of her brother's opinion. She called a smile into her features, said she was just thinking of the same thing, and sent her woman to fetch Ellen into her apartment.

To those used to kindness and affection, every deprivation is grievous, and a heart pining under a change so wounding to sensibility, opens to every approach of the treatment it regrets: Ellen found herself soothed by this mark of attention, her tears dispersed, she went to bed, and her mind, hurried by the events of the day, being now composed, sunk to rest. But however ready her Ladyship had been to oblige her brother, she had not in this case been civil to herself; the admitting Ellen to her room was, in some degree, to admit her to her confidence; for *her* woman, who was her privy counsellor, had as many things to amuse her Lady as Winifred had for Ellen.

Doctor Macshean had already found the secret of conveying his amorous vows, through Mrs. Gibson, and though he had not *now* a vast deal of gold to give her, yet, as she knew her Lady abounded, and as she saw it was very probable both Lady and gold would in time be his, she very courteously delivered the letters and messages he continued daily to send, and entertained her lady with a number of good qualities, with which she kindly endowed him, as well as with many pertinent remarks on his handsome person and pleasing address.

Those who have fixed their private affections, where they do not choose publicly to avow a partiality, and those only, know the value of a confab, at bed time, with a favourite servant; Lady Margaret was resolved not to be deprived of such a treasure, and therefore, as Ellen was attached to *her* maid she proposed sending for her, in pure kindness, which gave her great credit in the opinion of her brother, who sent a card to Code Gwyn, with a request, that Winifred might attend her young lady, and, at the same time, a light cart carried a hamper of fine old Madeira, for Sir Arthur's own drinking, from his Lordship, and a large canister of very fine tea, for Lady Meredith, from his sister.

But neither Madeira, tea, nor any of the advantages which promised to result from the patronage of the Earl could dispel the regrets which filled their hearts for the absence of their favourite; with a tear on each venerable cheek, Lady Meredith went herself to the house-keeper's room to inform Mrs. Griffiths of Lord Castle Howel's message. Mrs. Griffiths received the news of her niece's advancement, far otherwise than her Lady had done that of Ellen.

For the first time in her life joy superseded respect; she hastened to consult her brother, old Griffiths, on the mutual assistance necessary for them to give their niece; and as fast as the old man could hobble from his pantry, they returned to Lady Meredith, who remained in the house-keeper's room, with the lucid drops still distilling from either eye.

The two old servants readily consented Winifred should go to her lady; Edward brought out the contents of his leather purse, and Mrs. Griffiths ransacked her drawers for the remains of her old finery. Winifred was called for, but no Winifred was to be found in or near the house; Mrs. Griffiths fumed, and Lady Meredith, considering the sending for her as a proof that Ellen was not yet reconciled to her good fortune, was angry at her absence, and impatient for her return; as she was not, however, to be found, the servant was dismissed, with a grateful card from Lady Meredith, and as much of Winifred's wardrobe as Mrs. Griffiths could find, with an addition from her own hoards, that she might not disgrace either her Lady or her relations.

In half an hour after the servant was gone, home came Winifred; not as usual, singing till the woods echoed her wild coarse strains, nor with her natural hop, skip and jump; but silent, slow, and heavy – she entered her aunt's room.

Mrs. Griffiths, who had not much of the virtue of patience in her disposition, began to rate her roughly for her absence, and demanded where she had been, in a key, that reached the hall. Winifred, out of humour and irritable, answered in equal tone.

The duet was in alt; one stormed, the other half crying, half scolding, made up in volubility what her aunt possessed in authority, and it was not till Lady Meredith had twice raised her mild voice, either party could be silenced.

Winifred confessed that she had been out all day, but to where, or with whom, she was stubbornly silent, and was retiring in great sullenness when Lady Meredith bid her prepare to follow Ellen to Castle Howel.

All traces of ill humour immediately vanished, she laughed, sung, and capered, but suddenly stopping—

"Cot Almighty safe us, sure my mistress is not coing to stay at that tiflish place."

"Devilish place!" returned Mrs. Griffiths, "'tis the finest place in the thirteen counties; I was with my Lady there forty years ago."

"If it was with Cot Almighty, Cot forgive us, I had rather, come back to Code Gwyn; but, to be sure, if Miss Ellen is there that is enuf."

Lady Meredith desired Winifred to be ready early next morning, and Mrs. Griffiths having ostensibly inventoried all the articles she had selected to send with her to Castle Howel recommended it to her to devote the remaining time to getting her things in nice order.

But Winifred had other concerns to settle; she first met Joseph Wilks, by appointment, in the great barn, and gravely assured him, that all matters must end betwixt *him* and *her,* for, that her mistress would never have Lord Claverton, and as she was resolved, to live and die with her, desired he would take his handkerchiefs and buckles, and get another sweet heart.

Joe was astonished; he had made love to Winifred by order of his Lord, the girl, tho' very far from handsome, was young, playful, and innocent; Joseph had somehow persuaded himself into a liking for her, and as he had a little of the coxcomb in *his* disposition, as well as his master, his vanity was humbled at her sang froid.

He attempted to persuade.

"No, no, Mr. Joseph must not think to come over her."

He threatened to hang himself.

"It matters not, Mr. Joseph."

He would marry the first girl who would have him – but all his rhetoric was to no purpose, till he swore he would leave Lord Claverton, as soon as he had saved money to stock a farm, and live at Code Gwyn. This mollified the fair damsel, who then consented to keep his presents, and suffered him to accompany her on a secret expedition to Code Gwyn village.

In the way Joseph was *too* happy not to be very fond, and as Winifred looked on her marriage as a settled thing, she was easily persuaded there should be no secrets between man and wife; his blandishments obtained what all Lady Meredith's authority, and her aunt's scolding, had failed to do, the history of her morning's excursion.

Mr. Meredith's man had been before day at Code Gwyn, on a secret message to Mrs. Winifred Griffiths, to beg she would directly come to Mr. Evelyn, who was very ill.

Mr. Evelyn was too great a favourite not to be at all risks obeyed; but what was poor Winifred's consternation to find her friend with his eyes swelled almost out of his head, his hair disordered, his hands trembling and burning, and his whole frame speaking at once grief and disease, hardly articulate, he stammered the name of Ellen, and burst into tears.

Winifred had not slept – the night had been almost as tedious to her as it could be to him, and on account of the same object, she therefore wept too, and a few minutes conversation let her into a secret she had never suspected, and engaged her in a cause, which so accorded with her own wishes, that she swore vehemently, both in Welch and English, she would die by it.

Evelyn declared he could not live without Ellen, and his confidant said, it was not fit he should.

Evelyn detested all Lords – Winifred supposed they were a parcel of outlandish tivels.

"Oh, what shall I do, Winifred, if I cannot hear of my dear Ellen?"

She promised she would walk barefoot to Castle Howel but he should.

Winifred communicated this confidence to Joe, with her opinion, that "true lof was petter than cowld," in which he accorded, and, after a promise on her part, to meet him again in the parlour, when Sir Arthur and Lady Meredith were gone to bed, he returned back, and she proceeded to the rectory, according to agreement.

She went up the back stairs to Evelyn's room, whom she found extended on the bed and his eyes shut.

"Fat, are you asleep, Mr. Evelyn, Cot pless us? Cet up I have news for you."

Percival opened his eyes, but, in attempting to rise, fell back with such violence as alarmed his confidant; he, however, in a faint voice, begged she would tell him her news directly.

It was with visible joy he heard Winifred was to follow Ellen, he entreated her to let him know every thing that happened, and above all, to conceal the secret he had entrusted to her from all the world, even from Ellen herself, and not tell the dearest friend she had, he was sick of love.

Winifred swore, as she had done before, without the smallest inward reproach; for as Joseph was to be her husband, she had no idea it was any breach of confidence to tell him all she knew.

Miss Meredith's foot on the stair, coming to enquire after Evelyn's health, shortened her visit; and, after promising to write to him by David (the rector's man) away went Winifred.

Chapter IX

Possessed of Winifred's declaration, that Ellen would not have Lord Claverton, Joseph communicated it to his Lordship, and received five guineas in reward for past and earnest of future services; the terms he was on with his sweetheart gave him an excuse to visit Castle Howel as long as Lord Claverton chose to stay in the country, which, his Lordship resolved should depend on events.

In the mean time, as the whole family now at Code Gwyn were his aversion, as the intense coldness of the weather prevented his going out, and as, indeed, he would have no pretence for staying if he was able to travel, it was, in the present posture of affairs, the most convenient plan he could adopt, to be too much indisposed to leave his apartment, and as Mrs. Griffiths was a person he now chose to be well with, he patiently listened to her dissertations on water gruel and white soups.

Joseph's last interview with Winifred was very tender, he, consequently, knew every syllable that had passed at the rectory; and the five guineas in his pocket was a stimula to industry he was resolved to deserve; but he was too artful, at this interview, to drop a word in favour of his Lord. No, all Joseph's wishes were centered in the little farm, with his dear – Winny! and as he confirmed this assertion with many fashionable oaths, they separated in mutual good humour, and unbounded confidence, on *one* side, at least.

The noble owner of Castle Howel now experienced there *were* amusements more grateful to his feelings than even

Botany; he pointed out to Ellen the different classes of learning and literature that enlightened the world; described the progress refinement and luxury had made in modern times; spoke of the immortal Shakespeare, and quoted several beautiful passages, suitable to her comprehension, and so adapted his information to the experience of his fair pupil, that after a long morning passed in the library, Lord Castle Howel had the satisfaction to perceive the restless absence of thought, with which she had at first heard him, gradually change into eager attention; *her eyes* sparkled with pleasure, the rapidity of her questions and the quickness of her apprehension flattered and delighted *him,* and often did he regret, that the tyranny of custom forbad him to undertake the *sole* information of such a mind himself.

In the evening his Lordship taught her the gamut, both vocal and instrumental. She played on the harp a number of tunes by ear, and accompanied it with her voice, but the *science* of music was a matter she was totally unacquainted with; how this and other female attainments came to be unknown to the Miss Merediths, will appear in the course of this history; *all they knew* they had taught Ellen.

The hour of retirement was less irksome than the preceding night; she had sufficient subject for recollection, equally new and delightful, and her only wish, after the welfare of her friends at Code Gwyn, was, that Percival Evelyn could witness and share in the expansion of her mind.

Winifred arrived early next morning, and the Lieutenant and Doctor Macshean rode over before dinner.

The Earl received them with the utmost cordiality, and the reader will suppose Lady Margaret was not less condescending.

In the mean time Lord Claverton was deliberating on the step he should next take; Joseph was shut up with him the most part of the day – and as it was purposed Ellen's school education should take place when the Christmas recess ended, it was settled between Doctor Macshean and his noble Patron, that Bath was the precise place likely to renovate a constitution, injured by the hot climate from whence they were just arrived; and preparations were accordingly began for their departure.

The communication between the families of Castle Howel and Code Gwyn, became every day more frequent; the Miss Merediths were good horse-women, and Ellen delighted to see them; the severity of the weather was the Earl's objection to *her* riding, but he was pleased when his sister took her in the chariot to visit Code Gwyn, because she returned more cheerful and happy.

A Nobleman of Lord Claverton's rank in the neighbourhood, was also an object for politeness. The Earl rode over to visit Sir Arthur, and invite Lord Claverton to Castle Howel. The cultivation of this acquaintance was of too much importance to Lord Claverton's views to be neglected; he accepted, with great satisfaction, an offered corner in the Earl's carriage, and during the course of the visit, Lord Castle Howel understanding he meant, as well as themselves, to make some stay at Bath, very politely pressed him to accept of the same convenience thither, which the reader will be sure, he as politely accepted, and immediately wrote to order his carriage and servants to meet him there.

Every thing thus in train, Winifred, full of her importance at the fine Castle, of the fine cloaths making for Ellen, of the fine vows of her lover, and a long etcetera of finery – entirely forgot both Evelyn and her promise. At every excursion to

Code Gwyn, as Ellen was the oracle of the parlour, Winifred gave her orations in the servant's hall.

Sir Arthur, who, from his sedentary life, greedily devoured every bit of news, kept Ellen at his elbow from the moment of her arrival to her departure, asking a thousand questions; while she, who knew no pleasure superior to his amusement, stored up every anecdote she heard, and every occurrence that happened, for his entertainment.

Lord Claverton saw there was no possibility of obtaining a moment of her attention, and therefore became, with the family, an auditor of her sensible prattle.

Winifred, on her part, held forth to the servants, in their different ways, with an air of profound knowledge; she told her aunt, that all *her* experience would not carry her the day through at Castle Howel; and, as to her uncle, "Cot help the owld man, his white hairs would stand on end if he had as many sorts of liquors to cork and uncork as the putler at Castle Howel; the cook, Cot knows, was a dish washer, and the tairy mait mate coot putter enuff, but nothing like the putter at Castle Howel."

"And so you have learn'd," said old Griffiths, "already to despise your native home. I foresee thou wilt return as ragged as a colt."

"Cot help you, uncle, ragged! why there's no end to the riches at Castle Howel."

Old Griffiths shook his head in token of incredulity and disgust, and the rest of the male domestics followed his example.

Mrs. Griffiths called her an upstart ignorant wench; she warranted she could manage as good a family as any in the Country.

The maids felt themselves doubly hurt, first, in having their abilities degraded, next, in seeing their old fellow servant so finely dressed, and so full of airs; so that poor Winifred, abused by all, was obliged to seek consolation, where, indeed it was always ready, from Mr. Joseph, and declared she would not ask to come again with Miss Ellen, among such a low set; yet, as often as the carriage was ordered she made the same request, repeated the same stories, with the same effect, and left Code Gwyn with the same declaration.

At length the day being fixed for their departure, Ellen chose to go on the Sunday to take leave of her friends, and, with the little vanity natural to her sex, had her hair dressed by Lady Margaret's woman, wore a new green satin habit, with a white beaver hat, and green feathers, and attended by Winifred, in a drab cloth Joseph, a black hat and handsome band. They met the family at Code Gwyn church.

Every eye was turned from the *Creator* to the *created*; it was not that Ellen looked more beautiful, but she was finer and more *unlike* themselves.

Lady Meredith and her daughter's hearts dilated, the pew door was thrown open, they handed her in, and even the good Rector suffered his attention to be a moment taken from his duty.

Mutual gratulations however soon subsided; the respect she had always been taught was due to a place of worship, solemnized her features, but her eye glanced involuntarily to the Rector's pew, where Evelyn used to sit; no Evelyn was there; she eagerly explored every part of the church, and still no Evelyn was to be seen.

She coloured.

What! did Percival Evelyn know she was coming to Code Gwyn, for the last time, for she did not know how many months, and was he not desirous of bidding her farewell? – "Well, who cares!" and she sat down in the middle of the Psalms.

"I have not seen him since I left my grandfather's! no, not once! and my uncle, I have not seen him either! and it is now above a fortnight."

"Pray, aunt Mary, where is Percival Evelyn?"

"Lord, child, did you not receive my letter about him?"

"Letter! no: I never received a letter in all my life, when did you send it?"

"Above a week ago, Mr. Joseph, Lord Claverton's man, promised to give it Winifred for you."

"Then I am sure he forgot it; but what of Percival?"

"Why, my dear he has been dying."

Ellen turned pale.

"But he is better now and will dine with us – my brother thought him too weak to sit in the cold church."

Ellen's face changed to the deepest scarlet, and she fixed her eyes on the pictures in the prayer book, without attending to the service, till roused by Lady Meredith at the end.

Nothing, during the ride home, occupied Ellen, but Percival's illness; and though Lord Claverton was eagerly waiting to hand her out of the carriage, and though her Patron had explained to her the propriety of attending to the laws of politeness, she could think of nothing but Percival. Winifred having seen Lady Margaret's maid always attend her Lady immediately on her alighting, and willing to shew her fellow servants her improvements, actually pushed before Lord Claverton.

"Where," said Ellen, without taking the least notice of the Peer, or any other being, "where is the letter my aunt Mary sent, by Mr. Joseph, about Percival?"

Winifred coloured; it was the first thought she had given Percival since she left him sick at the Rectory, after having entered into a solemn engagement, to do him all manner of kind offices with her mistress, but as she was too great a lady at Castle Howel to be visible in any part of the house where such bumkins as the parson's man had access, she had not been in the way of receiving a single message from, or in the recollection of saying a civil thing of, the forgotten Percival: Winifred's, though simple, was not a bad heart; her conscience smote her for her breach of promise to Percival, but no letter had she received from Mr. Joseph, and therefore none could have been forgotten.

"Give me the letter directly," said Ellen, rushing by Lord Claverton, up stairs, without even thinking of Sir Arthur.

"What letter, and where are you going, Ellen?" asked Lady Meredith.

Winifred followed her mistress to her room, and Lord Claverton, who understood more of the matter than any other person, retired to his, and rang for Joseph. They had very little time to arrange affairs, before Winifred rapped, and desired to speak one word with Mr. Joseph, who, on being interrogated about the letter, confessed (with many protestations of sorrow, for his carelessness) that he had lost it out of his pocket, on the road to Castle Howel.

She, whose partiality for Joseph was far from decreasing, was easily persuaded to forgive; but Ellen, impatient, uneasy, and anxious to know every thing about Percival, declared he was a very idle young man, and never should do any thing for her again.

Winifred called Cot to witness Joseph was a fery onest lat, and would not hurt a worm; but her rhetoric was thrown away.

Ellen's displeasure continued, and she went to Sir Arthur with tears in her eyes, and her cheeks glowing with anger. Immediately after Mr. Meredith and Percival entered, the latter supported by his reverend friend.

Ellen shrank from the paternal embrace of Sir Arthur, and stood aghast.

The countenance of young Evelyn was, as before described, always pale; but it was the paleness of sentiment, a thinking habit, and a pensive turn of mind; his face was oval, perhaps beyond the exact line of beauty; his complexion clear brown, and his eyes large, black and piercing, which, with his dark eyebrows and eye lashes, gave a most interesting turn to his countenance; he was prepossessing and agreeable, and, far beyond mediocrity, handsome. But this was the shadow of his former self. His eyes, no longer brilliant, sunk in his head, his face thin and yellow, his lips parched and burning with hectic fever, his voice tremulous, and an universal weakness pervading his whole frame – he gasped for breath, and unable to answer the kind enquiries of the family, sat down on the nearest chair.

Ellen looked round, the glance of compassion, of sorrow, met her from every eye.

She burst into tears.

"Percival, my dear Percival," cried she, running towards him, "what is the matter? How long have you been ill?"

Percival tried to speak, but failing in the effort, turned away his head.

"What!" cried she, half turning to Mr. Meredith, "can't he speak? Percival, won't you speak to *me,* to Ellen, your own Ellen?"

Without turning his head, the blood faintly mantling into his face,

"You have forgot ME, Ellen, *quite, quite* forgot *me."*

Ellen did not answer, her arm rested on him, and his hand involuntarily clasped hers, as it hung over his shoulder. He then began to answer his friends, and say, how much better he was; he breathed freer, and although the observations Lady Meredith could not help making, were not the most pleasing, either to Sir Arthur or herself, yet, as this was to be the last interview, and as she loved Percival, she chose rather to *seem* not to *see*, than be *obliged* to *censure.*

They were in this situation when Lord Claverton made his appearance. Strange effects have been related from looking on the Gorgon. Lord Claverton did not actually turn to stone, but all the colours of the rainbow were by turns predominant in his face.

Lady Meredith endeavoured to divert the attention of Lord Claverton from the young pair, *and them* from each other, but having tried all ways she could think of, gave the matter up. The dinner was the most silent meal they had ever made, and was dispatched with that impatience of restraint, which a family, in the full confidence of each other, must be supposed to feel, on the eve of separation, in the presence of a stranger.

Lord Claverton felt he was himself that restraint.

The pauses in conversation growing longer and more frequent, could not be misunderstood. No man was better acquainted with the etiquette of fine breeding, yet, in this instance, he could not prevail on himself to leave to themselves a family, whose insipidity was his aversion, whose plain manners were his contempt; for, opposite to him sat Ellen and Percival, solely occupied by each other, and seeming to wait with impatience the moment when the many eloquent things, spoke in their mutual glances, might be put into words.

"*That* moment' said the haughty Peer, inwardly, "they shall *not* have." He endeavoured to enter into conversation with Catherine.

What was now the subject of her studies? Would she honour him with a commission to send her books of any kind?

Catherine thanked him, but she had enough for her life time; besides, there were no new Romances.

A silence ensued. He was still more unfortunate in his next effort.

"Had the early lambs suffered by the cold weather," was a question to Miss Agnes, from which he had great hopes.

It was answered with a formal "No."

Again a dead silence.

Mr. Meredith vexed, and really offended, at a restraint, which grew more intolerable every moment, asked Lady Meredith if she would not order coffee, and, as soon as it was over, taking Ellen and his mother in each hand, and bowing to Lord Claverton, he led them out of the room; they were followed by the other ladies.

Poor Percival sat with his eyes fixed on the door, which closed after them; not being asked to go, he wanted resolution to move, and endured a three hours silence the picture of despair.

Sir Arthur did indeed enter into a kind of forced conversation for some time, but fell insensibly into his evening nap.

Lord Claverton still persevered in his plan, which Percival's modesty assisted; for though not considered, by the Peer, of importance enough to be spoken to on any other occasion, yet *now* he condescended to address a few insignificant questions to him, and so contrived to render him his entertainer who was the object of his hatred.

At length, supper, and Lady Meredith with her family,

relieved all parties. Ellen's eyes were red and swelled, she drew her stool between her grandfather and grandmother, and, grasping a hand of each, sat totally absorbed, in her own reflection; and although Lord Claverton had the mortification to remain quite unnoticed, that mortification was much softened when he observed she was not more attentive to any other part of the company, except indeed at the moment when Mr. Meredith and his eleve departed, when her adieus were more tender and oftener repeated than sat entirely easy on him; he, however, consoled himself in the certainty that this would be the last interview, at least for some time, with the formidable Percival, for the next day he accompanied her to Bath, where Lord Castle Howel's carriage set her down at the first school in that polite city.

Chapter X

Thus, then, a new world was opened to our heroine; the well qualified governess of this little seminary was a woman, whose reputation, as a female writer, had been established, without estranging her from the duties of her situation; and she wisely employed her excellent senses in the cultivation of the human mind.

Under so good a judge, both of matter and manner, the improvements of her pupils was, as might be expected, rapid and systematical. Mrs. Forrest, though prepossessed by the beauty of the young stranger, immediately discovered the deficiencies in her education. Ellen, on her part, was confounded, to see ladies, much younger than herself, perfect mistresses of accomplishments, for which she had but just began to acquire a taste; comparing herself with her new associates, how ignorant, how contemptible did she appear; what time would it not require, what application, to become what they now were.

With the playful avidity natural to young minds, used to a regular succession of instruction, she saw them varying music, drawing, reciting in different languages, and fine works, to all which she was a total stranger.

Unable to bear a comparison so humiliating, tears filled her eyes, and dropped on her white bosom.

The sensible governess was not less attentive to her new charge, and drawing the most favourable conclusions from the observations she had seen her make, insinuated herself into her confidence, by a judicious mixture of instruction and compliment, and described, with such apparent ease, the gradations through which a perfect knowledge of all female accomplishments were to be attained, and so entirely entered into the true spirit of politeness, by contriving to raise her pupil's opinion of her own ability, as she impressed her with respect *for* and attention *to* herself, that all her uneasy sensations subsided; she wrote a short letter to Lady Meredith, and then joined her schoolmates in perfect good humour.

Lord Castle Howel gave every charge relative to his protegee; he obtained as a great favour, that Winifred should be admitted into Mrs. Forrest's family, but all conversation was strictly forbid with her young lady. The truth is, that though Ellen approached as near perfection as most heroines of her age, yet she certainly had a Welch accent, which, to the refined ears of Mrs. Forrest, and her ladies, sounded a little uncouth; and, as Winifred's was a barbarous jargon of neither Welch nor English, but a bad mixture of both, which she plainly saw would never be got rid of, she prudently conditioned for their entire separation.

Ellen's cheek crimsoned, and a tear of regret filled her eye at this sentence, but a moment's recollection, when Mrs. Forrest explained the reason, changed her regret to gratitude for such early attention to a defect her own ear reproached her with, whenever she spoke, or was spoken to, by her polished school fellows. Winifred was not indeed so acquiescent, but as murmuring had no effect, she quietly took her station in the laundry, contenting herself with making faces, nodding, winking, when she saw her young lady, and laying out the contents of her purse in fruit, which, as it was a breach of Mrs. Forrest's laws, she took great delight in supplying her with.

When our young novitiate made her fare well courtesy to

her friends, Lord Castle Howel felt a vacuum he could not easily account for; he had been lately amused by a pursuit, that superseded even his botanical experiments; he had spared no time, pains, or expense towards bringing the most beautiful production of nature to the high perfection he foresaw she would reach; he placed her where (for this end) she was to pass a considerable time, in a temporary seclusion from the world, and his visits were no longer necessary, or indeed proper.

To observe, and to assist, in the expansion of a young and ingenious mind; to watch the opening talents; to foster the seeds of virtue; to "teach the young idea how to shoot,"[3] is such an exquisite feast of reason, no wonder Lord Castle Howel's mind rejected in the instant all its former avocations, and recurred only to the hours passed in such delightful employment. Restless and uneasy, he proposed an excursion to Bristol Wells, before they returned to London.

Lord Claverton, though he appeared inactive, and even inattentive, to what was going forward, never lost sight of his original plan; from the instant he beheld Ellen he marked her for his own; rude and ignorant as she at first appeared, her graces softened on his observation; what she might be *made* struck *him* no less forcibly than it did Lord Castle Howel, though without the same disinterested ardour to assist noble work of nature.

To be Lord Claverton's toy, his amusement, as he had early planned, it was no matter how *little* Ellen knew; but to be his ostensible Mistress, to shew him the envied possessor of grace, ease, understanding, and such beauty! she could not know *too much*; it was indeed cursed impertinent of Lord

---

[3] Quoting "Spring" from James Thomson's *The Seasons* (1730).

Castle Howel to be meddling; an old fool! surely he might lay out his money to more advantage; and so thought both Doctor Macshean and Lady Margaret; but the more attached the Earl continued to his young favourite, the more difficult of access she would prove to him; to wean him, therefore, from an object on which his mind voluntarily turned, when Lord Claverton could so much better dispose of that object himself, was a point too desirable and important to be neglected; he knew the Doctor's views in the Castle Howel family, and the prudential caution with which he proceeded was an example not lost on the Peer; the Doctor indeed was a Socrates in love.

Although Lady Margaret assured him she had realized something very comfortable for a matrimonial garnish, she had only assured him, and he was resolved to have proof; for he had no reason to flatter himself his alliance would be eligible to the Earl, and, as in case of the worst, there were many snug little things to be procured by interest, as well for medical as other men, he was determined to be slow and sure; Lord Claverton, therefore, easily convinced Doctor Macshean, it was absolutely necessary to proceed immediately to London, and Lady Margaret, who was as anxious to retain her conquest, as his Lordship could be to secure his; became an immediate convert to Mr. Macshean's opinion; her nervous complaints returning, she could not live without Dr. Warren; she retired to her apartment the same evening, and continued growing worse till the hour was fixed for their departure for London.

The Earl employed the last morning in selecting, from the different shops, a variety of useful and ornamental trinkets; which, with a purse very liberally filled, he sent Ellen, after he had taken leave, and Lord Claverton, with great apparent modesty, entreated Lady Margaret would have the goodness to present Miss Meredith, in *his* name, a very elegant little watch, and fosse montre, as a faint memorial of the happy hours he had passed under the hospitable roof of her venerable grandfather.

Ellen's heart ached, separated from every being and every scene which happy childhood had endeared to her memory, Lord Castle Howel was the rock of her confidence, a superior being, to whom she looked up with a mixture of affection and respect: she dropped involuntarily on her knees as he took her hand, "Be sure you write to me, Ellen," said he, raising and pressing her to his bosom. "And me," said Lady Margaret.

Lord Claverton coloured, he even trembled, as he kissed the fair hand of Ellen, whose eyes followed the carriage till it was obscured by the dust of the London road.

A calm succeeded the busy scenes, which, for the last four months, totally occupied our heroine, very favourable to instruction and to recollection; the avidity with which she received the former, rendered her a great favourite with her governess; the mortification she felt at her own deficiencies, was a spur to emulation, and the idea of surprizing the friends she loved with her acquirements, a constant incitement to application.

No longer in habits of the robust exercise in which she had hitherto delighted, her person grew delicate, and her air became (from the unison of improved mind and body) easy and elegant; her manners, still charmingly vivacious, were soft and politely refined; she had naturally a sweet as well as strong voice, under Ruzzina it became possessed of all those thrilling graces, which melt on the ear, and reaches the soul of harmony.

The harp, from her early practice, was the instrument she

soon most excelled on, but her general improvements in music were astonishingly rapid.

Winifred, though kept at humble distance, continued, nevertheless, to make Ellen the confidant of Mr. Joseph's constant passion, by shewing her the letters she received from him; it was not indeed in nature so passionate a lover should forget a mistress, of whom his Lord so often reminded him; nor could Ellen help understanding how frequently Lord Claverton spoke of the pleasant hours he passed at Code Gwyn, and that he proposed being at Bath early in the Spring Season.

That Nobleman continued to keep up his acquaintance in Grosvenor-Street; and Doctor Macshean having satisfied himself as to Lady Margaret's prudent acquirements, took a house in Conduit-Street, which he elegantly furnished, and in which he gave handsome entertainments to select parties.

By means of his Patron, and Patroness, he was getting into snug practice; he kept one maid, and two men, at board wages, jobbed his horses, generally dined with Lord Claverton, in Portman-Square, and supped with Lady Margaret, in Grosvenor-Street.

Habits and customs of many years may be suspended, but will not soon be totally eradicated – the Earl, by degrees, returned to his botany; this, however, did not lessen the pleasure of Ellen's correspondence, or prevent his punctually and affectionately answering her letters.

The Lieutenant was an inmate of his house, and fellow labourer in the botanical experiments, but although few noblemen might, with more certainty of success, ask a favour of the Minister, his mind was so strangely abstracted from common occurrences, that it never once struck him, how desirable to a young officer promotion was; and the

Lieutenant, though panting to be employed, was too diffident to drop a sentence that would remind him of it.

Lord Claverton was often favoured with a sight of Ellen's letters, heard of her improvements, and languished for an opportunity of again beholding a face, that (in spite of all the blandishments with which quality and fortune are surrounded in London) was ever before him.

Nobody was more eager to pay court to every new beauty to admire, to toast; nobody entered with more gout and less delicacy into every fashionable intrigue, than Lord Claverton; his fortune large and independent; his title and family ancient and respectable;his face handsome, and his person, for a man of quality who had been seven years in the guards, still tolerable. It is not to be doubted, but there were fathers, guardians, and brothers, who had particularly distinguished him, he visited every where – but the fair Ellen swam on the surface, she floated on his imagination, and whatever variety or beauty met his eye, fancy painted *her* in colours more glowing, and all that pleased in the many combined in her.

Intrigue, the business of his life, when compared to the tranquil possession of Ellen, was no longer desirable; the style of her writing was polished and animated, and what most charmed him, was, that the same innocence and inexperience which inspired and kept hope alive, ran through all.

A Machiavel in intrigue, no point escaped him that led to the haven of his wishes, and, in consequence of his politics, Ellen and Winifred had letters by the same post, which, as they are originals, we beg the reader will accept in their native dress.

"Dear Ellen,

Never let the noble heart despair, as we say at sea; for here, when I had been all the year lagging at Lord Castle Howel's elbow, and often dining with the first Lord, without his so much as mentioning me. To be sure, he did not think of it, that I must say, but, God help me, I thought enough of it, I'm sure. Well, all of a sudden, Lord Claverton sends for me: "My brave lad" said he, and he took my hand, "you are so taken up with the Earl, you forget your old friend." So, you may be sure I apologized – but mark. Says he, I remember how you fought in the Lion, when you was wounded, And so I was, Ellen, I thought I should have gone to David Jones's locker. Now, says he, I don't like such a brave lad as you should lye by, and to go to the Admiralty, and there lies a commission for you. Well, Elen, I could not speak, but away I scampered, and now am Captain of the Hyslop, and we are stationed in the East Indies, I shall go down to take leave of my good father and mother; Lord Claverton is coming to Bath, and conveys me so far on my way; you may be sure I will bring you a cargo of diamonds from India, as big as Potatoes.

From your affectionate uncle,
Lewis Meredith,
Captain of the Hyslop Sloop of War.

Before this letter was read quite through, in the presence of the governess, the voice of Winifred, remarkably shrill, was heard at the door of the room.

"As Cot shall help me, and pless me, and I wish I may co to the tivil himself, if I don't speak to Miss Ellen; why, sure you are worse than the children of Isralitish, not to let me carry my mistress coot tidings, about my master's son, the Captain, who, as Cot shall safe me, will soon be an Admiral, and a Commodore."

"But I tell you, no."

"Tell me nothing, I shall tell my mistress," and in bounced Winifred, her face in a glow, and an open letter in her hand, which she eagerly presented to Ellen, who, in conformity to the rule of the school, handed it to the governess.

"As Cot shall judge me, Miss Ellen, that's very civil of you; if you won't read my letters yourself, I am sure you need not cive it to other people; pray, Miss, read it yourself, and you'll see what a precious coot creat man Lord Claverton is; my Cot! my Cot! I would cive forty coot shillings to be at Code Gwyn when the news reaches there."

This was the exact chord, it vibrated on all Ellen's feelings.

"My dear, dear grandmamma!"

"Ay, and my old master! As Cot shall safe me, he will not want his wheel chair. Oh, what a brave man is Lord Claverton."

"How happy will it make my aunts!"

"Yes, and the Reverent too; aye, and Mr. Percival – I dare for to say, with Cot's plessing, he will co beyond sea, with the Captain. Oh, what a fine man is Lord Claverton!"

Such a period has elapsed since the name of Percival has been mentioned, the reader will conclude he has not been much the subject of our thoughts, that, however, is a secret which time only must discover – it called a blush into Ellen's cheeks, and suddenly stopped her rapturous expressions of joy.

Mrs. Forrest having slightly run over Winifred's letter, returned it to her, saying, it was not of importance enough to require Miss Meredith's perusal.

Winifred received it with an air of pique, and a sly wink at Ellen, which meant, "we'll read it together however."

The hours of rest were literally less so to our heroine than any she had hitherto passed at Bath, she got into a chain of recollections which did not befriend sleep, and early in the morning Winifred was at her bedside with the letter, which, as it is the duty of a faithful historian to relate facts, I must own she had not fortitude to decline reading – it ran thus.

"Me derast Winny!

"Ever sens I saw your butiful eys, I never gets any rest nor never goes no were, but wat i think on you, as for a good noble master thank God i have that, an now I must tell you my Lord is very grate with the king, an he need only ax and have, and he has axd the king to make the noble leftenant a Captain, and to be certain if that is not prefering him i dont no wat is, it is with some peple out of site out of mind, but God forbid that should be my case, or my master's, tho' to be sure Lord Castle Howel mite a' done it over and over, but some people will not do themselves good, nor anyone else either; an my Lord says to me, Joseph sais he, I wish I could just peep in at Code Gwyn, just to see old Sir Arthur, wen the Captain goes home, and sweete Miss Ellen, and then he sighs and moans – Oh! Winny, if there is one tru lover in the herrth, it is my master, and me – we shall be at bath in a week at furdest.

I am till deth do us part
Your true lover
Joseph"

"What a noble man is Lord Claverton," whispered Winifred, fearing to awake two young ladies, who lay in the same room.

"He is very good indeed," said Ellen, "I could not have thought–"

"As to that old fusty odd mortal, Lord Castle Howel–"

"Hush, Winifred, I won't have you speak disrespectfully of him."

"As Cot shall safe me, Miss Ellen, I belief you hate Lord Claverton, for making my young master a great man."

This exclamation put an end to the conversation, for Winifred's voice and colour was sure to rise with her passions, and the ladies were disturbed.

From this period Ellen began to expect the arrival of the Captain and his Patron, a kind of perturbation and suspense agitated her, and the seeds of vanity, afterwards conspicuous in her character, shewed itself for the first time. She was unusually attentive to her dress, and practised an infinite variety of graces in order to astonish Lord Claverton.

At length the expected visitants were announced.

Lord Claverton had heard Ellen was taller and much improved, but by the admiration with which he appeared to be struck, it would seem this was the first time he had ever seen her.

Her hair, no longer partly shading and partly displaying her white neck and forehead, in a profusion of wild ringlets, was dressed in the nicest order; her fine falling shoulders inured to braces, now, of themselves, fell in the most graceful form; her shape, which was only small and strait when she came to Bath, was forming into woman; her eyes, in which a saucy vivacity was used to play, now withdrew from his ardent gaze, and dropped in modest dignity on the floor. The Captain saluted her in his blunt way, with,

"Ellen, you look like an angel, and 'tis an angel only can speak my gratitude here," leading her to Lord Claverton.

Ellen courtesied – "Permit me, my Lord, to thank you for my uncle, Sir Arthur, for Lady Meredith, for–"

"For yourself, dear angel," interrupted Lord Claverton, in a transport he could not repress.

Ellen blushed, Mrs. Forrest offered her congratulations, and the conversation became general.

As the Captain was impatient to pay his duty to his parents, that he might be ready to sail – and Lord Claverton saw, that without the particular favour of the governess he could not hope to be admitted, when his friend was gone; he assailed her in the vulnerable part, by a judicious and sensible critique on female writing, in which he contrived to give hers a delicate preference.

However acceptable to the woman, and flattering to the author, the praise of a man of Lord Claverton's sense and rank; however soothing to the vanity to which the wisest of the sex are a little inclined, Mrs. Forrest's own strict conduct, as well as regard to the sacred trust reposed in her, by the parents and guardians of her pupils, rendered her very difficult of access, but Lord Claverton's mind was, as before said, a daring and inventive one, he soon hit on an expedient to remove those impediments.

There are, the polite world *well know*, a description of women, who, having done every thing in their little power, to scandalize one sex, and dupe the other in their youth, carry their propensities so far into age, as to become odious to society; and there are also even among these, *some*, who have art enough to shield themselves from general detestation, by a profuse expenditure of ill gotten wealth; by playing high, giving splendid entertainments, opening their doors to an indiscriminate mixture of company, and making their houses convenient and agreeable to all parties; by these means they are sure of getting by degrees into some sort of estimation; – Ladies beginning to get a name, such as mistresses made wives; ladies beginning to lose a name, such as wives made mistresses; old women with money who want husbands; young ones, with none, who want any thing that offers; gamblers of both sexes; fortune hunters, old debauchees, and military smarts, are sure to grace their assemblies; if a great deal of money is either won or lost, the high bred ladies will swallow the bait; and so the house of a wretch, whose character is not only notorious but dangerous, becomes the fashion.

Mrs. Elderton, an Irish lady of this description, led the ton at Bath, Lord Claverton was her very old friend, and it was not in nature for her to penetrate further into his designs than he literally intended. Mrs. Forrest, she said, was a charming sensible woman, she wished to see her school, and Lord Claverton begged to escort her.

Never was any thing so delightful! She invited the amiable governess and a select number of her lovely pupils, to her public dinner. If Mrs. Forrest had a foible it was fondness for fashionable company, and though ill natured people talked freely of Mrs. Elderton, who would not ill natured people talk freely of? Mrs. Forrest thought her extremely amiable, and from this period she and her ladies were often invited to Mrs. Elderton's large parties, and often supplied by her with tickets for all public places; as she could not object to such flattering attentions from her, and as Miss Meredith was a particular favourite, she was always one of her companions. Lord Claverton, who was every where, took care to be at hand, to pay the most respectful attention to Mrs. Forrest, and the most oblique ones to Ellen.

It had been intended by the Castle Howels to visit Ellen, on their return through Bath, but an event happened that detained them in London the whole year – this was the indisposition of Miss Capus (for she had never assumed the title of Castle Howel) the unhappy woman had long been afflicted with a dropsy, which, at length, baffled the art of medicine. When the Doctor pronounced her doom she began to think of the bourn from whence there is no return, and fervently implored Lord Castle Howel would deign to pronounce his personal forgiveness; his refusal added strength to her naturally peevish and obstinate temper, she wearied him and Lady Margaret, and finding both inexorable wrote to the ladies, Frances and Gertrude, for their influence in favour of a dying penitent.

"Dying! and is the Witch really dying? and is it yet possible we may live to see an heir to our family honours we do not detest?" cried the elder maiden.

"I forgive every thing if she will but die!" answered the younger.

"What does she say?" resumed Lady Frances, looking at the letter. "She cannot die in peace till she is forgiven by the Earl."

"Bless me," exclaimed Lady Gertrude, "was there ever any thing so foolish, not to let the creature die!"

Pen and ink was called for, and both the ladies signed a short letter, requesting their nephew to let his wife die! and to give them the earliest notice of the happy event, as they would immediately leave their seat in the North, and, notwithstanding the length and expense of the journey, join him in London.

Rather forced into the measure than convinced it was necessary, Lord Castle Howel took a reluctant journey, where love, in his juvenile days often carried him, and exchanged forgiveness with his sick wife. But the lady did not, as the sage maidens seemed to expect, expire immediately, her disorder turned so perversely favourable, it was five months doubtful whether the strength of her constitution would not at last conquer.

During this time Ellen was pursuing her studies, and Lord Claverton not an instant neglectful of his – he had gained what he considered so great an advantage in his familiar access to Ellen, that he did not doubt, with the aid of Winifred, but his business was in a fair way; but the same object always seen in the same party, and the season being arrived when it is the fashion for people to run from Bath with as much avidity as two months before they run to it, surmises began to be dispersed about the few remaining card tables, not exactly to the credit of Mrs. Elderton, and tending to injure her new friend, the governess; of this Lord Claverton was one of the first to be acquainted, and as he possessed the happy art of turning most common events to his own advantage, he was also the first to communicate it to Mrs. Forrest, who was charmed with his candour, and considered his immediately leaving Bath (which he protested he did solely on her account) as a very proper and delicate compliment. Thus then he left Bath in high favour, and proceeded to his house on the forest in as high spirits, to prepare for the reception of the little charmer, who he was resolved to allure thither, when he returned, which he intended should be very early in the winter; but fate had otherwise disposed of her.

It was August before Lord Castle Howel could send his aunts the account of his enfranchisement; it was September before they arrived in town; in October Mr. Meredith brought a card from Lord Castle Howel to request Miss Meredith might be consigned to his care.

It is impossible to describe the wild sensations of joy our

heroine felt at this unexpected summons; she could hardly believe she was indeed going home to Code Gwyn, to see all the dear relatives on whom she still doated; nor was Winifred less delighted; they ran from room to room, embracing and congratulating each other; the cloaths were hastily packed, not without some little murmuring from Mrs. Forrest, who really felt regret at parting so suddenly with a pupil for whom she had the most perfect friendship; the chaise was at the door before six the next morning, and, attached as Winifred was to Joseph, she even neglected to apprise him of their journey.

The carriage, though they travelled post, bore no proportion to the celerity of Ellen's ideas; she remembered every town they went through on their way to Bath, slept at the same inns, and, at length, eagerly recognised the turning from Castle Howel road to Code Gwyn; but at the stone style of the church there was no Percival – Winifred looked too, "Well, Cot forcive me!" cried she, recollecting her broken promise.

The carriage passed with great velocity, and soon stopped at Code Gwyn. The same placid benevolent countenances and affectionate hearts – the servants, the house, exactly in the state she left it, raised a thousand tender sensations in her mind – she flew rather than stepped from the chaise, the servants were clamorous in their joy, and the family mingled tears with embraces; Winifred was received with vast deference in the servants hall, and even her uncle and aunt called her Mrs. Winifred. Ellen fancied she saw a furrow more on her grandfather's cheeks, and sometimes a pensive glance shoot from Lady Meredith's eye, but as joy and tenderness were most predominant, this was the fancy of the moment, she retired early by Lady Meredith's desire, and never did innocence enjoy more sweet repose.

Chapter XI

The next morning the momentary observations made the preceding night were renewed, an unaccustomed gravity presided in every countenance.

"Set by me, my love, my own Ellen," said Lady Meredith, taking her hand.

"Well, my child, you have been a traveller, does not our plain house appear little and contemptible, after–"

"Dear madam, what are you saying? – Little! contemptible! 'tis a paradise I wish to live and die in."

Lady Meredith kissed her forehead, "But there are changes, my dear, in life."

"Changes! What changes! What do you mean? Speak out, my dear grandmamma."

Lady Meredith hesitated. "I knew I could not, your uncle will retire with you, he will read you some letters."

Ellen stood up – "This moment, then, dear Sir," said she, "don't keep me in suspense."

He accompanied her to another room – But it is now necessary to carry my reader back to some family anecdotes which we have barely hinted at.

The want of an heir in the Castle Howel family was a subject of the severest regret to every part of that branch of it in which the title and estates were now vested; on the demise of the present Earl it returned to the descendants from a second son whose representative, a libertine on principle, had actually, with secret and false professions of love, deceived both his cousins, Lady Frances and Lady Gertrude Howel, at the same time that an artful and low-bred woman had drawn him into a private marriage; the children of this low union were the presumptive heirs of Castle Howel; the father braved the resentment of the injured ladies, the wife scoffed at, and the sons derided it. At the death of Lord Castle Howel's wife the exasperated virgins disclosed the full extent of provocation to a hatred so inveterate; and it was then that they entreated him to be the avenger of their injured honour by taking a wife from whom they might hope a disappointment to their wicked cousin; both ladies offering to settle their whole fortune on the issue of such marriage.

Lord Castle Howel fancied himself attached to Ellen, merely as a beautiful and amiable child; but now, urged to make choice of a wife, from family reasons, his heart claimed a different interest in her, and that choice instantly fell on Ellen.

He mentioned her to his sister, and to his aunts; – Lady Margaret, in her heart, little caring who possessed Castle Howel after her time, was only solicitous to retain the good things of it, as long as she could, to herself; it was, therefore, a very unpleasant thing to hear her brother talk of a wife at all; but, if he must marry, certainly the young thing he chose would be more governable than a town lady; and, seeing it was not to be avoided, entered, with a tolerable grace, into an animated description of the fair Ellen to her aunts.

When old ladies get certain matters into their heads, it is marvellous with what address they conduct them; they would not suffer his Lordship to sleep before he wrote his proposals to Sir Arthur Meredith, enclosing the card to Mrs. Forrest; in consequence of which our heroine returned to Code Gwyn.

This proposal, then, was the grand spring, on which all the

movements at Code Gwyn depended. Mr. Meredith opened the business with becoming gravity, he read the Earl's letter through with as little variation of voice as if it had been a church brief, when finished he laid it down, and looking anxiously at Ellen, saw such unfeigned astonishment in her countenance, such a vague indefinite attempt at recollection, that he asked if he should read it again, and again went through it with the same inflexible gravity, and laid it down, waiting for her answer.

"What is all this," cried Ellen, "I cannot understand you; is it Lord Castle Howel, who has been so good to me, that writes this?"

"There is no other Lord Castle Howel, Ellen."

"And has he been disgracefully married? And is his wife now only dead? I never before heard he had one. And is it possible? Can so grave, so wise a man, act so much like a simpleton? Me! Does he want to marry me! Such a thoughtless giddy girl as me! Uncle, are you not very sorry?"

"Sorry, my dear, for what?"

"That so respectable a being should be so very ridiculous."

"Then," said Mr. Meredith, still more gravely, "you will not accept his Lordship's offer?"

"Accept it, no, to be sure, you would not wish me to marry any body yet, much less an old man!"

"But he is an Earl, Ellen."

"So much the worse, his folly will be more conspicuous."

"If the *folly* of the act is your principal objection, suppose we could prove it one of consummate wisdom?"

"Nobody doubts your logic, uncle, when your heart is in the argument, but I hope that is not the case now."

"And why, my dear, do you hope so?'"

"Because I feel I shall be very stubborn."

"That is not like you, Ellen, to be premeditatedly stubborn."

"I cannot help it, I will not be married."

Mr. Meredith arose, "Am I to give this definitive *will not*, to my father and mother?"

"No, I will go to them myself directly; or, if you please – but, uncle, tell me, upon your honour, do you think they wish me to marry Lord Castle Howel?"

"You ask me on my honour, Ellen?"

Mr. Meredith changed colour, hem'd, and drew Ellen's chair nearer his own.

All the concerns, engagements, and interests of this family, had hitherto been conducted with such confidence in each other; so little reserve, either among themselves or towards the world; the *todays* were so exactly like the yesterdays, so little seemed to be hoped from the future that could lessen the enjoyments of the present; so little to fear, except in the eternal separation, for which every member of it was in some degree prepared, that Ellen could only suppose the apparent agitation of Mr. Meredith proceeded from some interest he took in the affairs of Lord Castle Howel; or, that he was disappointed in her rejection of so splendid an offer. In the former case, her own heart, open to sympathy, and generously alive to every sensation of pity, was ready to adopt his inquietudes; but in the latter, as ambition, or a desire of riches, had not yet biased one thought, she sat down predetermined to combat his prejudices, and retain her own freedom.

It was thus Ellen accounted for Mr. Meredith's change of countenance, and reflections like these occupied her during a silence, which, in spite of every effort on his part to conquer his feelings, preceded what he had further to say.

Poor Ellen! little did she foresee that the last happy hour she was to spend at Code Gwyn was already past, that the mornings of tranquillity, the noon of ease, and the evening of peace, had abandoned the habitation of Sir Arthur Meredith and his forefathers.

Before Mr. Meredith could speak, a tear dropped from his eye and fell on Ellen's cheek, but ashamed of a weakness, degrading, as he thought, to manhood and Christianity, again he hem'd, and in a voice, which, though tremulous at first, soon acquired its usual strength, he informed her, that from various and accumulating expenses, some of which could not be avoided, Sir Arthur had been induced to borrow money of a *rich neighbour*. "Perhaps," said he, sighing, "it would have been better we had not been so readily supplied; had any difficulty attended our borrowing, we should have recollected the still greater difficulty of repaying. My father's infirm state of health; your father and mother's death; my mother's grief, which a long time endangered her life; my own natural indolence of temper, are no excuses, though they were complicated causes of our negligence. In short, Ellen, –"

The equality of Mr. Meredith's temper here gave way to the excess of his feelings! again the big tear dropped on the cheek of his equally agitated auditor, who, totally unacquainted with money concerns, and never having heard of pecuniary wants, except any of her school fellows had been particularly profuse, wants which the liberality of her patron, and the generosity of her own heart, enabled her to supply, could comprehend very little of what Mr. Meredith wished to disclose; she understood, indeed, for the first time, that Sir Arthur had not every thing in his own power; that Lady Meredith was not happy; that her uncles and aunts must therefore be in affliction, and that the origin of these evils was borrowing money of a rich friend. All this was new, but it was enough for Ellen, the relatives she loved were in distress, to overwhelm her.

"How mistaken have I been," said she, "I thought the blessings and comforts of the world were made on purpose for the good, I knew you were all good, and did not doubt but you had every thing you wanted."

Mr. Meredith sighed. "We may not, Ellen, be in possession of this family mansion another year."

Ellen started.

"We have notice of the foreclosure of the mortgage."

"Mortgage! Who, what is that? Not live in our own house. How can my grandpapa live any where else? it is impossible, he will die, he will break his heart; his wheel-chair, you know, would not run, without danger, except the floor was very even."

"That, that and my dear mother's feelings, is all that afflicts me; for, as to the rest, as my house—"

"Oh, dear! I dare say we could, all live very easy there; but who is this Mortgage? What right has he?"

Mr. Meredith then explained the meaning of mortgage, and foreclosure, and, to her further astonishment, informed her, that their kind friend, John Morgan, Esquire, was the gentleman whose occasions for money was, at this time, so pressing, that though it was, as he declared himself, with extreme reluctance and distress of mind he put them any inconvenience, he could not possibly do without it. Mr. Meredith stated the impossibility of raising the money, the most to be hoped for was to join his father in assigning over the whole estate, reserving only the mansion-house, and the grounds belonging to it, for the life of his parents, and even this he doubted whether Mr. Morgan would or could agree to. He continued, that it was proper she should know the very narrow compass in which all their future hopes of comfort lay, before she finally resolved to forego the prosperity and advantage which were offered to her in Lord Castle Howel's alliance; he trusted, that while he lived he should have a peaceful asylum for her beauty and innocence; but his life was an uncertain tenure, and desirous as he hoped he always should be to put his firm trust in the God of righteousness, he owned, that when he looked on Ellen, and recollected the state in which *his* death would leave her, he dared not express his feelings: "My health, my dear Ellen," added he, "is already impaired."

Ellen fixed her tearful eye on his pale face, and resumed Lord Castle Howel's letter; the surprise and astonishment which at first filled her was no more, she read it over in anxious search of something alleviating of the poignancy of her feelings.

"Has Lord Castle Howel power?" asked she, in a half whisper, "to remove these misfortunes?"

Mr. Meredith gently took the letter from her. "He has it amply in his power to shield you from sharing in it."

"And is that all?" cried she, with vivacity, as if a load of anguish had been removed from her heart, "then never mention his proposal more. But you see that he still promises to be my Patron and protector, a much more honourable as well as suitable character for him. If, indeed, he could have made my dear grandfather happy, and satisfied that ugly man who I always hated, though he used to bow so low and flatter me so much, I believe I – I – But as he can't, you know uncle, we will pray to God, and trust in God, and none of us can tell what may yet happen."

The happy eagerness with which Ellen satisfied herself it was not in Lord Castle Howel's power to make her family happy; and the joy that darted from her eyes, when she declared she would hear no more of his proposals, were such convincing proofs, not only that the dazzling offer of making her a Countess had no weight, but that her heart recoiled from the disproportionate union; Mr. Meredith could not prevail on himself to hint what really was true, though he was too generous to urge it as a plea in favour of the marriage, that Mr. Morgan's necessity would certainly give way to his respect for a family allied to Lord Castle Howel, besides the likelihood that his Lordship would assist so old and respectable a relation of his young bride; but these and many other flattering probabilities which might follow, was disregarded when he saw her heart was averse; convinced that if she acceded to the Earl's proposal she would add to the wretched list of young females, who, with the best of dispositions, bound to men for whom they have no predilection, feel *too* late they have hearts as well as hands, he resolved to communicate his sentiments to his father, and spare his niece any solicitation on a subject, against which his own heart revolted.

The calamity that threatened the Code Gwyn family was not likely to remain concealed from domestics, who would be such sharers in the common misfortune. Mrs. Griffiths cried so violently in communicating it to Winifred, that it was necessary for her to take a portion of her own double distilled peppermint water; and Mr. Griffiths was too sick to take his morning pipe.

"It signified nothing," the bailiff said, "to manure that meadow, or crop this field, it is too good for old Morgan."

A general lassitude and despair blunted the edge of industry, and in the common aspect of domestic management, things, in the vulgar phrase, were actually going to rack and ruin.

A little flower garden, which Ellen and Percival had made, in a corner of the paddock, was the only spot that shewed a careful manager; the thickset hedge, set by herself, was cut in the nicest order, and particularly thriving; the small parterre, edged with box and mignonette, which forming a double cypher of P E and E M, was filled up with the choicest flowers in succession, and appeared in continual bloom.

Ellen observed her garden as they drove up to the house, and longed to revisit the scene of her childish labour and amusement; as soon, therefore, as Mr. Meredith left her, she took her hat and began her little walk; crossing the paddock, she was overtaken by Winifred, with swollen eyes and grief-worn countenance, her sighs, not quite so gentle as the zephyr, nor her moanings so soft or harmonious as the dove, little affected her generous mistress, who, truth to say, had already forgot the mortgage, foreclosure, the offered marriage, and even the affliction of Sir Arthur, and walked along with her eyes fixed on the spot she was approaching, every other faculty totally absorbed in that of thinking.

"The tivel tak riches, and all false hearted people," quoth Winifred.

Ellen was silent.

"That Squire Morgan is a tivel in garnet; no wonder his house his haunted by a great black tog in a winding sheet."

Ellen advanced to the wicket.

"Why to be sure, Cot Almighty will let the tivel fetch him in a whirlwind; his own tear sweet taughter was left to be starved alife, and now, you see, he has no chick nor child."

Ellen stopped, and gazing on a beautiful passion flower, that twined round every bush in the garden, softly and sweetly sung,

"Alas! where with him I have stray'd
I could wander with pleasure alone."[4]

"Are you there, Winifred?"

"Yes, Ma'am," whined Winifred, who though she had expended her stock of sorrow, thought, on the strength of her aunt's example, she must still be doleful.

"Don't you think it very odd, Winifred?"

"Yes inteet, Miss, Cot help us all out of our misery."

"Why, what's the matter?" cried Ellen, surprised.

Winifred flared, but presently conjecturing that it was possible Ellen was not yet acquainted with the impending misfortune, and that it did not signify whether she was or not, as it was not in her power to do any good.

"Nay, I am sure, Miss, I don't know what is the matter, but that lazy tog of a gartner have let all my holly hogs and polly hanches die."

"But don't you think it very odd, that –"

"Hod, no, Miss; I think nothing hod in this world, since David, the Parson's man, married the still room maid, of Castle Howel."

David at this instant appeared, with a spade and watering pot, but kept aloof.

"But, Winifred, what is become of Percival Evelyn; is it not very odd he is not here with my uncle?"

"Not hod at all, Miss, because he is gone to college."

---

[4] Misquoting William Shenstone's *A Pastoral Ballad* (1743). The original has "Alas, where with her I have stray'd…"

"To college!"

"Why, to be sure, Miss, because, poor poy, you know he has not cot a prass fardin of fortin, and so, as my aunt says, our poor tere Reverent does all the coot he can for every poty, and so he is to be his curate; half a loaf is petter as no preat."

"God forbid," said Ellen, seriously, "Percival Evelyn should ever want bread."

"Amen! amen! pray Cot, Miss; and I'm sure it would be a marcy if Mr. Joseph and Lord Claverton was to hear of our troopless and our miseries and come to—"

Winifred was never guilty of thinking, but if she had studied for an unfavourable moment all her life to mention his Lordship, she could not have succeeded better.

"Lord Claverton!" said Ellen, scornfully.

"You forget, Miss, how many fine places he treated you to at Bath."

"I hate him."

"And you forget, Miss, he made your uncle a Captain, but the sin of ungrateful is worse even as death."

"Ah! Winifred, so I had – but I wish I could see Percival Evelyn; don't you think he will make a very handsome parson?"

"Humph, well enuff for a parson!"

"What does my uncle's man wait for?"

Winifred immediately bawled out "Fine times for you, Mr. Tavy, to be standing with your hands in your pockets, I suppose your wife works for both."

Nature speaks the same language every where. David, who had been a kind of dangler to Winifred, and had often experienced her mild temper, expected, as he had presumed to marry another, he should not escape without a satirical fling, he took no notice of her, but leisurely advanced to the little garden, and began to work.

"And pray who set you to work here? I dare say the parson's garden will employ you."

"Why, Mrs. Winifred, nobody set me to work, but I am not like some folks, say one thing and do another – I like to serve Mr. Percival when his back's turned as well as when I see him; and so," bowing to Ellen, who having been two years in England, and being moreover dressed in a superior style he had not presumed to accost, although he had formerly been one of her favourites, "and so, as he said, he valued every little seed set in Miss Ellen's garden more than gold, I promised I'd take care of it and I think, Mrs. Winifred, (leaning on his spade, and looking proudly round) I think I have kept my word."

The hint of broken promises called the colour into Winifred's guilty cheeks; she could not help recollecting certain tokens, and certain promises; all of which she had most unconscionably suffered to slip her memory. But it requires a greater mind than hers to feel a fault and own it, particularly to an inferior, for, so she who was addressed by a Lord's valet, considered the parson's man of work; with as haughty a look, therefore, as she could assume, she endeavoured to hide her guilt, and turned out of the garden, leaving Miss Ellen and David to look at the improvements and talk of Percival. This was a subject not easy exhausted – it would have lasted a long summer's day without intermission; and Ellen was summoned to dinner before she was tired of David's store of anecdotes of what Percival said, how he looked, and what he had done.

Chapter XII

The affectionate reception our heroine met from the family, on her entering the hall, added to a harmony of spirits, which seemed to have taken possession of her in the garden; and after dinner she brought down her store of baubles and trinkets, and made presents from them to all the family; not a word was said either of Lord Castle Howel, or Mr. Morgan, and the week passed with tranquillity.

After church, on Sunday, the family dined at the parsonage, where Mr. Meredith had been making some alterations – he had turned his study, which adjoined the large parlour, into a bed chamber; he had been very attentive to the raising of the gravel walk even with the glass folding doors, and had also made folding doors to the entrance. Lady Meredith's eyes filled, as her son explained to her, in a whisper, these several alterations, and Ellen actually gasped for breath when a recollection of the conversation with her uncle, suggested the use intended to be made of them.

The image of Percival, the anticipation of his return, the many secretly projected rambles, which, for the last week had kept her mind in a kind of rapturous delirium, now dispersed; and in their room, her venerable parents, deprived of all the natural comforts of their inoffensive lives, driven from the seat of their ancestors, their large family thronged into the parsonage, and subjected to inconvenience and mortification – appeared in such terrible colours, that, unable to repress her emotions, she hastily left the side of Lady Meredith, and ran to an arbour in the garden where a violent burst of tears relieved, without removing from her mind, the sad images fancy had raised there.

By the thickset hedge before her lay the road to Castle Howel, on the instant she raised her eyes a servant, in the Earl's livery, approached, he pulled off his hat and rode on. This little incident carried recollection back to Lord Castle Howel. His kindness had inspired her with a grateful affection, and his knowledge both of men and books had impressed on her mind a respect superior to what she felt for any other person; she wept to think, that, perhaps, she was now the object of his anger, and for ever deprived of his friendship.

She raised her eyes a second time, and saw Squire Morgan trotting by towards the parsonage, he saw *her* too, but not with his usual servile look, he turned his bent brow hastily from her, and without the smallest inclination of his head passed on.

By an impulse as sudden as unpremeditated she also darted towards the house: Mr. Morgan, the suppliant humble Mr. Morgan, who would never take a chair before every individual of the family were seated, now sat in great state in the arm chair, with his hat on, though in the presence of Lady Meredith, who was smelling her salts and trembling every limb – his voice no longer soft and insinuating, but stern and discordant.

"Sir, I have never received a shilling interest for any of the sums I advanced, people will make me pay and I must be paid."

"The proposal I made you, Sir," answered Mr. Meredith, "of leaving Code Gwyn house and lands to my parents, during their lives, on condition of my relinquishing all future claim."

"It won't do, Mr. Parson, it won't do; I have lent more than the value of the estate, and must immediately take it into my own hands to bring myself home; I began the world with half a crown, and have no money to spare."

"If that is really so," said Lady Meredith, faintly, "it is but just Mr. Morgan should take care of himself. How long, Sir,–"

"I am sure I am very much concerned, Madam, but your Ladyship will please to recollect I am an humble, a very humble man, my money has been got by dint of hard labour, I have no pretensions to gentility."

"Say no more, Sir, say no more," sighed Lady Meredith.

"You may stay a month or two, or even till Christmas."

Lady Meredith drew out her handkerchief, and Ellen throwing herself on her knees, hid her face in her lap and wept aloud.

Miss Meredith never, in all the romances she had read, met with any misfortune which was the consequence of running in debt, nor had she heard of a single knight who was armed against a foreclosure; but she had long considered Mr. Morgan as the demon of avarice, and not doubting but this was his hour of triumph, was secretly praying for a whirlwind to carry him away.

Miss Agnes wept because her mother wept, for let what would happen she had a very comfortable stock of wool and cheese.

Mr. Morgan arose and was stalking towards the door, when, casting a contemptuous glance at Ellen, "I am sorry to see your granddaughter returned on your hands, what good will her fine learning do her now? Aye aye, I have seen many such freaks in my time, Lord Castle Howel would have done a more charitable thing to get her a good service."

At this instant the sound of a carriage was heard, Mr.

Morgan had hardly time to untie the silk handkerchief from his neck, and take off his hat, before Lord Castle Howel, his aunts and sister were in the room.

Nothing could equal the Earl's astonishment at the scene which presented itself, Ellen still kneeling. "What," said he, looking round, "can be the meaning of all this?"

Lady Margaret, whose cue it was to be very fond of Ellen, caught her in her arms, while the old ladies, with delighted looks, were examining her through their spectacles.

"Dear Lady Meredith, may I, without being impertinent?" said the Earl,—

The agitation of Lady Meredith's spirits, the mortification she had suffered from Morgan's behaviour, the agonies of her heart at the prospect before her, and now the sudden appearance of the Castle Howel family, so humiliating to all pride of circumstance overpowered her weak frame; in making an effort to rise, she sunk senseless on the floor; the cries of the affrighted Ellen rent the air, she screamed till she was black in the face, and, before Lady Meredith was recovered, had a convulsion fit.

The two old ladies were frightened out of their observations; Lady Margaret assisted the Miss Merediths in taking care of their mother, and the Earl himself carried Ellen to the garden.

Mr. Morgan, who heard as *he* supposed from good authority, the Earl's wife was dead, and that he would marry immediately had concluded Ellen was sent home and done with.

Lord Claverton's designs being insidious and wicked, were of a stamp so accordant to his own principles he was presently master of them. But Lord Castle Howel's actions being the entire result of innate honour and refined sentiment, were enveloped in a mystery he could not penetrate; facts, however, were stubborn things. If his Lordship had got a bride, and one of the strangers was her, she was of too antient a date to lessen the interest of the beautiful Ellen, on whom he looked with delight at his entrance, and for whose distress he seemed to suffer so much. The crafty observer, therefore, had now to fear, the beauty of the granddaughter would raise a friend to rescue the estate out of his hands. It may here be asked, if avarice was Mr. Morgan's motive for calling in his money, why he should not rather rejoice at an event that promised payment without so unpopular a step, as the foreclosure of the mortgage? And thus we answer.

According to the old assessments of the estates, the mortgage and interest really amounted to its value, but when it is remembered, the tenants and their descendants had, at their original rents, lived and died in their farms, allowing for the increasing value of landed property, the advantage of seizing on a complete manor, at the price it would have fetched five hundred years back, must be obvious; besides this, enveloped in the deepest recess of a heart devoted to avarice, fraught with hypocrisy, and swelling with malice, lay concealed schemes, and motives too black to be at once unravelled.

It had been the cautious policy of this man's life to lay his plans, and bring them step by step to light; this caution and policy were now in their full vigour; he instantly changed his measures, all the impenetrable prudence which had frosted over his features before the Earl entered vanished; the silk handkerchief which gave him, purposely, a ruffian-like appearance to Lady Meredith, now served to rub an uncommon redness into his eyes – he followed the Earl into the garden, where he found him recovering and soothing the poor Ellen, who no sooner saw Mr. Morgan, than she shrieked out, "Oh, save me, my dear Lord, from that wicked man."

Mr. Morgan bowed to the ground.

"What man, my Ellen; be composed, nobody shall hurt you."

"But he will hurt my grandpapa, he will kill my dear grandmamma, he is going to turn us all out of Code Gwyn, and take our house from us, and my uncle will be obliged to keep us at the parsonage. Pray, my dear Lord, if it is at all in your power," and she slid down on her knees.

Lord Castle Howel turned pale with astonishment; he knew the rapacity of Morgan's character, the fawning servility of his deportment had not imposed on him; he penetrated the thin disguise of affected humility, and never deigned to take the smallest notice of him, except what his own sense of politeness enforced, when he sometimes joined the hunt, and partook his public dinner.

Mr. Morgan again bowed very low, "My Lord, I humbly crave your Lordship –"

The Earl, impatient to administer consolation to the venerable matron within, as well as to set at rest the heart of Ellen, requested Mr. Morgan would go to Castle Howel directly, promised to follow him in six minutes, and having hastily consigned Ellen to the care of Lady Margaret immediately joined the Merediths.

The result of a very short conversation was, Mr. Meredith's getting into the carriage with his Lordship, who begged the ladies would take tea at the parsonage, and he would return to escort them home.

Lady Meredith, though never in London, had all inbred politeness, that rendered her the ornament of whatever society she was in; she apologized, with a truth and grace that spoke to the heart, for the scene they had witnessed; and desired Ellen to make tea. The old ladies, charmed with the appearance of her health and vivacity, were exceedingly pleased both with their company and repast, and though it was nine before the carriage returned, they were far from thinking the time tedious.

Mr. Meredith's dark and expressive eyes shewed the essence of meekness and good humour, three hours before they had streamed in sympathy, with the sorrow of a beloved parent – they now beamed with placidity and content. He apologized to the ladies for his stay, after he had in silence pressed the hand of his mother to his lips, and to his heart, and with a look of unutterable tenderness folded Ellen in his arms. Lady Meredith perceived a change in their favour; and Ellen, inexperienced as she was, concluded Lord Castle Howel was the good genius of the hour. The old ladies had invited her to accompany them, but the carriage brought Mr. Meredith without the Earl, or an intimation her company was desired. She was delighted at the sight of her Patron at such a critical period, relying implicitly on the goodness of his heart, and easy in the confidence of his power; but, strange as it may appear, his offer of marriage never occurred to her mind; it had astonished, and, for the moment, perplexed her, but the entire silence on the subject, observed by all the family, the parental character in which Lord Castle Howel had become so dear and respectable, so kindly reassumed at the parsonage, together with some secret ideas, totally averse to marriage with him, had expelled an event so transient and unexpected.

When the coach drove up to Code Gwyn, Winifred waited to receive her mistress with more meaning than was usually discernible in her large black eyes; and, not a usual thing,

Ellen, Countess of Castle Howel   113

close behind stood old Griffiths and his sister, with an equal quantity of treasured wisdom in theirs.

Mrs. Griffiths whispered to Lady Meredith, and old Griffiths taking the Reverend by the button, led him across the hall in close confab. Ellen had ascended half the stairs, with Winifred in attendance, when Lady Meredith desired she would accompany her, in the parlour. It was very seldom Ellen thought of the right or wrong in her grandmother's commands, and still seldomer, she disobeyed them; she turned with alacrity, and then for the first time, saw something more than usual in the looks of her servant.

"Cot pless your dear soul, co into your room, here has peen the tivel to pay, Cot save us," whispered Winifred.

"What's the matter?" asked Ellen.

Now if any of the young ladies (supposing this story should have the honour to be perused by such) has known what it is to think particularly well of a young male acquaintance, and should fancy the secret was known only to themselves, such young ladies will know, on all occasions of surprise, fear, or joy, the mind instantly reverts to the *favoured subject*, and concludes, he is in some degree or other connected with it.

Percival Evelyn stood before Ellen's mental eye, as she uttered, "What's the matter?"

"Ellen, you are waited for," said Lady Meredith.

"Cot Almighty pless us, they won't let us speak – I have had a letter."

"From Percival?"

"No, as Cot is my judge, Miss, from his petters."

"Ellen, you are not used to keep my mother waiting," said Mr. Meredith gravely.

"There now, tivel take it, the Reverent must put in his hoar!"

Percival's betters, thought Ellen, as she turned quick, down stairs.

Lady Meredith and her son were already with Sir Arthur. The heart of affection when it has joyful tidings to communicate, is generally very brief, there needs no rhetoric, no ornament of speech to varnish a tale of happiness. Lady Meredith was weeping in the arms of her husband – Mr. Meredith and his two sisters were kneeling at his feet, their joyful emotions divided betwixt thankfulness to heaven, and gratitude to him who had been the blessed means of saving them from distress; Miss Meredith and Ellen joined the rest of the family; the servants caught the enthusiasm; it was Sunday, and therefore there was no dance, but the old harper struck up, "Of a noble race was Shenkin." All was harmony and good humour till after supper, when Winifred being summoned, Mrs. Griffiths stationed behind Lady Meredith's chair, as her brother was behind Sir Arthur's, and the rest of the domestics dismissed, her Ladyship took a letter out of her pocket, and requested her son to read it.

Winifred, half crying and half scolding, her usual way of argument, protested against this. For why? The Reverent had no control over her, she was twenty-one years of age, and, moreover, as coot as a married woman.

"A married woman!" exclaimed Sir Arthur.

"I mean by contraction," answered Winifred, pertly. "Cot safe me, tis fery hard I can't receive a letter without all this hollobolo."

Mr. Meredith, who had been running his eye over the paper, now turning sternly, converted the voluble part of her argument into tears and loud sobs.

"When you receive letters in which the honour of any part

of this family is concerned, you are answerable to us all; how dare you, or your correspondent, presume to name Ellen Meredith in your scrawls?"

Ellen's first suspicion, that Percival was the source of all this bustle, recurred with additional force; conscious that she thought of little but *him*, her natural inference was that his thoughts were as busy about her. Winifred had confessed she had entered into a kind of league with him, and though, when absent in England, he had no means of reminding her of her promise, yet it was not unlikely he would do it, when he heard they were returning to Code Gwyn. This idea in her head, she sat blushing, while Sir Arthur and indeed all the family, were impatiently urging Mr. Meredith to read the letter, which, after drawing his chair nearer, hemming, snuffing the candles, he began as follows.

"Mi dearest Miss Winifred."

Ellen ventured to look up, *that* could not be Percival's style to *her* servant.

Mr. Meredith went on:

"Mi art is broke by your cruel unkindness, and mi Lord's art is as bad hoff."

"Poor tear Mr. Joseph," sobbed Winifred.

Ellen looked amazed.

Mr. Meredith resumed.

"We came to Bath, all to see our true lovers, and Madam Forrest told, us the bitter news that you, was fals arted."

"A wicked woman," sobbed Winifred.

"Indeed, Winifred," said Ellen, "you are very impertinent, I wonder how you dare call Mrs. Forrest a wicked woman?"

"Why did she call me fals arted, Miss, tell me but that? Cot safe me, what's coot for the coos is coot for the canter."

"Silence," said Sir Arthur, sternly, "go on, son."

"Which was the most bitter to me, has my Lord has got a promise of an exciseman's place for me, where of we might have a comfortable being of our own, and moreover kept our little farm too."

Winifred gave Mrs. Griffiths a nod, "you see, aunt—"

"And my Lord has been beautifying his fine seat, and new gilding, and painting, and laying out the ground, all for a sarten young lady, that shall be nameless."

Every eye was now fixed on Ellen, but as Ellen returned the look without a trait of confusion, Mr. Meredith went on.

"For, you know, Winifred, I never tell secrets, but my Lord can think of nothing, nor talk of nothing, but Miss Meredith."

"No more he can, I'll take my affitavit," cried Winifred.

"Any more than I can of my dear Winifred, and certainly we shall both die, if you break your vows and promises."

"Oh, Cot forbit. Amen! amen!"

"So now I beg if you have a spark little of love for your poor constant Joseph, you will write me word, by the return of post, as follows: Why you went in such a hurry from Bath? what you are now doing? whether that sauntering fellow, Evelyn, is still with the prig of a parson!"

Mr. Meredith stopped, and as poor Winifred, notwithstanding her partiality for Joseph, and her good thoughts, through him, of his Lord, really loved and respected all the Code Gwyn family, she could not hear the last sentence without feeling the utmost confusion.

"The prig of a parson!" repeated Sir Arthur.

"Aye, aye, aye aye," cried old Griffiths, shaking his white locks over Sir Arthurs shoulder, "this is a brave husband you have got, hussey, who makes his game of God's minister."

"Of our Reverent!" added Mrs. Griffiths, with a look of horror.

"The sauntering fellow, Evelyn," said Mr. Meredith, resentfully.

"I wonder what poor Percival has done to him," joined Ellen.

"Go on, go on, my dear brother," said Mary, "this will be a charming subject for me to write to Miss Jones."

"And whether you tell Miss Meredith, how dear my Lord loves her, and whether she loves him ever so little, and whether she has any other sweetheart, and whether you can persuade her to come with you to the coppice to meet my Lord and I."

"What does the man mean?" cried Ellen, with unfeigned astonishment.

"Meet him! a miscreant! it is out of the practice of romance to meet a man by appointment!" said Miss Catherine, in an accent of disgust.

"Is there any more?" asked Lady Meredith, impatiently.

"Only the signature – Your loving husband, tell deth, Joseph Wilks."

"Meet in the coppice," said Mr. Meredith, "then I suppose this worthy spouse elect of yours, was apprehensive Mr. Evelyn would be sauntering in the way of his noble employer and himself."

Winifred had not a word to say, the prig of a parson struck her dumb; but her tears were always ready, those she shed in great abundance.

"Oh, thou shame of thy family," said old Griffiths, with indignation, "thou viper, not only to abuse the noble blood that nourished thee, but join a rag-a-muffin of a footman to reduce sweet Miss Ellen to be ruined."

Of this accusation Winifred knew herself to be innocent; her own vanity confirmed every profession made by her lover, not once had she suspected either the honesty or sincerity of his addresses, and Ellen being beyond comparison the most beautiful creature she had ever seen, and being sincerely attached to her, it was natural to suppose her charms had, at least, made as indelible an impression on Lord Claverton; indeed, as Joseph had said and sworn it, the matter was so far past doubt, that had they continued at Bath till his Lordship's arrival, and he proposed, as was intended, a double elopement, either the danger or impropriety of the measure would have prevented her. Innocent therefore as to intention, and of an irritable temper, she entered into a vindictive explanation, in the course of which, by her defence both of her lover and his Lordship, she discovered to the family, what was entirely hid from herself – that Joseph and his Lord were pursuing a regular concerted plan; which, but for the sudden recall from Bath might have ended in the ruin of both mistress and maid. But, as it nevertheless appeared she was the innocent dupe of secret villainy, she was consigned to the reprimands of her uncle and aunt.

"What, ben't I to undress Miss Ellen?" cried she, as she was leaving the room.

"Not till you are sensible of the errors of your conduct," answered Lady Meredith.

It was now too late to enter into any farther discussion of the letter with Ellen, but the occurrences of the day were of too interesting a nature to permit the other part of the family to part, before every particular had been canvassed over among them.

John Morgan, the rich Squire, who, as Catherine described

him, bought every body's estates, and lived in a corner of his own house, feared by many, respected by few, and loved by none, left his native village, Code Gwyn, an indigent adventurer; his father, a dissolute pauper of the Parish, got the then Rector who had taken some pains in having his son taught reading and writing, to recommend him to a person of respectable connexions of that country, who was then a successful and opulent Merchant in London. Martin, the paternal name of the now Squire, was fortunately engaged by Mr. Morgan as under porter, where he ingratiated himself first into the good opinion of his master, a plain fair meaning man, who raised him from his menial servant to his principal trust in the business, and next into the heart of his only child.

Miss Morgan was motherless, and her father's excessive fondness, by keeping her constantly at home, deprived her of the advantage she would have imbibed by associating with well educated young women.

Martin was handsome, and, even then, could bow very low where occasion suited. He did not run away with Miss Morgan, but he took care to alarm her father with fears for her life, if he refused his consent. The old man had a good deal of Cambrian pride about him; he withstood his daughter's entreaties, but her tears conquered him, and he consented to their marriage. Martin succeeded Mr. Morgan in his business, and buried his wife the same year, by whom he had an only daughter, who, in hopes of making a woman of fashion, he kept at a capital boarding school till she was eighteen, when his father-in-law, who had retired to his estate at Code Gwyn some years, died, leaving all his fortune to him, and his granddaughter on condition of their taking the name of Morgan, which, as that of Martin was by no means deficient in notoriety, and Code Gwyn the place his vanity wished to shine at, notwithstanding his mean origin, was a very acceptable clause in a will that left him, with his own savings, one of the richest men in Britain, and as soon as an act of parliament changed John Martin to John Morgan, he took possession.

Elizabeth Morgan was mild, sensible, and virtuous; she accompanied her father to Code Gwyn, and the late Mr. Morgan having lived in habits of friendship with the Merediths, Edmund, just then returned from College, fell passionately in love with her. Sir Arthur would not hear of a connexion so degrading, notwithstanding the immense wealth of her father, and *his* views were much higher for his daughter.

Mr. Meredith honoured his parents, and inherited their pride of blood; but, spite of all his efforts to conquer his attachment, it increased with every interview.

Sir Arthur's objection was an affront, though he was as much averse to the match as himself, Mr. Morgan secretly vowed never to forgive.

The young lady was far from encouraging Mr. Meredith's passion, though she was in habits of intimacy with the Miss Merediths then about her own age.

Her pleasant manners and sweetness of temper conquered the dislike the neighbourhood entertained against her father; every body took notice of and invited her to their houses, and she was a frequent and favourite guest of Lady Margaret Howel's. The fair Elizabeth flattered the hopes and pride of her father; he knew enough of the world to be sure his daughter with £80,000 would be received into families, whose blood might be traced to the Conqueror, though the poor proud Code Gwyn family, had the impertinence to remember his leaving the hovel in which he was born, to seek better bread than they gave his parents; fond of the aggrandizements of his daughter, she never made a connexion he did not immediately canvas in every light, to try whether it promised to lead to the desired point.

The first glance from the eyes of Elizabeth determined the fate of our young parson. Naturally of a studious pensive turn, his mind retreated from futile amusements: he studied much before he saw Miss Morgan, and after he had seen her, she mixed in every sentiment, and he saw her in every line he read. He had a little taste for drawing, her face, in all attitudes, ornamented his study, her eyes were pencilled on the margins of even his sermons, and he wrote the initials of her name in the blank leaves of all his books. His walks were within sight of the house, and if, after a ramble of three or four hours, he saw Elizabeth, he returned satisfied. This often happened, for all her amusements were solitary walks, in the most sequestered parts of the neighbourhood; but her health grew daily worse. Her father, angry at the ravage sickness made in her lovely countenance, and alarmed at the consequence, instead of soothing, reproached, and threatened the fair invalid. He took it into his head Meredith was the secret source of her disorder, and vowed to give his fortune to hospitals, and turn her out of doors, if she thought of that beggarly parson.

Elizabeth wept and trembled, without answering her stern father, who, as her health still declined, became every day more fretful.

Meredith, shocked at the change in her looks, and unable to conceal the anguish of his soul, often absented himself from her and became a prey to despair. During one of these self-inflicted penances, he was surprised by an abrupt visit from Mr. Morgan, who vociferously charged him with having stolen his daughter from his house that morning.

The surprise and grief which took possession of Mr. Meredith's countenance were proofs sufficient of his innocence; and Morgan, forgetting for a minute his animosity, informed him, that his daughter, after bidding him in a more tender than common manner good night, had gone early to rest; that, in the morning, on her not coming to breakfast, he searched her apartments, where she had not been in bed; that on opening her wardrobe, they found she had taken best part of her cloaths; and, in fine, that she had left his house.

Our parson's countenance brightened at this. So visible and increasing had been her dejection, he had, at first the strongest apprehensions for her fate; but she lived, and he trusted had happiness in pursuit, not, indeed, *with him*, that was self evident; but *self* was not, in this interesting hour attended to. Morgan secretly triumphed over the parson, who, he conceived must be terribly galled at the disappointment; and he became more reconciled to the elopement of his daughter, since he found the poor Meredith was not her companion. He, however, immediately set off for town, but though enquiries nor even money was spared to discover her, she was not heard of till eight months after, when he received anonymous information, that the corpse of his daughter lay at a house on Highgate hill, from whence he was requested to take it for interment.

It was not in human nature for a father to be unmoved in such a situation; he hastened to the place and found his only child dead. The people of the house were strangers to her and her connexions; she had been removed there for air, a month had been paid in advance for the lodging; and a man and woman servant had attended her, who disappeared within an hour after she died; and though every thing about her bore the appearance of elegance, and even affluence, they had so dexterously managed, as to escape without suspicion of their intentions, till after a violent bustle, a silence, which continued more than an hour, induced the landlady to open the chamber door, where she found the lady dead, and the apartment cleared of every thing that could possibly lead to the discovery of the thieves, for that they had been guilty of theft admitted not a doubt.

Mr. Morgan wept and raved as he contemplated the corpse of his child; and after passing two hours in vain regrets he had ever been a father, almost distracted, left the scene of mortality. But tho' change of place could not remove the reproach from his mind, which he endeavoured to appease, by such a ridiculous parade of funeral grandeur, as served to gratify his own vanity, and swell the undertaker's bill. But the deceased left a more lasting monument of his hard heart than the expensive one he placed to her memory in the parish church where she died. He liberally rewarded the people of the house, and paid them a high price for their good report; he took every possible means to conceal the harshness of his conduct from the world, and making a precipitate end of his concerns in town, hastened to his Welch mansion, where, he flattered himself the event would not be known. But rumour, with his hundred tongues, told the fate of the young Elizabeth in a thousand different ways – Meredith heard all, and found one sad certainty, the woman who possessed his warm heart was no more; a fever seized his brain, followed by a nervous debility that totally incapacitated him from performing his functions, and for three years left his spirits quite sunk, his health impaired and all his affection for woman buried with his adored Elizabeth.

Mr Morgan's regret for the untimely death of his daughter was changed into a detestation of her memory, by some discoveries made in applications to him after her death; he never would hear her name mentioned, and, dead to every generous feeling, devoted his life to the accumulation of riches, and the gratification of his passions – he was in the constant habit of lending money to people in distressed circumstances, and of conceiving a vicious inclination for modest women, and it was not seldom he made the husband and father give good security for money he pretended to advance to the charms of the wife or daughter.

The Code Gwyn estate groaned for the axe, no wood had been cut but for domestic use for more than a century back, it was, as poor Brown would have said, "full of mind capabilities."[5] The manor was extensive, the ground rich, and finely laid out; the mansion house, it is true, was out of repair, but Mr. Morgan's keen eye ran it over, he knew how little, with the old materials, and wood and lime on the premises, it would cost to build a new one; then, to turn the haughty Merediths out of their vaunted antient home, was a gratification which he never lost sight of! He insinuated himself into Sir Arthur's confidence by an affected gratitude for the charities bestowed on his family, and in the zeal of apparent friendship, supplied the easy improvident Baronet with sum after sum, till, like a thunderbolt, the notice of foreclosure shewed them the gulph before them; and the wolf, having gained his point, dropped his sheep's skin.

---

[5] A reference to the landscape gardener, Lancelot "Capability" Brown (1716-83), who told clients their estates had "capabilities" for improvement.

Mr. Morgan, not content with ruining the Code Gwyn family, vented the concealed rancour of his heart in reproaches and insults; and these were so often repeated, that they reconciled themselves to the removing to the parsonage, to avoid any further intercourse with their narrow minded creditor. Yet, to leave the house where their ancestors lived and died, to break up their family, to take the bread and asylum from their grey-headed domestics, to assign a set of honest dependants to the mercy of a rapacious miser, to become a tax on the duty of their son, no longer to behold objects which time had endeared to their view, was terrible. Every part of the family dreaded the impending misery, yet all were solicitous to conceal from each other their feelings.

The meeting of Mr. Morgan at the parsonage, was at the request of Mr. Meredith, whose last hope rested on a doubt old Griffiths had suggested, of Sir Arthur's right to mortgage one part of the estate; but the money had been advanced, and, therefore, however the point of law might stand, he was not of a turn to dispute payment, although he thought he might honourably avail himself of this suggested advantage so far as to retain the possession of the manor during his parent's life; but he had to do with a man well acquainted with the honour, or, as he called it, the folly of his debtors.

The reader has seen the success of the meeting; we have now to follow them, from Mr. Meredith's account, to Castle Howel.

During the ride from Code Gwyn, Lord Castle Howel made himself master of the rapacious views of Mr. Morgan, as well as the supine negligence of the Merediths; he well knew what money Mr. Morgan would advance was on perfect security, and worth any other person's while to do the same; at all events, he resolved the house and grounds should be left in the possession of the old people for life, *that* being settled, he eagerly asked, if Ellen had yet been made acquainted with his proposals.

Mr. Meredith's answer to his Lordship's letter had not reached London before the impatience of the old ladies, to say nothing of his Lordship's, induced them to leave it; the question, therefore, at such a period, was extremely embarrassing, as it must lead to an explanation, which might entirely frustrate all the plans the Earl had been concerting in their favour.

Lord Castle Howel observed his embarrassment, and felt it was no good augur for him. He was silent while Mr. Meredith was considering how to soften a refusal his natural frankness forbid him to conceal – but the more he considered, the more he found himself at a loss.

The Earl, then, with a forced smile, said he feared Ellen's heart was not in his cause, he saw he was rejected, but hoped he had not been urged too warmly – Mr. Meredith would forgive him – he meant in reference to the circumstances of the family.

Mr. Meredith coloured. "My Lord, you little know either Ellen or the family, had they been capable of urging such a motive, I should have been spared the pain I feel in conveying to your Lordship – but I have written to you."

"Forgive me," answered the Earl, "we will say no more on the business," and he turned the conversation to the improvements on his own estate.

When Morgan was admitted, after what had been settled in the coach, Mr. Meredith was surprised to hear the Earl desire him to send the demands on the Code Gwyn estate to his attorney, and it should be paid.

Do I hear right, thought he – "The whole mortgage, my Lord?"

"What, you know I am not rich, and wonder to hear me talk of paying off mortgages? But I take this to be a good thing, or Morgan would not have it."

Morgan bowed the lower, to hide his chagrin, and Lord Castle Howel ordered a bottle of Madeira, "Come, Morgan," said he, "you are disappointed, I know, and to confess the truth, so am I, but here is a bumper, to better luck another time."

"My Lord, I beg your Lordship to believe," again bowing.

"Believe, why I know it," replied the Earl, "but as I *will* pay the money; and as you receive it, drink your glass and make the best of it."

Morgan could not possibly contradict an Earl, who was not in his debt, and therefore become quite friends with Mr. Meredith, and after begging his Lordship would not think of an attorney, in a business which should be settled exactly as his Lordship pleased, humbly took his leave.

Meredith would have made acknowledgements, but the Earl forbid him, and without again mentioning Ellen they parted.

Every thing now went well at Code Gwyn, but this calm was of short duration, for David, whose wife had lived at Castle Howel, brought news that distressed them all, that the Earl was indisposed. Ellen, alarmed, was every hour for sending messengers to know if he was better – the answers, each more unfavourable than the other, pained her heart.

"If he should die!" said she, to Lady Meredith, who was at that instant thinking of his disinterested kindness.

"Aye, my dear, if he should, you would know the value of the friend, the protector, you have rejected."

Ellen protested no event would or could make her more sensible of his worth than she was at that moment.

"Would you not be grieved, then, my dear, to think, that instead of adding to his comforts, you had shortened his days?"

"Who, me, madam! Me shorten Lord Castle Howel's days! Can you think me such monster? Him, to whom I owe so much! who has been so good to *you* – No, I would die to give him comfort."

"Die, Ellen," cried the lively Mary, "if you give him comfort it must be in living for him!"

Lady Meredith sighed, Sir Arthur folded his hands, as he usually did when particularly moved; Ellen threw herself at his feet, and in the instant she was embracing his knees, formed a resolution as strong as heroic.

VOLUME II

Chapter I

Dear Percival,

I dare say, *you* remember as well as me, the last time I saw you, when we were walking round our little garden, I promised not to marry without you approved it. I suppose you will think it very forward in me to talk of such things, but you know I was just turned of fifteen *then,* and I am *now* seventeen, which makes a difference, tho' still I think it a very foolish subject for *me,* but here (I am almost ashamed to tell you) that Lord Castle Howel, who you know I dearly loved, wishes – I declare I am glad I am writing instead of speaking to you, for my cheeks burn like fire, and I am sure I hardly know what I write, but any thing is better than breaking one's word. Oh, Percival, we have had sad doings, what would you say, to see my poor grandpapa and grandmama, and my uncle and aunts, and all of us turned out of Code Gwyn, and crammed into the Parsonage? Poor old Griffiths and Susan cried themselves almost blind, for what you know could they do? And the old Harper must have gone to the parish; and that, as he says, would be a sad thing, for a man who had laced cloaths, and played before my grandpapa's father, when he was knight of the shire, then there is the old Bailiff – but indeed none of these would be so bad off, as my grandpapa himself, for you know he loves a large room, where his chair can travel as he calls it, and the largest room in the parsonage will hardly hold us all to dine when he is not there, and as to the poor dogs, there is no kennel for them either, and my grandpapa could not part with Bruin and Whitefoot; as to me, I have not minded dogs since Lord Claverton killed Lion, which you know you gave me when he was very little, and I was little too indeed. Well Percival, but I dare say you are shocked as well as me at the idea of my marrying, and yet Lord Castle Howel has behaved so kind to us all, and taken our estate out of the power of Mr. Morgan, who is turned out a very bad sort of a man, that I think you would rather I married *him* than any body *else*. I wish he could marry one of my aunts, I'm sure he would be very happy, and you must know I have refused him, but he is so good, and so ill, and tho' my uncle Meredith who oftener visits him, than any of the family, won't say it – yet I know they think he would be well and happy if I *relented,* that's an odd word you will think, but 'tis my aunt Catherine's, who is always using odd words. Now dear Percival, I should break my heart if Lord Castle Howel died, but I would not save *his* life, by breaking my promise to *you,* so pray answer me by return of Post, and whatever becomes of Ellen Meredith, she will always esteem and love Percival Evelyn, and wish those happy days they spent together, had not so soon been over. Oh, Percival, our garden is in beautiful order, I walk there till I am low spirited, and always leave it in tears, but dear Percival advise me, tell me if you give me up my promise.

              ELLEN MEREDITH.

After hastily folding and sealing this letter, she recollected that she neither knew his address, nor how to get it to the next Post town unknown to the family. Winifred was the only resource in such an exigence, she was directed to get Evelyn's address from David, and as Winifred was rather hardened as to consequences, vowed she would carry it to the post-office herself, "if it rained cats and togs, cot forgive her for saying so."

Accordingly, away went Winifred to the Parsonage, and sure of David in any thing concerning Evelyn, desired him to direct the letter.

Since Winifred's disgrace, and the cause of it, was known she became a person of much less consequence among the domestics of Code Gwyn and the Parsonage, David was sulky; how did he know but 'twas a trick to write to her London fellow, to carry Miss Ellen off.

Winifred was on the point of breaking out, but recollecting she should be betrayed to the family, called in her old auxiliary, *tears,* wondered how he could use an old friend so, asked if he thought Mr. Evelyn would be concerned in carrying off Miss Ellen? "No to be sure," was the surly answer, and he took the pencil she offered and scrawled the direction.

Poor Winifred's evil planet reigned; Mr. Meredith, from the study window, saw her trip over the field to the back wicket of the garden, she had at that period the misfortune to stand very low in his opinion, and although knowing the integrity of David, he could not guess how he should be made a party in her treachery, yet he had no doubt but the letter he saw in her hand was one, designed for Lord Claverton's footman, and darting round, met her as she was coming out of the garden. Never was poor waiting damsel in such a fright, she had not power to hide the letter, but stood trembling with it in her hand, positively denying she had such a thing about her, till exasperated at her falsehood, he snatched it from her, but his astonishment and confusion nearly equalled hers, when instead of Joseph, he saw it addressed to Percival Evelyn.

"And who wrote this letter?" said he in a voice of rage.

"Cot Almighty knows, sir" answered Win, for I am sure I never saw it in my porn days; tivel take me, but I believe 'tis all witchery."

"Hold thy lying tongue," cried Mr. Meredith, and calling to David and his maid, charged them to keep her prisoner, till his return from Code Gwyn whither he directly rode. Ellen was walking in her beloved garden, and he was so lucky as to find his father and mother alone, his face was so clear an index of his mind that Lady Meredith saw something extraordinary had happened before he produced the letter.

"Ah poor Ellen" exclaimed Lady Meredith, showing the direction[6] to Sir Arthur.

Mr. Meredith looked more surprised.

"Shall we open it?" continued Lady Meredith.

"Certainly" answered her son.

Sir Arthur examined the impression, it was a fine *Hope,* an appendage to the watch Lord Claverton had given her; his looks did not entirely approve of breaking the seal.

"It is justified, sir, by our regard to the honour of our family, and affection for this lovely branch of it; it is indeed necessary, for how are we sure, that poor ignorant creature, Winifred, is not, even in this measure, the dupe of some plan of Lord

---

[6] I.e., the address

Claverton, whose libertine designs" – Mr. Meredith's colour rose as he spoke.

Lady Meredith broke the seal herself, at the same time assuring her son she had in *this* instance, no suspicion of Lord Claverton. When the letter was read, Sir Arthur folding his hands turned to his lady.

"What pity!" said he.

Lady Meredith did not answer.

"I did not suspect this" said her son, "but I am confident the letter may be sent to Percival."

"Oh, no! poor lad," answered Lady Meredith, "it is too much."

"I am confident it may," repeated Mr. Meredith, and he was justified in the assertion, by his thorough knowledge of the youth, whose mind he had formed to the practice of every social virtue; he persisted in advising the letter to be sent, positively affirming from what he knew of his Eleve's disposition, that his answer would promote the object of their wish, more than all they could do.

Lady Meredith had not quite so much faith in the self denial of a young man of twenty-one, but she no longer opposed the trial; Mr. Meredith returned with the letter to the Parsonage, and in the presence of Winifred sent his servant with it to the post town, telling her coldly, that when he took it from her, he suspected it was for her friend Joseph; but as it was for Mr. Evelyn, he had no business with it; he added, she need not say any thing to Ellen, and offered her half a crown. There were but two ways of bribing Winifred, one was a secret in the possession of Joseph Wilks, the other in that of Percival Evelyn; she put the half crown scornfully on the table.

"Not tell my mistress, but, as Cot shall safe me I will, if I lose my life for it."

Mr. Meredith smiled at the pert toss of her head, as she left the Parsonage, but after all, and when she had made the very most of the story, Ellen was neither surprised nor alarmed, indeed she had wished, she said (she knew not why) to conceal it from the family; but that was foolish, for as his answer must come by post to Code Gwyn, it could not be kept secret, but none of these reasons, which she explained to Winifred, could satisfy *her*; she protested against the behaviour of the Reverend, and vowed the house was "Cot pless her, no better as a prison."

A tedious eight days passed before Percival's answer arrived. In that interval Lord Castle Howel had been thought in some danger from a low fever, the old ladies (alarmed at his situation, and provoked at the assurance of a little country Miss's refusing the offered hand of the Earl of Castle Howel), were constantly urging a fresh choice, and teasing both him and themselves by their impatience to return to London, where each of them had pointed out, among their acquaintance, young brides in abundance, whose mothers, aunts, and cousins, were remarkable for the number of children they brought into this wicked world; to these arrangements Lord Castle Howel turned a listless ear, his choice had been made, with too much real feeling, to be soon transferred, and he was convinced, by the pain her rejection inflicted on him, that the early impression Ellen had made on his mind, was as much the result of passion as philanthropy; he dwelt on her perfections, the joy which darted from her eyes, when she saw him at the Parsonage, the confidence with which she disclosed her sorrows, and asked his assistance, was ever before him, not having then received Mr. Meredith's letter, he was transported to receive so many proofs of affection from her, and the disappointment was from that circumstance more bitter, the agitation of his mind increased by the old Maderia, of which he had drank several bumpers, without recollecting it was a liquor he had not accustomed himself to, at an hour he usually idled away at the tea table, threw him into a fever, but he was now recovering his health, tho' with a languor on his spirits, that was very distressing to the two spinsters.

On the eighth day the expected letter arrived at Code Gwyn. Winifred was on the look out, tho' not, as she flattered herself, unobserved, for as the connexions of the family at the mansion, with the great world were very circumscribed; what few letters came, were left at the Parsonage, but *this* Mr. Meredith chose should go to the house by the Postman.

Ellen was reading 'Zadig' to Sir Arthur and Lady Meredith, and the two aunts were sitting at work, when Winifred entered, pretending to look for something; it was post day, Ellen understood Percival's answer was come. Oh! what did that answer contain? her voice faltered, her colour went and came, she trembled – Zadig dropped on the floor.

Mr. Meredith, as if by accident, came in, and in his usual expressive face Lady Meredith saw the intelligence just conveyed by Winifred.

"What's the matter with Ellen," demanded he, "is she not well?"

"No – yes, not quite, I—"

"Are you fatigued with reading, my dear?" said Sir Arthur.

"A little, I believe."

Lady Meredith advised a walk in the air, Ellen gladly rose and ran up stairs.

Winifred followed, threw the letter on the table, and vanished –

Ellen locked her door, and took up the letter – she knew the hand – her eyes filled – she trembled and laid it down again – after a shower of tears, again she took up the important letter – but wanting resolution to open it, again it was laid on the table – she walked to the window – her heart beat violently – she traversed the room; and became more composed – again the letter was resumed – she examined the seal – it was a plain cypher of E – "dear Evelyn" whispered she, and pressed it to her lips – she carefully tore the paper round the seal and opened the letter – its contents were short. She read,

"What advice can poor Percival Evelyn, the child of bounty, the object of charity, give his adored Ellen Meredith, your promise Ellen is no more – I give it up – you are free – let your heart be your monitor, but whatever your situation or mine may in future be, remember, while I have life, you have one sure unchangeable friend, who will rejoice in your prosperity, and on whose poor all, both soul and power, you may in adversity depend."

P. E."

An agony of tears succeeded the reading of this letter, and it would be hard to say whether she was pleased or displeased at its contents – he had given back a promise, she considered as the only obstacle to her rendering her own and the Castle Howel family happy – but she did not feel more happy *herself* for this enfranchisement, she wept over her liberty, and grieved that she had asked it, – dinner was announced – she could not eat, and begged to be excused going down – her request was complied with, Mr. Meredith guessed rightly the purport of the letter, and it was judged delicate and proper to submit to herself, the manner in which she would bear the first disappointment of her heart.

Tea time came, Ellen was still in her room – a carriage drove up – she heard it, and all over nerve, ran trembling to the window. Lady Margaret alighted.

"My fate is determined!" said she bursting into a fresh flood of tears. Lady Meredith knocked at the door "Lady Margaret Howel my dear is come to take leave of you, and has brought you a number of fine things, how is your head? will you come down?"

Ellen accepted her offered hand, and looking up met Lady Meredith's eye, so humid, so compassionate, so tender, she threw her arms round her neck and could only sob.

"My Mamma, my dear, my only Mother, pity your poor Ellen." "Pity!" replied the venerable matron," I admire, I almost envy my child."

Ellen pointed to the letter.

"Do you mean, I should read that letter, my child?"

"Not now, but take it with you, and never let me see it again."

"My heroic child," said the fond parent embracing her.

Encouraged by the sweet voice of maternal approbation, and self assured, by the consciousness of a sacrifice so dear, a modest blush suffusing her cheek, she followed her respectable relation into the parlour.

Lady Margaret saluted her, with rather a constrained politeness, and answered her anxious enquiries after the Earl, with a cold and formal bow; her brother she said requested Miss Meredith would do him the honour to accept a few trifling remembrances he had brought to Castle Howel for her; these trifles were a profusion of fine laces, muslins, and other elegant materials for female dress. The Miss Merediths could not help admiring them article by article, but as Ellen sat lost in thought, Lady Margaret continued – The Earl lamented he could not take a personal leave of the family, Sir Arthur will tell you Miss, how much my brother is your friend; he regrets he is *only* your friend."

Ellen was still silent.

Mr. Meredith hoped the neighbourhood were not going to lose them immediately.

The Ladies, Gertrude and Frances would not, she answered, perhaps ever see Wales again, and they were naturally desirous of visiting some very old friends, this was probably the only unengaged day, and she had taken it to pay a farewell visit at Code Gwyn.

The family were properly sensible of the honour, but Ellen was still silent.

Lady Margaret took one dish of tea, made her exit with a few fashionable courtesys, and was handed to her carriage by Mr. Meredith, who stood some time looking after the chariot, in a reverie, from which he was roused, by an invitation to walk with Ellen, she led to her little Garden, where with swimming eyes, and plaintive voice she pointed to his notice, the beautiful shrubs, and flowers, the cypher[7] and every ornament love had contrived to adorn it: without seeming to observe the effect the fond reverie had on her mind, he liberally praised both the plan, and cultivation of the charming spot; they had now walked round, and returned to the entrance. Ellen looked

---

[7] The floral display forming Ellen's and Percival's initials

alternately at her uncle, and at the garden, she put her spread hand before her eyes, but the trickling tears would not be concealed, she hastily quitted the garden, and locking the little wicket, requested he would give the key to Evelyn.

Mr. Meredith took the key in an attentive silence, and accompanied her back to the house; as she turned to the stairs, he kissed his hand, and motioned towards the Parlour, she stopped, he saw her heart was struggling with itself, "have you done with me my dear Ellen?" said he in a voice of sympathy.

After a moment's hesitation,

"No sir," she replied, "If you have patience." – He instantly followed into the gallery, where with a graceful modesty she opened her heart; confessed that from the moment she knew she had affections, they were placed on Percival Evelyn, told him of her promise, her letter, and his answer; lamented Lord Castle Howel had made a choice so unworthy of him, that he had not continued her friend, and protector, "but what" added she in an elevated tone and gesture, "what is the whole life of such an insignificant as me, compared to one hour of so good a man as Lord Castle Howel, of my dear venerable parents, of my aunts, and of you my dear worthy uncle; you who are the orphan's friend, and the father of the fatherless, from this moment I devote all my little faculties to gratitude and to duty, – you will still love Percival and advise him to his good. – If the Earl will accept me, and if you my dear uncle will tell him, I have *now* no will but his." She stopped and paused.

Mr. Meredith looked at her with pleasure and admiration, but not with surprise, her conduct was exactly what he expected would be the result of her letter to Percival, but though it was of more importance than he chose himself to think on, he forbore to commend, or even answer, what she had said; and only seriously replied, he was at her devotion, and would say or do whatever she wished.

"Then I believe, sir, I believe I have said enough for Lord Castle Howel, but do you, my uncle, my friend, excuse me to the dear assembly in the Parlour, say every thing for me; but I, indeed I cannot see them tonight." Mr. Meredith embraced and left her.

The pleasure this communication gave the Code Gwyn family may be conceived; besides making their situation happy, Ellen, the pride, the darling of their hearts, would be secured from distress, and an earnest of the same security to themselves; she would be a Countess! and the charms of mind, and person, which so delighted *them,* could not fail of exciting general esteem. Lady Meredith cautioned her family not to show an excess of joy, "we must," said the considerate parent, "respect the sacrifice, tho' we rejoice it is made."

Mr. Meredith executed his welcome commission, with delicate propriety. The Earl embraced him with warmth, and put a diamond of value on his finger, – Lady Gertrude took a pair of gold buckles, out of her own shoes which had been her father's, and insisted on his wearing them. Lady Frances had a locket set with brilliants, in which was a lock of beautiful auburn hair, which she said was cut from her own head, a *very few* years back, he must take that for *her* sake, – Lady Margaret contented herself, with bestowing on him many *precious words,* the projected visits were given up, the coach ordered, and the Ladies returned with Mr. Meredith to visit their destined relations.

Nothing could be kinder than the Ladies; nothing more engaging than the fair Ellen, an immediate return of the visit was pressed by Lady Margaret, in consideration of the Earl's health, and the blushing Ellen consented to be of the party.

The next day, Lord Castle Howel had the happiness to receive his young bride elect at his Castle; and that day month was blessed with her hand at Code Gwyn church, every house of entertainment within ten miles of Castle Howel, and Code Gwyn, were opened on the joyful occasion. The two spinsters vied with each other in brilliant presents to the bride, in honour to their family, and in private benefactions to the poor, in honour to themselves.

This splendid wedding, of which Winifred had not the smallest expectation, almost turned her brain, not that Ellen's advance in rank, or riches, was a matter of any wonder, for nothing in this world, or indeed in the next, could, in her opinion, equal the deserts of the mistress she perfectly adored; but, as Ellen was too much attached to her old favourite to exchange her, notwithstanding her want of skill in the mysteries of the toilette, for a very clever young person, who was an adept, – the consequence and advantages she derived from her situation were more than the equilibrium of her little mind could well bear.

The Earl, charmed with every movement of a heart, where innocence and honour so entirely presided; was also partial to the oddities of Winifred; he insisted on her being retained, with the more regular lady's maid, and that *she* should have the pre-eminence.

Sir Arthur Meredith now at ease in his circumstances, his beloved grand-daughter so happily established, his Lady happy and gratified, felt himself renovated. The ladies dressed better, the servants were again merry, Mr. Jones, the apothecary, who had withdrawn his visits, when a certain foreclosure was in agitation, now renewed his attendance at the Mansion, and Mr. Morgan's bow was more frequent, and lower than ever, tho' all intercourse with the family was declined on their part. As to the Castle Howels, they, as is usual with people of quality, who are at the top of happiness, wanted to be still happier. The old Ladies had not been many years from home, and now the object of their journey was in part obtained, they wished to accompany the young Countess to London; to go to court, see the public places, and visit their old friends. Lady Margaret had wishes too, but though not exactly the same as her aunts, yet as they ultimately pointed London-ward, she chose to echo them.

Lady Castle Howel, whose lively disposition we have before mentioned, found elegance, affluence, rank and all the luxurious appendages sit vastly easy on her. She heard too much of the metropolis, and all its fascinations to object going there; besides the Ladies who were perfect mistresses of etiquette, insisted her presentation at court was an indispensable ceremony, attached to her rank; and the Earl was too proud of his charming bride, and too much gratified by the admiration she excited, to wish to hide her in the mountains of Wales; a grand retinue was therefore ordered, and the day fixed for departure.

But, although Ellen was now every inch a Countess, she had not forgot her duty and love, for the dear circle at Code Gwyn; she asked the Earl's permission to take her maid and spend one day with them, previous to her departure.

It was bleak December, the days short, and unpleasant, and the road bad; the Earl existed but in the light of his beautiful wife, but her gratification was dearer to him than his own – he advised her to stay the night, with her beloved relations –

the family he observed were so worthily united, they would have a thousand little nothings to say, which a stranger would restrain; "enjoy your good friends, my Ellen, visit the scenes dear to your infant affection, speak kindly to your old domestics, assure your venerable parents, I consider them as mine, and will receive you a second time from them myself, tomorrow."

The Countess felt the kindness of this plan, and charmed her Lord, by her sensible acknowledgments. The Code Gwyn family were apprised of her visit, and an universal holiday prevailed; Mr. Meredith dined, but would not sleep at Code Gwyn; the Countess remonstrated, "the night was dark and cold, and it was the last she should pass there" – he was not to be prevailed on, but said, he would be ready for his breakfast next morning, before she left her room.

When Winifred attended to undress her, she was remarkably silent, and on being interrogated by her Lady, as to the *cause,* protested, that "she believed, the tivel had always something to do at Code Gwyn; "I desire, my Lady, you will ax me no questions, for as cot shall judge me, if I speak, they will cill me, and if I don't, I shall purst" – "Well," replied the Countess, "I want to know none of your secrets, I suppose you have heard from your old sweetheart."

"Ay, Ay, well, well, cot pless, and save old sweet hearts, I say, amen, amen, pray cot – name o cot, I am not afraid of apparitions, if people will preak their hearts, and tie, other people can't help it, cot forgive us all our sins, and our iniquities."

"You are very pious tonight, Winifred."

"No, cot help me, I must not speak, put if I was to tell your Ladyship –"

"I won't hear another word," said the Countess, sportively.

Winifred sighed, and went away praying to cot, to forgive her sins.

The Earl was at Code Gwyn by two, and on account of the short days, declined staying to dinner; they departed amid the tears, and benedictions of the family, and servants, the former from affection, the latter, partly from regard to their young mistress, and partly from the generosity of the Earl.

The day was clear, and light, Ellen prattled away; the Earl 'conversing with her, forgot all time, all seasons, and their change;' he was contemplating with delight the flattering change in her lovely countenance, which tho' deluged with tears, at parting with her friends, was already restored to its usual serenity, when a scream, and exclamation from Winifred, who sat at the back of the coach, called all Ellen's blood into her face, and turned him pale.

"Cot have mercy on us, pray cot, and forgive our transgressions, avaunt satan plese cot."

They were passing the Parsonage, it stood on the top of a steep hill, the weather had been frosty, and the drivers were obliged to slacken their pace; Ellen bended forward, and saw the object that excited Winifred's exclamation.

Percival Evelyn, or rather the pale emaciated shadow, of what he *was*, stood at a chamber window, supported by David, watching with eager eyes the passing vehicle.

The Earl, extremely displeased, and attributing the agitation visible in Ellen, to Winifred's exclamation, asked sternly if she had seen a ghost.

Certain recollections, at this moment particularly troublesome to poor Winifred, and a natural fear of ghosts and hobgoblins, having heard that Mr. Evelyn was actually dying, levelled all distinction.

"Cot forgive you my Lort, for using such pad worts, and plast femys,[8] but cot is abof the tivil still, and cot knows, what is a lort before satan, any more then a poor sinner, for costs[9] to be shure if they want to be tied in the red sea, may tear a lort to pieces with crace of cot."

"The wench is mad!" exclaimed the Earl. The Countess had by this time recovered her surprise, the sight of Percival, at such a period, and in such a situation, so unthought of and so unexpected, could not fail to agitate her; but a moment's recollection convinced her of the impropriety of shewing the concern she felt for another man, in her husband's presence; that she *did feel* it – was an injury to her own peace, but to betray it, would be an insult to his honour – every soothing word from the Earl, was a reproach to her heart, and she had the heroism to make a secret vow, in that moment, never to mention, or hear mentioned, the name of Percival Evelyn; yet, not even the consciousness of acting right, could recompose her spirits, and she retired to her chamber as soon as she alighted at Castle Howel.

Winifred was bursting to speak of Evelyn, "Oh, my Lady!" cried she, "did you see the poor tear dying Mr. Evelyn? who" – she was struck dumb with astonishment, when Ellen commanded her, on pain of utter displeasure, to avoid ever mentioning a name *once* so *dear*.

"Cot be coot unto us, poor sinful souls, what, not when he ties? as he certainly will, must not I speak, when he is dead and cone, in the peaceful crave, and his cost comes in a whirlwind, like a roaring lion?"

---

[8] I.e. blasphemies
[9] I.e., ghosts

"Living, or dead, I will not hear him mentioned," answered Ellen, much agitated.

Winifred had patched up a kind of truce with her conscience, by resolving to make a confession of some *secret* sins to her Lady, in which Mr. Evelyn's name *must* occur, but Ellen's determined manner deprived the poor penitent of this consolation, and she left her in such terror of mind, that she actually gave the dairy maid two yards of ribbon, *almost as good as new,* to sit up with her all night, and it was not till she left Castle Howel she fancied herself safe.

The next morning the Castle Howel family set out for the metropolis. The newspapers had announced the marriage of "the right honourable the Earl of Castle Howel to the beautiful Miss Ellen Meredith" and the curiosity of the beau monde was in consequence excited; their arrival at Bath, where Ellen wished to see her governess, and old school fellows, was proclaimed by the usual music, ringing of bells, &c. and Mrs. Forrest and her ladies were very early in their respects.

At the sight of Mrs. Forrest, Winifred Griffith, whose head had been in a constant vortex of new cloaths, fine sights, and dignity of station, so infinitely superior to any thing she had ever seen, or expected; remembered there was such a man in existence as Joseph Wilks, whose kind letter (which brought her into such disgrace at Code Gwyn), yet remained unanswered, and that in the aforesaid letter, certain things were alleged as coming from Mrs. Forrest, at which she had taken great offence; she also remembered, that during Miss Meredith's residence at Bath, she was forbid to attend on her; but times were changed, she had now the honour to be first woman to a Countess, one, who from the superior gifts of fortune and nature, seemed formed for the adoration of the multitude; and although poor Win had the ill luck to be disliked by every soul in the family but her Lady, on account of her uncouth language and manners which appeared vulgar, and her promptitude to speak whatever she thought, on all occasions, which appeared bold and assuming, yet, the Countess's protection gave her the highest degree of consequence, and Mrs. Forrest's name was carried to her, as she sat lolling at the window, and sipping her coffee.

The aforesaid recollection tempted Winifred to give herself a few airs; but the respect she knew the Countess had for her late governess luckily restrained her; she was however resolved to exhibit her consequence, and at the same time gratify both her vanity and passion (if what Joseph Wilks had inspired her with, might be so called), by learning some particulars of him.

Mrs. Forrest was therefore shewn to *her* apartment – and with the affability always attendant on good sense, and good breeding, was much pleased to see such a desirable change in the circumstances of one, whom she had considered as a domestic of her own; she congratulated her, with such unaffected good nature, that all Winifred's projected *hauteur* was in an instant forgotten.

When Mrs. Forrest enquired of the Countess, Winifred, who really was a thorough good hearted creature, and proud, as well as fond of her lady, launched out into descriptions of her state, and grandeur, ostentatiously displayed all the paraphernalia, then unpacked and concluded by saying (what to her was really a wonder) that she was not the least altered, but better tempered than ever.

Mrs Forrest smiling, said, she was much mistaken, if any change of circumstances would alter so sweet a disposition, her elevation did not surprise *her,* she was sure Lady Castle Howel need only be seen, to be universally admired; for her part, she had always expected Lord Claverton would have been the man, and believed he was sincerely mortified, he had not made his proposals before Lord Castle Howel – the Countess, to be sure, could be no more than happy – but Lord Claverton was such an elegant, polite bred man, and *younger* than Lord Castle Howel.

Winifred interrupted her, to ask, when she had seen Mr. Joseph?

"If you mean Lord Claverton's valet, he brought me a card yesterday."

Winifred coloured up to the ears, pleased to think she should so soon exhibit her state to Joseph, but her joy was of short duration. Mrs. Forrest informed her, Lord Claverton had been very much indisposed, that he had often done her the honour to call at her house, *before* his indisposition, and that his servant had brought her an apology, for his not making his bow, before he left Bath.

"Dear me! dear me! how sorry," Winifred *said* she was for poor Lord Claverton, and how sorry she *really* was, that Joseph had gone *without* her seeing him or at least without *his* seeing *her;* but there was some comfort he was at London, where she also was going, and no doubt, her true lover would soon find her.

The moment Mrs. Forrest was announced, she was admitted, the Earl politely thanked her, for her care of his lady.

Ellen loved, and respected her governess, as every young lady will, who has the good fortune to be educated by accomplished women, whose own faultless example illustrates their precepts; and she received her with open arms. Breakfast was

Ellen, Countess of Castle Howel 149

served in the Countess's apartment, but the Earl at her request joined his aunts and sister.

After exhausting chit chat enquiries, Lady Castle Howel recollected Lord Claverton had been at Bath, and asked if he yet continued there; Mrs. Forrest had too proper a sense of the rule of right to say a syllable more of him, than merely to answer the Countess's questions, which were, simply, when he came, and when he left Bath.

Mrs. Forrest's nice sense of virtue and propriety was blended with an excess of good nature – Lord Claverton, in prosecution of his darling scheme, had returned to Bath. An adept in every art of penetration, he found her weak side, if indeed it might be so called, and contrived to be so *unhappy,* so *inadvertent,* and so off all kind of guard, when he found Ellen was removed, it was impossible for her to avoid the discovery he *intended* she should make, of his being *desperately in love;* and as he had so much honour on his tongue, and she so much in her heart it was also impossible she could doubt, either the sincerity, or honour, of his professions; proud of the confidence of a nobleman of his rank, and pleased to look forward to the elevation of a young creature she loved, and whom by contributing to bring about a match of such consequence, she should serve and oblige – she became familiarized to the event, and spoke, without reserve of Ellen to his Lordship, as he did of his passion to her.

The sudden recall from school, was a matter of mutual surprise and conjecture; every possible cause, except the right, was canvassed, and Joseph directed to write to his true love for information; how *she* was engaged, the reader has seen, and as Mrs Forrest thought his Lordship's health was affected by the unaccountable mystery, that had attended Ellen's removal, she easily persuaded herself, he was an amiable unfortunate lover.

Lord Castle Howel being in comparison of his Lady, and even of Lord Claverton, an old man; the match so suddenly concluded, the inadvertent enquiries from Lady Castle Howel after a lover so superior to her husband, in Mrs. Forrest's opinion, were corroborating that the attachment was, tho' unpropitious, *mutual,* – she took leave of her late pupil with sentiments of compassion, too strong to be confined to her own bosom; these she confided to a female friend, who had a friend, who had two friends, whose friends were dispersed, over the whole polite circles, then at Bath, the natural consequences of which were, that when the Earl and his bride, with the ladies of their party, went to the rooms in the evening – the merest Chit there knew that Lady Castle Howel was a beautiful young girl, *forced* to marry an *old man,* when she was breaking her heart for a *younger one.* It is true, her Ladyship's look and manner, positively contradicted this, as never did peace and content more visibly eradiate a human countenance, – but rumour's hundred tongues established the fact.

Thus in the full bloom of health, with a temper sweet and lively, a disposition to please, and be pleased, attached to her husband, by whom she was adored, fond of gaiety and splendour, of which she was in full possession; the sensible world chose she should be the most wretched creature living, the men swore, "it was pitiful, wond'rous pitiful," she was a charming creature – and Claverton would have her in the end. The women saw nothing in her, but a baby face which would soon be spoiled by the quantity of paint she wore, and all the little world, then at Bath, was so good as to be extremely agitated, about the fate of a young creature, who herself felt, and really was, one of the happiest women in existence; who laughed, danced and chatted away the hours; while Lady Gertrude, and Lady Frances, accompanied by their niece, were visiting beauties of the last century; and retracing men, and things, *now no more.*

Chapter II

The week thus spent at Bath, was in fact, an entree into the greater world, of London, for as every body visited the Castle Howels, and as these *every bodies* had *their* correspondents, to whom they sent their opinion and description, together with a full and particular account of all the reports, true and untrue, in circulation respecting this phenomena in the world of beauty; and as besides, which the world is in possession of so many daily blessings, ycleped[10] newspapers, before she reached the metropolis, Lady Castle Howel was better known to the haut ton, and every Coffee house, than to her most intimate friends.

Meanwhile, Lord Claverton was confined to his house, a prey to ill health, ill humour, and unsuccessful passion. Joseph Wilks was still prime minister; not that Lord Claverton had an atom of regard for Joseph, or Joseph for his Lord; but as the one was not more apt in planning, than the other dexterous in executing, and as habit becomes second nature, there was a kind of compact between master and man, which promised to be more lasting, than such compacts generally are.

Joseph, who was raised from a private in the guards to his present honourable station, tho' very illiterate, had a great share of what is called mother's wit: he was taught his letters at a charity school, which he learnt to put together on the drum head; as he was a great man's great man, before he could

---

[10] I.e., called

write, application supplied the place of instruction, and he was self learnt to scrawl such letters as we have seen in the course of this history; he was a dashing fellow, and in no small degree a newspaper critic, – as the papers went through his hands, before they reached his Lord, he had it in his power to give the first information of every paragraph, that would amuse, or entertain him.

The moment his lordship's bell rung, Joseph appeared with the papers, and almost out of breath read the Bath news.

"It is said a beautiful new made Countess sighs in the arms of her old Lord, for the object of her first attachment, and it is whispered that Lord C—n left Bath, in delicate regard to the feelings of the new married pair."

The spear of Ithuriel, when it detected Satan at the ear of Eve, had not a more instantaneous effect on the father of intrigue, than the paragraph had upon this his true son; and a letter from his friend Mrs. Elderton completed the business.

From the time Ellen was sent to Bath, he marked her for the sweet companion of those hours, his constitution would no longer permit him to devote to intemperance; his whole heart fixed on a design, in which he knew not of a competitor, he thought he had nothing to do but to watch the fine fruit, till an opportunity offered to gather it for his own table. The more secure he had been, the more vexatious his disappointment; but the Bath news renovated his hopes; as to Ellen's loving Lord Castle Howel, that was out of the question, and a thoughtless young woman, married to a man she did *not* love, was a fair field for intrigue; whether partial to him, or not, no matter, – the world was taught, to believe so, the scandalous chronicle had established the fact, and volumes wrote on the subject could not do it away. Self love indeed, was mortified in the consciousness that the reports, as far as concerned him, were false, but that was by no means an argument why they should always continue so. Dr. Macshean, still his medical attendant, and always his tool, retained his influence in Grosvenor-Street and he himself resolved to become a favourite of Lady Margaret's, which he well knew, thro' his friend the doctor, would be a very easy matter, and he instructed Joseph to be more in love than ever with Winifred, or whatever damsel might happen to attend Lady Castle Howel.

Meanwhile the unconscious Countess was in raptures at every thing she saw; the towns, so superior to any thing she had passed thro' in Wales, the elegant accommodations on the road, the respect paid to their retinue, the grand and populous avenues to the metropolis, were all objects of wonder and of pleasure.

Lord Castle Howel's house appeared nothing extraordinary, perhaps, to those who had seen some of the superb edifices, which adorn the court end of the town; but it was spacious, convenient, and nobly furnished. Seddon never credited his taste more, than in the new decorations of the bride's apartments, – her dressing room, library, closet, and even powdering room, were more useful than showy, and yet more tasty than either: she looked delight, and gratitude, at her husband, when he gave her possession of them, and the next day, from habit of employing herself, was found very busy with Winifred, at the hour the knocker was in perpetual motion; but this was an error she was not likely to retain; simplicity of dress, reading, music and work were soon obliged to give place to more fashionable avocations; the house was thronged with visitors of all descriptions, she saw a vast number of pretty women, and agreeable men, who appeared as desirous to cultivate her friendship, as if their very beings had depended on her. When the ladies declared it was impossible to exist without dear Lady Castle Howel, and the men swore life was no life where she *was not,* could she be less than pleased? When women of the first fashion, were so anxious to fill up every moment of *their* time, encroaching even on the hours allowed for meals, and rest, in dressing, public amusements, and gaming, the three grand pursuits of the superior women of the age; how was it possible *she* could be so stupid, as to prefer any of the obsolete amusements, which had filled a long summer's day, and winter's evening, in the mountains of Wales? Had she been fortunate enough to have one *friend,* one adviser, not warped by affection, not partial in indulgence, she might perhaps have selected from the multitude, who crowded her parties, a circle, in whose society she might have escaped the almost inevitable evils, which however well the polite world may please to be with themselves, are monsters of their own growth.

But Ellen had no friends; she had only a tender husband, affectionate relations, a profligate lover, and a numerous acquaintance.

The points of the compass could not differ more than the three ladies, who undertook to chaperone Ellen into life.

Lady Gertrude, and Lady Frances Howel, were toasts forty years before Ellen was in being; they were born within an hour of each other, and tho' in the early part of their lives, when pleased with *themselves,* they were ready to dispense to others the smile that glowed from the heart to the coral lip of beauty; they were never even *then* remarkable for their sisterly attachment; one sentiment only seemed to be mutual, and this one was the subject of their first animosity. Their cousin, a wild handsome young fellow of that age, famous for his infidelities among women, and his courage among men, laid a bet with some of his dissipated companions, that he would make love to his two cousins, one a starched prude, the other a wild coquette, and be successful with both; he won his wager; and what aggravated the injury done two young ladies of character, he was, at the same time, actually married to his mother's dairy-maid.

His mock addresses however were not so guarded, but the twin sisters were jealous of each other; and indeed, nothing but their mutual suspicions could have blinded them to the perfidy of their lover.

The resentment of the then Lord Castle Howel, and his family, were justly levelled against Mr. Howel, but the *laugh* of the country was against the ladies, and so strong they persuaded their father to leave Wales, and live wholly in London, which he did for the remainder of his life; but whether the story travelled with them, whether they were not *quite* so charming as they now described themselves to have been when young, or whether *experience* of the falsehood of *man,* steeled their hearts against their fascination, they were now in the sixty-fifth year of their celibacy; retaining, if not their virgin beauties, all the propensities that had formerly distinguished them; perpetually jarring, contradicting, and reproaching each other, and agreeing in nothing, but their wish to disinherit their cousin, they had spent their long unsocial lives without love, and incapable of friendship.

Lady Gertrude (the prude) took on her to select a set of acquaintance for the young Countess, who might have sat for Hogarth's pictures, in the society of old maids; consisting of widows, whose last hopes were buried with their husbands – wives, whose faces and manners had effectually secured *them* from temptation, but whose tempers had suffered the severest trials, from the folly of their handsome acquaintance; antiquated virgins, a few fretful old men, whose wit was out of fashion, and a few *as* fretful who wished to bring *theirs* in.

"These now, my dear," said she, "are people whose countenance will protect you from the nauseous adulation men of this age pay to weak young women; you will meet none of the bucks, as they are called; none of the idle red and blue coats that annoy people of superior ideas almost every where; no, what men you see there are sensible, rational beings, from whom you may acquire improvement and receive instruction; keep to such characters, and your own will remain unimpeached."

"I dare say," replied Ellen, colouring extremely, "the ladies and gentlemen you mention are very amiable; but I shall never think of having any other protector for my character than my own innocence and my Lord's honour."

"When you have been a certain time initiated into the society I have mentioned, you will think differently, – it is necessary in the great world, not only to *be* innocent, but to *seem* so."

"Be and *seem*! indeed madam, I shall think any time very ill bestowed, that is devoted to the distinction – to me, it is exactly one thing."

"Well, Lady Autumn and her sister, Miss Pendergrass (both of whom I remember very handsome) and *are* very clever, have left their cards, and I will introduce you to their assembly; you will be charmed with the decorum and solidity of their conversation, and I have too good an opinion of your understanding to suppose you will not prefer *them,* to any other acquaintance you can make."

Ellen acquiesced with Lady Gertrude's sentiments, who left her fully satisfied she would follow her advice.

"My sister has engaged you to a mighty stupid party, niece," said Lady Frances, with a youthful affectation of levity, "you will be bored to death; I never could bear the assemblies of that Lady Autumn, tho' I suppose they are not now quite so insufferable, as when poor Autumn was living; what a life did she lead that poor man one evening, merely for kissing my glove."

"Kissing your glove madam!"

"Gallantry child, mere gallantry; then the first hour after we were seated, while she made tea (ladies made their own tea then) I was very young, but I remember it extremely well, there were we hipped to death with her lamentable jealousy, and as to Bab Pendegrass, if you happen to shew your white teeth before her, you are undone (Lady Frances's teeth were in tolerable preservation, which having displayed, she went on) first because her own (when she had any) were, I remember, (and I was quite an urchin) *black* as jet; and secondly, because Sir Solomon Spindle, who has been her dangler, off and on, these forty years, will be sure you mean it to him, and ogle you accordingly."

Lady Frances wore that day, a new clear muslin robe, trimmed with Pink, and monsieur (who was very famous for assisting nature) had so managed the dressing of her hair, that both in warmth and size, it supplied the want of a cap, and she was at this moment contemplating her figure before the glass, which *still,* in opposition to her sister, who was rather corpulent, retained a youthful slim appearance, – "take my advice, and I'll introduce you into the pleasantest set of beings on earth. First, there's Lady Daub, a woman of exquisite feelings, tho' she has been obliged to disguise them a little on account of her Enamel – *there* I remember, I first saw the haughty, gallant, gay Lothario.'

"Lothario, Madam, pray who is that?"

"Why my dear that is Lord Merriot, that was – the dear duke of – that is – a nobleman, who has been in the practice of making love, long before I was born, and has still some new thing to do, and to say, to every fine woman he meets; if I had not made a vow never to marry–"

Ellen could keep her countenance no longer; the Earl had in their airing thro' Hyde Park, been stopped by this dear Duke, who certainly did say a vast number of *new,* surprising things in praise of *her* beauty, but who nevertheless had so provoked her risible faculties, she could not help offending against the laws of politeness, by bursting into a fit of laughter, which offence, to the astonishment of Lady Frances, she *now* repeated.

Now, be it known unto all pert, handsome, giggling young women, the most dangerous thing they can do, and the hardest to be forgiven is to laugh at an old coquette, at a time when she is new dressed, before a glass, and well with herself.

Lady Frances's little grey eyes struck fire, she cast a contemptuous glance at our laughter, and left the room.

Her look, and manner, frightened Ellen out of her mirth, and much disconcerted, she repeated to Lady Margaret the whole conversation.

"My aunts," said Lady Margaret, "have been so long immured, at their Castle in the north, they forget how times and fashions alter, the people they talk of, are like themselves *out of date* – but if you do not accompany them in their visits, it will be a heinous offence, and you will meet many of the first people at Lady Daub's. When once you have been presented, and the ancient Ladies gone, you won't mind company; your old friend Lord Claverton and Dr Macshean (who both dine with us today) when my Lord chooses to stay in his study, will make up our whist table, and attend us to the Opera; we may receive, and pay a few visits, but I wish this racketing life was over, I am weary of it, an hour with one agreeable friend is worth all the public places in town."

The reader will perceive the change *one* friend has made in Lady Margaret.

Her plan was worse than the old ladies, "shut up at whist with Doctor Macshean, Lord Claverton, and Lady Margaret, monsterous!" Nothing was ever so pleasant to Ellen, as the racketing life Lady Margaret had very lately began to hate, and she secretly dissented from the whist proposition; the entire confidence she placed in her Lord, made her long to tell him the conversation of the morning, but it was time to dress for dinner.

This article of dressing was the only thing she disliked in her new arrangements, her dishabille was elegant, and she was always, even at Code Gwyn, clean, why therefore her hair was to be deranged, after it was once put in order, why one elegant dress, was to be changed for another, merely because it was dinner hour, she could not understand and was provoked at such a waste of time, but this error was also one that required a very short time to correct.

The Earl led the Countess into the drawing room, a little while before dinner was announced, and presented the gentlemen both to her and his aunts.

Lord Claverton trembled; Doctor Macshean, who had not seen her since they left her the first time at Bath, could not help breaking out in a rapturous exclamation, when he saw the beautiful Romp of less than sixteen, now changed into a tall graceful woman, whose elegant figure, and fine proportioned limbs, seemed put together in the most perfect symmetry, to set off a face as faultless, as at that instant, was her gentle heart; she had already acquired a taste and manner in dress, which more adorns a beautiful woman than the most costly Jewels, and she derived from her excellent understanding, a confidence in herself that supported her rank. The blush of modesty suffused her cheek at first sight of any stranger, but the world will allow, a young lady entering into high life in London is in a very fair way of getting over all faults of that kind.

Doctor Macshean still adhered to a cautious humility of manners before the Earl, and nothing could be more respectfully attentive to the Countess than Lord Claverton, he also contrived without any appearance of adulation, to make his politeness acceptable to the two spinsters, who both declared he was the best bred man they had seen since they left the north; another instance of Lord Claverton's knowledge of the human heart, since he reconciled two such contradictions in his favour.

Parties were proposed, and engagements made for the opera, plays and masquerades, all which places Ellen longed to be at.

Lady Gertrude appealed to Lord Claverton whether it was proper the bride should be seen about, before she was presented.

Lord Claverton did not exactly know the sentiments of the

rest of the family, and could not answer more positively than, "certainly, except indeed in certain cases."

"Certain cases," said Lady Frances, impatiently, "our cousin the Duchess is not in town, as she is the person of highest rank in the family, it is proper my niece should be presented by her, but sure there is no necessity for us to keep house till she arrives."

Lady Margaret saw no reason to hurry.

The Earl wished Ellen's opinion.

"Oh, don't ask me, for tho' I don't know what is right, I shall certainly give my vote for the opera and plays."

Lady Gertrude frowned, but as a favourite singer was announced for that night; with such champions to support her, Lady Castle Howel ventured to make her party, from which her ladyship did not however choose to be excluded.

Lord Claverton had the honour to hand the bride; the Earl took care of his aunts, and Doctor Macshean had the felicity to press the fair hand of Lady Margaret.

Out came the glasses – neither sex are in this polished age, so vulgar as to see with the naked eye.

The men having examined every feature, with but one opinion of her beauty, formed many of her appearance, and attendants; that Lord Claverton was a happy dog, and that Lord Castle Howel was an old fool, were settled points.

"What an old stupid fellow! to let his wife's lover be on such familiar terms in his family," cried an emaciated young nobleman, whose lady had recently eloped with her footman: "very good," answered Sir Harry Whiffle, "how would you have him avoid it, if the Lady is resolved?"

"In that case to be sure," joined a red-faced Counsellor, "he has no resource but Westminster-hall."

"Oh, damn it!" said General Spindle, "he deserves it for marrying – what can a man expect, who parts with his liberty? I dare say, she might have been had on easier terms."

General Spindle was one of these generous creatures, who always kept one pretty woman or another, in great style, pro bono publico, he was duped, bullied, and laughed at, by half the celebrated courtesans of the age, but what of that, he had not parted with his *liberty!*

The Ladies were divided in their opinion of her beauty, some thought her too tall, others not tall enough; with some she was too much in the em bon point, with others too thin; one thought her handsome, but lamented the wanted animation, others thought she affected intelligence of countenance, but was not at all pretty; they all however agreed, she was very bold, to make her first entree into public with a favoured lover – they were sure she was very imprudent, but would invite her to their parties nevertheless.

Ellen, in the mean while, fancied herself in a land of enchantment, and her unfashionable attention to the music disgraced her still more than her imprudence; the first opera was the most delightful thing in nature, except the second, the third was still more charming; and so, having been presented, under a load of family jewels; the Queen having admired, and the King saluted her – there was no longer an objection to her seeing every place, and every thing; and to do her justice, no young Lady of fashion ever made a more liberal use of the bon ton parole; her morning levees were crowded with fashionable milliners and mantua-makers, all of whom had some exquisite thing, just imported, or invented, which no Lady but herself was to see, to whose civility she was too much obliged not to give an order; every half hour teemed with petitions from distressed families, or verses from indigent poets; every day produced a fresh list of engagements, and every visit an addition to her acquaintance.

Lady Gertrude reminded her, of Lady Autumn's assembly, where she found the company very fine, very solemn, and very stupid, till cards a little inspired them; she cut into a whist party, a very sentimental grave old gentleman chatted to and challenged her to bet, in so civil a manner, she could not refuse; in two hours she had lost one hundred and fifty guineas – and then declined playing, having, as she frankly confessed lost all her money.

The sentimental Gentleman begged she would do him the honour to make him her banker.

Ellen was too ignorant to understand his meaning, he explained, "what sir, and so run in debt," said she, with vivacity, " Oh, no."

The Ladies with great difficulty concealed their contempt, the poor thing was so very silly.

Ellen now looked for Lady Gertrude, who she found at the same table with her friend Lady Autumn, and most unconscionably was she fleeced by her very old acquaintance.

"I have lost all my money, Madam," said Ellen, showing her empty purse, and laughing.

Lady Gertrude sat reddening over her cards, without regarding her.

The other table was immediately full, all parties were as intent on their cards, as if their existence was at stake.

I wonder, thought Ellen, looking round, when the conversazzioni begins.

Just then Lady Gertrude directed her servant to be called, in a voice in which there was neither sentiment or good humour, and she was hastily quitting her dear friend Lady Autumn, without one trait of antient friendship on her countenance.

Ellen joined her, "dear Madam you would not leave *me.*"

"Oh, I forgot, I beg pardon," and she stalked as fast as possible to her carriage, and the instant it moved from the door, began a regular, and succinct account of the games she had played, the cards she had held, and the bets she had made; in all which she had not made a single mistake, or deviated in one instance from the rules laid down by Hoyle; that therefore Lady Autumn and Miss Pendergrast must have cheated.

Ellen was astonished; cheat! Lady Autumn, cheat!

Oh! Lady Gertrude observed, *that* was no such an unprecedented thing, Lady Autumn was always famous for it.

Heavens! thought Ellen, what an acquaintance to preserve one's character.

It was near two when they got home, and the first evening Ellen had spent from the protecting side of her fond Lord; he welcomed her with the sincerest affection, and heard of her loss at play with no more apparent regret than she herself told it, – he immediately replenished her purse, and in the greatest good humour, listened to her account of the manner in which she had passed the evening.

I have before said, Ellen's natural disposition was lively, it was perhaps so to excess. In the enjoyment of every indulgence that can render a gay, dissipated life delightful; the object of admiration wherever she appeared; never addressed at home, but in the soothing voice of affection, or abroad, but in the insinuating one of flattery; *followed, imitated,* and courted by all the gay world; in high health, and in the full glow of conscious beauty; is it to be wondered, that spirit, that natural vivacity, which rendered her life at Code Gwyn one continued scene of sportive amusement, should, *so* situated in London, sometimes *exceed* the exact limits of *discretion?*

She was an excellent *mimic,* the Earl had often been amused, when between themselves, she would imitate his aunts, in their peculiarities and disputes; forgetting now, that although Lady Autumn had, as Lady Gertrude said, "cheated a little,' she was that Lady's most esteemed friend; that Miss Pendergrast was her constant correspondent, and had been in former times her *confidante;* or that the whole of the company who were invited on purpose to meeting Lady Gertrude, were her particular intimates: she sat down, and with great cleverness, as well as good humour, gave so striking a specimen of the *persons, manners* and *conversation,* at Lady Autumn's assembly, that Lady Frances, who had declined going, and Lady Margaret, who had taken that pretence for staying at home, and the Earl, who all knew the people she described, burst into convulsive fits of laughter; even Lady Gertrude relaxed her solemn features into a smile.

"Be merry and wise," says the old proverb, but show me a witty creature under eighteen, who ever was wise when merry; encouraged by the success of her imitations, on she went, and though last, not least, concluded with *Lady Gertrude* herself, whose inward vexation, before she left the card table, and invectives against her friend's chicane, afterwards were indeed *fair* subjects, tho' not herself *wise* ones.

Lady Gertrude arose with indignation, "really Madam," said the enraged maiden, "you have been taken out of your sphere, you should have been an actress."

Lord Castle Howel reddened, but Ellen's good humour was invincible.

"And I should have liked it vastly," replied she, standing up and composing her features; "let me see, what was it my Lord first taught me, 'She never told her love, but let concealment like a worm 'ith bud, feed on her damask cheek;' and then I forget what followed, something about green and yellow melancholy, but the best was at last, 'she smiled at grief,' now that's what I shall always do."[11]

A jaundiced imagination sees its own colour in every thing, Lady Gertrude felt that Ellen's irony was just, and well applied, tho' her countenance wanted not circumference, it had yet a good deal of both green and yellow in it, which all the washes (and they were not a few) she had employed herself and her woman, many years in making, could not remove; and she doubted not but Shakespeare himself was now introduced to insult *her*: without giving the salutations of the night, therefore, she took a taper off a side table, and stalked to her apartment, leaving her sister and niece laughing, both at *her* and her *friends*.

As soon as she was out of sight, the incorrigible Ellen took her taper, and having lighted it, with the same indignant look, finished her imitations by stalking to her dressing room, exactly in Lady Gertrude's manner, the Ladies again burst into fits of laughter, but in separating, Lady Frances observed, "all this was very impertinent."

---

[11] Quoting Shakespeare, *Twelfth Night*.

Chapter III

Lord Castle Howel had amused himself several mornings, with purchasing a number of elegant books, to furnish Ellen's library, and requested she would look at them; her answer was as simple as true, "she would be very glad to do it, but really she had – Not time."

"Not time?"

"No, indeed! I have not" – and a loud rap at the door confirmed in part the assertion; it was a Lady of high rank, come to drop a card, previous to an invitation to her ball, and the instant after the Duchess of ___ called and was admitted; this Lady's visit was, it is true, short, but as the Countess was *at home*, it was followed by a succession of idlers, who occupied the whole of the day, till it was time to dress for dinner – and in the evening, at the request of Lady Frances, she accompanied her to Lady Daub's.

Here were crowded rooms, and a numerous assembly of people of high distinction; Lady Daub herself was a dowager of quality, whose face had been literally *masked* the last twenty years of her life; on that mask, the roses and lilies were in perpetual bloom; she had confined in a corner of her mansion several fine women, whom she had brought into the world, but who, in no other sense, had reason to call her mother; they were *too* full grown, *too* handsome, and *too* amiable to be shown to the world; and she *too* sensible of the injury she did them, to bear their company when alone: – alone! did I say, that was a situation in which Lady Daub never found herself, but when her mask wanted repair.

At the assembly of such a woman, some old fashioned readers may suppose, few of the well informed cultivated beings, who *credit* the list of fashion, would be found; but such is the prevalence of custom, such the rage for dissipation, and such the necessity of *killing time*, that many of the most amiable of that description, were mixed in the transient crowd that entered and retired.

Lady Castle Howel, and Lady Frances were among the *select party* invited to supper; the gay Lothario was also one of the chosen, as was the all accomplished Lord Charles Dash, his son, and Lord Claverton.

Lord Castle Howel's inveterate head ache prevented his being ever in those late parties; there was dancing in one of the lower rooms; a pharo table in another, and the rest filled with card parties.

The Countess cut in, but her ears were attracted by the sound of the music, and she, as usual, lost every thing she staked; Lord Claverton stood behind her chair. "I have lost all my money," said Ellen, "somebody will have the goodness to take my place." Lord Charles Dash begged he might try her luck for her.

"No, pray don't, I always lose."

Lord Charles took her place.

"Oh, Lord Claverton, I am glad to see you, will you join the dancers?"

Lord Claverton, with an air of transport, led her down stairs, and they were dancing with great spirit, when Lord Charles and Lady Frances joined them, with a full purse; "you have been fortunate, Lady Castle Howel." said Lord Charles, "here are your winnings."

Ellen drew back, Lady Frances explained, that Lord Charles

having merely taken her cards, if he had lost, it would have been a debt of honour due from her; she accepted the purse and continued dancing.

The reader may believe, Lord Claverton lost no opportunity of paying his court to his fair partner, – he did indeed play off all the artillery of sighs, looks, short absences and sudden recoveries, &c. &c. but he might as well have been at the pharo table, dancing was an exercise Ellen both excelled and delighted in; and as it was the first amusement of the kind she had been at, since her arrival in town, enjoyed it too much to attend to the soft nothings of a man so perfectly indifferent to her: when the last dance was gone down, there was a short interval before supper; they sauntered to the pharo table, and in ten minutes Ellen won the bank; this was the first moment she felt an inclination to game, it was impossible not to be pleased at winning two thousand guineas, in so short a time; Lord Charles and Lord Claverton congratulated her on her success, – supper was announced before she had time to lose back any of her winnings, and there was no play afterwards.

At four o'clock she found the Earl waiting in her dressing room.

"You have been well entertained, my love," said he, showing his watch.

"Yes, I have been dancing, and am quite tired."

"Dancing! have you, and pray who had the honour to be your partner?"

"The honour was Lord Claverton's, but I believe he was heartily tired of it, for you know he is a poor creature, and I would not let him sit down. Oh! but I have been at cards too; see, my dear lord, how rich I am," taking out the loaded purse, a quantity of guineas fell on the carpet which she ordered

Winifred to pick up, without troubling herself to count the number; her pocket book was next displayed full of notes – this was the first painful sensation the good Earl had felt since his marriage; while she continued losing small sums, without caring about them, he knew the rage of gaming would not hurt her; but such a flow of success would have the double *ill* effect, of rendering her anxious to obtain it in future, and lessening her estimation of the sums she had hitherto reckoned capital; – he was lost in a disagreeable reverie, when Ellen complained of fatigue, and they retired to rest.

"Well," said Lady Frances, when they met at four the next afternoon, for Ellen's head had ached, and she was too much fatigued to rise before, "and how did you like Lady Daub?"

Ellen declared she frightened her.

"Frightened you! she is one of the politest women of the age."

"Oh! I don't mean her manners, it was that shocking unnatural red and white."

Lady Gertrude, who had not been cordially reconciled to the Countess, since Lady Autumn's night, smiled contemptuously, "yes, Lady Daub's red and white has a fortitude *time* has no power over."

"Is she a very grave person, Madam?" said Ellen.

"Far from it" replied Lady Frances, "she is just of my disposition."

"And of your age, too?"

"I am not so old as Lady Daub, she was a woman when I wore white frocks."

"Well! I should not have thought that; but does she never smile?"

"No, I defy her to do that,' said Lady Gertrude.

"Make as free with your *own* friends as you please, sister," interrupted Lady Frances.

"You should give that hint to Lady Castle Howel, sister," answered Lady Gertrude, spitefully.

"I give it to you, Ma'am – but don't you think the Duke delightful, niece? and his son, Lord Charles?

"He plays his cards well, I dare say; he won my money back even in less time than I lost it."

The Earl, on whom the event of the last night had made an unpleasant impression, now joined, "but on the whole, Ellen, how did you like your entertainment?"

"Charming! delightful! there were many very sweet women, and some agreeable men, and I made several very pleasant new acquaintances."

Lord Claverton was announced, he received the thanks of the man, whose peace he was meditating to ruin, for his politeness to the Ladies of his family, and came to offer them tickets for the professional concert.

"A concert! Oh! pray let us go," cried Ellen, "I have not been at a concert yet." The Earl tenderly anxious for her health, reminded her of her head-ache, and the fatigues of the last night.

One *was gone* and she had quite recovered the other.

"You complained of want of time, my Ellen, had you not better devote this one evening to your library?"

"Oh, reading, she was sure would give her the head-ache." Lord Castle Howel sighed at the remembrance of the happy days, past in the library at Castle Howel, but could not prevail on himself to oppose, any further, the wish of a wife he doated on, and therefore agreed to accompany her.

When once the mind of a young woman has taken a bias

for pleasure, unrestrained by a fear of consequence or a prudential regard to expense, it is in vain to expect she will be either sated, or even gratified; amusing, good humoured, gay, witty, and pleasant, Lady Castle Howel's company would have been courted without the personal charms, which were sure to attract a crowd of fashionable men, wherever she appeared; a round of engagements employed every hour of her time, and a constant routine of amusements, every avocation of her mind.

Joseph's attendance on Winifred was continued, but with little advantage to his employer, for the Countess had no *time* to talk to *her*, or to hear, as formerly, the *wonderfuls* she had to say – but his Lordship's close attendance was talked of every where, and by every body but those most concerned.

At length the happy intimation was given, that the Countess was pregnant, the Earl's fondness could not increase, but his anxiety for the welfare of Ellen did, he remonstrated anxiously, and tenderly, against fatigue and late hours, and was joined by the two old spinsters, who entreated her to retire into the Country. But the country had *now* no charms for Ellen.

She had a list of engagements that would last till the hour of her accouchement, besides her own nights, which were always brilliantly attended; but she constantly promised to return home at an early hour, and *as constantly* broke her word; she had made a set of intimates of women, who were at the head of every thing, the business of whose lives seemed to be, that of getting rid of their husband's estates, but they were women of *character*!

She played high, and her losses were so frequent, that the Earl, with great delicacy, informed her he was unable to answer such frequent demands.

Thunder struck and amazed, she turned pale, she had judged of the riches of her husband by his liberality, and supposed one as inexhaustible as the other.

Lady Gertrude entered, she found her near fainting, and terrified least her disorder should bring on an event that would frustrate all their hopes, drew from her the cause, and immediately supplied her with money to discharge every debt of honour, with advice to her not to play again.

Ellen had selected one among her acquaintance, to whom she was in the habit of speaking of all her affairs, *secrets* she had *none*; the honourable Mrs. Morley, Lord Durant's eldest daughter, married to a rich banker, with whom she was, on account of her expenses, at perpetual variance; Ellen told that Lady what had happened, ingenuously regretted her extravagance, and resolved to leave off play. Mrs. Morley burst into a fit of laughter. Ellen could not divine the cause; her friend assured her, the Earl was *humming* her; – he does not like you should spend so much money, and he knows the simple goodness of your heart so well, he takes this method of interesting your feelings in his own cause; he *must* be rich, *he* or his musty old sister, never lived at any expense; but come, we shall be late, Mrs. Hewart's doors are open early; I teased Morley out of five hundred to day, and am resolved to be a bold adventurer tonight, "allons."

Mrs. Morley *was* bold and successful, Ellen caught the infection, instead of paying her debts of honour, she lost all the money Lady Gertrude had given her; Lord Charles Dash, one of her creditors, walked up, he condoled with her on her repeated ill fortune; but "heaven is just," continued he, "those charms alone are more than should fall to the lot of one happy mortal," and he seized her hand, from which she had just drawn her glove, and with a freedom he had never before attempted, imprinted on it a kiss.

Overwhelmed with shame, regret and mortification, she wanted, for the moment, power to assert her own dignity.

Encouraged by her passiveness, and invited by the embarrassment he knew she was in (for Mrs. Morley had, in mere kindness, told him how the Earl had treated her friend) he fixed his eyes on hers, and drawing his chair near her, whispered an inundation of nonsense, every period ending in the word *love*.

Poor Ellen felt, in that instant, every sensation of anguish the human mind could feel in such a situation; pride, shame and virtue struggled in her bosom, her cheek glowed, but when she looked on the face of the unfeeling insulter, and recollected she was in his debt, without means to enfranchise her honour, *shame* was predominant.

Lord Claverton, *constant* to the settled point of all his desires, was an anxious and interested observer of this scene; he well knew Lord Castle Howel's fortune would not support his wife's extravagance; he saw with pleasure she was sinking deeper and deeper into the vortex of dissipation; on her propensity to play rested *his* chief *hope*, – he wished to see her embarrassed, and in debt, but not to Lord Charles Dash – the designs of his Lordship were too palpable to be misunderstood, and the eye of jealousy too keen not to see through every disguise, – he could not bear any other man should take a liberty he dared not to think of; he saw Lord Charles's presumptuous hope in his eyes but how to rescue her, in that moment, from a situation so desperate?

It happened that Ellen at that instant looked up, her brow, no longer the throne of *Momus*, was contracted and overcast;

a tear trembled on her eyelid, and her cheek lost its lovely bloom, – Lord Claverton could not bear this, he advanced to her, and presented his pocket book – "Lord Castle Howel, Madam, requested me to deliver you this, and expects you at home as soon as possible."

Ellen glanced her eye at the book, she saw it was not her husband's, and her first impulse was to return it to Lord Claverton, – in the vague, indeterminate manner in which she held the book, Lord Charles had also an opportunity of seeing Lord Viscount Claverton's name; – rage filled his lordly bosom; Ellen met his eyes, they were so hateful, and his touch (for he had again taken her hand) so petrifying, that she received the book, and took notes out to the amount of his debt, and turned from him without speaking. Mrs. Morley, exulting in her own success, declined going home, – the Countess, who was too much agitated however to stay for her, ordered her servants, and on the first flight of stairs met Lord Claverton, "Oh my Lord" said she, half sobbing, and involuntarily giving her hand, "from what a situation did you relieve me!" He respectfully bowed, restraining every desire to imprint his lips, where so late he had seen Lord Charles's.

Ellen happened to look behind her and saw Lord Charles leaning over the banister, she quickened her step, and handed by Lord Claverton got into her carriage, "I shall see you soon, my Lord," – he bowed – Lord Charles brushed by, and the vis a vis drove off.

Lord Castle Howel was subject to inveterate head aches, which obliged him, as soon as he was seized with them, to lay down, during these paroxysms, he could not bear the least noise, – he happened, unfortunately for our heroine, to be in one of these fits at her return, – she resolved, during her ride home, to confess her fault, tell him of Lord Claverton's kindness, and vow never more to touch a card; but after sleeping on the matter, she found *confession* of aggravated faults *not quite so* pleasant. Lord Castle Howel was not recovered, and the repetition of a story so reprehensible might bring on a relapse; the old ladies complimented her on her early return home the night before, and she could not resolve to tell them how little merit she had in that matter.

Lord Claverton did not appear next day, it was one of her nights, neither he nor Lord Charles attended, they had both cards, and were used to be among the first, – she, however, declined play, to the infinite pleasure of her doating husband; never were the ladies more pleased with her, and never was she more deserving their favour, – the event of the last evening left an impression on her mind, which the more she indulged, the more she was shocked.

A thousand men had sworn she was divine; had told her of the lustre of her eyes, the beautiful transparency of her complexion, her fine turned arm and Medicien form, her grace, her wit, had been the theme of praise from the million, but there was a decorum observed in the flattery, the harsh strokes were softened off; the innocence of her look, and propriety of her manners, awed libertinism; and in the midst of gaiety, no word, no action, escaped, to inspire hope in the heart of depravity, from one, whose life and conversation had been under the influence of pure minds, and faultless examples: if she acted without foresight, it was because she wanted experience, to point out dangers *she* did not know existed; if she talked without thought, it was because she was used to look inward, where she found no one sentiment condemned by conscience, or restrained by delicacy; but now she had the "debtors pillow," his debasement, his anxiety, and her purity, recoiled, from a recollection of the voice and manner of the professed debauchee, who had insulted her with sentiments, as humiliating as hateful. Many were the times and opportunities, when Lord Charles might have availed himself of being alone with her, to give the conversation the same indecent turn, had he not been restrained by respect; that *respect* she had deprived herself of; and the consequence of making her only proper protector acquainted with his presumption, might be fatal.

So far from loving play, cards were her aversion, before an inconsiderate compliance with fashion tempted her to game; could they be less so now, when the consequence was so injurious to her peace and honour?

Mrs. Morley's insinuation that the Earl had been guilty of duplicity, in his assigned reason for not supplying her with money, had not gained the smallest degree of credit, even when it seduced her into so fatal an error; and now, seated by her husband, whose eyes fondly fixed on her spoke tenderness unutterable, the calumny pierced her heart; and she endeavoured to reconcile her feelings to her conscience, by renewing those attentions he so well deserved, but which dissipation had deprived him of.

Lady Gertrude hinted, she was expected to be more with her guests; she complained of fatigue, and begged her ladyship would apologize, – the company were as usual select for supper; Lady Castle Howel knew nothing of expense, *that* was the department of her complaisant sister-in-law, she was only solicitous to have her table look as well, or better, than other persons of her rank; it was particularly magnificent this night, but besides Lord Charles Dash, and Lord Claverton, Lady

Ellen, Countess of Castle Howel

Margaret found another *absentee*, Dr. Macshean had not attended, nor any more than the other gentleman, sent a card; the company stayed late, but Lady Castle Howel's indisposition was an apology for her early retiring.

Ah! how unconscious was she of the sorrows that awaited her; how often did she afterwards regret, that an eternal sleep had not for ever closed her eyes; doomed to weep for the mere inadvertencies of heedless youth, as for the blackest crimes.

Lord Charles Dash was, in respect to modern dissipation, an improved picture of his illustrious father; the most noble, and puissant Duke of Dash, Marquis Squandervelt, Viscount Sterling, Baron Dunder, knight companion of the most noble order of the garter, of his majesty's most wise and honourable privy council, and one of the first, and most ancient ornaments of the British peerage. Lord Charles Dash, second son to the above mentioned noble personage, was six foot high, colonel of a regiment of horse, and a member of parliament; he swore fluently, gamed immoderately, made love indiscriminately, won more money, fought more duels, ruined more women, and was more the *thing*, than any Lord of his standing in the kingdom: it is needless to say he was an immense favourite of the ladies.

The noble Duke his father, it is but justice to allow, did all in the power of example, to render his sons as famous as himself, – he had three leading traits in *his* character, – he borrowed every man's money, seduced every man's wife, and broke every man's confidence, on whose weakness or credulity he could practice; he shortened the days of two amiable wives, women of virtue, character and fortune, and he was now kept in the most servile subjection by a low bred woman, who had neither.

Had Lord Charles's understanding been dignified by more noble pursuits, it would have been respectable, he had read much, made the grand tour; conversed with an elegant fluency, not only in his mother tongue, but in the languages of most of the European courts, and to finish his portrait was immensely rich.

In an age, when Sir Robert Walpole's axiom, that every man had his price, may be almost transferred to the other sex, Lord Charles Dash's success will not be doubted; but excess of dissipation had so far blunted the keen feelings which had carried him headlong in pursuit of all that was fair and new, –it was not *mere* beauty, no; nor modesty, that could *now* touch a heart, surfeited with sweets; it must be something extraordinary, out of the common run: one whole month, he had followed a child under fourteen, whom at last having purchased of her venal parents, at a very high price, he returned to them, and the town, after three days possession: he had even felt a momentary desire for the English Ninon after she had passed her grand climacteric, – the lady, who well knew how to make the most of his folly, accepted a handsome gratification for receiving him, and a still handsomer one for dismissing him.

He was invited by Lady Daub, on the first night of our heroine's appearance at her assembly, to see a rustic, whom the Earl of Castle Howel had married, for the avowed purpose of propagating the species, a mere girl, ignorant, and inexperienced, but extremely beautiful.

He found her to surpass all he had expected in the last description, but, tho' young, and new to the circle of fashion, graceful, easy and sensible; he was introduced by the Earl himself, at an accidental meeting in Hyde Park, but did not then see enough of her to be sure Lady Daub's picture was not overcharged, – he was however a lost man, from the instant he became sufficiently acquainted, to be treated without reserve, and taking it on the credit of usage le monde, doubted not, but a young girl, who for riches would marry an old man, might, on certain conditions, be induced to intrigue with a young one, – this settled maxim left him at liberty to sigh, and look, and look and sigh, – to plan, – to reconnoitre – and, as occasion offered to act: with an air of the utmost indifference he won her money, and with an insinuating politeness offered revenge; still he was fortunate; they doubled stakes, fate was still obdurate; he pressed her to go on – she had already exceeded the limits of her purse – she ventured and was still a loser; – overwhelmed with shame and vexation, she apologized for not paying him – he entreated she would not mention a circumstance that rendered him happy.

An opening was made at the loo table, – he asked her to change her luck – fortune could not always persecute so lovely a votary! – he entreated he might be her banker, and putting his purse into her hand, led her to the loo table.

The party received her with every expression of politeness, and the secret joy a certainty of winning inspires – she hardly knew what she was doing, or going to do, she however reckoned what money was in the purse, and (with a heart aching with a sensation, which could be neither called regret, or self reproach, and yet an indefinable mixture of both), sat down, her honourable friend standing at her chair back. For some time she won, and inwardly exulted, she could at least pay off part of her debt of honour – she arose and ordered her servants; on looking round the table so many crestfallen visages met her eye; so many voices entreating her stay; her servants not being ready, and a something in her bosom which pointed her going with a large sum, from a table where she had sat so short a time, as selfish, she reseated herself, and lost every shilling, both of what she had won, and what Lord Charles had lent her; become desperate by this sudden turn, she played on credit, till the indolence of her adversaries towards *her*, and their eagerness to *each other*, showed her of how little consequence she was, in her present stripped, and bankrupt situation, and her motion to go was no longer opposed.

Hardly able to support herself she was led to her carriage by Lord Claverton. It was to pay the debts incurred at the loo table, Lady Gertrude had supplied her; for shame of the amount of the sum she owed Lord Charles, confidence in his politeness, hopes that the Earl's liberality would soon enable her to pay him, or perhaps the more rational design, of taking some fond moment to confess to him, and him alone, her extravagant folly, prevented her mentioning the whole amount of her debt. With such a scheme in his head, as the reduction of the young Countess, brought nearer perfection than he could have hoped in so short a time; how could so noble a spirit be otherwise than enraged, when another noble spirit insinuated itself between him, and his prey? He heard of Lady Castle Howel's penchant for Lord Claverton, but as from his Lordship's extreme caution he appeared to be rather an observer, than an admirer, concluded the report was either untrue, or which was just the same, the intrigue over – when therefore with so little ceremony, Lord Claverton put it in her power to pay her debt of honour to him; which to say the truth, had been done in so delicate a way, that the eye of candour might have imputed it to honourable friendship; he, who judged of other men by himself, and had long been acquainted with Lord Claverton's disposition and character, had no doubt but his Lordship's designs were similar to his own; too proud for contention, too peevish for contradiction, and too much in love to act with reason or consistence, he set himself down for an injured man, and Lord Claverton for the person who had injured him.

The Viscount's sentiments were equally vindictive; both their noble bosoms burned with rage, and panted for revenge; Lord Charles sent Lord Claverton a challenge, which, tho' fighting was a trade he had resigned, he accepted, and made every preparation for the glorious on-set, neither of these great minded noblemen once recollecting, there was a husband in the world, to whom they were offering injuries human nature could not bear, or honour forgive.

Chapter IV

The meeting took place in Hyde Park, at eight on the evening their absence so much surprised the Ladies in Grosvenor Street; Lord Claverton was dangerously wounded, and Lord Charles set off for the Continent, till the event should be known.

Most unfortunately for our heroine, Lord Charles had an humble friend, who flattered both his vices, and his follies; from this man none of his great designs, or achievements were concealed; he had progressively been the confidant of his admiration; his hope, his expectations, and finally of his jealousy, which with additions, suggestions and inferences, Captain Durell (not being enjoined to secrecy, or bound to veracity) took special care should be fully comprehended at every breakfast table in the fashionable circle; but had not the affair been thus en train, it would have been impossible to conceal it from the family, whose honour, and whose peace, was thus wantonly exposed to the idle and malevolent gossip of the town; for Lord Claverton, constant to his medical friend, had entrusted him with the duel without hinting at the cause, and directed his attendance in the Park.

Dr. Macshean was not wanting in medical skill, but perceiving from the situation of the wound, and the weak constitution of his patron, that it would be attended with danger, immediately sent for two surgeons, and a physician of the first eminence to his assistance.

Neither were *these* gentlemen enjoined to secrecy, so that the duel, with what particulars Captain Durell chose to add, was not only in private circles, but in every Coffee-house in town.

The two letters we subjoin were carried to the bedside of Lady Frances and Lady Gertrude Howel, while Dr. Macshean and Lady Margaret were shut up in her ladyship's dressing room, and the Earl was reading in his closet.

For Lady Gertrude Howel.
Lady Autumn and Miss Pendegrass most sincerely condole with Lady Gertrude Howel, on the unfortunate denouement in her family; Lady Autumn expressed her ideas as delicately as she could to her friend Lady Gertrude, on the unequal alliance, certainly Lord Castle Howel might have found a bride under the prudent direction of Lady Gertrude, more approximating to the opinion of his friends, as well as more suitable to himself; but what can be said? Miss Pendegrass supposes a divorce must ensue, she is shocked at the depravity of the age, two illicit connexions at once is a refinement on vice, decreed for the beautiful Countess of Castle Howel. Lady Autumn hopes the report of the Earl's fortune being deranged by his wife's extravagance is not true.

For Lady Frances Howel.
Dear Fanny
I am dying with the tooth-ache: (Lady Daub's teeth were *all* of Parkinson's manufacturing) or should have flown to you; your sufferings, my dear creature, must be intense, and I feel them very sincerely, but the thing itself is no more than I foretold; if men will make wives of girls, who should be dressing their dolls, they should expect the consequences, but that sly devil, Lord Charles! I declare, I am seriously angry with him,

to take advantage of such a poor simple young thing; as to Claverton 'tis an old affair I find, Morley was in all her secrets, adieu come to me as soon as possible, that I may tell you every thing I've heard.

Yours,
Hermoine Daub

The ladies rubbed their eyes, and read the notes over and over without understanding a syllable. Lady Frances being the most alert of the two was soon in her sister's room.

"I have the oddest letter from Lady Daub," said she.

"Read this note from Lady Autumn," answered Lady Gertrude.

Their astonishment increased, they hurried down stairs, Lady Margaret and Dr. Macshean joined them; – the Doctor's information of the duel was circumstantial, but from his own knowledge he could speak no further; each of the spinsters ordered her chair.

At Lady Autumn's, Lady Gertrude heard that her niece had intrigued with Lord Claverton, both before, and since she was married, that she had forsaken him for a lover, who had it more in his power to support her extravagance – that however Lord Claverton having furnished her with money to pay some play debts, it had betrayed the connexion to Lord Charles Dash, who challenged Claverton and killed him.

Lady Gertrude's astonishment is not to be expressed, and prone as she was to take the worst part of every story that reached her, a constant observation of the conduct of Lady Castle Howel, from the instant of finding her at her grandmother's feet till that moment, had given her so different an impression of her heart, notwithstanding her occasional levity, that she could not help treating what her good friends, Lady Autumn and Miss Pendegrass were saying with every mark of incredulity.

The Ladies were resolved to convince her of her family misfortune; they were perhaps apprehensive, she would not only remain under her present security herself but communicate it to the rest of the family, for whose honour, they protested, they were too much concerned to suffer it to be injured, by a wicked young woman. Captain Durell was therefore sent for, and he, on authority of Lord Charles's confidence, declared, that he knew he had supplied Lady Castle Howel with several different sums of money, to a large amount; that Lord Charles was a man of the world, and attached, as he certainly was, to the fair sex, yet it was not to be supposed he would part so liberally with money, for which he was to receive no consideration; the Captain would be grieved to advance any thing to a lady's prejudice on mere conjecture; but he thought he might venture to assert, Lord Charles knew in general, what he was about; with respect to Lord Claverton, that matter was beyond a doubt, and Lord Charles, when he sent the challenge, declared to *him* that Claverton intrigued with Lady Castle Howel who had jilted him.

Lady Gertrude was really affected; "If this be true," cried she, sighing at the probable disappointment of all her hopes.

True! Miss Pendegrass declared it was past all doubt, and that she had always observed a certain cast of countenance in Lady Castle Howel, that disgusted *her*, and believed, she had spread her snares for more than Lord Charles and Lord Claverton – Sir Solomon Spindle—

Lady Gertrude interrupted her with impatience; "what day

did this unfortunate affair happen?" – "The duel, Captain Durell informed her, was yesterday, but the transaction which occasioned it was the day before, at Mrs. Stewart's. Lord Charles having liberally furnished Lady Castle Howel with money to pay some play debts, accidentally saw Lord Claverton give her his pocket book for the same purpose.

"Good God!" exclaimed Lady Gertrude, "some mistake, some inexplicable mystery is in all this, for I myself gave her money to pay play debts the same day."

Lady Autumn and Miss Pendegrass laughed out at this, and congratulated their friend on being added to the number of dupes made by the little Welch novice.

Lady Gertrude took rather an abrupt leave, and ordered her chair to Lord Claverton's, where she found the street covered with straw, the hall door on jar, and the porter in waiting, who put her name on the slate, but could only say, his Lord was ill, without a syllable that led to the information she was in pursuit of.

Lady Frances, on her part, found her friend's dressing room crowded, the company highly diverted with every thing but Lord Claverton's danger, which as it involved Lord Charles in some difficulties, was really tremendous – *here*, it was, tho' entirely believed, treated as a thing of course, and from seeing Lady Frances abroad, half the company concluded, the family would think of it in the same way; Lady Daub however, seeing her Fanny look very grave, took her into her closet, and eagerly repeated *her story*. "Lord Charles, who, dear creature, was but too generous, had been very lavish of presents to Lady Castle Howel, and among other things of great value, gave her a pocket book, in which were bank notes to a very considerable amount, that happening to see Lord Claverton take out a pocket book at Mrs. Stewart's, he fancied it like, and indeed it proved to be the one he had given Lady Castle Howel; "now you know Fanny," added her ladyship, in the prettiest lisp imaginable, "that was too bad – Lord Charles challenged and killed Lord Claverton. I am sorry the girl did not know better, they say, my dear, she is with child, can you guess at the father?"

Poor Lady Frances could not speak for some minutes, but as hers was the sort of mind that, a little conscious of its own faults, was, if not more lenient, more credulous, to those of others, she implicitly believed the whole story, and far from feeling any delicate embarrassment on the occasion, resolved to be, if possible, the person who should first carry this pleasant news to my Lord.

She was however mistaken, for tho' she reached Grosvenor-Street long before her sister – the business was done.

Mrs. Morley, who could not, at this juncture, for the world, visit the Countess, was however not under the same difficulty with Lady Margaret, having called, in her way from Lady Daub's, at every door where she could get admittance at that early hour, and having, to her infinite gratification, found the matter was past doubt, and Lady Castle Howel's sun set, she ordered her footman to rap with great caution at the Earl's door, and enquire for Lady Margaret Howel.

Mrs. Morley's name was announced, Lady Margaret was for being denied, but the Dr. who could (if he would have spoken out) have cleared the matter as far as related to Lord Claverton, had yet his doubts about Lord Charles; the rage in which his patron prepared for the duel, convinced him *he* at least *thought* he had cause for jealousy, he was therefore curious to hear what Lady Castle Howel's most intimate friend would say on the subject, and at his instance she was admitted.

Mrs. Morley was too pretty to be ever out of humour with her own features, yet on such an occasion it was proper to *seem* sad, she entered with a demure step, and down cast look, and being seated, sighed and drew out her handkerchief.

"Lady Castle Howel is not up, Madam," said Lady Margaret – "but,—"

"Oh! my dear Lady Margaret, don't name her, poor unhappy woman, 'tis all over you know, one can't ever think of visiting her; but how are you? and how is the good Earl?"

The good Earl was at the door, he was crossing to his Lady's dressing room, but on hearing her friend's voice, supposed she was already down; at his sudden entrance Lady Margaret turned pale, and Mrs. Morley reddened; his ideas were confused, something he thought had been said about Lady Castle Howel, he could not understand, and the looks, both of Mrs. Morley, and his sister, were alarming.

"What is the matter, Madam?" said he, hastily, "you were speaking of my Ellen!"

"Ah! my Lord, your tenderness, your well known indulgence," answered Mrs. Morley, in a whining tone, "for that ungrateful –"

Lord Castle Howel was not disposed to be trifled with; "who? what did she mean?" asked he in a stern terrific voice.

Mrs. Morley was awed – she hesitated.

Lord Castle Howel was in agonies.

Dr. Macshean then calmly said, he feared Lord Claverton was dying.

"What is that to me? or Lady Castle Howel?"

"Lord Charles Dash challenged him."

"Why am I tortured about that? Where is my Ellen? Where?" his looks betrayed the perturbation of his mind, and Lady Margaret endeavoured to sooth him, by saying, the Countess was yet in bed.

Winifred was called; who said she was in a sweet sleep, "cot pless her."

Mrs. Morley was now more herself, she shrugged her shoulders, cast up her eyes, and sighed as if in detestation of one party, and compassion for the other.

"For so fine a face," said the Earl, peevishly, "I never saw one so unhappy in expression."

Lady Frances at this instant entered, and with a vast deal of dignity, took her nephew's hand, was glad to see him bear it so well, and asked if he had got to the truth of the story.

That there was a story to be told, in which he was concerned, was evident, altho' it was not designed he should understand it, he therefore only replied, he would thank Lady Frances to tell it the way *she* had heard it, which she very obligingly did, and to her honour be it spoken (for such a tale) with very few additions of her own.

The Earl was thunderstruck, he trembled with indignation, and every throbbing pulse bore testimony to his feelings, but let my reader not believe the horrid story, thus unconnected, and unsupported, could find credit in his manly breast – Ellen intrigue! The innocent, the chaste, the modest Ellen! for so she had always appeared to him, she a mercenary intriguer! she whose little foibles (the effect as he believed of the pernicious examples of a dissipated age) he had even imprudently indulged! and who, when she signified her want of a greater sum than it was convenient for him to advance, was so cheerfully supplied by his aunt, – she accept money, or presents from a professed debauchee, impossible! he declared his life and fortune should be devoted to the searching out, and punishing the base inventor of so daring a calumny – He demanded Lady Frances's Author.

A whole room full of morning visitors at Lady Daub's—

"And yours, Madam?" to Mrs. Morley.

She had heard from so many, it was impossible to recollect: now that was a little fib; but as Mrs. Cowley says, fine ladies don't mind fibbing; she knew very well, who had told her; Captain Durell was indeed a married man, but as Mr. Morley was a friendly creature, who kept a good house, and had often a set of jolly fellows about him, and as moreover, Mrs. Morley had a passion for admiration, he found it convenient to be violently in love, without the mortification of disobliging the Lady.

To her then, as in duty bound, he flew with the news, as soon as Lord Charles set off, by which means, Mrs. Morley had the happiness to be one of the first circulators of the story *herself*, and was actually the person who carried it to Lady Daub's.

The Earl, however, swore he would not rest, till his wife's fame, and his own honour was avenged – he called for his hat and was going out, tho' he had not exactly determined where.

At the foot of the stairs he met Lady Gertrude, just getting out of her chair, so apparently disordered, she was obliged to rest on her servant; and occupied as the Earl was, by his own feelings, he could not help offering his arm – slow and silent, they ascended; every tongue in Lady Margaret's dressing room, being set going the instant the Earl left it, were stopped at his unexpected return.

"Oh!" cried Lady Frances, "here is my sister, we shall now know what she has heard."

"She heard!" answered the Earl, "is the demon of detraction let loose in the world! do you suppose she has heard!"

Lady Gertrude, with a deep sigh, and great gravity of countenance, replied, she had heard *too much*, and then enquired of Dr. Macshean after his patient.

The Doctor shook his head, and Mrs. Morley applied to her salts in the prettiest manner imaginable.

The "I have heard *too much*," the sigh, the shake of Lady Gertrude's head, almost annihilated the Earl; without understanding why, he sat down, as in expectation of something dreadful, with his eyes fixed on his aunt.

This was entirely a family concern; perhaps as no person knew the secret terms Dr. Macshean was in by the favour of Lady Margaret, *he* might be excusable for staying, but what detained Mrs. Morley?

When domestic misfortunes begin to be discussed before a third person, they become, from that instant, at once *judge* and *accuser*; they gratify their curiosity, at the expense of your feelings, and their malevolence, at the expense of your passions; you cannot withdraw a confidence you have unthinkingly reposed, without making them your bitter enemies; they remember the extravagance you utter in your agony, but forget the incitement, – their pity is a triumph over your misfortunes – and their consolation an insult to your distress. Mrs. Morley fancied she had rendered herself of importance sufficient to excuse *her* stay, and she was dying with curiosity, to hear how the family consultation would terminate.

Lady Gertrude however was more guarded than her sister had been, she made Mrs. Morley a formal courtsey, and withdrew, followed by the Earl. Mrs Morley now chose to be very attentive to Lady Frances, a servant delivered her sister's compliments, and requested her company; still there was one lady left, the one she came to condole, but scarce had she got a word from Lady Margaret, before a second messenger demanded her presence; there was nobody now but Dr. Macshean, who considering her as the cause why he was not admitted to the family confidence, was ill disposed to *entertain* or be *entertained* by her; he must visit his patient he said.

"Oh! do let me set you down, my dear Doctor."

He gravely told her, his own carriage waited; she had nothing now for it but to order her servant, and the Doctor handed her to her coach.

Lady Gertrude had by this time entered on her history, which agreed in the main points with Lady Frances; the difference was only in the pocket book, which, at Lady Autumn's was Lord Claverton's; and accidentally seen by Lord Charles, whereas, at Lady Daub's it was Lord Charles's, and given by Lady Castle Howel to Lord Claverton; but all agreed, there had been a duel about the Countess, between two lovers, one of whom at least it was presumed must be a favourite.

"Good God," said the Earl, impatiently, "why do I suffer my heart, to be wrung in this manner, when an angel, on whose brow sits truth, and ingenuity, can and will develop every transaction in which she is concerned, to the confusion of her calumniators, and to the satisfaction of her friends."

He started up, and was eagerly proceeding to Ellen's

room; Lady Gertrude's prudence again stopped him, she had *resolved* all the likely consequences of this disagreeable business in her own mind; of worldly wisdom Lady Gertrude had more than her share; of worldly affections none – the disappointment of her heart had shut up every avenue to the softer attachments; resentment, jealousy, slighted love, and wounded pride, had all settled into a calm and most inveterate hatred; she had more pride, more sense, and more resolution, than her sister, in consequence of which, tho' in trifles they were for ever quarrelling, in *essentials*, *she* always carried her point, not by the coincidence (for she would dispute inch by inch) but by the weakness of Lady Frances.

To the hatred then she felt for her perfidious lover, life and all its enjoyments had been sacrificed; and as her sister had equal cause of displeasure, *hers* had been kept alive by the tenets pride enforced, both in the precept and example of Lady Gertrude; the hope of cutting off the man she hated, the family she abhorred, from the inheritance she knew they languished after, was the first consideration on earth to her. Allowing Ellen to be all she had heard, still she was pregnant, the main end of the Earl's marriage, as far as it concerned *her* was answered; what then might not be feared from the effect this discovery, whether true or false, might have on a form so young and delicate? All their present hopes might be in a moment blasted, and should the worst be proved, no future ones could arise.

To these reflections and conclusions Ellen owed the present protection of Lady Gertrude, who became her warm advocate, and pledged *her own* honour, for that of the Countess. The mind of man is easily persuaded to credit what it wishes, the Earl fondly acceded to all she advanced, and in spite of the recollections of Lady Frances, and the dead cold silence of Lady Margaret, triumphed in the innocence of his Countess.

Lady Margaret, not quite so sanguine about the heirship of the title and estate as her aunts, recalled innumerable instances of Lord Claverton's admiration of Ellen, and prior to her brother's widowhood foretold he would make her a Viscountess, – she had even hinted this to her brother, who far from being displeased, had once congratulated himself on having contributed to the endowments of a young woman, he was sure was born to move in an elevated sphere; she had often mentioned this to the Doctor, as well as her observations on his continued attention; but however ardent the Doctor's admiration of Lady Margaret, he was not subject to *weakness* many a *wiser* man *suffers* for; he was master of all the Ladies' secrets, but his own were uncomeatable. Nevertheless, on the credit of her own conjectures, Lady Margaret was not so sure of Ellen's innocence, as her brother and aunts appeared to be.

As to Lady Frances, the spirit of contradiction was raised in her, and a bench of bishops could not have inspired her with an atom of charity; she withdrew from the consultation to her own apartment, and made her woman confidante of the story; this person, who was a true waiting maid, could add *another* very *suspicious* circumstance which was, that Joseph, Lord Claverton's man, visited the Countess's favourite woman every day of his life; Lady Frances returned in haste with this intelligence, but all further proofs had by this time become unnecessary.

Lady Gertrude had exerted all her powers of rhetoric to

carry her favourite point, which was to conceal every circumstance of the affair from the Countess, till after her accouchement; to accomplish this, she requested the Earl would feign urgent business in the north, that they might immediately set out for her seat, where it would be impossible any of the slanders invented against her could reach.

Lord Castle Howel objected to the last part of the plan, tho' he very readily acceded to the other, on the ground that a sudden removal from the capital, without an explanation due to his wife's injured honour, would confirm, instead of contradict the slander; but Lady Gertrude was too deeply interested not to persist; how, she demanded could Lady Castle Howel's repose be undisturbed, while such a mortifying matter was in agitation? and Winifred passing the door at that instant, to answer her Lady's bell, they agreed to go to her dressing room, and inform her of the intended, and immediate journey. She had not yet left her bed chamber and the diamond ornaments she wore the preceding night lay on the toilet in her dressing room; Lady Gertrude, from a natural impulse of female restlessness, sauntered towards the table, and tho' she had seen them a thousand times before, looked at her bracelet, and admired the likeness of the Earl, who also approached the table; but reader, feel for his surprise, his anguish, his distress, when he saw, lying in her jewel case, as he was going to deposit the bracelet in it, a pocket book with 'Lord Viscount Claverton' on the cover; trembling he took it in his hands, and on opening, found a number of bank notes, which he well knew he had not given his wife, his agitation increased, he felt all the agonies which ingratitude and ill requited love can inflict on a sensible mind.

The faithless conduct of his first lady had opened on him

by degrees; she had robbed herself of his esteem, and he was not a man fondly to *love* where he could *not* esteem; before he suspected the fidelity of the *wife*, he ceased to respect the *woman*; but *here* he had treasured every hope of joy – entirely confiding in principles, he thought invulnerable, in innocence he had made it the business of his existence to adore, in sentiments he fondly believed came spontaneous from a heart devoid of guile; how could he support himself under a conviction of the guilty depravity of the woman he doated on? His lips turned blue, cold drops of sweat rolled down his forehead, and tears burst from his eyes, unattended by any of the softening, the soothing sensations which generally accompany them, – her voice, gentle as it always was, roused him, he started at the sound, and rushed out of the room, the pocket book in his hand.

Lady Frances became vociferous in praise of her own discernment, and her sister was obliged to use force, aided by her woman, to get her out of the room, before the Countess entered.

Lady Margaret, uncertain what measures her brother would adopt, tho' clearly convinced of his injuries, made an effort to get a way before she entered the dressing room, but could not.

Lady Castle Howel said, she "believed she had slept very late, but her dreams had been so troublesome she was fatigued instead of refreshed," – Winifred told her the Earl was there, "where was he gone?" Lady Margaret sat pinching the corner of her handkerchief; but so engrossed was Ellen by her dreams; and unconscious of any cause for her silence, she did not perceive it.

Lady Gertrude now entered, without one particle of compassion for her, whom she esteemed to be guilty, and knew to be ruined; but with sufficient solicitude about her favourite scheme, to hide all her real feelings, and to affect those which the exigence of the moment might render most politic; she had, in the short time she had been absent persuaded Lady Frances into the necessity of being quiet, or giving up all hope of an heir.

Lady Castle Howel, with a smile, which the harmony and innocence of her soul could only light up, gave her aunt the salutation of the morning, and her breakfast equipage being before her, desired Winifred to let the Earl know she was up.

Chapter V

Winifred returned, my Lord was gone out, the Countess was surprised "what, without seeing me?" – Lady Gertrude took a dish of tea, "some extraordinary business, I suppose," continued she, "but not to speak to me! this is really new, and I feel myself affronted," she had a headache, and would pay a few visits, and ride in the park, would Lady Gertrude go?

Lady Gertrude, equally fearful of leaving her by herself, lest any body in the house should drop any thing, or of her going out, where she would be sure to be affronted, said, after some pause, that she believed the Earl was engrossed by some particular business, which perhaps could not be settled without a journey into the country, and in *that* case, as they should be hurried, it would be best to stay at home.

The Countess acquiesced – she hoped the business was not of a nature to vex the Earl, and as to the journey into the country she should rejoice at that; – her harp was brought, she played, and sang; Lady Gertrude liked music, and Lady Castle Howel's voice was harmony itself; imperceptibly, and undesignedly, she soothed even the rugged heart of Lady Gertrude, who, while she was warbling a plaintive sonnet, could not help feeling some concern for the fallen state of so charming a creature. – When she ended her song, as if fate was inspiring her with a presentiment of what was to happen, and as if she knew how important it would be to her to make a friend, she began speaking of her situation, and declared her resolution to suckle her own infant, – a subject so grateful to the person to whom it was addressed, added to her cordial temper of mind for the moment, her eyes, 'unused to the melting mood,' was surcharged with a *stranger* – a *tear* actually stood on her cheek.

Lady Castle Howel saw it – and unable otherwise to account for so new an exhibition, concluded her Lord was ill; the fright and agony this fear threw her into is not to be conceived, it was in vain Lady Gertrude assured her he was well, or that she called Lady Margaret to witness it; "where was he? why did she not see him? why would they not send to him?" tears, hysterics, and at length faintings succeeded.

As the day passed, and no tidings of the Earl, the Ladies were themselves alarmed; night came, horrible was the darkness and suspense it brought, no creature in the house went to rest; Lady Castle Howel's senses became disordered, she was in a burning fever, and by day light the next morning, quite delirious.

Messengers were dispatched every way that could be thought of, and Dr. Macshean greatly recommended himself to the Ladies by the share he took in their misfortunes.

On the third day of the Countess's illness, which was every moment expected to occasion the entire destruction of the family hope, two packets were left at the house, one a blank cover addressed to the Countess, in which was enclosed the pocket book, the other to Lady Margaret. With a letter of attorney properly executed, and a short note to his aunts, requesting them to pay every humane attention to the unhappy woman who bore his name, till after her delivery; when if Lady Margaret considered her unworthy of future personal protection, one thousand pounds a year should be paid to her order, provided she resigned the infant to *his relations*; said he had taken a step that might appear unaccountable to them, with a hope, and it was a unique one, of weaning his heart from remembrances that distracted him; when that was effected, he should go to Castle Howel, he desired his sister to write occasionally, but strictly forbad her even to mention his wife.

Ellen's good constitution, contrary to expectation, and almost hope, aided her recovery, without the dreaded effect, and she was restored to sensations something less poignant, tho' painful in the extreme; Lord Castle Howel's absence was still unaccounted for, in a way that could satisfy her, she could not doubt his being alive, of this she was assured from all quarters, and the whole family with their domestics proved it; as there was no mourning worn, – but if he was gone abroad, – on business of importance to himself, that which was of consequence to the husband, could not but be interesting to the wife, and even if it were necessary to conceal it from her, out of kindness, how little did such precaution agree with his total neglect of her! Not a line, not even a message had she received; she wearied herself and all about her with conjectures; Winifred was suffered to attend, on condition only of not entering on a subject, now become the common topic of conversation, even among the servants; Joseph was forbid the house, and no letters taken in but what were carried to the ladies for inspection.

So entirely was Lady Castle Howel taken up with her situation, and suspense, it had not occurred to her since her illness, that there were in the world beings of any importance but her Lord; she, who in the midst of gaiety and dissipation wrote once a week to Code Gwyn, had now been near a month without recollecting there was such a place in existence.

Ill news flies swifter than a carrier Pigeon, the rumours spread in the neighbourhood of Castle Howel, and from thence to Code Gwyn were shocking.

Lady Meredith, who knew the heart she had formed, treated them at first with contempt; but when post day came, and the next, and the next, without a line from Ellen; when the orders at the Castle proved the Earl's absence; when she heard from the housekeeper, that Lady Margaret's commands were positive from *herself*, without the form assumed since the Earl's marriage, "as your Lady desires," &c. &c. dismay seized the whole family, and days now passed without admitting the light of the sun into the best apartments.

Young Evelyn had taken on him the clerical habit, and accepted a curr[12] in a different part of England: Mr. Meredith thus deprived of his beloved companion resided wholly at Code Gwyn, and attended the duty of his church from thence.

The honour of his family, impeached in the character of that branch of it, so dear, and so distinguished, tinged his cheek with shame; and the misery, which is the sure consequence of a breach of the moral duties of society, and which, if guilty, must be the lot of the unhappy Ellen, filled his sympathizing heart with anguish; hours did the miserable family pass, in regrets that they had suffered so amiable, so dutiful, so affectionate a creature to sacrifice herself for them; for *now*, all the splendid allurements of her marriage had lost their brilliancy.

"Oh!" said the old Baronet, "how happy had I been now in your little parsonage, with all my children about me, before dishonour had blasted my name, with my age's comfort blooming as a cherub in my bosom!"

---

[12] I.e. a curacy

"We had but a little while to live," joined Lady Meredith, bathed in tears, "that little might have been passed in peace; we have not more *now* to leave our children than we should have had *then*, and Ellen, dear unhappy Ellen! Oh, my child! my child, comfort was in her looks, alas she may now want comfort herself."

"She who was the soul of innocence" said Catherine, "who never breathed a sentiment that would disgrace the brightest heroine of antiquity."

Miss Mary wept.

Agnes declared the house had been a desert, since Ellen was made a Countess.

"Not even in her infancy," continued Lady Meredith, "was she subject to the faults common in other children, I never knew her tell a wilful untruth, or be guilty of an act of disobedience."

"Disobedience! my love," said Sir Arthur "it was the pleasure of her life, to render *ours happy*, obedience was nature in her, Oh that I never had parted with her."

"What may be her sufferings, friendless and unprotected."

"But why is she unprotected?" said Mr. Meredith, with spirit; "if she is innocent she–"

"I will venture my soul on her innocence," replied Catherine, rising, "and if I were a man–"

"I will be that man," eagerly interrupted Mr. Meredith, "I condemn myself for wasting so much time in unavailing sorrow and conjecture, even if she is guilty."

"Oh! my dear son," cried Lady Meredith in an agony of grief, "do not even *suppose* it: Ellen, my gentle, kind, affectionate Ellen! the orphan child of my Arthur, his living picture! Oh, no, it cannot, cannot be."

"Yet the depravity of the age of which we are happily ignorant, the luxury, the dissipation, all fascinating, all potent to so young a mind, – then the *integrity*, the *honour* of the Earl," Mr. Meredith sighed as he made these observations.

"If you wish me to live, to exist," answered Lady Meredith, "think of Ellen as I do; could a few short months do away a life of innocent rectitude? could the mild, the benevolent principles of Christianity, taught by you, with such care and attention? could the honourable lessons she has imbibed from the lips of her grandfather? could the example, the precepts of all our inoffensive lives; could not all these support her in the practice of virtue, even though opposed by a torrent of vice?" Mr. Meredith had no wish to oppose these sanguine hopes of his mother, his prayer was, they might be realized; he proposed setting off to London, to see, and know her real situation, as soon as a substitute for his church duty could be found; and he arrived just as Ellen was recovered sufficiently to think of airing in the park.

Her intention to go out was violently opposed by the Ladies of the family.

Ellen was astonished; what, not to air! not to call on her particular friend! but a propos of friends, bring the porters list, – astonished as she had been two minutes before, it now increased, not a single name had been left; "what does all this mean?" asked she with great anxiety; "has not Mrs. Morley been here, nor Caroline Holt nor the Wilmers? nor–"

"Nobody, so that you see, Ma'am," said Lady Margaret drily, "you have no visits to return."

There was something in Lady Margaret's manner which spoke *more* than her words.

"Well," answered Ellen, spiritedly, "as I see there is a

mystery I am not to develop, and as you say, *Ma'am*, I have no visits to return, I will at least breathe the fresh air," and she rang for her carriage, when in bounced Winifred, regardless of the haughty and imperious constraint, insisted on by the maiden Ladies, who, since the Earl's departure, had governed her with a rod of iron.

"As Cot shall be coot unto me, my Lady, he is come, he is come, to safe and defend us from the hands of the Philistines; Oh Lort," she cried, throwing herself at her Lady's feet in a fit of devotion, "plest and praist be thy name, for efer and efer, my prayers are heart, he is come, he is come."

"Where, where?" cried Ellen, darting to the door, in expectation of her Lord.

The Ladies were enraged at Winifred's rebellion, "who is come? who? were you not commanded not to mention any thing that happened out of your Lady's apartment?"

"Oh the Cot of heaven forbit, I should not tell my poor Lady, she will be deliveret out of the paws of Satan." At this moment they saw Ellen fainting in the arms of her uncle, and Winifred, instead of attending to his repeated calls for water, crying, and clinging round his knees; the Countess had not doubted, but the step she heard, rapidly advancing up the stairs was her Lord's, her heart palpitated with joy, and unable to proceed further than her dressing room door, she waited with expanded arms and expecting heart, to receive him; at sight of her uncle, she was seized with a mixture of joy and disappointment, she trembled, and turned away, but in a moment recovered to a sense of duty and affection, and throwing herself in his arms, was asking after her venerable parents, when perceiving he also had an ashy cheek, that his eyes were suffused with tears, it directly struck her that one or other of the beings she most loved and revered were no more, the idea sunk in her heart, and she dropped lifeless on her uncle's bosom.

The old Ladies were as usual in terror, they blamed Mr. Meredith, scolded Winifred, and were as busy about Ellen, as the respective postures of himself and her, with Winifred kneeling, and clasping her arms round both, would permit. Ellen was conveyed to a sofa, and before her recovery, Mr. Meredith understood it was the Ladies' wish he should speak to her only on the welfare of the Code Gwyn family, till he received further instructions from them.

The weakness and lassitude which the late severe indisposition had left on our heroine, was increased by the event of this morning; life could with difficulty be kept in her, while Mr. Meredith was answering her fond and anxious inquires after his father and mother; one by one she made him inform her of the welfare of his sisters and then finding herself much exhausted, was persuaded to lay on her bed – and Winifred, spite of her tears, entreaties and promise to obey orders, commanded to retire.

Lady Gertrude continued with her, and Mr. Meredith withdrew to hear the history of his niece's dishonour, from two women devoid of candour, and deaf to the small still voice of female charity.

The dissipation, extravagance and thoughtless turn of the young Countess were exaggerated; the tenderness, indulgence, and an unlimited confidence of her husband, adduced in aggravation of all her faults; with the history of the gaming incident and the money given her by Lady Gertrude, for the express purpose of paying debts, still owing; then came the finale of the duel, with all its criminal and corroborating train of circumstances.

A thunder bolt could not have more stunned the simple Welch parson; such a series of iniquitous imprudence, to be practiced by such a novice, was carrying human depravity beyond what he had conceived to be in nature; again, and again, he asked, and again, and again, was indulged with the heart wounding recital. Dr. Macshean was announced, he confirmed every title of the story, as far as facts went, but though Lady Margaret had, in a language he perfectly understood, convinced him there were unanswerable reasons why the Earl should remain in his present opinion of his Lady, he had not the heart to confirm any part of the inferences respecting Lord Claverton, who still languished, with *very* faint hopes of recovery, ignorant of the consequences of his universal gallantry, he had once expressed his hope that the duel would not injure the honour, or peace, of the Countess, and had inquired about her with much solicitude; but the Doctor forbore to hint at her situation, from apprehension of the ill effects it might have upon him. That his Lordship was a passionate lover, was a secret he had long been master of, but that he was (as inferred by the world) a *successful* one, was by no means clear to him; but tho' he did not *confirm*, neither did he *deny*, the facts laid down by the Ladies, and Mr. Meredith left the house, with a heart too full for utterance, tho' pressed to dine and make his home in Grosvenor Street.

Unmindful where he was going, he walked at a great pace, revolving on the black tale he had heard, at length, tired of his thoughts, his walk, and the world; he entered a Coffee-house near Charing-cross, and called for tea.

The hour was now five; a paper lay before him, the first paragraph he read was,

"A certain beautiful Cambrian Countess is recovered from

her indisposition, without any very fatal consequences; a divorce will immediately take place, when the frail fair, is expected to abandon her chere amie, Lord C–n, and march under the banner of a noble soldier."

Captain Durell happened to sit in the next seat, and read the same paragraph in another paper, with great volubility, to an elderly gentleman; no man in fact could be so well qualified for a public reading of the said paragraph, as he was the fabricator of it himself.

"Do you think Lord Charles will marry her'?" said the elderly gentleman.

"Marry," replied the Captain, "for a little while, perhaps; no, no, my friend, Lord Charles is not to be so taken in. I have a letter from him in my pocket, which explains his sentiments pretty clearly on that head."

Meredith's Welch blood was boiling, he could no longer contain himself; "give me that letter, sir," and his eyes flashed fire.

"Sir!" exclaimed the Captain.

"I ask your pardon, sir, but it is of importance for me to see the letter you say you have from Lord Charles Dash, relative to" – here fortunately his emotion was too strong for speech, he attempted to finish, but the effort died on his parched tongue.

The Captain eyed him from top to toe, turned on his heel, whistled an Italian air, and left the coffee-room.

Meredith arose to follow him, but the tremor of his soul shook every limb, and he returned to his seat almost breathless.

The gentleman who had been speaking to the Captain, now with great apparent good humour addressed him.

"The Captain is very profuse in his communications; Lord Charles has an excellent confidante." Meredith groaned.

"You know the Lady perhaps," a deeper groan.

"She is very handsome, but her affair with Claverton was known before that old Castle Howel married her – he is ruined, they say," a third groan.

"Her extravagance was without bounds, I have known her lose thousands at a sitting. Have you any letters for me waiter?"

"None, sir", "very hard that"; turning to Mr. Meredith, he continued, "These fine women give a man a damned deal of trouble, but if one gets them at last, the *trouble* you know, sir (winking) is amply repaid!"

Meredith, for the first time, felt a sovereign contempt for the folly of the sex, who could sacrifice to the vice or vanity of so despicable a being, he arose and was leaving the house, when he heard the veteran say to another gentleman,

"Poor fellow, some relation of Lady Castle Howel's I am sure, she is like him, devilish fine creature, do you know her?"

The person answered "he had not the honour."

"Damned extravagant, should have had her myself else."

Meredith's first impulse was to return and chastise the folly, as well as wickedness, of the hoary braggard, but a moment's reflection, and a recollection of his sacred function, soothed him into the patient bearing of an evil, for which, in its present state, he saw no remedy.

Blasted in her character, abandoned by her husband, what hope of happiness or peace to her, in a world where she was despised? What hope of salvation to the soul, where once every virtue lived, but from a seclusion from the vanities that had undone her.

He came to London intent on vindicating her innocence, of clearing her fame, but the facts were too glaring to doubt or disprove. "Unhappy girl!", he exclaimed; as he touched the knocker of Lord Castle Howel's door, "how shall I carry thy shame to the hearts of my parents? yet there it must be buried."

He was admitted to the eating room, the family were at dinner, he was invited to join them, but his heart was too full to think of eating, he declined the invitation and retired to an adjoining room.

Winifred, who had not ceased watching the door, from the time he went out, now came in on tiptoe, her eyes swollen, and in evident fear of interruption.

"Cot pless our dear reverent," sobbed she, bathing his hand with tears, "for the lofe of Cot take us with you to Code Gwyn, let us co from the tribe of faro, Oh! my tear Lady."

"Ay, Winifred, your Lady and you have made a sad hand of it, – you have acted very unwisely."

"Yes, indeed, Cot help us, we have brought our pigs to a fine market; there's Mr. Joseph's poor Lort is dying, Oh!" (weeping) "if my Lady knew it she would preak her heart."

"Indeed!"

"Yes, inteet, and here's our Lord gone away Cot knows where, and there's the two cross ould tivels, and Lady Margaret, and Dr. Macshean, such a crew – and to be sure I must not say my soul's my own; no more it is, inteet, nor pody neither, Cot help us, and send us back to Code Gwyn; Cot he knows I had rather knit and spin all day, than live here in this cumbustion, and as to my Lady 'tis no kindness to her, that keeps her here. Lady Margaret says, and Cot knows she is as *pad* as the rest, so she need not give her pribbles and prabbles;

she had better mind how the Doctor gets in and out of her chamber, but Cot help us sarvants, we must hear and see, and say nothing."

"But what does Lady Margaret say?"

"Cot rot her, a nasty painted old belzibub, she says as my Lady shall put off her Ladyship, and troop to her *old* hole at Code Gwyn, because, as why, 'tis the fittest place, as soon as she has brought to bed, if the child (pray Cot bless the baby) is a girl, and take her brat with her, and if (by crace of Cot) the dear baby is a Lord; why then the old ones are to carry him away, and so part mother and child."

"And did you hear Lady Margaret say all this?"

"That I did, and I'll take my affadavit; and beside."

The dinner party being now broke up, Winifred made her escape, praying that the reverend would take her, and her Lady, "back to Code Gwyn, and leave lords and ladies to go to the tivel."

Mr. Meredith's family honour, his pride, his affections, were equally wounded in this communication of Winifred's; a moment since he resolved to carry her back, disgraced as she was, to her natural home, but in her present interesting situation, and of which till now he was ignorant, how could he do *that*? how answer to the dignity of Castle Howel, to the honour of the Merediths, for an obscure birth, of the legal representative of a noble, and ancient family? an obscurity that might lay the foundation of future doubts, and rob the innocent of its right, – for whatever were the depravities, of which the Countess was accused, the state of her pregnancy admitted no doubt of the legitimacy of her offspring, and he knew the family were too much interested in the event, to neglect any thing for its welfare and preservation; in *that* welfare and *that* preservation Ellen's health and peace was now the primary object; there was therefore no room for the interference or protection of her friends, no immediate reason to fear, however attached she might be to her errors, she would in her present situation relapse into them, or that, if she was so culpably disposed, she could effect it under the guard of the Ladies, whose apparent kindness was also secured by the interest they must take in her well doing; – all these reasons co-operating with the several circumstances that had occurred in the course of the day, and which leaving impressions on his mind, that confirmed the history of Ellen's ill conduct, certainly blunted the fine edge of those tender feelings for her, that had brought him to town, he coincided with the wishes of Lady Gertrude and Lady Frances, that he would leave the Countess and her affairs exactly in the situation in which he found them, till after her accouchement, when they promised, should no change of sentiment in the *Earl* prevent it, she should be delivered to the protection of her own family, with the handsome allowance assigned by him; – this agreement was witnessed by Dr. Macshean, and guaranteed by Lady Margaret, and as nothing further could now be done in the affair, as Mr. Meredith knew how anxious his father and mother were to hear from him, and as he felt it impossible to write, in terms that would not impeach his veracity, without risking his mother's life, he resolved, to the great satisfaction of the Ladies, to return to Code Gwyn, with the same expedition he had left it. Some shrewd people will liken the journey of Mr. Meredith to the old distich of 'The king of France, with twenty thousand men, went up the hill – and so came back again,'[13] for say they, what has

---

[13] Better known today as the nursery rhyme, *The Grand Old Duke of York*

he done? has he made a single inquiry on behalf of his niece? has he made the smallest attempt to clear her fame, to vindicate her innocence? No, Mr. Meredith was a plain, sensible and a learned man; he was moreover a Christian, in whom there was no guile; he served God, and he loved his fellow creatures; there was, in his opinion, no exigence in the human system that could excuse a falsehood, no motive that could justify one; he was the last to suspect and the first to forgive an injury, no scheme of present advantage, or future ambition, occupied *his* mind, he took no pains to search out the debasements of the heart, it was always enough for him to recognize its virtues, whether *feigned* or *real*; finding in himself no disposition for detraction, he suspected it not in others; when any flagrant act was pointed out to him, his indignation was warm, he reproved, he punished, but at the first dawn of repentance *he forgot*; had he lived in the great world, his credulity would have been a fine field of amusement to the *witty*, and a prey to the designing, – at Code Gwyn it was neither, his example was so respectfully followed, his precepts so truly attended to, and his simplicity of heart so beloved, that an imposition on *him* would have exposed the perpetrator to general resentment; how then could a man so void of guile himself, doubt a relation so attached to probability, so confirmed by circumstances, and so solemnly witnessed by people of (as far as he knew or believed) as great veracity as himself? and certainly the ladies had no interest in defaming the Countess, nor indeed, excepting a few embellishments, did they do it, for they implicitly believed her guilty.

The conversation at the Coffee-house was purely accidental, a Captain in the army! the confidential friend of a Lord! could *he* be suspected of falsehood? and the old gentleman, 'tis true, his folly was the most conspicuous thing about him, but he had no apparent end to answer in reviling the Countess, at least none our Welch parson could discover. The duel was a fact, Lord Claverton not expected to survive, Lord Charles fled, and the Earl had repudiated his wife; he had seen the fatal pocket book, which still lay in the jewel case on the toilet, open for any inspection, and having no cause to doubt gave up even the hope, to find her worthy the protection he nevertheless resolved to give her.

Meanwhile Winifred desperate in resentment of the injuries offered her, and intended to be offered her mistress, and courageous in the certainty they had *one* friend now in the house, clamorously insisted on being suffered to attend her, complaint of her behaviour was brought to the Ladies in the hearing of Mr. Meredith.

Some events at Code Gwyn, in which she had been suspected, recurred to his mind, and a transient suspicion of her integrity, shot across the bosom of candour, it was however *but* transient.

This creature loves her, poor poor Ellen! is it come to this? must she then be deprived of the sight of the *only* one who does; while he thought he pleaded for Winifred, the comfort and consolation of Ellen was only in his mind, he entreated she might be suffered to attend her lady.

The Ladies had strong objections, they argued with passion.

Mr. Meredith would not give up the point, he reasoned with humanity.

They adduced the danger of her imprudence and likelihood she would, by betraying the discovery, defeat all their hopes; he hinted the natural terrors incident to her situation, the satisfaction it must be to see herself attended by the companion of her infancy, one of whose fidelity she was assured.

Fidelity! they were surprised at the expression, from a man of his cloth, what could fidelity infer from a servant to a woman in Lady Castle Howel's situation.

He apologized, and begged to change it for affection.

They were gloomy and dissatisfied.

But tho' the very essence of mildness in his general conduct, there were points on which Mr. Meredith was immoveable; he felt there was a degree of tyranny, in depriving Ellen of her chosen servant, and substituting another in her room, not warranted by the Earl's orders, and therefore not justifiable in them; and as to think and speak was to him one and the same thing, he with equal respect and resolution, remonstrated against so indefensible a measure; the result was Winifred was ordered in, and restored to her place on condition of secrecy.

"What" cried she "is the reverent then going without us, are we not to co home with you to tear Code Gwyn?"

"*She* might go," Lady Margaret said.

Poor Win's tears were always near, she began to cry and kneel, but Mr. Meredith insisted on her leaving the room.

"If indeed she *wished* to leave her Lady."

Win shook her head and wept aloud.

"There was no objection."

"Ay, ay, I see how it is, satan has set his clofen foot on my poor Lady, and her own flesh and blood is turned against her, but as for poor Winny Griffiths, she will bag her pread from door to door, and carry the tear little paby on her pack, before she will leave her, and as to you, Mr. reverent, you may be ashamed, with a parcel of ould cats to—"

"Old cats," repeated Lady Gertrude, rising with dignity and resentment.

"Cats!" said Lady Frances, her eyes flashing fire.

"This creature should be turned out of the house," said Lady Margaret to Dr. Macshean.

"Petter not Madam," answered the enraged Winifred, "I shall say a thing or two wherever I am, some folks won't like, so you'd petter let me alone, I care for nobody in the house, but my mistress; and if it was paved with cowld I would not stay a day after her, Cot knows I lofe her too well to tell her any thing to vex her, and a petter and more firtuous Lady never lived."

The Ladies smiled contemptuously.

"No, nor died neither for all your pad looks, and with the crace of Cot it will come out, and then our reverent will be ashamed to leave us in the jaws of destruction," so ready to burst with passion, exit Winifred.

The Ladies agreed, nothing could make Lady Castle Howel partial to so ignorant a creature, but being in her power.

Mr. Meredith modestly adverted to the infant attachment she must have formed, to a girl who had always attended her.

Neither of the three Ladies had any idea of infant attachments.

Winifred returned with a message, her Lady was up and requested her uncle would take his tea in her dressing room. After repeated charges to beware of what he said, he followed Winifred.

Ellen fondly embraced him, and again enquired with anxious tenderness after every part of the family.

Spite of the censure and indignation of his upright heart, he could not see her in her present situation, young, beautiful, far advanced in a state the most endearing, as well as interesting to a husband, who had abandoned her, lost to peace, to fame, and to honour, yet unconscious of the precipice on which she stood, without being extremely moved; he turned his face away, but tears would flow, hers accompanied his, and a silence ensued broken, only by the audible sobs of Winifred, who not having been bid to withdraw, stood behind her Lady's chair.

Lady Castle Howel recovered her serenity before Mr. Meredith resumed the part he was enjoined to act, and with great tenderness said, she had been extremely affected by his agitation when first she saw him, supposing it occasioned by some melancholy event at Code Gwyn; but relying on his assurances, that all were well there, she could now account in a different manner for the distress that seemed to overpower *him*, "you weep my dear uncle, and it is for me, my situation, left by my Lord at a time when" – she hesitated, a crystal drop trembled thro' the silken lashes of her eyes, "ignorant of his fate, shut out of his confidence, an alien from his heart, a constraint on all my actions, is no doubt affecting to my friends; my Lord they *say* is well, he is under no dreadful misfortune – he has his intellects – is at liberty, *can* write to those who share his confidence, – and these also are permitted to address *him*; what I suffered from my fears for his safety, the righteous God, whom you my dear uncle taught me to fear, can only witness."

Mr. Meredith shuddered, he looked at her with abhorrence; what, thought he, has she then acquired confidence to appeal to her God, with a load of unrepented iniquities on her mind! he met her eye, his own, armed with the calm severity of an accusing angel, he intended should flash conviction into her guilty soul; but her steady, undismayed, yet sorrowful glance, spoke no guilt, no conviction; on the contrary she construed the severe expression of his naturally serene eye into resentment for her treatment.

"I knew you would feel for your Ellen, but who, or whatever has been the cause of my sorrows, I forgive them; it has awakened me from a lethargy, in which all the blessings heaven so liberally bestowed on me were lost; I had almost ceased to regret our happy parties at Code Gwyn, and I thought – no, I did not *think*, till (deeply sighing) it was too late; my conduct certainly estranged me from the warm heart of my dear Lord, yet had he but compassionated the youth, the caprice, the weakness of her he honoured with his name; had he waited but a little" – she paused, while Mr. Meredith, all attention, sat in expectation of a full confession of her guilt, she continued, "but these are vain regrets, and it is my only consolation that my heart is cleared from the guilt of intentionally offending him, that my gratitude and affection is yet inviolable, and that however faulty I have been, the punishment he has inflicted is unjust and excessive." She stopped, waiting but waiting in vain for Mr. Meredith's answer, he was lost in the perplexity of her speech, to him it appeared mysterious, and equivocal! confession, and justification! in the same moment, and in the latter part false in every particular; if guilty, how could her gratitude and affection be inviolate? or how could she impeach the justice of a punishment so mild, for actions so atrocious?

Finding he did not answer, she again recurred to the family at Code Gwyn, regretted she had ever left it, and anxiously asked if he thought she should be allowed to revisit it.

He believed it was not intended to restrain her, after a certain event, from going where she pleased.

"After! is my Lord then for ever gone? will he not return to sustain and comfort me? what never! am I never to be forgiven?"

"There are offences, Ellen, which it is not in the power of an honest man to forget, tho' Christian charity may induce him to forgive."

"You make me tremble, sir, are mine of that black description? what have I done? for God's sake tell me! uncle, – my heart,—"

"Yes, Ellen, *your heart* will inform you."

She started.

Mr. Meredith arose, he advised her to be composed; said the business being finished which brought him to town, he must immediately return, and embracing her, bid her farewell before she could recover from her consternation.

Chapter VI

Winifred's sorrows however would have vent, she wrung her hands, and wept aloud, "the reverent was gone; they had no friend to stand py them, they were poor miserable wretches, and Cot know'd whether their lives were in safety."

Ellen stood the picture of despair, she repeated "your heart will inform you." She traversed her apartment, Winifred still lamenting their hard fate, to be left behind by the reverent.

"My *heart*," said Ellen, looking steadfastly at Winifred, and bursting into tears.

Winifred threw herself on her knees, "for the Lort almighty's sake, my tear laty, let us co home, what matter the reverent, we shall be as welcome at Code Gwyn as him, and there we can tell our own story, and prove all the lies that has been hatcht."

"And pray my good Winifred," said Ellen extending her hand, with that cordiality which is sure to flow from a sorrowful heart, when it meets sympathy, "pray what has been said? what lies have been told?"

Winifred kissed the white hand thus extended, and forgetting all the old ladies' precautions, her own promises, and the consequences of the discovery; stole to the door, locked it, and beginning from the fatal night at Mrs. Stewart's rout, repeated the story in as many different ways, as she heard it; with however the same conclusions, that Lady Castle Howel intrigued with Lord Claverton, that Lord Charles Dash was in love with her, and had challenged him; that Lord Castle Howel had discovered the intrigue by a book with papers in it he had found, that he was gone abroad, but that he was to be divorced as soon as her lying in was over; to these succeeded a long list of things that were to come to pass, collected from what the servants dropped, and what Win, by dint of industry, could overhear, with here and there a conjecture of her own converted into facts.

To conceive Lady Castle Howel's agitation the reader must be as innocent and as injured as herself.

Her heart had severely reproached her, for the folly and imprudence of running in Lord Charles's debt, because it had exposed her to the insult of his degrading passion, she had also been severely mortified at a retrospect of the last card assembly, where she had not only squandered the money given expressly by Lady Gertrude to pay play debts, but had contracted new ones; but as to the transaction between Lord Claverton and her, it had never recurred to her thoughts as criminal, nor could she imagine how it could lead to slanders of so shocking a nature; so much had her mind been occupied by the unexpected events that had happened since, she had not once thought of his Lordship's debt, the book with the remainder of the notes she remembered to have laid on her toilet, from thence Winifred removed it to the jewel case; but too ignorant, and let me add, too innocent to enter into every circumstance, as the world had chose to discuss it, instead of sinking under the discovery, as the ladies expected, her soul rose superior to misfortune; conscious of innate integrity, her heart revolted against her Lord.

"He took me, it is true," said she, "from obscurity, he expanded my mind, and added a polish to the valuable instructions I had from infancy been in the habit of receiving; he brought me into the great world, loaded me with finery, and taught me how much easier it was to be splendid than happy! He led me into temptation; and deserted me when there! He left his wife to the injuries and scorn of the pitiless savages, who call themselves well bred; he consigned me to women without hearts, and men without honour!"

"Ay, Cot knows" cried Winifred, "and if it was not for the expected heir –"

Ellen's colour rose, "I am degraded in the opinion of my venerable grandfather, and his virtuous wife will no longer receive me to her heart!"

"To be sure she will know all, the reverent was never coot at keeping secrets, I warrant the old tivels will send him home primful."

"My aunts will blush to hear me mentioned!"

" Ay, I dare say Miss Meredith is comparing you to all the women with hard names in her old books."

"My uncles think on me with indignation!"

"Yes inteet, the reverent for that."

"I have nothing left worth preserving; but the innocent burthen I carry!"

"And that will be taken from you the instant it is porn; if it is a Lort, the ould ones will have it; if a Lady, Lady Margaret and the Doctor will."

Ellen walked about the room in agitation.

Lady Gertrude rapped at the door.

Winifred said, her Lady would not be disturbed! An answer so rude and unusual alarmed her; she retired to communicate it to her sister and niece, lamenting that she had been prevailed on to suffer Winifred's attendance.

Lady Frances, having advised the measure, was sure, if any thing had transpired it was from the Welch parson.

Lady Gertrude denied that with warmth, she knew he had too much good sense.

Lady Frances thought him the greatest fool she ever saw.

Her sister coolly gave it as her private opinion that Lady Frances was not a competent judge.

Lady Margaret was just then whispering an important something to the Doctor, so that she did not give her sentiments, but as neither of the aunts chose to retract theirs, they waxed both warm and loud! their replies and rejoinders became less and less suitable to their quality, and matters wore a very unpleasant aspect – when one of their women came in to inform them, Lady Castle Howel had ordered the carriage to be at the door at six in the morning, and bid a footman enquire where Mr. Meredith slept.

All animosity now forgot in the common cause, Lady Margaret joined in consultation of what was to be done; the Doctor, it was decreed, should pay the Countess a visit, he sent his name and was admitted.

To his enquiries after her health, she answered decidedly *well*, and withdrew her pulse from his touch.

He observed it was a cold evening, and asked leave to stir the fire.

She was suffocated with heat, and begged he would not give himself the trouble.

Winifred came in with an account of Lord Castle Howel having taken all the horses with him.

Confirmed by the Doctor.

Ellen directed them to get hired horses.

The Doctor remonstrated against her using hired, or indeed any horses, going out would actually endanger her life, and he concluded his harangue by hinting it was the Earl's wish she should not leave her own house.

"*My* house!" repeated she, indignantly.

Winifred re-entered and said her uncle left town in an evening coach, as soon as he parted with her.

Confirmed by the Doctor.

Her countenance, in which a haughty indignation was blended with sorrow, fell at this, she sighed bitterly, and turning to the Doctor, said whatever constructions might be put on the question she was about to ask him, she would be obliged by his candid answer, – he bowed, – she asked if there had really been a duel between Lord Claverton and Lord Charles Dash.

He bowed affirmatively.

"On my account, sir?"

He bowed again, but doubtfully.

The Countess then courtesy'd, and retired to her closet, and the Doctor joined the Ladies.

All now then was discovered, and delicacy, according to Lady Margaret's opinion, out of the question; it was proper she thought to acquaint her with the power invested in them, and what line of conduct it was expected she should adopt.

Lady Gertrude, still politically apprehensive, wished to use gentle means, but allowed it was improper to suffer her to go abroad without some part of the family.

"And what part of the family, madam, would undertake so honourable an office," said Lady Margaret, "as the chaperoning such a woman? would you, Lady Frances?"

"*Me*," replied her Ladyship, "no, I am too volatile, Lady Gertrude will not I dare say object to an office for which her gravity so well qualifies her."

Lady Gertrude frowned, – "if she should assume spirit enough to insist on going out, I cannot see how we can prevent her."

Dr. Macshean presumed, that acting by authority of Lord Castle Howel, she might be legally restrained.

"Where should she go?" asked Lady Margaret, "she has not a friend in the world! the pride of the Merediths will reject her, the people she called *friends* here, would not be seen to speak to her; Morley will never let her in, and Lady Mappleton has sent Caroline to her uncle's at Durham, to prevent her seeing her. Where can she go?"

Where indeed! but the mask had dropped, Winifred no longer fearing the tyrants, who so late made her tremble, was still recollecting and still relating, the many malevolent speeches of the Ladies and their creatures.

The contempt of Ellen's authority in the family, the utter neglect of her Lord, the ruin of her character at Code Gwyn, which was the world to her; were a catalogue of injuries that roused into action every faculty of *her* soul; she recollected her husband's unbounded tenderness, his arguments to dissuade her from a too excessive pursuit of pleasure, and regretted she had not attended to them; her extravagance, which had dissipated what would have rendered whole worthy families happy, filled her with shame, and the gentle reproofs she had disregarded aggravated her repentant sorrow; but with all this, as no angel was more free from the impurity of which she was charged, the pride of conscious innocence, and injured honour repelled the momentary humiliation of self reproach, she felt herself falsely accused, condemned and deserted without being heard.

"My Lord has abandoned me," she said, "but I will not desert *myself*," and the next morning entered the breakfast room where the Ladies and Doctor Macshean were in close confab; the air and manner she was enabled to assume astonished them, they involuntarily rose, and struck by the apparent fortitude of her looks, but in contempt of her character instantly reseated themselves; Lady Margaret took Ellen's usual place; she felt the affront, and on a servant's answering the bell, ordered a breakfast equipage to be brought to the sofa, where she seated herself.

The two parties finished their morning repast in gloomy silence, and Ellen ordered her work stand.

Mrs. Morley was announced; she had figured to herself the poor guilty degraded Countess, suffered to remain in the house thro' the intercession of the Ladies, only till her accouchement, judging of what her own feelings would be in such a situation, when having no resources within herself, she should be deserted by the world, and confined to the narrow limits of her own apartments; she fancied grief would have fed on her beauty, mortification humbled her pride, and shame sunk her to the level of the guilty; instead of which, with the radiant dignity of conscious innocence on her brow, the pride of insulted honour flushing on her cheek, and the collected consequence of innate gentility, she saw and felt the real Lady of the mansion was in her place.

Among Winifred's numerous communications, she forgot the intimacy that had taken place between Mrs. Morley and Lady Margaret; Ellen therefore could not but take this visit to herself, but the frivolity of mere fashionable attachments had no longer charms for her: Mrs Morley was her companion, nay, her seducer, in scenes she blushed to recollect, her thoughtless gaiety amused in the moment but disgusted in the retrospect, and the absence of friendship and sympathy evinced in her neglect robbed her of all the regard she had felt for her; she nevertheless, with the good breeding natural to her, arose. Mrs. Morley courtesy'd with an involuntary respect, extorted by the manner of our heroine, she blushed, and her eyes unused to be withdrawn on *any* occasion, sought an object where to rest, free from the piercing glance of the elegant Countess; in Lady Margaret's she found so much, both of information and confidence, that turning short, without speaking, she ran up to her friend, shook hands, and tho' she had aired with her the preceding morning, talked of the age that had elapsed since she saw her, and was immoderately rejoiced to find she was not tormented with the head-ache, of which she had complained.

Ellen smiled; the flow of words, warm professions, the friendly actions that *mean nothing!* amused without mortifying her; she had no regrets for such little enjoyments and the less they became in her estimation, the more her thoughts recurred to deprivations of more moment. She resumed her work.

The opera, concert, play, court dresses, visits, &c. &c. were discussed with exactly the same attention to the Countess, as if she had not been present.

Lady Mappleton was announced.

Lady Margaret coloured, "we must not receive her here," and darting an angry glance at Ellen, left the room, followed by Mrs. Morley and the two spinsters.

Lady Mappleton was a widow of quality and fashion, a woman of excellent morals, unimpeached character, and sound understanding; she was related by marriage to the Castle Howels, had been left early in life a widow, with two sons and three charming daughters; Ellen had been introduced to, and well received by her, but not till after she had got into a circle of acquaintance and engagements that prevented her following the bias of her heart, in accepting the advances to friendship and intimacy of Caroline Holt, Lady Mappleton's only unmarried daughter. In the vortex of dissipation in which she was constantly immersed, there was no time to cultivate sentiment with the less dissipated; Miss Holt's card was oftener on her table than that of any other person, and she was always pleased to see her, but it very seldom happened she could pay the attention she felt due to this amiable girl.

Lady Mappleton was visited by most of the description of nobility, who mingled mind in their connexions; her select parties consisted of the most brilliant geniuses of the age, and her musical meetings, where her daughters were performers, considered among the first private concerts; yet Lady Mappleton, and her family, always found leisure for the elegant attachments of the heart; and to these Lady Castle Howel would have been an invited welcome guest, had she been mistress enough of her time to accept it; but Lady Mappleton had too much sense, and experience not to foresee the ill consequences of Lord Castle Howel's indulgence, and his Lady's thoughtless extravagance; tho' all her penetration, of which she had a great deal, and observation, of which she was not sparing, had never suggested to her, the probability of the Countess's commencing intriguer.

Miss Holt's partiality for our heroine, was warm from a benignant heart; tho' of a grave turn herself, she loved her vivacity, and (tho' a woman) admired her beauty; she could not bear the shock of hearing in all parties of Ellen's infamy, and therefore prevailed on her mother to send her to visit an uncle in the north, from thence she wrote to request she would call in Grosvenor-street, to enquire the fate of Lady Castle Howel.

Lady Mappleton, and her family, were the only connexions, which now, awoke from her delirium, Ellen regretted; Miss Holt had been indeed as neglectful of her as Mrs. Morley, and most likely from the same motive, but there was a purity, a modest consistence, in the character of one that properly censured the imprudence, which the levity of the other authorized; to the censure of strict propriety Ellen bowed; but she despised the vain triumph of accidental character, – she felt acutely the misfortune that deprived her of the honour and comfort of Lady Mappleton's countenance and advice; her proud heart, which repelled with indignation the affronts of Lord Castle Howel's family, would have melted in the society of a matron, whose goodness of heart, and fine sense, were at once an earnest of candour and a symbol of justice; the former she was sure would not be denied her, and she had no cause to deprecate the latter, she sat ruminating on the good effects of such an interview, and was tempted to go to Lady Mappleton, and in presence of the women she despised, throw herself at the feet of the one she respected, and implore her protection and advice; but while she hesitated, the servants called the carriage, she hastened to the window, her Ladyship at that moment looked up, Ellen's heart sprang to her eyes; she courtesy'd, but had the grief to see, – tho' Lady Mappleton steadily observed her, she did not return the compliment, but drove off, without condescending to notice it ; she turned from the window to give way to her tears, and perceived Lady Margaret at her back, who, having seen both the compliment, and Lady Mappleton's neglect of it, who visibly enjoyed the ill natured triumph.

Whether Lady Margaret had any point to carry in making her desperate, whether any consequences could be derived of

Ellen, Countess of Castle Howel

advantage to her from a repetition of the supposed imprudence, which had robbed her young sister-in-law of every blessing in life, will appear in the course of this history; certain it is, had she been as much bent on *driving* her to extremities, as her aunts were in *avoiding* them, she could not have taken more effectual methods, nor have succeeded better.

In Ellen's establishment, a favourite servant of Lord Castle Howel's was by her own desire, placed as her footman; this man, who was proud of the distinction, and who, by his constant attendance on his lady, was better qualified for the office he assumed than anyone of the family (Winifred only excepted), was her advocate from the garret to the cellar; but as Lady Margaret admitted no doubt herself of Ellen's guilt, it was not to be hoped she would permit a menial servant to give his opinion of the matter, when that opinion so entirely contradicted hers.

Philip was therefore discharged in disgrace, and forbid to hold acquaintance with any of the servants; of this circumstance Winifred was reminded, by seeing him pass the window, while her Lady was pensively looking out, and Ellen insisted, with great spirit, he should be restored.

Lady Margaret's answer called forth a reply, that reply provoked a rejoinder; and spite of all the efforts of the two spinsters to prevent matters from coming to extremity, it ended in Lady Margaret's insisting on Ellen's giving up the situation she was so unworthy to fill, and retire to her own apartment, with an humble sense of the lenity shown her – and then, in her presence, ordered the servants to pay no regard to any commands she might have the temerity to give them.

Winifred unfortunately snapping her fingers at this, and saying, "the servants, Cot almighty be plest and praist noes petter how to sarve Cot, and obey their true and rightful mistress," was bid to be gone immediately, and the Earl's delegated authority produced to enforce these orders.

Ellen read the letter over, and silently returned it to Lady Margaret, while Winifred raised her voice in vociferous protestations, she would tie on the spot before she would leafe her Laty.

Dr. Macshean entered the room.

Sorrow, pride and vindictive anger, swelled the bosom of the fair Countess, the tear that anguish forced into her eye, was repelled by scorn; her form was raised and she really looked over them all.

The Doctor's conscience smote him, it reproached him for being, in some degree, an accessory to injuries that might occasion the death of the loveliest woman of the age, and of the heir of a noble family; he had recently left the bedside of his patron, whose mind weakened by present and appalled by future danger, unveiled some secrets to the Doctor, which convinced him, tho' the Countess might be imprudent, she was not guilty.

Winifred, still vociferous, grew louder and louder; the Doctor whispered Lady Margaret, and proved his ascendency by the effect of that whisper; Win was ordered out of the room, but suffered to remain in her place.

Ellen declined the officious civility of the Doctor, in haughty silence, and withdrew, with a fixed resolution to avoid all further intercourse with every part of the family.

She reached her apartment, with her head and heart full; the treatment she had received, in the presence of Lady Frances and Lady Gertrude, gave her an earnest of what worse she might have expected, if the situation, on which all the family hopes hung, was not her protection. To be considered as a convenience, a mere vehicle, to gratify the vanity and resentment of one part of the family, and the whim and caprice of the other, – till their own ends were answered, and *then* to be spurned from them, and have her child taken from her, for whose fate she already began to feel an interest, was more than the philosophy of eighteen could bear.

She would write to her grandmamma, openly and explicitly; she would implore the protection of her grandfather, who with her uncle, would resent her ill usage. Ah! but they were in Lord Castle Howel's debt, would his resentment not be excited by their interference? would he not withdraw his friendship? would he not consign them to the merciless stone hearted Morgan? and what end after all would it answer, but expose them to insult and distress; her character was injured on circumstantial evidence only; but what was her simple *no*, to the *yes* of the multitude; if that *no* was not believed; her grandfather would disgrace himself by receiving her, if it was, he might be ruined by opposing *his* confidence to Lord Castle Howel's prejudices; "no," said she, "my uncle condemned without hearing me, he has carried his opinions with him to Code Gwyn, my heart is in the eye of God, – and my fate is in his hands, I will quit this house, and never return to it, till my honour is cleared from the injurious imputations cast on it, but I will not involve my friends in my disgrace."

Winifred, her faithful friend and counsellor was present, watching with staring eyes, and distended mouth, every turn of her countenance, the "I will quit this house," was the happiest tidings she could hear, hating every thing in a place, where she had experienced such extreme of good and ill fortune, and where she was, when out of her Lady's presence, exposed to all the second hand airs of the Ladies women, no change in her opinion, could be for the worse.

"Cot be plest and praist! Oh, my poor aunt Griffiths always said, 'London was the tifel's drawing room!' When shall we cet out? how shall we travel?" and twenty other questions poured from her voluble tongue, and she immediately began to pack up without waiting for the answer, Ellen was indeed little disposed to give.

The provocations she had received, the resentment that glowed in her bosom, and the punishment her absence would inflict on at least some part of the Howel's, solely occupied her.

Winifred, however, proceeded in packing up the most valuable portables, among which she did not forget the jewel case, which she placed in the midst of a bundle of cloaths without Ellen's observation.

After a silence of some minutes;

"Where can we go?" said Lady Castle Howel.

"Where but to Code Gwyn, Cot pless us," answered Winifred, still busy.

The Countess started. "Aha, no! Winifred, Code Gwyn! we cannot go there."

Down dropped the bundle out of Winifred's hands, "Not co to Code Gwyn! Why, where in the name of Cot almighty shall we co, then? I am sure if we don't co there we shall be like the tove out of Noah's hark, wandering about without a pit of resting place to put our foots upon."

Ellen felt her desolate condition, but, as she fancied she had, with great coolness and solidity, weighed all the arguments for returning, or not returning, to Code Gwyn, and as the latter had predominated, to free herself from questions which in her present irritated state of mind were very vexatious, she told

Winifred, with unusual severity, her commands must be obeyed, without inquiries of any sort; on the contrary, if she wished to go to Code Gwyn, or any where else, she was at liberty.

Winifred's joyful note was in an instant changed, her tears as usual were the prelude to a volley of words, she wanted to co no where, not she, Cot help her, it did not signify what became of her, she would even stay and wait on the ould cats.

Ellen warned her not to give so much licence to her tongue.

Winifred vowed she would never speak again.

"I leave this house," said Ellen, "tho' clandestinely, *not* guilty; I shall not want fine clothes, you must therefore prepare things only suitable to a private gentlewoman, mere necessaries, and endeavour to find where Philip is."

Winifred knew, it was at a little shop, kept by a Welch woman in the next street, where, when permitted to go out, he had made a visiting acquaintance.

"I think I may trust him," said Ellen.

"Trust him! lort my Laty."

"Forget my Lady, Winifred, I shall wish to be concealed."

"As to the matter of that, I wish I could not remember you ever was a Laty. Oh my Cot! poor tear Mr. Evelyn."

Ellen's face and neck crimsoned, his name had more than once within the last painful hours died on her own tongue, but she had checked the vagrant thought with her utmost effort, and now, after the momentary thrill of pleasure, the long disused sound raised in her throbbing heart, rebuked Winifred severely, and solemnly charged her never to offend in that way more.

The girl's own recollections recurred to Evelyn's love for her mistress, and in that moment she thought Mrs. Evelyn could not have been so unhappy as the Countess of Castle Howel, but her usual promise to do so no more, made her peace; and she went to seek Philip to concert measures for their departure.

Philip was a plain mannered, well meaning Welchman, son of a tenant to Sir Arthur Meredith; and though taken very young into Lord Castle Howel's suit, where he was a great favourite, always retained a love and respect for the hereditary landlord of his kin; Ellen was known to be the pride and idol of the Code Gwyn family, before whom Philip, among the rest of the tenantry, had been used to bow; the warmth of his vindication of her in a family, where as the principals admitted her guilt, it was not likely she would find many advocates among the dependants, had cost him his place, but had it also cost him his life, he would have been the same honest champion.

Winifred soon found her old fellow servant, with whom indeed she had, in disobedience of Lady Margaret's positive commands, held *daily* conference from that of his discharge.

To Philip's great regret he had engaged himself to a gentleman, who was gone to Edinburgh to marry a Scotch heiress, and had left him the care of a new carriage, not quite finished which was to convey in the packing trunks the wedding paraphernalia; confidence thus reposed would render his leaving his new master's service a breach of trust, for which he would be answerable to the law; this set Winifred into her old habit of tears and lamentations.

"Lort be coot unto us, poor miserable Laty as my mistress is! what is poor woman's without a man! Cot help them, when they are wandering about without house or home!"

"God forbid, Mrs. Winifred, that should be my Lady's case, why don't she go to Code Gwyn?"

"Oh Cot help thy foolish head Philip, why our tivel of a

reverent, Cot forgive me, has peen here and believed all the ould cats said, and—"

Philip begged, with tears in his eyes, she would say no more, and having considered a little,

"I cannot leave the trust reposed in me," continued the honest servant, "but if as you say my Lady wishes to be concealed from my Lord's family, and has not resolved where to go, if she would condescend to ride in the carriage any part of the way, I will lose my life before she shall come to harm, and will be ready when she pleases."

Winifred's April day countenance cleared up, she protested Philip had the wisdom of Solomon, and even of Mr. Joseph! who poor tear soul she had not seen in all her troubles; she would go and advise her Lady to take Philip's offer, and return as soon as she could escape Lady Margaret, who to be sure, like other cats, she believed in her conscious, could see in the dark.

Ellen, whose resolution strengthened every moment, waited her return with great impatience, and immediately accepted the offers of her old servant; Winifred, notwithstanding her Lady's commands, could not bear the thoughts of leaving any of her finery, which, from her own hankering after new clothes, she supposed the old Ladies would seize for their own use, was industrious enough to convey in bundles, most of the wardrobe to Philip's lodging, "they were any where safer than in the hands of the Philistines;" those intended for travelling he packed up by her directions, and all being ready, the carriage waited at the corner of the street. Exactly at eleven which was the family supper hour, and Ellen, eager in the prosecution of a plan, formed and executed under the influence of contentious passions, followed her servant to the hall.

As Winifred had, within the last two days, many extra occasions to pass the porter, and as she had in view the object of passing him for the last time, she found it convenient to be very civil, and as he, who like many other quality appendages, was better fed than taught, had time to be very gallant to all the maids, and particularly so to Winifred, when his purple face was a little flushed, which was generally the case at this hour; she relying on his amorous advances, went boldly up to the street door, the corpulent gallant waddled after her, in the scuffle he threw down his candle, and the lamp being near exhausted, Lady Castle Howel passed unobserved, while Cerberus took his sop from the lips of Winifred, who very calmly returned down stairs, through the servants hall, up the area and immediately joined her mistress, who was already in the coach, which, as soon as they were seated, drove off.

Chapter VII

Our travellers were hardly off the stones, when two things of great importance to people of common understanding, who begin a journey, but which had not been once thought of by our heroine, gave rise to some uneasy sensations.

"I never travelled but three times before in my life," said Winifred, "and that was when your ladyship went –"

"No more ladyships, Winifred."

"Cot pless us, I forgot, but pray what must I call you? *Miss* Ellen won't do."

Our heroine had not thought of the necessity of fixing on a fictitious name, that of Holt was the first that occurred, "Mrs. Holt, and you Winifred must change yours."

Winifred was rejoiced at that, hers had such a Welchy vulgar sound she chose to be called Maria.

Ellen had no objection to Maria; but she thought Jenny, as being something in the sound approximating to Winny, better.

Jenny! Jane! oh dear that was as bad as her own, she begged it might be Maria, or Charlotte, or Bella, or—

Ellen bid her chuse what she liked.

Winifred liked Maria vastly, and yet some how, she thought Charlotte genteeler, because it was the queen's, and queens knew what was good for themselves, so if her Lady pleased she would be Maria Charlotte.

"Maria Charlotte!" repeated Ellen, "do you think I can call you by two names?"

"No; one at a time was enough, and if her ladyship—"

Ellen was quite angry but Winifred, or Maria Charlotte, was too much in alt to be easily let down.

"I was going," continued she, "to say I never moved but three times, and that was from Code Gwyn to Bath and back, and from Code Gwyn to London."

"Ah," said Ellen, "*that was a removal* indeed!"

"I wonder where we shall move next, may be into our craves, but Cot of his mercy forbid we should be buried among strangers."

If the reader considers the youth and situation of our fair heroine at this period, friendless, and going from her legal home, into a world where she was as much a stranger to manners as to men; they will not wonder this grave reflection of her volatile servant gave rise to the most gloomy ideas; to die in the approaching hour of danger was fearful! but to die without one of the dear relatives, in whose hearts she had lived! to be buried among strangers! – "Ah!" she exclaimed bursting into tears, "what a fate is mine!"

The idea of being "buried among strangers," lowered Winifred's spirits, notwithstanding her acquisition of Maria Charlotte, and she continued silent, while her Lady's recollection carried her to another painful subject.

People she knew could not be so much as *buried* without money, of which useful article she had very little, she took out her purse, the whole contents of which was some loose silver.

The same reflection had more opportunely occurred to Winifred in the morning, which now unavailingly troubled her mistress in the evening; and she had studied ways and means to prevent so disagreeable an evil, as a light purse at the commencement of a long journey; for as to her own stock, her propensity to finery always kept that low.

In packing the jewels, she had seen Lord Claverton's pocket book open, with the notes half out, she found their value, and knowing her mistress's situation, without one scruple of conscience, gave a fifty to Philip, from whom she received the change; and now ostentatiously displayed it to Ellen, who had no more doubt but it was her own saving, than *she* had it was her mistress's absolute property.

Ellen had formed no plan but that of leaving Grosvenor-street, and by concealing herself and the so much desired heir – avenge the insults of the Castle Howel's, till her honour should be cleared; how, when, or by what means that was to be effected she could not foresee, but as in the sanguine hope of innocence, she considered it as an event that *would* certainly happen, *where* she spent the intermediate time was a matter of perfect indifference; at all events, the carriage and her old faithful servant attending, was an opportunity which seemed to be thrown in her way by providence; and, only anxious to escape, from a bondage she considered as tyrannical as unjust, was too much occupied by resentment to pay any regard to consequences.

At the end of the first stage, Philip appeared at the coach door for directions.

Winifred had considered the matter deeper than her mistress, she had no pride to goad *her* on, no resentments to urge, no affections to interest *her*; Mr. Joseph indeed was of some little moment, but not enough to divert her from the perilous situation, in which Philip's absence would leave them; she therefore said, they would go on, this ready answer was not only a relief to herself and her Lady, but to the poor fellow himself, who dreaded leaving them at that hour, so near town, alone and unprotected, and rejoiced to find they were not yet to separate, he ordered horses on, and again mounted the coach box.

This stage was travelled in entire silence; what was next to be done, where to go, and how to support her existence, during, and after an approaching interesting event, were at first pigmies, but now increasing to giants, in Ellen's imagination, and they were in the parlour of the inn, with their little baggage round them, before the silence was broke.

Every blessing of life is enhanced or lessened, every misfortune increased or alleviated by comparison; the inn where they now stopped, would on the first journey from Wales to Bath, have made Winifred eloquent in its praise, but she had since travelled en suit with the Earl of Castle Howel, where an out rider prepared accommodations at the inns, and the domestics, with the landlord at their head, obsequiously waited their arrival.

"What a paltry inn is this," cried she, fretfully to Phillip, who brought in the last packages.

Philip calmly answered, that being a stranger to the road himself, he had left the choice of inns to the driver.

He was a fool for his pains she said; was *this* a place fit for *her* Lady and *her*?

Philip was very sorry it was not better, and anxious to exonerate himself from blame, went to the Landlady, and insisted on a superior apartment.

The Postillion from London, understood he was conveying a new carriage under the care of a servant, and he could not be ignorant that the women he took up in Grosvenor-street were the connexions of that servant; these observations he as usual repeated to the next driver, while they were changing at Barnet, who brought it on with him to the next inn; Philip's demand, therefore, to have the best apartment was coolly answered, that it was engaged; but it happened the waiter had carried in a glass of water, and heard Winifred address "her Ladyship."

There was a certain dignity inseparable from the manners of Lady Castle Howel, that confirmed the idea of her quality, which being carried to the landlady, immediately procured the engaged apartment for the accommodation of the mistress, who did not give the change a thought, to the great satisfaction of the maid, who thought of nothing else.

Winifred, whose pride suffered at the most trifling omission of the attention and respect she had been lately used to, finding the good effect her Lady's quality had on the people of the inn, forgot the precautions given her by Ellen, and vauntingly communicated her name and rank; she had also forgot how incompatible with that rank it was to travel in the present style; a new cased coach, with one man servant, not her own, on the naked box, a pair of hack horses, and a prating waiting woman, were sorry appendages to a coronet; and accordingly excited a curiosity at the inn, that added in no small degree to the scandalous chronicle of our heroine's actions.

In the mean time, Ellen began seriously to consult her maid about their future operations; Winifred was incapable of advising, she recommended it to call Philip, who being a *man*, and a *traveller*, must be *better* informed.

Philip had indeed several times journeyed from Castle Howel to London, and back; he had also attended his Lord twice to Bath, but his honesty and faithful intentions recommended him much more than his mental qualities, or good travelling information. Philip was however called to the consultation, and took his station behind Ellen's chair.

A dead silence ensued.

Philip waited in a kind of pensive attention for what he supposed would be his parting instructions from a Lady, for whom he felt a mixture of respect and compassion.

"Where," said Lady Castle Howel, "would you advise us?" – the word *advise* died on her lips.

Philip's fingers beat a tattoo on the back of her chair.

"What in the name of Cot, are we to do Philip?" cried Winifred, her eyes fixed on his, interrogatively.

Philip would go to the end of the world with his Lady, if he could do it without betraying his trust; but as that obliged him to go to Scotland, –

Winifred's eyes extended to their utmost size: "What and leave us! can't we co too?"

Winifred's fright suggested to Lady Castle Howel, that if they travelled in the coach as far on the road as they found it convenient, or till they passed some place she should like to stay at, Philip might go on, deliver up his charge and return to them; she accordingly proposed, and he, to their mutual joy, accepted her offer; she saw in this poor fellow an attachment, which desolate as she now was, pleased and comforted her, – they proceeded, journeying to the north, till she found her strength near exhausted, and the rough road to Northallerton, where they slept the third night, having particularly affected her, she with great reluctance told Philip her intention to stop the next day.

With this separation in view, both mistress and maid entered the carriage the next morning in very low spirits.

"Cot be coot unto us," cried Winifred, "two helpless women alone in a strange country, with not a friend to hold their heads, cot help us, nor a man to stand by us; lort preserve his poor servants," and she looked wishfully thro' the glass at Philip; "as to this country, my Laty, the trees, and fields, and broad rivers, – our high brown mountains in Wales!"—

Ellen sighed.

"Wou'd to Cot of his infinite mercy, we were there, for as to this road, to my mind –"

Ellen wept.

Winifred longed to give way to her old habit, from the instant she was out of sight of Grosvenor-street, but the fortitude of her Lady, and fear of offending, restrained her under the sanction of example, however, it now burst forth, in the most bitter wailings, at their cruel fate, mixed with tenderness for her Lady, and invectives against the she tivels of the Castle Howel family, nor indeed did the Earl escape.

Ellen's mind, the seat of delicacy and rectitude; no longer irritated by a treatment wounding to her feelings, nor hurt by the privation of dignity and respect attendant on the character of the Countess of Castle Howel; out of hearing of the sarcastic sneers of Lady Margaret, and the provoking pity and ill acted friendship of the old Ladies, reverted to a bitter reflection to her situation, and a retrospect of all the circumstances that had led to it.

In the hour of dissipation, in the very moment in which she had been betrayed into the embarrassment which induced her to accept Lord Claverton's offered assistance, her heart smote her, and altho' her inexperience of the world, and ignorance of its etiquettes, blinded her to the consequence, there was a something so retrograde to her spirit, and sense of honour in pecuniary obligations, that nothing but the immediate insult from Lord Charles Dash would have prevailed on her to accept it; not that she had the most distant suspicion he could have a latent design in seizing a moment so critical to oblige her.

He had succeeded so well in concealing from every part of Lord Castle Howel's family, his passion for the Countess, that the Earl was always pleased to see him at his house, or in attendance on his Lady; who on her part considered him in the interesting light of an old acquaintance, and one to whom she was obliged; his former passion, so eloquently pleaded by Joseph and Winifred, but so entirely reprobated by her friends, if at all recollected, it was with such a mixture of indifference and incredulity, that it was not in the texture of a mind, at once so thoughtless and candid, to harbour a sentiment on that account, that could take from the obliging respectful attention he paid the whole family.

With Lady Margaret, it has been observed, he stood in a high degree of favour; and even the incident, that according to public statement, had dishonoured her brother, could not deprive a man of *her* partial esteem, who still continued his patronage of Dr. Macshean.

There are indeed some ladies in this liberal age, who have such prodigious regard to the virtue of their *own* sex, they will forgive, receive, and often love, a known seducer! while their extreme purity shrinks with indignation and contempt from the unhappy victim of his art! Lady Margaret was of this description; she made great allowance for *male* offenders, but abhorred all *female* frailty.

Lady Castle Howel was entirely clear of a thought that could injure her honour, or her character, if laid open to the world; but now that the pride natural to a young and falsely accused wife was no longer insulted; that she had taken the step most likely to punish those who had personally offended her; she could not help feeling and lamenting the folly that had led her from *real* into the pursuits of *imaginary* happiness.

When she recollected the distress from which the generosity of her Lord had relieved her family, and the narrowness, not to say poverty, from which he had raised her; when she thought on the splendid sphere in which he had placed her, and remembered how in mere wantonness of folly she had squandered his fortune; how she had disregarded the assertions of a man, whose integrity of soul was conspicuous in every action, and believed those of such a reptile as Mrs. Morley; shame and regret overpowered her; and this shame and regret led to feelings still more painful.

Her character was lost, and she could not but feel, that *this*, a privation of the first importance to woman, stamped also disgrace on a husband, who adored her, who seemed to live but in her sight, who had often in transport vowed the possession of her was a talisman against all temporal evil, – that she endeared to him every other blessing, – that his house was a terrestrial paradise, and she the angel who irradiated it.

And when she reflected that he had torn himself from her arms, all his comforts changed to bitterness; that he had abandoned his family and his home, unable to meet the one or endure the other; that his extreme sensibility had perhaps impelled him to hide both his shame and sorrow from the world, in some solitude, where they preyed on him with redoubled force; his leaving her, which she at first deemed an act of cruelty, appeared one of mercy.

"Ah!" cried she, "believing me guilty, what hindered him from spurning me from his house? no, he chose rather to become a wanderer himself. – Oh! my dear Lord, where, where are you? why cannot I throw myself at your feet, to implore pardon of my folly, and to vindicate my innocence; what will become of me?"

"For the lofe of Cot," cried Winifred, "let us turn back."

"Back!" answered Ellen, "to Lady Margaret, to – Oh, never!"—

"No, no, not there, my tear Laty, but to Code Gwyn."

They were now just within sight of Durham; the sun was setting and left on the beautiful hills which surround this charming neighbourhood, a sombre majesty that render such views particularly charming at the close of day; the scene caught her eye, she involuntarily put her head out of the coach window, a chariot was passing, a voice exclaimed, "heavens! Lady Castle Howel."

Surprised and disconcerted she hastily drew in, "Who could that be?"

Before Winifred had time to answer, by some mismanagement of the Postillion, the carriage overset.

Winifred had excellent lungs, which she did not fail to make use of on this occasion; Philip was thrown off the box, his collar bone broke, and so bruised he could not move.

Winifred's shrieks, which now finding her Lady did not speak, grew louder and more terrific, either reached the carriage which had passed, or the attention of those within was not withdrawn from Lady Castle Howel, they immediately stopped, two Ladies alighted, who with their servant came to their assistance.

Winifred's head and shoulders were out of the window, crying for help; her Laty was teat.

"Heaven forbid," said the younger Lady, affected almost to fainting.

Winifred's grief was echoed by the surrounding woods.

The elder Lady proposed putting the lifeless body, as it then appeared into the chariot, when a middle aged person in a shabby black coat, sauntered on by the inside of the hedge, he immediately closed a book he was reading, and hastened towards them.

Perhaps there never was seen a more interesting figure than our heroine at this moment; her hat was off, her fine hair, which had not been dressed (as the term is) since she left London, only combed out of the powder, hung in beautiful disorder over her shoulders; her eyes indeed were closed but her long eye lashes, and fine eye brows contrasted to the most beautiful complexion in the world, together with her situation, combined to excite compassion, admiration, and curiosity.

The stranger felt her pulse, and to the great joy of all the little group, declared she was not dead. He took a lancet from his case of instruments.

"It will be sometime, Madam," said he, addressing himself to the elder Lady, "before you can reach Durham; with your leave I will take a little blood from the young lady.

"The lort be praist for ever and ever," cried Winifred, "you are a Doctor!"

The blood dropped very slow from the orifice.

"The Lady," said the man in black, "is really in danger. I live not a quarter of a mile up that lane; permit me, madam." —

Mrs. Dean Holt, the Lady in whose way fortune had thus thrown our heroine, replied, the accident happening just as her carriage was passing, she had stopped, but the Lady was a stranger to her.

"Bless me!" cried the Doctor, looking at Miss Holt, who was weeping over Ellen, – but thought he, if she is a stranger, why should I wait for leave? and he immediately led the way to his own house.

"Nancy, my dear," said he to a smart handsome brunette, about his own age, "get the chintz bed ready."

"What for? who is this? what has happened?"

"Hoot; do you think I can answer questions, do you see the condition the Lady is in."

The chintz bed was soon ready.

Dr. Gordon, our benevolent host, was the son of a Scotch manufacturer, who tho' he got his son instructed in the rudiments of a scholastic education, at a small expense, by the clergyman of his own town, found no small difficulty in supporting him at the college of Edinburgh; the young man's application was intense and indiscriminate; it was uncertain, not, what line his father *would*, but what he *could* fix him in, and like many of his countrymen, he attained a smattering of all sciences without being master of any; he knew a little of physic, less of theology and still less of law; yet had a diploma, was ordained and admitted a member of the faculty of advocates, having embraced each of these professions in turn, without attaining a settlement in any, he was imprudent enough to fall in love, and marry clandestinely the daughter of a very great man, who had fourteen children, without a sixpence of *siller* among them, but who being fifteenth cousin to Sir Hector Mac Burlish, of the North Highlands, did not choose his daughter should marry the son of a mechanic.

Sir Hector however gave him a small living, he removed to the highlands, and getting also an appointment to a free school, became at once teacher of the gospel and of the A, B, C; but unfortunately happening to offend a Lord, who was cousin to another Lord, who had married the relation of a great man in the south, he was marked for ruin; a prosecution was commenced against him for observing on a text from scripture, namely, "he that giveth to the poor, lendeth to the Lord; "now" said our irreverent reverend, "if that be the case, the Lord above certainly owes our Lord nothing."

Those who imagined the Doctor had nothing to apprehend from such an expression, are poor ignorant beings, not enlightened by the practice of some Scotch lawyers, who far from that troublesome regard to honour, and the established laws of their country, which distinguish every *society*, whatever effect it may have on individuals, in *our* southern hemisphere, associate themselves in a body, to make black white, and white black, at the nod of him who has the crumbs to distribute. A prodigious *great* man, who if he had not been a great man would have been a very *silly* one; but who as it was, if not a luminary of the law, to dazzle posterity with his blaze, will be at least remembered as the rushlight of *this* age, and serve like a will-o'-the-whisp to warn the *next* of the filth, and quagmires thro' which he has waded; this great man was determined to ruin poor Gordon.

He talked! gods how he talked!

A few old fashioned men, said it was against the law; but the question was not between plaintiff and defendant, it was between the law and the lawyers; the law carried it, but poor Gordon was ruined notwithstanding; he was banished from the milk and honey country, and having tried various means of procuring a subsistence, put off his divinity, by which he would have starved, and took to physick by which he now just managed to live.

Chapter VIII

But the chintz bed waits while we are talking of Scotch laws, parsons and physick.

To this gentleman's care, and to his chintz bed, was the beautiful Lady Castle Howel now obliged for shelter and protection; she received more fright than personal injury from the accident, but was nevertheless sensible of that ready welcome, that always enhances the kind offices of hospitality.

Mr. Gordon mixed up a draught from his medical stores, which as soon as she was laid on the chintz bed, he made her swallow.

The Ladies who had lent their carriage to convey her to Gordon's, anxiously asked, as they found he was a medical man, if, referring to her situation, she was in any danger; Gordon answered with the true physical equivoque, if certain effects followed the accident which might be feared, there probably would be danger, if not, which might be hoped, there possibly would *not*.

Mrs. Holt was a very good, tho' remarkably proud woman, her niece, the amiable Caroline, then on a visit to the Dean her uncle, we have before introduced to the reader; she had been on a short excursion with her aunt, when accident occasioned a meeting with Lady Castle Howel, and a renewal of subjects she had travelled so many miles to avoid.

Any stranger who saw Ellen two months before, the pride of her family, the model of fashion, the rage of admiration, and who saw her now without friends, shew, or attendants, except one poor maid, and an accidental footman, would at least have made a moral reflection on the vicissitudes of human life.

Caroline Holt did more, she so effectually pleaded the cause of humanity to her aunt, as to prevail on her to stay at Gordon's, till a doctor from Durham could arrive.

The good Lady therefore returned to the chamber where Ellen lay in a restless doze.

Mrs. Holt was exceedingly shocked and embarrassed, at having been witness of the accident, as she did not well know what step to take with respect to the family; – those who judged of this Lady from sight, could form no idea of her disposition, for never was sensibility, good nature, benevolence and piety so entirely disguised by a haughty demeanour, and harsh countenance.

Ellen's story was universally known, and Mrs. Holt held her in all possible contempt; yet she could not hear her groans, and see her lovely face distorted by pain, without feeling the most lively compassion, and perhaps some little curiosity to know if she was so very bad as the world reported.

When Ellen was a little composed, and Gordon gone to give his assistance to Philip, she entered into a whispering gossip with Winifred, who had gained great credit by her fortitude while her Lady was in danger; but from her she could not understand any thing more than her own hatred of the Ladies of the Castle Howel family, and her regret they did not go to Code Gwyn; not that Winifred kept any thing back out of prudence, but that she told every thing so indiscriminately, it was hardly possible to discover whether she was ignorant of her Lady's levity, or the Lady innocent of any levity at all; but be it as it would, Mrs. Holt naturally concluded, she among the rest, would be one of the subjects of her future communication, and did not think it absolutely necessary all the world should know, Dean Holt's lady, a Bishop's daughter! was watching by the bed of a frail female; and therefore sharply rebuked Winifred, recommending it to her to be taciturn.

Poor Winifred did not know what taciturn was, she thought she might say any thing to a dear good lady, who was kind to *her* Laty; she expected a plain Mrs. would be proud to know she had the honour to assist a Countess; it could not occur to her there *were* Countesses on whom many a humble woman would look down, much less that her Lady was in that unfortunate predicament.

Dr. Ferguson now arrived; and having acquainted himself with all Gordon had done with respect to Ellen, paid some of his most elaborate compliments to Mrs. Holt, in the course of which he made so many bold advances, to know who and what the patient was, who he perceived to be both young and handsome, that she, ashamed of her own urbanity, abruptly withdrew, under the pretence of laying down till her carriage arrived.

Gordon then requested the Doctor to examine the fracture of the servant which he had set.

If Dr. Ferguson had not made some slight alteration in dressing and medicines, he could not have shewn *his superior skill*, and as they were very slight, we forgive him.

VOLUME III

Chapter I

Mr Gordon, whose soul was sociability itself, now invited Dr. Ferguson to a glass of wine and excellent biscuits Mrs. Gordon had learned to make in the land of cakes.

"This," said the Durham Doctor, with a serious pompous accent, "is a very bad accident, pray who is the Lady?"

"She has the finest countenance I ever beheld," replied Mr. Gordon.

"I suppose she is a person of rank?" in an interrogatory tone, said Dr. Ferguson.

"There is such an interest in the combination of her features," continued Gordon, "that – "

"She is well attended," interrupted Dr. Ferguson.

"If I had found her in a ditch," replied Gordon "her look would have convinced me she had a mind."

"Mrs. Holt is, I presume, acquainted with her," said Dr. Ferguson. "I never saw such a form; did you remark her hand and arm?"

"She is unquestionably a superior creature," answered Gordon.

"So I should suppose," replied Ferguson, "and very able to pay handsomely for our attendance."

"Pay!" exclaimed Gordon, "your journey from Durham

may be of importance, as it takes you out of the immediate call of your patients, but as to my poor assistance, I am already paid."

"What, Mrs. Holt," answered Dr. Ferguson, with a significant nod, "she is a noble spirited woman."

"Very likely" replied Gordon, drily, his Scotch pride somewhat hurt.

"This is excellent wine, I have the honour to drink Mrs. Gordon's very good health, and these biscuits are extremely pleasant," Dr. Ferguson filled his glass to a bumper.

The toast was one that in water would have warmed the heart of Gordon, and he returned the compliment to Mrs. Ferguson.

"And so Mrs. Holt has already made you a present."

Gordon's Scotch pride became again troublesome, he played a voluntary on the table with his fingers in allegro.

"The lady is her acquaintance," said Ferguson, "no doubt, Mrs. Holt's connexions are all in the first line, what became of the equipage?"

"The equipage and Mrs. Holt's connexions, may be together, for ought I know *or* care," replied Gordon.

"Nay, no offence I hope, good Mr. Gordon, surely brethren in a profession should be candid with each other; it is true, you have had the most personal trouble with the lady, but as I was called out of my bed, and rode six miles in the dark, to the imminent risk of my life and property, and have the same danger to encounter on my return; not to mention my rank in the medical world, which you know is always considered in the fees – I shall have great reason to be offended if Mrs. Holt does not at least double the sum she gave you."

"You have yourself said," replied Gordon, "Mrs Holt was

a noble spirited woman, and I dare say she will satisfy you for your attendance, but the patient is an utter stranger to her, and the carriage breaking down in her sight is the only introduction to her acquaintance."

"Ay, ay, she knew the arms and livery."

"She must be a witch then, for the carriage is cased up and no livery servant attending."

"Very likely, it is become a fashion for ladies when they travel post, to be attended by a servant out of livery."

"But this lady was not travelling post, nor in her own carriage."

"No! you surprise me."

"No, the coach belongs to Archibald Frazer, and his servant was following his master with it to Scotland, who is going to marry Miss Louisa Cambell, one of the prettiest girls, and best reel dancers in Perthshire."

"Who then is this lady?" asked Dr. Ferguson, in astonishment.

"This lady is most probably one of those uncomfortable beings, whom the Lord has determined to make use of her own limbs; in common, and to take the cheapest manner of being carried, when her occasions call her to any distance; I believe she was a passenger only in the coach."

"Very extraordinary indeed, Mrs. Holt should be so liberal for a stranger," said Dr. Ferguson.

"Too extraordinary to be true," answered Gordon, whose anger was fast waning into contempt; "for I assure you, I have received none of the pecuniary rewards, which appear of so much consequence to you."

"Sir, I despise your insinuations," cried Dr. Ferguson, rising in a rage.

"Despise the sentiment that provoked it," said Gordon with a smile, that more disturbed the placid smooth round face of Dr. Ferguson.

"Very well, very well; order my carriage; I shall take an opportunity of letting the Dean and his Lady know, a man of my rank and character is not to be called out to attend on stragglers, mail coach passengers, or *riders* in return carriages; nor inveigled into consultations with Scotch quacks, mere dabblers in the profession, I shall – " and Dr. Ferguson flourished his cane.

"Look ye, Dr. Ferguson," said Gordon, rising and advancing towards him, "I am a peaceable man, my principles would be dishonoured by a paltry broil, but I am *but* a *man*, I have *passions,* and am not *always* master of them, and I advise –"

During this address the colour of the peaceable man rose, his voice naturally low and somewhat inarticulate, acquired a strength and clearness that was not quite agreeable to Dr. Ferguson, whose choler sinking as his adversary's arose, involuntarily retreated as he advanced, till he reached the extremity of the room.

"I advise you to have more wit in your anger, and more method in your madness, than to insult a man, whose unworthy veins are filled with the *blood* of the race of Gordon; a race, d'ye see, *mark me, sir,* perfect lambs in their love, but lions in their wrath."

The blood of the Fergusons had a contrary tendency, the Doctor was apter to show the lion where he had *power*, and the lamb where he was *powerless.*

He had however in the present instance outshot his usual cunning; no apology (and he offered a multitude), could do away the words, "Scotch quack, dabblers in the profession,"

&c. &c. – Gordon's resentment was only restrained by the reflection, that he was under his own roof, and Ferguson besides had the protection of the Dean's lady, he therefore permitted him to retire, and having again looked in on the invalids, and found his own assistance not immediately necessary, according to his usual and invariable custom, reposed his troubles in his Nancy's bosom, and retired to that rest which is sure to be the reward of a day spent in the active discharge of *moral,* and not unmindful of the *religious* duty, which enjoins us not to let the sun go down on our wrath.

Mrs. Holt's carriage came for her very early, but she found her ill opinion of Ellen was not proof against the humanity of her nature, and did not leave her till noon, when Gordon assured her, in the old style, she was "as well as could be expected."

On her return home, Caroline was as grateful for her condescension as if she had been acting the kind Samaritan to herself. Mrs. Holt confessed she was interested for the unhappy wanderer, but thought it right to be informed of the circumstances in which she had left the Castle Howel family, before her name appeared publicly in her affairs. Miss Holt accordingly wrote to her mother a particular account of the accident, and begged to know whether it was possible for them to take any notice of the unfortunate Countess.

While this letter remained unanswered, Mrs. Holt continued an attention to Ellen, that became more interesting every interview; and although she did not permit her niece to be of the party, yet the pleasure she took in repeating to her the conversations she began to hold with Ellen, to whom however she did not announce herself, made Caroline impatient for her mother's answer. It at length arrived, and entirely deprived the poor fugitive of their accidental protection.

Lady Mappleton wrote from Windsor, where she then was, that on hearing of Lady Castle Howel's elopement, she had called in Grosvenor-street; and tho' she condemned the severity of Lady Margaret, on the principle that exposing the Countess, bad as she was, reflected a disgrace on the family, and must shock the Earl when it reached him; yet she could not but allow they had extreme provocation, for, that she actually did elope with her own footman, all her best cloaths had been found at his lodgings, which he left, but not discharged; on pretence of his going to place, the day, or rather night, she quitted Grosvenor-street. Her ladyship said she went from town on purpose to be out of the hearing of what filled every body's mouth; and concluded with charging her daughter to have no sort of connection with her.

Mrs. Holt and Caroline looked at each other, but as there was no doubt on their minds, and as she was out of danger, they agreed to drop all further concern with or about her; the thing was too plain, the servant was with her and all confirmed.

The deprivation of Mrs. Holt's company was a sensible mortification to Ellen, whose hours of confinement were from her own reflections dreadfully heavy.

Well has it been said, every present misfortune is aggravated by a recollection of past happiness, particularly if the former be in consequence of our own imprudence.

Ellen began, before her accident, to retrace the late occurrences of her life; but tho' her tenderness for her Lord, mollified by resentment towards him, mortified pride, and the vindictive spirit it inspires, had not ceased to represent the conduct of the Ladies of the family in the most odious light; but *now*, sick and helpless, thrown on the benevolence of strangers, pride was no more, and anger, sated on its own banquet, no longer spread the glowing veil over *causes,* but exposed *them* and their baneful *effects* together; repentant, humble and resigned, she bowed to the decree of providence, nor shed one tear for any past enjoyments, but to the recollection of the dear relatives of Code Gwyn.

The years past under the protection of her virtuous family, were winged with happiness and peace, and she retraced their rapid progress with poignant regret; the few months that intervened were also winged; but one was the gentle motion of the summer breeze, the other the irresistible whirlwind; on the one, memory feasted with delight; from the other it shrunk with abhorrence. The remembrance of grandeur disgusted her, for had it not torn her from the innocent, cheerful and laudable avocations of her blameless life? from the endearments of her family, and the companions of her youth? had not its baneful tyranny forced from her heart, the only image in which it delighted? and had not the vacuum been usurped by phantoms that had nearly been her destruction? she could not indeed repress a sigh, a tear, that accompanied the image of Percival Evelyn, as it now rushed on her mental view, but a moment's reflection told her the sad, the unavailing retrospect, injured a man whose generosity had been a common source of benefits to her family; to whom her dear grandfather owed the privilege of breathing his native air; who preserved to Lady Meredith her accustomed dignity; who continued to her aunts the protection of the roof of their ancestors, and her uncle the power of dispensing blessings to his honest neighbours; and above all to cultivate the genius, and improve the talents of Percival Evelyn. "Ah, sure," would she say, "he at *least* deserved respect, his advice ought to have governed, and his command been obeyed by one for whom he had done so much."

Philip, under the care of Gordon, was now convalescent, and able to pursue his journey; he took leave of his Lady, who had at this time no use for a man servant, and engaged to make such settlement with his master as would enable him to obey her summons, whenever he could be of service to her. Winifred, who was purse bearer, was ordered to give him ten guineas, which it was painful to him to take, but would not have been respectful in him to refuse.

A short time recovered Ellen from the effects of her accident, and her return to health was hailed by the unaffected joy of the honest Gordons, in whose skill and humanity she perfectly confided, and determined to await with them the approach of an hour, when the soothings of friendship are almost as necessary and welcome as the skill of the Doctor, and was more particularly important to a young creature hitherto cherished in the bosom of family love, who had not only the deprivations so dear to regret, but to combat the natural fears of an event, which had cost her own mother her life.

The Gordons watched every motion of her countenance, and as the lovely patient continued to gain on their liking, sympathy, the sweet offspring of heavenly emanation, caught the languor which overspread her features, it glistened in their eyes, it melted in their bosoms, and rejoiced, when in an hour of youthful oblivion, an arch sally broke from her dimpled mouth, and the ray of innocent cheerfulness beamed in her eye.

Mr. and Mrs. Gordon were plain people, affable in their tempers, and contented in their stations; they never had any children, and were so entirely shut out from the world that their particular affections centred on a few birds, two small dogs, and a large cat; but Ellen had become a potent rival to the dumb favourites of the house; and tho' it certainly would be very wise to despise so frail a thing as beauty, yet, spite of mamma's, grandmamma's, cross aunts, and freckled cousins, we fear a beautiful face is a letter of recommendation, read in every language, and admired by every nation under the sun.

Ellen was blessed in a very superior degree with this letter of recommendation, graced with the most obliging temper and winning manners; to these were added the idea of superior rank, for Winifred was perpetually boasting of her Lady's quality, and all the etcetera of elegance, which, notwithstanding her eagerness to leave Grosvenor-street, she secretly regretted; she had indeed in her communications, which were most liberal, kept back the *name* of Lord Castle Howel's family, but as nothing, in Winifred's opinion, in the world was so lovely, so wise, or so good as her Lady; so there was nothing great, she did not think at her command, nor any *good,* she did not deserve; in exaggerating the ingratitude of Lord Castle Howel she protested that many and many a coot Lort lofed the crount[14] Miss Ellen Meredith trot, – there was Lord Claverton, –

"Lord Claverton!" repeated Gordon.

"Claverton!" echoed his wife.

"Ay Cot save him! Lort, why count Claverton poor man! he is killed now by Lord Charles Dash, Cot forgive him, pray Cot! But I hope in the Lort, I shall lif to see him hanged for killing poor dear Mr. Joseph's master, who prought him up, for Mr. Joseph's father was Lord Claverton's own servant."

"Claverton!" again repeated Gordon.

"But this is a Lord," answered his wife.

Ellen's bell rung, and put an end to the conference.

---

[14] I.e., the ground

Chapter II

With strong understanding, and fine sense, Lady Castle Howel was very deficient in what is sometimes understood by the phrase *common* sense, she felt as much gratitude to, and love for her hosts as the finest feelings of the finest language could depicture; yet it never occurred to her that the very best of all sorts of provisions to court her appetite, choice fruits and foreign wines were more than a poor Doctor could properly pay for, it is true she was extremely moderate in the quantity, but it was Gordon who catered in the quality of her table, and as both herself and servant were treated in a superior style to what was usual at the Doctor's, his last guinea was changed before he began to think about the circumstances of his guest, "certain," he said he was, "if she was poor she was not born so, and it was not possible she could incur misfortune by any fault of her own."

Mr. Gordon was very well read, and had an insatiable desire after knowledge; he had a large collection of ill bound books, lying in great disorder round a room he called his study, where it was his practice, to write in the morning the business of the day, that he might get it off his hands, the only thing in which he was methodical, if we except an unvaried attachment to his black coat, which was always put on the day it came from the tailor's, and worn till it would no longer hang decently together; he was of a cheerful, tho' studious turn, and his sociable temper was the result of an entire philanthropy of heart; he was as most Scotchmen are, fond of music, particularly the compositions of his own country; he played a little on the flute, and sang Ramsey's songs with peculiar taste; in his studies, music, and songs, Ellen became by degrees his constant associate, but neither reading, music, nor good humour will pay tradesmen's bills, or keep a good table, out of an income of fifty or sixty pounds a year.

Mrs. Gordon sent to an opulent farmer's wife to borrow two guineas, and the answer, without the loan, was, that "she would serve Mr. or Mrs. Gordon by night or by day, but as for hussies, who were big with child, the parish ought to provide for them; and indeed she would advise Mrs. Gordon to take care, she did not nurse a snake in her bosom!"

Mrs. Gordon was a very friendly good woman, but she was not perfect; fretful at the embarrassment their guest brought on them, she imperceptibly began to think it would have been quite as well, if the accident had not happened; and having been always used, whenever a difference of opinion occurred, to bring her husband round to hers, either by fair reason, or by tiring him out of opposition, found herself not a little hurt, that in this instance he was invincible, and her neighbour's hint, as well as her own observations of her husband's fondness for the society of their guest, which was growing fast into a first object with him, raised some sensations in her bosom altogether new, and by no means to be envied.

When the fiend jealousy gets possession of a woman's heart its power becomes entire; all the gentler and more amiable passions vanish; peevish and dissatisfied she no longer chatted with Winifred, or personally attended Ellen; Gordon was the first to observe this change in his wife, and attributed it to their embarrassed inconstancies, which tho' he knew he must retrench, he wanted resolution to go about.

Ellen's situation as she now drew very near her time, was also an inducement to his straining every nerve to serve her, he had treated her with such tenderness, and she had such confidence in his skill, he knew it would extremely shock her to hint at a removal, and yet, without money or means, what was to be done?

Mrs. Clover's suspicions and insinuations being against a person, who from Gordon's embarrassment must be supposed to be poor, made great way in the parish, and prodigiously scandalized a Methodist preacher, who occupied one of farmer Clover's barns every Sunday; the baker, the brewer and the butcher were alarmed, and the Doctor's house thronged with visitors of that sort, till poor Mrs Gordon grew quite outrageous.

"What does that greasy man want?" said Winifred, in her usual pert thoughtless manner.

"Money," answered Mrs. Gordon, roughly.

"Well, and why don't you cive it him?" said Win, smartly.

"Because," replied Mrs. Gordon, "both my money and credit are gone, in supporting you and your fine mistress."

"The Lort be coot unto me," said Winifred, "and so I dare say you have, and I never thought nothing of the matter; as to my Laty she never thinks of money."

"More shame for her, other people's husbands are I suppose to think for her."

"Ay, Cot help her, any poty's husband is petter as her own.'

Mrs. Gordon coloured, she believed so, but *she* was not to be made a fool of.

Win's understanding was literal, she suspected nothing of Mrs. Gordon's jealousy, tho' the want of money being explained she was perfect mistress of that, and went immediately to her Lady with an account that poor tear Mrs. Gordon had neither money nor credit.

Ellen turned pale, it was the first moment the expense she had been to the Gordons occurred to her recollection; she took out her purse to examine the state of her finances, – shame and mortification were the result, it did not contain sufficient to pay the nurse who attended her, much less to make compensation to the Doctor for his trouble, and the board of herself, and servant; she turned out her little stock upon the table, looked at Winifred and sighed.

Winifred sighed responsively, and took out of her pocket half a guinea, and some loose silver.

"We are sad contrivers, Winifred," said Ellen, "to venture on the world with such a poor stock to support us."

Winifred wiped a tear from either eye.

"What shall we do?" continued Ellen; "have we nothing we can sell to pay these honest people?"

Winifred made no answer but ran out of the room, and instantly returned with Lord Claverton's book, "Cot forgive me! pray Cot!" said she opening it, and displaying the notes, "praise the Lort for his mercy! amen! amen!"

Ellen shuddered, every part of that unfortunate transaction rushed into her mind; the film was removed, – she had seen and felt the impropriety of her conduct, and the pocket book now struck her as the ghost of her departed happiness and fame; she turned pale, her lips quivered, and a tear trembled in her eye.

"Cot of his plessed mercy, safe me!" cried Winifred, "what is the matter? shure and shure, I thought you would be glad to pay poor Mrs. Gordon, and I'm sure she wants it pad enough of all conscience; she sent Bett to farmer Clover's, to barrow two kinees yesterday morning, to pay for the white wine for your whey."

Ellen breathed a sigh that went to the heart of her faithful servant, who intending to comfort her went on.

"And here, Cot pless us! is enough to make us all happy, see my Laty shall I carry him this, let me see f-i-f – ay fifty – lort what pot hooks and hangers, these pank notes are, – now for my part give me coot yellow goult and hard silver. – Oh lort! help, help, my mistress is tead!"

Ellen's emotions had really so overcome her that she fainted.

Winifred's outcry brought in Mrs. Gordon, she left the bank notes scattered on the table, and flew to her mistress.

Mr. Gordon was unfortunately gone out, and all the compassion of his wife's nature, swallowed up by the green eyed monster; instead of attending to Ellen, she was amusing herself with looking over the book, and the notes, when Mrs. Holt entered.

This Lady had been two stages on the London road with Miss Holt on her way to town, and was returning to Durham, escorted by a friend of the Dean's.

It was now near two months since she had condescended so much as to enquire after our heroine: Dr. Ferguson represented to his numerous patients how ill he had been used in being sent at such an hour, to visit a woman who came from nobody knew where, was with child by nobody knew whom, and lived nobody knew how; all these nobodies made the Dean and his Lady ashamed of being charitable, but as they agreed the disgrace was less, particularly to Miss Holt, than if the nobodies were taken from the *who's,* they contented themselves with stopping his resentful communications, by a handsome present, and troubled themselves no more about the unworthy Countess.

Gordon's maid servant happened to be running across the meadow, in the instant Mrs. Holt was passing, and she felt an irresistible impulse to enquire after the Countess.

"How is your master?"

The girl out of breath answered, still running, "well."

"And your mistress?"

"Well."

"And the Lady?"

"Just dead."

Mrs. Holt immediately alighted and walked over the meadow in great agitation, and the door standing open entered the Doctor's mansion.

The first thing she saw, was Ellen fainting, and Mrs. Gordon looking at a pocket book with bank notes; Mrs. Gordon's attention to her guest, she could not but see, was greatly lessened, but she confined her observations to her own mind, poor Ellen being now recovering was on the point of leaving the room, Winifred stopped her.

" Oh tear mattam what dye call it, is it you? Cot pless your tear coot soul! My mistress have longed to see you."

Ellen's eye and extended hand confirmed her servant's assertion, and Mrs. Holt sat down.

The Countess looked on the notes and burst into an hysterical flood of tears.

Mrs. Holt took up the book, and seeing the name, started and laid it down again, "ay, madam," said she, shaking her head, "this is a sad witness, good morning."

Mrs. Gordon saw there was some mystery in all this, and followed her out. Mrs. Holt felt herself very much affected, "poor undone creature!" escaped her; and was heard by Mrs. Gordon, who ejaculated, " God forgive her!" "amen," said Mrs. Holt, and in the open indignation of her heart, sentences dropped from her that fully confirmed Mrs. Gordon's ill opinion; who waited her husband's return brimful of jealous spite, resolving her house should no longer be polluted by the residence of a creature she persuaded herself he preferred to her.

Meanwhile Ellen bid Winifred take that horrid book from her sight.

"What! must not she take one note for poor tear Mrs. Gordon, who had no money or credit,–"

"Not one!"

"Who, poor tear, paid all our pord and lodging, who was refused two kinees Bett tried to borrow!"

Ellen's temples seemed bursting, "take my watch, these rings, any thing but that book."

Winifred obeyed, but exclaimed as she went, "mercy and cootness! what would she say, if she knew all the money we have spent came out of the book."

But tho' Ellen's heart recoiled against using Lord Claverton's money, she was roused into a reflection on her situation respecting pecuniary matters. That Mr. Gordon and his family should be embarrassed was a reproach not only on the generosity but on the justice of her principles; and she immediately summoned Winifred to consult on measures, to repair the injury she conceived she had done them.

Winifred, then to her surprise, produced the jewel case, and she was extremely displeased at this second proof of worldly wisdom; but the maid, who had no such delicacy, feeling, or understanding, obstinately vindicated herself on the score, that

Ellen, Countess of Castle Howel 271

they could not even be buried without money, and that, Cot pless her! she had paid tear enough for jewels.

While they were separating the jewels, that had been presented to Ellen, from the family ones, Mrs. Gordon entered, "so," said she, throwing herself into a chair, "my husband is arrested; my dear Gordon, who I have lived with so many years in peace, must go to a prison at last."

"God forbid!" said Ellen, very much affected.

"Yes, and what vexes me is, it is not a debt of our own, we are always taking *other* people's troubles on ourselves," and Mrs. Gordon glanced a look at our heroine, as she intended, of great significance, but tho' it was lost on the person for whom it was designed, Winifred found the speech and gesture quite in her way, and understood their full meaning.

"Good God!" exclaimed Ellen, "I am very much grieved, and wish it was in my power – "

"You *wish* it was in your *power!*" answered Mrs Gordon, in a mixture of astonishment and rage.

Ellen sighed, "I have nothing but these jewels."

"*What* do you say, Madam?"

"I have nothing but these jewels, and have indeed some doubts whether they belong to me in strict justice, but if you can dispose of them,–"

The reader will please to recollect, a quarter of an hour before, Mrs. Gordon saw in Ellen's possession, a, pocket book with several bank notes, two of which were for £500 each, her *wish* therefore she had it in her *power* to serve Gordon, to whom she was so much obliged, and so much in debt, together with the baneful passion before mentioned, were provocations that might irritate a firmer mind than Mrs. Gordon's; her husband whom she loved entirely, under arrest, their credit stretched to its utmost limit, and fresh demands coming in every day, while the person, to support whom they had involved themselves, had a profusion of bank notes, and *wished* it was in her *power* to assist them, was too much.

"I touch your paltry baubles," retorted she, "no indeed, I dare say you stole them from some fellow, whom you have duped worse than my poor Gordon, if they are *worth* stealing."

Ellen stood amazed, the notes never recurred to her recollection, tho' she had that instant sent them away.

"I want no favour of such an ingrate – You have money in plenty; ill enough got, I dare say, but that does not matter; pay me for your board and lodging, and for my husband's attendance and trouble or *you* shall be arrested *too,* and since you have taught him to prefer *you* to his lawful *wife* you may go to prison together for what I care."

From a heart filled with anger, jealousy and distress, these violent expressions were not perhaps unnatural.

When Winifred heard her Mistress insulted by the Ladies of the Castle Howel family, her own feelings were wounded, she had ten times more pride in her rank, than Ellen ever had herself; and thought higher of her than any mortal living; but as she had been brought up with a strong sense of respect to her superiors, her resentments were generally confined to private invectives, with now and then impertinent mutterings, which however under her subordinate impressions were accompanied with fear and trembling. But this was a scene perfectly new; here was a woman, who she fancied she had taught to believe, as much of Ellen's infallibility, as she did herself; and who she had taken as much pains as possible, without actually betraying her name, to convince, she had under her roof a woman of the first quality, which indeed, till her mind became tinctured with jealousy, Mrs. Gordon was ready enough to believe, an inferior woman! the wife of a little village Doctor! presuming to abuse Lady Castle Howel, and wound her ears with insinuations of the most contemptible nature!

Winifred's eyes darted rage, her red cheeks turned pale, she gnashed her large teeth and going up to Mrs. Gordon fiercely asked, " If she knew who she talked to."

The jealous wife was not a jot behind her adversary in spirit or rage.

"No, I don't," replied she "for as to your bombast about her quality, I don't mind it *that,"* snapping her fingers.

"You don't," answered Winifred, trembling with increasing passion, from a two fold cause; first the indignity offered her mistress, second as it betrayed, notwithstanding all her injunctions, she had been babbling.

"No, a pretty story you trumped up, about Lords and Ladies; think any Lord would suffer his wife to be affronted by his old aunts; and as to Lord Claverton, if he was Captain Claverton, I know him better than you; he marry! he was lawfully married twenty three years ago, to a school fellow of mine, who I dare say is living yet, if *he* has not killed her, which however I would not swear.

I suppose some Lord took your fine Lady into keeping, and it was natural enough for his *sister,* and perhaps his *wife,* to turn her out of doors; no modest woman would go vagabondizing about the country in that situation that could help it."

"Now Cot of his creat cootness and mercy forgive me, pray Cot! and defend us from satan the father of lies! I shall certainly be your teath Mrs. Gordon."

A hungry tigress was Winifred, in looks and actions; at this moment she flew at Mrs. Gordon, who no way deficient in good will, sustained the attack, and attempted to return blow for blow, and scratch for scratch, but the Cambrian heroine overpowered the Caledonian one, who called out lustily for help; and at the entrance of her husband with a bailiff, who had him in his possession, and Mrs. Clover, who accidentally called in, she was found pinned into a corner by the victorious Winifred, who still unsated with vengeance, accompanied every assault with one or other of the provocative speeches, – "Stole the jewels! – duped your husband! – kept! – Lord Claverton married!

"Murder! Murder!" cried Mrs. Gordon but no sooner was she rescued from her conqueror, than her spirit renewed; she threatened her antagonist with a prison, and very eloquently avenged her wrongs on the head of the distressed Gordon; declared she had only asked the *woman* for her own, which to be sure Mrs. Clover thought very right; hinted at the barbarity of a husband's preferring the company and interest of another woman to his own wife, which Mrs. Clover declared was monstrous wrong; and finally concluded with an account of the bank notes, which tho' she had seen, and tho' she told her of her husband's arrest, she refused to pay a farthing, for all the trouble and expense they had been at.

"Tis the way of these creatures," said Mrs. Clover, "they don't care who they fleece, and many an honest woman suffers for them."

Mrs. Gordon's feelings were all in the most sensitive state, her flowing tears asserted to Mrs. Clover's sentiments.

For Mrs. Clover's part, she never suffered any flirt to come into her *house,* Dick Clover was bad enough abroad, God knew! a poor woman suffered enough without having creatures brought home; she could not help saying, she had a better opinion of Mr. Gordon, than to suspect him of such doings; but indeed she wondered how Mrs. Gordon could be blind so long, *poor woman! her heart* ached for her.

If any of our readers have known what it is to be in the hands of a bailiff, at a time when the sweetness of a mate's temper is disturbed by jealousy, they will feel the full force of this conversation, which bore the harder on poor Gordon, as it was the first time he discovered the least trait of that troublesome passion in his wife's disposition and he was entirely at a loss to account for it now; his kind heart sank as he understood, in process of her complaints, how much the feelings of our heroine had been hurt; and although she repeated to her good neighbour, with the quality stories the maid had, as she said, crammed her with, a list of the improbabilities of their truth, which indeed were many; the *good* opinion he formed of her was obstinate, and his own distress ceased to afflict him, as he considered what so pure a mind would suffer in such a situation.

"Where is the Lady?" said Gordon, impatiently. Both Lady and maid had left the room.

The Bailiff observed he had waited very long; and as neither money or bail were offered, he thought Mr. Gordon had better mind his own business, than talking of Ladies.

Both the women coincided.

Well! would Mrs. Clover be so good as lend him twelve pound? or suffer Mr. Clover, who was willing if *she* consented, to become bail?

"Do, dear Mrs. Clover," said Mrs. Gordon.

Mrs. Clover wondered how Mrs. Gordon could ask such a

thing of *her,* when she *herself* had just been convincing her what a *bad man* her husband was, he was a larned man, and ought to know "a house divided against itself, could not stand;"[15] she should not suffer her Dick to be any body's bail, not to save his own father, and she thought, Mr. Gordon should have spoken to *her* before he asked Dick; but indeed *one* bad husband made another, and therefore she would be very careful how she let Mr. Gordon come to Rye farm; and so she wished them good day; leaving the man and wife to the painful conviction, that however other people may be pleased to interfere in their disputes, or to share in their prosperity, they will be sure to have their distresses all to themselves.

The Bailiff was impatient, and Mrs. Gordon, at the sight of her worthy husband going to be taken from her, would have forgot her jealousy, had not Ellen's *power* to assist them, without the *will,* recurred to her distracted thought.

She burst into tears, wailing and invectives, while Gordon in despair of friends, was providing to go with the Bailiff; when her conjugal affection conquering every thing, she declared she would accompany him, and ran up stairs for her hat.

"This poor Lady," thought Gordon, "so near her time, what will she do?"

Mrs. Gordon returned, and putting a fifty pound note into the officer's hand, desired he would take debt and costs, and release her husband.

The man stared! rubbed his eyes! but it really was a bank of England note, and he hastened away with it to his employer.

Gordon supposing Ellen was in her chamber, and had given

---

[15] Quoting the Bible, Mark 3:25.

his wife the note, calmly reasoned with her on her behaviour; but how was he surprised and hurt to hear, that passing the door she saw the pocket book lie on the table, and urged by the necessity of the moment, had taken out the one of smallest value in the absence of the Lady.

"So then," said he, " you have not only injured this poor Lady, but robbed her! where is she?"

Mrs. Gordon neither knew nor cared, she said, in a voice that however contradicted the latter part of the assertion; for finding she had left the house, her heart which was a good one at bottom, had already begun to relent.

Her husband had never been angry with his Nancy before, not because he had not discovered faults in her, but because her good disposition and intentions threw a veil over them; but tho' he was the best tempered man in the world, there were provocations he could not resist; these were such as portrayed inward depravity, such he thought he now perceived, and he left her, with an indignant look, to search for his injured patient.

After going through all the apartments, he again passed his wife with the same angry countenance, to search in the garden and about the house; he crossed the meadows to the road, then went back to the village, made enquiries of every being he met, returned home again, questioned the maid, without speaking to his wife, and hearing nothing of Ellen, sallied out again in the same pursuit.

As the evening closed, the blackening clouds portended a storm, but neither rain, thunder or lightening appalled the good Gordon, who wandered about till midnight, when he returned, grieved, weary, wet and disappointed.

Mrs. Gordon affected and even frightened at her husband's

uncommon anger, and loving him too well to be easy when not friends, began to recollect herself, and not quite satisfied in her own mind, at the liberty she had taken with the property of another, carried the change as soon as she received it from the officer to Ellen's apartment.

She now saw Lord Claverton's name in the pocket book, and suspecting he was the identical Captain who both she and Gordon once knew, it gave rise to a train of reflections and suggestions.

What could possess Lord Claverton to be so profuse to a young Lady in the situation of their lodger? except she was either his own child or pregnant by him.

"My God!" said she, "if she should be his daughter."

Mrs. Gordon had no sooner stumbled as she thought on this strange discovery, than she became eager to establish it as a fact, and longed to communicate it to her husband, which having no present opportunity of doing, she returned to Ellen's chamber, and seeing the keys were left, proceeded to open the trunks, in hopes to find something that might confirm her idea, that our heroine was Lord Claverton's daughter.

Ellen, whose longest excursion since her residence at Gordon's, had been round the adjacent fields, and whose situation proscribed a certain style of dress, had worn nothing superior to muslin wrappers, these were however, so fine and elegantly laced, that they were considered as dishabilles by Mrs. Gordon, who was not in the habit of seeing rich cloaths.

Dress, and the etceteras appertaining to it, is a subject on which the female mind, from Catherine, the empress of all Russia, down to the water cress girl, whose bare legs are drenched in water in the coldest winter, delights to dwell: Mrs. Gordon feasted with infinite pleasure on trunks of fashionable costly cloaths, such as she never saw or imagined were worn; and among her other researches discovered a number of complimentary notes, addressed to The right honourable Countess of Castle Howel, which Winifred had converted into cases for lace, ribbons, &c. &c.

This discovery superseded the other, but it ended in combining them together; she had now no doubt but Lord Claverton's daughter was Lord Castle Howel's wife, and all her jealousy was converted into fear of the consequences of offending even the waiting maid of so great a Lady.

But where could she be all this while, and in such weather? and where too could Gordon be? his long stay could only be accounted for, by his having found or met her, and doubtless they were taking shelter from the weather, but Mr. Gordon's return involved them both in anxious perplexity; the discovery of Ellen's rank did not surprise him; nothing could raise her in his opinion, the accidental advantages of high birth and great riches, however desirable, were of less value to him than the amiable qualities of heart for which *his* gave *her* credit.

Mrs. Gordon endeavoured, for the first time in vain, to bring him into temper, he wandered in silent displeasure from room to room, and as soon as day broke, set off again on his hitherto fruitless search.

Chapter III

Never was consternation equal to Ellen's at Mrs. Gordon's behaviour, nor any thing so unaccountable to her as the transformation of the meek, friendly hostess into a fury, raging with invectives and inflamed with jealousy. Her heart oppressed with a succession of harassing events, her delicacy hurt and her feelings wounded, occasioned a kind of momentary delirium; in the midst of the battle she rushed out.

Mrs. Gordon's threats, when her husband and the officer entered, filled Winifred with fear and dismay; to be sent to prison was a thing she of all others thought the most dreadful, and therefore made her immediate escape, and happening fortunately to take the same path as her Lady, soon overtook her.

Ellen was walking on a slow solemn pace, tears trickling down her pale cheeks, her eyes now on the ground, and now lifted to heaven.

"The Lort look town on two poor sinners," sobbed Win, her hair about her ears and her cap in tatters.

Ellen turned round, and with a serious melancholy look reprehended her, for her incorrigible loquacity.

"Did I not charge you to keep my secret? why do you think did I change my name?"

"If ever I told that she wolf a letter of your name I wish the tivel may take me, please Cot this plessed moment."

"What does that signify, you have told all my family concerns, which is of much more consequence."

"As to that, sure you are no discrass to your family, and I

told the woman that she might keep her tistance. Cot pless us, sure it was not fit she should come with her pribbles and prabbles to you."

Ellen said she saw there was nothing to be done with her, but parting.

Winifred cried and vowed, but Ellen commanded her silence, and walked on without attending to the path, solicitous only to avoid the houses, and resting now and then as a style or stumps of trees invited.

She had proceeded in this absent way four hours, followed by Winifred, when the latter, who began to feel, notwithstanding her disgrace, that it was very far past dinner time, motioned to speak, but was again commanded to silence. They walked on.

They were now on a wild desolate heath, which terminated in a very thick wood; they had advanced without any track beyond the middle, when Winifred seeing the aspect of the clouds, ventured to touch her mistress's wrapper.

"For the lof of Cot, Matam, don't let us run about like the wild peasts, I am sure it will be a night not fit to turn a tog out; our Lion, Cot save his tear soul, always used to set up a tivilish howl when the clouds looked so plack; Lion was a fery coot hanimal."

What a train of ideas did this mention of Lion's sagacity raise; talk of weather! Ellen would have gone straight forward, 'amidst the clash of elements, and the crush of worlds.'[16]

Large drops of rain fell; the Countess's morning cap, and Winifred's bare head were ill adapted to stand the shower; the thunder rolled, livid lightning flashed. Nature gave way.

Ellen appalled and tired, sunk in the arms of Winifred on

---

[16] Slight misquote of Joseph Addison's play *Cato, A Tragedy* (first performed 1713).

the ground; the same slow dropping of rain continued, the thunder burst nearer on their ears, and the lightning flashed unintermittingly from the dark sky.

"The lort safe us," cried Winifred, "if it please his coot majesty. Oh! when I was at Code Gwyn—"

Ellen groaned.

"And inteed, *Castle Howel* was not so pad as–"

Ellen's eyes were raised, a flash of lightning made Winifred as well as her hide her face, as soon as the momentary terror was over, "and for the matter of that, my room was pretty enuff in Crosvenor-street, the ould cats, to be sure, did not call us thieves nor—"

Another flash.

"Oh Lort forcive her sins and transgressions! But cuss their spiteful hearts, they–"

Another flash.

"Cot preserve us poor harmless creatures, that with the plessing of Cot would not hurt a worm; they as coot as said, we was pad women, and I pray to Cot the tivel may take them away."

Another flash.

Winifred could bear it no longer, torrents of rain descended, which a little allayed the severity of the storm, but soon wetted our wanderers to the skin.

Winifred, like sailors in a storm, now ventured to disobey orders; she lifted Ellen up and insisted on endeavouring to reach the wood.

"Name o Cot, there was no danger of tigers in a Christian country."

Ellen, wet, cold, and indisposed, alternately fevered with severe pains, and chilled by the weather, was supported by Winifred till they gained the skirts of the wood.

"I *can* go no farther," said she, almost fainting.

Winifred, we have observed, on all common occasions of grief, was noisy, thoughtless, and obstinate. In the danger of Ellen from the overturn, where her care was of such importance, she showed a fortitude, attention and perseverance, that astonished every body who saw her uncommon volatility.

The same motive for courage and presence of mind, namely, love for her mistress operated now in the same manner; having laid every thing she could take off over and under her, she crept to a little rising ground, to see if she could distinguish any light, or sign of inhabitants.

The night was exceedingly dark, except when a dash of lightening showed a transient glance of surrounding objects.

Winifred had got with great caution to the top of a little hill, and saw nothing but darkness visible, when a sudden flash discovered a man just by her.

Whatever fright she might receive from a transient view of a tall figure in a drab great coat, it is not to be expressed what effect hers had on him; her head bare; her neck scarcely covered, a white gown, and the ashy white of her affrighted countenance, contrasted to her wet black hair and large eyes, was truly terrific.

Winifred screamed, and the first idea that struck her neighbour, after he had exclaimed, "What in the name of heaven is this!" was, that it must be some poor wandering maniac, who thus exposed herself to the horrors of such a night.

He addressed her in a soothing tone of voice, but the more he endeavoured to compose, the more loud and dismal were her shrieks.

Ellen, unable to see, and ignorant of the cause that carried

Winifred from her side, concluded that the wood was the haunt of ruffians, and gave herself up for lost.

The flash that discovered the two night wanderers to each other was the last, but the rain continued to pour, and the darkness was still the same.

Winifred continued to shriek and retreat from the hill, towards the place where she left Ellen, but mistaking the exact spot, she exalted her voice in a different tone, and falling on her knees began to pray in her Welch dialect, to be delivered from costs and apparitions, and not suffer her tear mistress to fall into the hands of satan.

"Good God!" exclaimed the man who still followed her.

Several successive shrieks from Winifred.

"Good God! do my ears deceive me, is it possible; is this Winifred Griffiths?"

"Oh Lort! oh Lort! I peg a thousand and a million partons, for all my sins and offences; oh Lort defent me from costs and all teatly sins, and deliver my poor Laty."

Tho' the distressed damsel had mistaken the exact spot where Ellen lay, two trees only divided them, and the continued agitation of her servant, at last gave her an exertion to call faintly, "Winifred."

"Oh, my God!" cried the man, "that voice, that voice, I cannot mistake it."

"Oh, tear, no no, for the lof Cot, say no more, put co to the crave in lightning as come."

By this time the man having fastened his horse to the branch of a tree, found his way to Ellen, and kneeling down,

"I cannot be deceived, my soul is responsive to the voice that in memory yet cheers my solitary life, it is, it must be Ellen Meredith."

"Oh! tear, tear, don't touch my Laty, avaunt satan; Cot almighty is above the tifel still, Cot preserve my Laty."

"Amen, dear Winifred, do you not know me?"

"Oh the cootness of cootness presarve us from temptation, and fornication, and murder, and all teatly sins! yes, I know you fery well; and as to the locket you cave me for my mistress, with the true lover's knot in hair, as I hope to see your poor tear restless soul tied town in the red sea."

"Ellen, dear Ellen, speak. Oh Winifred, she is cold, she is dead; great God, have I then satisfied the longing desire of my fond heart, to have her die in my arms?

"Percival Evelyn!" said a faintly reviving voice.

"Ellen Meredith!"

The involuntary embrace was witnessed by the goddess of Chastity, the moon rose in conscious majesty to enlighten a scene on which sensibility might banquet.

"My Cot, my Cot, is it your copreal poty[17] Mr. Evelyn, and not your cost'?"

Ellen was very ill, the meeting in such a place, and at such a time increased her pain, she was she believed dying.

Evelyn, anxious and distracted, was determined to get some assistance, he mounted his horse, and having found a track, with charge from our heroine to take care of himself, rode on a smart pace into the wood, till he came to a shallow river, that, swelled by the torrent, rushed loud and foaming over the broad stones, on the opposite side, which at first appeared to be one huge rock covered with ivy and other creepers. A small glimmer of light, which glanced thro' different chinks, as they seemed, and became at last stationary, tho' he could not distinguish whether

---

[17] I.e., corporeal body

through a latrice or a fracture in a wall, inspired the welcome hope of obtaining help for the idol of his heart, and gave an additional strength to his lungs, he hallooed till the woods reverberated the sound.

A female voice answered from the opposite side.

Evelyn told his tale, and offered any money for accommodations for his sick friend.

The light disappeared, all was silent, he waited a few minutes, and then more impatient from disappointment hallooed, in a still louder voice; not being answered, he was on the point of plunging into the stream, when providentially he turned his head, and saw a light advancing by the water edge, on the side he then was.

An old man and two young ones with lanterns, came as they informed him, from the opposite side to his assistance, they showed him where was a safe crossing and offered their services to his friend; he soon returned to the spot where he had left the fair wanderer, and before the men got up had placed her on his horse, and mounted behind to support her.

They crossed the river, and following their guide by a steep and winding ascent, after great difficulty got round to the front of a very ancient pile of building; the old man gave a single knock which echoed thro' the wood; and the door was opened without a living creature appearing, which miracle was effected by means of a rope, passing through pullies close to the kitchen fire place, and saved the inhabitants many a cold facing of the winter weather.

Evelyn started and Winifred's fears, when she concluded for certain it was Evelyn's ghost returned, she ran up to him and felt his hands, to be sure *he* was, as she said, *he,* and being satisfied, whispered in terror, that this was one of the *magicians'* Castles Miss Catherine used to read of.

Evelyn bid her be confident, and they passed thro' a large quadrangle court to another door, where a knocker as massy as the first, was answered by the appearance of a clean elderly woman, followed by a young one, and lighted by a mean country girl; from this door they had to go thro' a long broad stone passage, so cold, it struck a chill into Winifred's heart, and the sound of their feet reverberating, persuaded her they were followed by a number of people, – she got very close to Mr. Evelyn, who with the assistance of one of the young men, were carrying Ellen, and turning her head with great caution, saw as she thought a row of armed men at small distances on each side, this was worse than the ghost, she could not even pray, and her fears were so strong she did not perceive, they were stone images placed in niches of the wall.

As the Lady was so ill the woman sent the girl forward to make a fire in a bed chamber, and ordered the men to put fresh billets of wood on the fire below.

The stair case was stone, extremely wide, the steps in many places broken and adorned with the same terrific figures that first annoyed Winifred; after ascending the winding stairs they had the same length of gallery, with the passage, which led quite round the building, to pass, before they came to one *habitable* room.

The old woman, who was distinguished by the appellation of Dame, had fortunately brought up a large family of her own, she put Ellen to bed with great tenderness, and having given her a bason of whey, in which she infused a few drops of poppy juice of her own distilling, watched by her bedside till morning.

Chapter IV

Except Winifred had been robbed, and half stripped by banditti, it was impossible for any body, not acquainted with the occurrences of the preceding day, to account for her appearance; she had neglected to gather up the cloaths taken off in the wood for the convenience of her Lady, so that she was now literally half naked. The people of the house were not more surprised than Percival; "for heaven's sake, Winifred" said he, when they met round the great fire, where being furnished with cloaths, while their own were drying, "how came you in this dreadful plight?"

Even Winifred was now quite down, strong as her constitution was, she could not bear up against such weather and fatigue as she had been exposed to; and her mistress being composed, she was sensible to a violent head ache, a sore throat, and a pain in her limbs.

"Oh, Lort! Mr. Evelyn, ax no manner of questions, for I am sure I am tying, but the witch that said my Laty stole the jewels, Cot, I mauled her."

Evelyn was struck to the heart, stole jewels! Ellen accused of stealing! was it possible such an insult could be offered to one who mixed in all his aspirations to heaven! He would have asked an explanation, but the words died on his tongue.

"What have you been boxing, young woman?" said one of the men, laughing, "are you good at that?"

"Not fery coot, Cot save me, at any thing now," answered she, wiping her eyes, "but I wish I was in a pig stye at Code Gwyn, that I know."

"Ah! Winifred, those were happy days."

"And nights too, Mr. Evelyn, the tivel's cloven foot covers all Englant I believe; tit you ever see such a night at Code Gwyn as this?"

"Many, Winifred; but you nor your mistress were never exposed to such a one."

"No, Lort help us! once is enough to kill a tog; I am sure I am fery ill. I know that." Another bason of whey was now administered to her, and the maid showed her to a small bed, in a room on the ground floor, where, as she had to pass the armed figures to go to it, she certainly would not have stayed, if she had been able to explore the way to her mistress; but as she durst not venture into the passage alone, and as she really was by this time very ill, she was obliged to stay.

Evelyn was also shown to a room, but his mind was in so perturbed a state, the waters of Lethe, instead of whey and poppy juice, would hardly have composed it.

Percival Evelyn had a confused remembrance of leaving a woman he was very fond of, and of being put to school with a clergyman's widow, who had a few more boys of the same age, under her care, and perfectly recollected being taken from her by Mr. Edward Meredith, and carried a long journey to Code Gwyn, where he soon became the companion of Ellen Meredith.

Mr. Meredith's attention to his morals and learning was incessant, and as he grew up the affection of a father, was blended with the instruction of a tutor, in so much that many people gave him the credit of being one; and even Sir Arthur once seriously questioned his son on the subject, and received a decided negative.

"What, or who you are my dear Evelyn," he would say, "as you have no *friend* but me, is of little import; if by telling you every particular I know, and they are *not many,* I could do you service, or give you pleasure, I would not one moment deprive you of either; but, when I tell you, that is *not* the case, and that the subject gives me exquisite pain, I expect you will rest confident, that though no tie of blood unites us, I will, in every essential sense, be a parent to you, and repel a curiosity that cannot be gratified, without hurting my feelings."

From this excellent man young Evelyn received every advantage. Mr. Meredith's education was liberal, his talents, understanding and learning qualified him to be private tutor to the first man in the kingdom, as his extreme modesty, his entire ignorance in the points enforced by a late noble tutor to *his son,*[18] his ill health and sedentary turn of mind, unqualified him to be a *public* one.

He was an exceeding good classical scholar, his books were well chosen, and, what does not always happen, they were also well read. Every human being has some favourite habit of relaxation and amusement, Mr. Meredith's was the improvement of his pupil, and he was overpaid by his docility, talents and gratitude.

As Percival was three years older than Ellen, he led in all their infant sports, and became her habitual protector.

There are some, and those among the most learned and liberal, who, at the same time that they recommend the sedulous application of every moment to the education of every [man] think very lightly of the time or application proper for the other sex, of this number were Sir Arthur Meredith and his son.

---

[18] See Lord Chesterfield's *Letters to His Son on the Art of Becoming a Man of the World and a Gentleman*, published posthumously in 1774.

The Miss Merediths had been taught to read and write in their father's house; Lady Meredith was herself very accomplished, she was perfect mistress of all the polite attainments of her day, but her large and increasing family engrossed with her duty and affection all her time and attention; and their circumstances, which rendered every expense that carried ready money out of the steward's hands an object, though it did not prevent Mr. Meredith's college learning and a liberal establishment there, was certainly a reason why Sir Arthur's opinion that "no woman need be a scholar," was adopted in the family, for Lady Meredith, with an affluent fortune would have thought very different. However, an established rule for his daughters could not be expected to give way in favour of an orphan grand daughter, and thus, while the whole attention of the reverend Mr. Meredith was given to an Eleve, who had no natural claims on him, his own niece was suffered to run wild about his father's house, every body petting, and every body, while they doated on her infant beauty and vivacity, neglecting a mind that wanted nothing but instruction.

Application to study was from habit second nature to Percival, but every holiday, every hour of recess grew insensibly dearer, because it restored him to the companion, who from his infant state, became a part of his vital existence.

A lad of seventeen will pointedly admire the charms of a girl of fourteen; he will delight in the society of a lively sweet tempered young creature, who also loves *him,* with as much warmth, and *more* sincerity perhaps than at the maturest age. Evelyn early saw the difference between his play fellow and other girls of her age; and had she not been so infinitely their superior, he would have thought her so. Thus cherishing a passion, which for *such* an object, had no chance of sating on his imagination, even when reason was called to the council of his heart, his time passed in a happy delirium of friendship and passion, till the attentions of Lord Claverton gave rise to the most tormenting sensations, and all the raptures of pure and unbounded love were swallowed in the pangs of jealousy.

It is true, no being stood in a higher degree of favour with the Code Gwyn family than himself; and while he was the unrivalled companion of Ellen, while she parted with him with regret, and met him with joy; while his eyes, and *his alone,* dwelt in ecstasy on her face; he forgot his obligation, his dependence, and his poverty. But the splendid advantages of his rival, turned his dejected thoughts on himself, – the comparison was misery. Lord Claverton's stay was attended with inconvenience, Mr. Meredith was obliged to live entirely at the Parsonage, and as no title or rank unadorned with internal virtues had attraction for *him,* day after day sometimes past without visiting Code Gwyn, and how could the humble Evelyn intrude where Lord Claverton was a visitor, without his friend, his patron, his protector?

Night, propitious equally to happy and despairing lovers, carried him to the environs of Code Gwyn, and he returned comparatively happy, if, after walking round the house, till his limbs were almost frozen, and laying his ear close to the window, he could distinguish the sound of her voice. To the sensible, the delicate, and really attached, voice is a part of the beloved object, which sinks into the heart of hearts, and is never forgotten; the gross, the cautious, or the worldly lover, will not understand this assertion, but it appeals to all of Evelyn's description for its truth.

Lord Claverton, at the time he first visited Code Gwyn, had the sickly remains of great personal attractions, he allowed himself to be in his thirty-fourth year, but really was in his thirty-ninth. He left England, one of those notorious officers of twenty-one, whose achievements in the guards are so well known, on account of declining a challenge from the brother of a young girl, his landlady's daughter, who he had seduced under promise of marriage. His brother officers *did not, could not,* blame him for the *seduction,* but the *not* killing her brother, or being killed by him, was an offence, the court of honour could not pardon; the young captain, it is true, was not fond of exposing the prettiest person in his corps to an unmannerly bullet. "Then marry, sir," said the spirited youth. "I am married already," answered the Captain. "When? and to whom?"

As the Captain *would* not, or *could* not tell, he was reduced to the necessity of evading the challenge, by a pretence that the challenger was not a gentleman, in as much as he kept a linen draper's shop, a misfortune that did not entitle him to commit murder; and the mother of the ruined girl, desirous to escape a second obligation to the noble Captain, having discovered the vindictive intentions of her son, gave information to a justice of the peace, which, with respect to him, ended the business.

But not so with the noble Captain, his brother officers sent *him* to Coventry; and the improbability of his continuing in a corps, where he was held in contempt, brought a number of impertinent people to his levee, who pretended they had as much right to receive satisfaction, in their way, as the linen draper had in *his*. The distressed hero applied to his uncle (father or mother he had not), Lord Viscount Claverton and his three cousins, the honourable Mr. Clavertons; but it was not possible to countenance an officer who would not fight a duel!

for the honour of the family. However, they got him leave to exchange his lieutenancy in the guards, for a company abroad, and out of the same regard to family honour, assisted him to escape the vigilance of his creditors, – among whom, to a considerable amount, were the linen draper and his mother.

Although the Captain's creditors did not follow him to the West Indies, his disposition did; but he had been challenged, sent to Coventry, and narrowly escaped a prison, to little purpose, if he did not profit something by experience; he indeed was cautious to intrigue with women who had no spirited relations; he kept *well* with his brother officers, and he took care to spend debts of any man's contracting but his own.

A long residence abroad, where his being a man of family, handsome and well bred, secured him a favourable reception, and the impossibility of escaping certain troublesome visitors, if he returned home, induced him, when the regiment was relieved, to keep on exchange, and he lived several years in that unhealthy climate, before he was at all affected by it.

But for two years previous to his return home, he had been in a very ill state of health, and being recommended a sea excursion, took the opportunity of going on a small cruise in a man of war, on the station, where his acquaintance commenced with Lewis Meredith, with whom, as before related, he visited Code Gwyn, to the great regret, and anguish of the youth, whose history his lordship has, undesignedly, interrupted.

What can escape the Lynx-eye of jealousy? Lord Claverton scarce trusted *himself* with his designs on Ellen, and it was with extreme caution that he disclosed any part of them to Macshean. But Evelyn, novice as he was, penetrated into his heart, *he* saw the passion which animated his countenance, when in her presence, and the entire apathy that took possession of it when she was absent; his mind, which now underwent a total change, panted for title, rank and riches, for with these he thought it was possible to obtain Ellen; Mr. Meredith designed him for the church, and opened to his hope the possibility of his one day succeeding in the rectory, but that *one day* was an eternity; what would become of Ellen, long, long before that?

An appetite for learning, all enjoyment of the present, and hope for the future, were now absorbed in a passion as hopeless as violent; what was existence to Percival, if Ellen was another's? *She* was light and life to *him;* he rambled through those walks, where she had hung on his arm, her voice sounded in every breeze, and wherever he looked, her face was before his eyes; sometimes in the violence of youthful despair he was tempted to put a period to his agonies and existence together, and once actually pointed the muzzle of his fowling piece to his ear; at others he would give way to sighs and tears, and more than once he had hid himself from Mr. Meredith, when in a state of insobriety.

These agitations of the mind preyed on his health, yet he rejoiced when he heard of Lord Castle Howel's intention, from *him* he had nothing to fear, from Lord Claverton every thing. He had taken leave of Ellen at Code Gwyn, the night before she was to set out for Bath, in the presence of her family, she wept, – and twice followed him to the door, merely to say, God bless you, Evelyn, – yet one look more was so much the object of his wish, that he slept not the whole night, and by break of day, he was in his usual loitering place at Code Gwyn.

Ellen's mind little less agitated, although not quite so well acquainted with the cause, deprived her too of rest; she was early at her chamber window, and the first object she saw was Percival, wrapped in his great coat, and leaning pensively against a tree, with his eyes fixed on her window; this was a moment worth a diadem to Evelyn, he easily prevailed on her to join him, and had the happiness to hear from her lips, in answer to professions in which his soul was blended, that *she* loved *him* better than any body in the world, except her grand-mamma – and – and the rest of her relations; after this it was no difficult matter to persuade her, she ought not to marry any body but *him,* or at least without *his* consent, which she solemnly promised she would not, – and on the faith of this promise they parted.

With such an object in distant view, Evelyn returned to his studies with redoubled ardour, and straightened as the Merediths were for money, his friend sent him to college, where he was nourishing his first passion still in his heart, with the warmest enthusiasm, when he received Ellen's letter. His answer gave her up, but his passion was the same; a fever was the consequence of the noble sacrifice to honour and duty, that left him in almost a dying state. Mr. Meredith, notwithstanding he knew the situation of his mind, insisted on having him to his house, where he might attend to every turn of his health himself, but as this was about the time of Ellen's marriage, forbid her name to be mentioned, during his slow recovery; he however found means through his old friend David, to hear every thing concerning her, and was watching for one look when seen by Winifred as before mentioned.

Evelyn had now time for meditation. Ellen was no more to be the solace of his thoughts, the object of his hopes, the latter she indeed was not, but the former she could not cease to be; he read her letter over and over, – the motives for her marriage were at once an oblation to his love, and a dagger to his heart. "*I* too" said, he, "have contributed to my own misery; I have been an expensive tax on the goodness of my friend, I still am, but will not remain so;" he threw himself at the feet of Mr. Meredith, opened his heart, and implored him to procure his ordination, that he might no longer be a burden to him.

Mr. Meredith assured him it was impossible he could ever consider him in that light, and less so now than ever, since the friendship of Lord Castle Howel had so essentially –

"Oh, my dear sir, spare me, spare me," interrupted he, "shall I then owe to the husband of Ellen Meredith?" – he stopped unable to proceed; his friend understood the delicacy of the unuttered sentiment, and went with him to the Bishop of St. David, who ordained, and introduced him to Dean Holt, then on a visit at St. David's, by whose recommendation, he was settled in a respectable cure, at the time he, fortunately for Ellen, lost his way on the heath.

The Dean introduced him to his family, and he was at this time, so great a favourite with Mrs. Holt, she had made him escort her and Caroline, and he was now returning to his cure; little did he think, when that Lady left her carriage in the morning, it was to visit Lady Castle Howel; and less could he expect to see her himself, in the situation in which he found her.

Ellen was unable to rise in the morning, but the pains which the old women declared were the symptoms of approaching labour, did not deprive her of the strength of mind, misfortune had taught her, – although the presence of Evelyn, at such an interesting moment, had perhaps saved her life, and although strong as her early attachment had been to him, it was impossible but she must feel, at a re-encounter so unexpected a variety of sensations, both pleasing and painful; yet, she did not forget that she was wife to a man of honour, and, that respectful as Evelyn behaved, words had dropped from him, that proved he yet thought of her, with more tenderness than was consistent with his sacred character, and her situation; besides this, what had she not already suffered, from false appearances, and what a handle might not her enemies make of an event so purely accidental; that Evelyn loved, and had been beloved by her, was, she believed, a secret known only to themselves, but it was therefore the more imprudent to remain in any situation which might sooth so improper a passion in him, or renew it in her. She got up as soon as her strength would admit, and her wrapper being washed and white as her own fine complexion, sent for Evelyn to her room.

He entered, as if sentence of death was going to be passed on him; he saw the woman he adored, who when he parted last with her was beauty's self, in the bloom of health, and spring of youth; now pale and languid, unattended by the appendages of splendour, unassisted by the friends of simplicity; he had *heard,* but did not *believe* she had forsaken the paths of honour; yet the situation in which he found her and her servant, was so strange, so inexplicable, that his own conjectures distressed and bewildered him, – but he saw her, heard her speak, and remembered nothing else.

Ellen also *saw* him, – saw him infinitely improved in his person and manner, but the same interesting countenance, and the same crimson glow that had ever animated it when his eyes met hers – she also coloured, hesitated, then was silent.

Percival yet stood before her, his eyes were indeed fixed on her face, but his imagination reverted to time and circumstances for ever gone; he burst into an agony of tears, and threw himself at her feet.

Ellen, Countess of Castle Howel

Ellen was affected, but tho' she wanted courage to address him, in the manner she intended, and her heart told her was right, she felt every moment more and more, how improper his stay with her was, she stammered –

"Rise, sir, rise Mr. Evelyn, this is no time, – no place, – I am a wife, – you must leave me."

"I know I must, Madam, else why this agony of soul? if I dared stay and watch over you, if I might guard you from insult and shield you from danger, should I feel as I do at this instant? Oh, God! why, why did I give you up that dear promise? why did I not rather claim the happy privilege of working, of begging for you?"

"I can't hear this, sir, you must leave me this moment, I am ill, I can't bear it; alas I have learned to suffer, but do not you, sir, Percival, dear Percival, do not you degrade your once loved Ellen; go, sir, I wish you happy, but I see you no more, no, not to save me from death."

She changed colour, trembled, gasped for breath, and could not speak, but motioned for him to go; Percival, who used to watch every turn of her speaking countenance, saw her agitation.

"Tell me Ellen, but where you came from, and where you are going, and say you will sometimes think of him, who will love you to death."

When Ellen went from Gordon's she had no design entirely to leave them, at least not that day; but revolving over her unhappy fate, had wandered on in inconceivable agony of mind, abstracted from every present object; Percival's question brought the whole occurrence to her mind.

"Go, Percival, go, sir," was her answer.

"Only say I shall hear from you."

"Why won't you go, Evelyn? how can you distress me so? if you were to be seen with me -"

"Beloved of my soul, can there be harm in letting me know where you are? how can I leave you in this situation? reflect *how* and *where* I found you, dear Ellen," and he again kneeled; the door opened and in came the old woman and Mr. Gordon, – he stood aghast.

As soon as it was day, the old hostess, whose name was Spackman, on presumption of her own judgement, sent her son to the next village for a Doctor; Mr. Gordon, who set out about the same time from home, happened to be enquiring after his patient at that place, and hearing a man talking at the apothecary's door, of some stranger ill at his mother's, listened, and to his infinite joy, heard of the lost sheep, and immediately took the lad's directions and set off.

Gordon's faith in our heroine was a little staggered when he saw a handsome young man at her feet, but the joy that lighted up her countenance at sight of him, was so flattering he could not remember a moment, the possibility of her having a fault; he gently reproached her for the uneasiness she had given him, "if you had gone to the world's end," said he, "I would have followed you, till I knew you were safe and well."

Percival drew near and offered his hand, "my heart," said he, "claims your acquaintance."

"It is a gentleman," said Ellen, in the frankness of her heart, "who was the companion of my childhood. I find my servant has been telling one half of my story and you shall hear it all. This, Mr. Evelyn, is Mr. Gordon, a gentleman to whom I owe –"

"Gordon," repeated Evelyn, "what, of Little Manor?"

Gordon bowed, "and did you receive a visit from Mrs. Holt yesterday?"

"What Mrs. Holt?" asked Ellen.

Gordon explained, that the Lady who saw her accident, and since often visited her, was Mrs. Holt, of Durham.

Ellen again coloured.

"I thought it was odd enough," continued Gordon, "you should be of the same name, but as she desired me not to mention hers, I concluded it did not signify telling her yours."

Ellen eagerly asked if it was Caroline Holt, Lady Mappleton's daughter, who rode with her in the chariot; Gordon did not know, but he was struck with the interest she seemed to feel for one who Mrs. Holt said was a mere stranger.

Ellen paused, and seeing Evelyn eagerly attentive, told Gordon his caution with respect to her was useless; for the Ladies knew her real name, which she confessed was not Holt; "you are surprised, Evelyn," continued she, with a languid smile, "but tho' I cannot be your acquaintance myself, I introduce you to Mr. Gordon, to whom you are at liberty to make what communications you please concerning me; and you, Mr. Gordon, may be equally frank to Mr. Evelyn; I feel myself ill, you must retire; you Percival must leave the house immediately, and as I am undetermined what step I shall next take, I charge you keep this adventure secret;" then extending a white hand to each, they bowed over it by one impulse and withdrew.

Evelyn returned to the door.

"One look, Ellen, it may be the last; I have before parted with you, but you was then in the protection of your family; *now –*"

"Don't tease me, Percival, you must go;" interrupted she impatiently, "I know your friendship, and I know Gordon's;

somebody has said, "poor is the friendless master of the world,"[19] now I have two friends, when I was mistress of the world, or at least, more of it than I made good use of, I had not one, but with the same author, I bless the exchange, and call it "gain"; you may correspond with Gordon, but I *will* not, *must* not hear your name mentioned."

"But you left Gordon, Ellen, left him ignorant of your fate, this man, whom you call your friend, he at least is not in my wretched situation; yet you left his roof, you exposed yourself to the extremest misery, and the apprehension of what may yet happen to you rends my heart."

"Rest satisfied Percival, I do not at present think I shall return to Little Manor, but wherever I go, whatever step I take, I will ask Gordon's advice, once more farewell," and a sweet blush diffusing the cheeks, which were stained by an involuntary crystal drop, "God bless my friend!"

Percival retired with precipitation, and Ellen exhausted, affected, and indisposed, threw herself on the bed.

Gordon was in the mean time, gone to visit Winifred, he found her with some degree of fever, and an ulcerated sore throat, which rendered her swallow and utterance extremely painful; she was rejoiced to see Gordon in that dismal place, and as well as she could, enquired for her Lady.

"If I tie, as Cot knows I may, you will take care of my Laty, and here is one Mr. Evelyn, Cot forgive my sins." As she spoke with difficulty, Mr. Gordon enjoined her silence, and having directed a gargle, left her to join Evelyn, with whom,

---

[19] Quoting Edward Young's poem *The Complaint: or, Night-Thoughts on Life, Death & Immortality. Night II. On Time, Death, And Friendship* (1742-45)

in earnest discourse, he walked round the outside of the court yard, and to their mutual surprise, found themselves in front of a neat modern building, with every appearance of fairy land about it, – it attracted their transient observation, but the subject of their conversation was of too interesting a nature, to be broken by mere passive objects.

After two hours passed in preliminaries of confidence, and unreserved friendship, Evelyn liberally rewarded old farmer Spackman for his trouble, mounted his horse and took his leave; and Gordon having taken abundance of pains to conceal the traces of tears from his eyes, returned to the house; he was met at the door by the young woman, who told him the Lady was very ill indeed.

In two hours Ellen was a mother, and Castle Howel had an heir, this event as to the birth of the child, and every circumstance to establish its nativity, Mr. Gordon took care to have particularly witnessed, and the infant being cloathed from the hoards Mrs. Spackman kept in careful preservation, for her Patty, was presented to his young mother, who had not yet entered her nineteenth year; who can describe the new, and exquisite sensations, that fill a mother's breast at the sight of her first born, – that is, such as God and nature have made mothers; not such as content themselves with the appellation only, and leave the duties of the maternal character to hired substitutes.

Ellen pressed the little stranger to her heart, she contemplated his features, with a mixture of sensations not to be conceived, she bathed his cherub face with her tears, and longed to have her faithful Winifred's assistance, in marking out lineaments of wisdom and goodness, in the most beautiful face *she* had ever seen.

Mr. Gordon now returned to the room, and told her, in a

whisper, her speedy recovery depended on herself; "if" said he, seeing her tears, "you give way to these sensations, I will not even answer for your life."

"Oh," said she, pressing her little one to her heart, "who will then be a mother to my child?"

"For his sake then you must be content, to give him to the care of a nurse."

"Oh, never! never! I will never part with him!"

Gordon looked very grave, "you know not what you say, – you have not considered."

"Oh, yes, I have, they may tear me to pieces, but I won't part with my child."

Gordon looked still graver, "It is impossible for you to nurse that child yourself."

"Why so, sir? how many poor weak women have I seen nursing their children; I am young and healthy."

"I tell you," said Gordon, peevishly, " 'tis impossible," but after a pause, "we will think about it, you must now let Mrs. Spackman put the child in her cradle, and compose yourself." Ellen would have answered, but Gordon was absolute.

When Gordon left the room, he casually inquired who lived in the modern house next door.

Dame Spackman told him, they had both one owner, that the estate was left to the present possessor, on condition of keeping the ancient mansion, which in the eighth Harry's time was a large monastery, in the situation they found it; that her husband was the hired farmer of what grounds were not let, and she had the whole care of the old house.

Ellen slept well, and the medicines he gave her, with the profound quiet of the room, contributed to her speedy recovery; she had her child constantly brought to her while awake, and on putting her curtain back the third day, saw Gordon had carried his point, the child was at the breast of a very hearty looking young woman.

Winifred was still ill, and as she was not in danger, Gordon thought it extremely lucky, "as her tongue" he said "was the perpetual motion."

Mr. Evelyn had agreed to call on Mrs. Gordon, and account for her husband's absence, from which she had suffered so much; and from her researches among Ellen's cloaths, being so convinced that she was in the first place *somebody,* and in the next, that being somebody, and so young and handsome, it could be no object to her to seduce her Gordon, had entirely conquered her jealousy; and the happy medium being no part of Mrs. Gordon's character, she was now as eager to see her late guest, out of renewed regard, as she had been to affront her, out of the mere vindictive spite of the green eyed monster.

She accordingly packed up the changes she knew would be necessary, with the very few child bed cloaths Ellen had provided, and begged Mr. Curate, as she called Evelyn, who tho' he had ten miles of indifferent road to ride, was her daily visitor, to take her to visit Mrs. Holt – as she still called her – this he gladly undertook, but having set her down out of a post chaise, returned without being seen by the family.

Ellen, by this time sufficiently recovered to sit up an hour in the day, was fondling her infant, when Gordon led in his wife; she was too much obliged to the husband, and indeed, understood too little of the meaning of her invectives, to retain resentment against the wife. Not so Winifred, who lay under the torture of a large gathering in her throat, who no sooner saw Mrs. Gordon than her ire rose, she attempted to speak; the words "witch" and "my Lady" were at last articulate, and the effort occasioned a favourable turn in her disorder, tho' both herself and Mrs. Gordon thought she was dying.

Mrs. Gordon's arrival was very convenient, for the Spackmans had received instruction to prepare for the reception of the owner of the mansion, who, with company, were on the road, and as Mrs. Spackman, tho' there were servants, and a housekeeper in the new house, always assisted in preparing it, she was obliged to absent herself from Ellen's chamber; Mrs. Gordon therefore took her place, and grew almost as fond of the little nursery, as the nurse who suckled it; Winifred now began to recover, and as soon as Gordon would permit her, went to Ellen's room.

The poor faithful girl, overcome with joy, fell on her knees by the door, she was forbid to go farther, and all her volubility, overpowered by her sensation, could only sob and cry.

Ellen wept too and pointed to her child.

Winifred then found her tongue.

"Oh the tear sweet angel of a papy, tivel take me put it is the picture of my old master, Oh, Lort! Oh, Lort! will you let the ould Cats have him?"

Ellen had pondered over that matter; bold in maternal affection, no longer hesitating and deficient in resolution, no longer wavering about her future destination, she had *arranged* and *resolved.*

If the child was claimed by his father, she supposed the law, and if not that, power would take him from her; of the importance to the family of an heir, she was fully acquainted; of their little regard to her feelings, she had proofs enough; but all other considerations absorbed in the new and delightful feelings of a mother, one point only seemed desirable, which was that of retaining her child.

"If they receive me at Code Gwyn," would she say, "their obligations to the husband will weaken the defence of the wife; and if they believe me guilty, will they not think me indefensible, in retaining the heir of a noble family from his father? alas in the spirit of integrity they will forget I am the mother, I will not go *there.*"

No longer delicate about the jewels, she considered them now as her indubitable right, and predetermined to send Gordon with them to London, to sell, and then retire into some remote part of the world, where she might enjoy her child in peace.

"Let who have him?" said Mrs. Gordon.

"What's that to you, name o Cot," answered Winifred; then addressing Ellen, "if they once set their ugly eyes on the tear papy, we shall never see him again as long as the world stands, no, nor after neither, for to be sure, all that tivelish clang will, please Cot, go to satan!"

"We shall see," said Ellen, profiting by the experience of Winifred's gossip, which had like to have cost her so dear.

"Well," answered Winifred, sitting on the ground at the door, and wrapping the skirt of her gown round her shoulders, "you may see and hear what you please, and Dr. Gordon says, I must not come near you with my throat, put tivel take me, if let the tear papy out of my own sight."

"Indeed but you will," said Gordon; "did not you promise not to say a word to your Lady, more than to ask how she did? Come, you shan't see her again this fortnight."

"Why, pray now, Mr. Gordon, what have I said?"

"Too much a great deal"

"The tivel take me, if I spoke one word,—"

"An't you a little afraid, Mrs. Winifred?"

"Afraid of what?" and she closed up to Gordon.

"Why, of that black gentleman, whose name you are so often taking in vain."

"No, Mr. Gordon, I defy satan and all his works, and the tifel take me if I am – afraid – of – of – of any thing but apparitions and costs, and to be sure this house looks like the ten of evil spirits."

"Well, get you down stairs, and settle that matter, as you can, for here you must not stay."

"That's very civil of you, Mr. Doctor, but I'd have you to know—"

"Tell it me below stairs then," said Gordon, putting her arm under his, and forcing her half crying, half scolding out of the room, – "well now, what would you have me to know?"

"Tifel take me, if you shall know any thing from me," and she flounced the door in his face.

Gordon insisted she should not yet repeat her visit, and seeing a number of servants busy, taking portmanteaus to the upper rooms, he also charged her not to let her tongue run.

"Tut, tut, tifel take me, if I care a pin for you, Mr. Gordon," bawled the enraged damsel.

Mr. Gordon then went home, which he had entirely neglected, to reconnoitre matters there.

Ellen, full of her intended plan, longed to communicate as much of it as was safe to Winifred; who being now convalescent, relieved Mrs. Gordon, and sat up with her, she took this opportunity to hold a confab which as it was to be a great secret, was divulged by Lady Castle Howel as she lay, and as Winifred knelt by her bedside, – the nurse, who suckled the infant, lay in an adjoining apartment, but, as the having the infant sleep on her own arm, was a great treat to Ellen, and as the looking at, and admiring it was as great a one to her maid, as soon as the consultation was ended, Winifred went on tiptoe to fetch him, and having laid him in his mother's arms, resumed her kneeling posture, and very soon mother, child and maid were wrapped in the arms of Morpheus.

Among other things Mrs. Gordon brought with her, she did not forget the pocket book, and having unpacked her bundle, laid it on the old fashioned, worm eaten cabinet, that stood in Ellen's room, where she had left it.

Winifred, whose natural fear of spirits fancied every noise that in the dead of the night had ever disturbed her to proceed from some supernatural cause, was now awaked by a something, that left her in no doubt of ghosts and hobgoblins, and overpowered her with terror; she plainly distinguished a rustling of silk, and a heavy, slow tread thro' the long dismal gallery, a door whose creaking hinges awakened her, shut of itself and shook the house, like the report of a cannon.

The rustling and footstep came nearer and nearer, – Winifred's hair stood on end, she trembled and turned pale, it approached the door, her jaw fell, after a moment it returned, the hinges again creaked, and the door made a second report, – Winifred then began to breathe and to pray.

Ellen, not quite awake, asked what was the matter, hugged her boy and again fell asleep.

"I knowed from the pecining[20] this was the tivel's ten" thought Winifred, "tear papy" looking on the child, "if thy hard hearted taty,[21] and his ugly ould cats of aunts, and that cross Lady Margaret, was carried away in a whirlwind by

---

[20] I.e., the beginning
[21] I.e., daddy

satan." – Again the rusty hinges creaked, the door opened, and the third time the house echoed its close.

The third of every thing, poor Winifred now recollected was ominous; the rustling of silk, the slow heavy step approached; more terrified than before she sunk down with her white face, large eyes and distended jaws, only visible above the bed, – the door opened, the taper happening to stand in the current of air was near being extinguished, the rustle of silk, the same step approached the room, a tall male figure in a paduasoy morning gown, a night cap and a strapped hat entered.

Winifred was all eyes. It seemed to examine the room, walked up to the empty cradle, stood with its arms folded and heaved a deep sigh.

"Ah," thought Winifred, "it will tear me to pieces, it is an evil spirit in the claws of satan."

Having lighted a candle it carried in its hand, it was returning, but stopped short at the cabinet, it took something in its hand, it started, walked quick to the taper, and Winifred then saw it had taken Lord Claverton's pocket book.

"Name o Cot," thought she, "what does it want with bank notes."

It quickened the taper, it lighted another, again examined the book, and groaned most piteously.

"Poor, poor soul," thought Winifred, "how it is tormented!" it now was turning to the door, having stood with its back to the bed – "his hour is out," thought Winifred, "Cot pe praist and blessed for ever and ever, he is coing back to the devil," and she began to respire more freely, but what became of her when suddenly looking round, it turned from the door and approached the bed.

Winifred trembled so much the curtains shook, and as the

figure advanced, the bed itself partook of the motion, – it undrew the curtain, Winifred shrieked, and Ellen started up in her bed with the boy in her arms. If when disguised by a large night cap, pale cheeks and haggard eyes, they recognized him, they were dumb with astonishment, what were the sensations of Lord Castle Howel when he beheld his *wife,* a wife so dear, so beloved, so injured?

Ellen's child was now her first care; her last thought before she slept, was on the means of preserving him from the power of her husband; that husband now stood before her, with power, and she doubted not, with inclination, to tear her child from her arms.

"No," cried she, with hysteric wildness, "you *shall* not have my child, I will die before I part with him."

"My dear child," said the Earl, in a voice scarcely articulate.

"Dear, who can he be so dear to as *me*? you shall not have him."

Winifred lost all fear of spirits, and throwing herself over her mistress, to the other side of the bed, clasped her strong arms round Lord Castle Howel, and dragged him with all her might away.

"Fat in the name of Cot is the matter fith you?" cried she, foaming at the mouth, "fat are you turned turk? or chew? or cristain? that you want my poor tear Lady's tear papy, – have you no bowels of measuration? do you want to commit murder? can't you let the ould cats co to the tifel their own way?"

The Earl, who was just recovered from a severe illness, could neither withstand the strength of Winifred's arms, nor the loud torrent of her tongue, which seemed to penetrate his brain; she was for driving him out of the room, still continuing her harangue, "why need you co with them to fire and primstone for ever and ever? fat signifies their Latyships to you? think Cot almighty cares a pin for Lorts or Latys?"

"Let me speak," said his Lordship.

"No, no, we ton't want your plashfemys, and your lies, and your tuels, and your tifels, we have had enough of them."

"Ellen, my dearest Ellen! my angel! my beloved wife!"

Ellen was sobbing over her infant, but her Lord's voice, in broken accents of tenderness, was congenial to her senses, and even assuaged the wrath of Winifred, who however retreated backwards towards the bed, to guard the tear papy.

Lord Castle Howel bent his knee, "I cannot approach you, I dare not look at my child, till you pronounce my pardon; dear injured innocence forgive me!"

Ellen's soul was the throne of sensibility, she gave her child to its nurse, who was by this time awake, and expanded her arms to receive Lord Castle Howel.

In the sweet delirium of conjugal reconciliation, we hope we may be permitted to leave man and wife, while we retrace some events, the reader is unacquainted with.

Chapter V

When Ellen's elopement was discovered, and the means she had used to effect it, nothing too bad could be said of her; the taking the family jewels was an absolute theft, leaving her court and other dress cloaths at Philip's lodgings, going with him, and not to Code Gwyn, were all so many proofs of depravity.

Lady Margaret was so weak, as to weary every body, with their domestic disgrace, and had it not been for the consolation that Ellen's son, if born in wedlock, let his mother be ever so infamous, would disinherit their cousin, the old Ladies would have gone distracted.

The scandalous chronicle however had scarce time to register the black scroll, before the lye direct was given to the major part of it.

Lord Claverton's slow recovery, and the extreme weakness which resulted partly from his wounds, and partly from the bilious disorder, which inquietude of mind always irritated, was so exceedingly reduced, as to give Dr. Macshean great apprehensions for his life; other physicians were of his opinion, and a voyage to Lisbon proposed as the only hope of renovation.

Lord Claverton's tedious illness was attended with so few comforts from without, or consolations from within, and the film which a long career of dissipation had spread before his eyes, having dropped, at the first proposition of the voyage to Lisbon, he had leisure to take a retrospect of the actions of his past life, in which catalogue, that which concerned our heroine was perhaps one of the least fatal. Yet in the intention, as it was among the most atrocious, as the intent, not the act, fixes the guilt; and, as in the midst of pain, and even in sight of death, his mind reverted to her, as the most attractive and lovely of God's creatures, he was incessant in his inquires about her. Dr. Macshean, in the consternation and even concern he felt, on account of her elopement, told him all, and raised a phantom in his troubled mind, no exertion on the part of the Doctor could dissipate, – the innocent, the injured and now miserable Lady Castle Howel, was ever before him.

The credit given to her intrigue with her footman, we must do the Ladies the justice to say, rested only with themselves; for tho' the indolence of some men, the interest, indifference, or ill nature of others, might prevent their contradicting a report received by the gentle sex! very few believed, what, however, they did themselves the honour to repeat.

Dr. Macshean was himself so convinced of her innocence, in that and every other respect, except her connexion with Lord Charles Dash, which from Lord Claverton's well known peaceable disposition, being roused so far as to fight a duel, he considered as wearing a face of probability, – that he did not mention it to his Lordship.

Lord Claverton had strong confidence in Macshean's medical and surgical skill; the doctor was that kind of accommodating man a bad mind might make its ally, without nice explanation, for tho' he professed much religious zeal, and affected strict morality, if an ill design had but the slightest cover it imposed on him, and where his interest was concerned, he was far from being troublesome in his scruples: such a man may be taken by the hand, and continued the first favourite of the Lord Clavertons of the age, as long as danger, distress, and death are kept in the back ground; but on the approach of either of the former, the patron loses the favourite, of the latter the favourite loses the patron.

It was not from Dr. Macshean; no, nor from the ready and capable Joseph, Lord Claverton's mind could find relief; had Lord Castle Howel himself been present, *to him,* tho' the man he meant to injure, he could have unbosomed himself; but as among 'the wicked there is no friendship,' the whole list of his Lordship's acquaintance, and it was graced with as many famous and fashionable names as any great man's porter in the purlieus of St. James's could produce, he could not select one companion, to attend the bedside of a man, whom his Physicians advised to take a voyage to Lisbon.

In retracing his first acquaintance with the object of his wishes, and his condemnation, he recollected Mr. Meredith, whose unaffected sanctity of manners he had ridiculed, the purity of whose sentiments were the object of his contempt, and whose religious duties he protested were mere priestcraft; but who *now* he recollected with veneration and respect, and from whom he hoped to receive comfort, – he desired Macshean to write, to request him to come to him on business of emergency, and enclosed a bank note for the expenses of the journey.

Lady Margaret Howel had wrote a most circumstantial account of her sister-in-law's elopement, as cruel as unnecessary, to Lady Meredith; her letter, however, tho' written with crow pens, on the finest French paper, and tho' interlarded with many expressions of pity, and compliments of condolence, was never half perused by any of the distressed family, – the three first lines, which mentioned, "Ellen's going off with her footman, notwithstanding the Ladies of Castle Howel family, had, in respect to her situation, suffered her to remain under their protection," and allowing "if there was an excuse for her conduct it was in her familiarity with the domestics of Code Gwyn, in the early part of her life, which she" Lady Margaret "exceedingly lamented," were quite enough. Lady Meredith took to her bed *without* speaking one word, and in fourteen days was followed to the mansion which is never mortgaged, by her weeping children. Sir Arthur's wheel chair was no longer of use, change of place was neither pleasure nor relief, to one, whose beloved companion died of a broken heart, and whose fondest hope was blasted by iniquity; the Miss Merediths were ashamed to be seen, even at church, and had not their brother been too good a Christian to suffer temporal affairs to abate his zeal in the service of his maker, he would have been the least qualified among them to administer consolation. Even the loud and cheerful mirth, which used to echo in the servants hall was changed into gloomy whispers, and the harper's occupation was over.

In this situation were the family at Code Gwyn, when Lord Claverton's mandate arrived.

"Oh, the Caitiff!" said Catherine, "what does he want?"

"His business cannot be so emergent as mine," said Mr. Meredith, throwing the letter down.

"Answer it however," said Mary, – it was still a rule with her, letters should be punctually answered. Mr. Meredith was little anxious about either the Doctor, or his patron, and therefore contented himself with writing, "that having had the blessing of seeing his dear mother released from the agonies of a breaking heart; and the misfortune to see his father struggling with calamity; no business, however urgent, could take him from a place where he was necessary, both as comforter and protector, he therefore returned the bill."

If Lord Claverton's conscience was before troublesome, in its remembrance of the Code Gwyn family, what was it on receipt of this letter? Lady Meredith, in manner, disposition, conduct, and form, was as much an angel as could be incorporated in mortal frame, that frame was dissolved and its agonized spirit now at rest, where he had no hope of ever meeting it; the dying saint was ever before him, she even took place of her lovely grand daughter, and having failed in procuring a confident, who could also be his comforter, he disclosed the feelings of his mind to Macshean, and clearly proved to him that Ellen was as innocent of any intrigue with Lord Charles as with him; he declared he should not rest, till Lord Castle Howel was convinced of her innocence; he insisted Macshean should inform the Earl of his declaration, and if possible bring about a reconciliation between them.

This however was a business easier promised than performed; for as a reconciliation between her brother and his wife was the last thing Lady Margaret wished, so to accomplish any thing she did *not* wish, was, at this juncture, the last thing the Doctor would undertake, – accident however did it for him.

Lord Castle Howel, as soon as he had wrote, as before mentioned, crossed over to Ostend, meaning to divert the anguish of his mind, by visiting the place where he had lived, and had still some valuable friends in Switzerland; he adopted a travelling name, and would have directly proceeded on his journey, but the excessive agitation of his mind, together with the fatigue of a tempestuous passage, threw him into a fever, which confined him near two months; and when he recovered, his letters announcing the Countess's elopement, occasioned a relapse, more dangerous than the first attack; on his second recovery he altered his mind, and resolved on returning to England.

He was giving some directions, at the hotel, respecting his return, when a carriage, with a retinue of servants, drove up, Lord Charles Dash, with another officer, jumped out, and in wonderful spirits passed the Earl without seeing him.

Lord Castle Howel was of a peaceable, retired, sedate turn of mind, he disliked duelling on principle, and even when he considered his wife as guilty, never thought of sanguinary revenge, either on her or her seducers, nor probably ever would, had not the sight of this young nobleman, and his subsequent conduct, met him in an irritable moment. Some English gentlemen, then at Ostend, were immediately summoned, by Lord Charles, for a dinner and hazard party; and unfortunately the best room having an occasional division, Lord Castle Howel was applied to, by the obsequious landlord, for leave to accommodate Lord Charles Dash with half that apartment, there being none other vacant in the house; his Lordship, perhaps a little curious about the manoeuvres of a man, who had so materially injured him, immediately consented, with the provision, however, the sliders should not be quite closed, in which the waiter took care he should be obeyed.

Lord Castle Howel had finished his dinner, and was sitting over his Burgundy, when Lord Charles and his party came to theirs. Amidst the noisy congratulations to Lord Charles on his arrival, he heard his own name, and drew nearer, to know how he, who was a personal stranger to the whole set, would be treated in his absence.

"So you fought Claverton, Charles, thou wilt not leave off, till thou art either shot or hanged."

"No matter, I will live all the days of my life, boy."

A loud laugh at the *new* sentiment.

"But what said old square toes?"

"Said, what he *did,* nothing."

"Lord Castle Howel is a man of honour," joined another voice.

"O damn his honour," replied Lord Charles, "I only want his wife."

"That I suppose is no longer a *want,*" answered the same voice.

"Oh faith, you are mistaken, I have a vast deal to do, for tho' I had every reason to believe she liked me, yet 'tis the veriest little prude."

"D—n Dash, how's that? why I thought both Claverton and you had her, that you quarrelled about who was the favourite, while she sung, *How happy could I be with either,*"[22] – singing.

"Claverton, ay, ay, he had her before the old fool led the *timid virgin* to Hymen's altar."

Another loud laugh.

"What! and so was jealous, eh Dash?"

"Damn the fellow, let's have no more of him, he is recovered, and if she is above ground, I'll have her yet, in spite of Claverton, Castle Howel, or the devil," – the slider opened, and Enter Lord Castle Howel.

One of the party only besides Lord Charles knew his person.

---

[22] Quoting John Gay's *The Beggar's Opera* (1728)

'Tis a wonderful argument in favour of moral integrity, that the most abandoned, vicious, and daring, be their self, or acquired, importance what it will, are always awed by its presence.

Lord Charles coloured, and got up involuntary, the gentleman who knew him, Captain Ireby, reached a chair, while the rest stared at him, at Lord Charles, at the sliders, and at each other.

Lord Castle Howel declined sitting; but addressing the company, said, in a resolute tone of voice,

"If the event did not justify the act, gentlemen, I should think you entitled to an apology for being by my own wish an unsuspected auditor of your conversation; my name, gentlemen," to those he did not know, "Lord Charles Dash will inform you, is Castle Howel."

"Well," said an incorrigible young red coat, "then you are rightly served, listeners never hear any good of themselves."

"Nor is it fit they should," answered the Earl "for the practice is a mean one, and should be discountenanced; but the ill I have heard is not respecting myself, it is one who was dearer to me than my life; whose character Lord Charles Dash has injured, although he confesses he has not yet vitiated her morals, which nevertheless he is yet determined, if she is above ground, to effect. Now I am no soldier, nor duellist, but I am the natural protector of a young woman who bears my name, and is within a few weeks of making me a father; she is, by Lord Charles's voluntary declaration, cleared of one, and that the most generally believed, stain on her reputation, she *may* be equally free from the other; but whether or not, I stand up her defender, from the avowed libertine designs of Lord Charles, and insist, he either retracts his declaration, and pledges his honour not to attempt hers, or, that he will meet me within one hour, as it is the fashion for one gentleman to meet another, and remember, that my sword, when drawn, shall not be sheathed till she has lost, either her husband who would protect, or him who would dishonour her;" and laying down his watch on the table he walked firmly out.

A silence ensued.

The incorrigible before mentioned, having first taken care to examine the adjoining room, burst into a loud laugh; and exclaimed, "what a d—ned hurlo thrumbo!"

"This is the drollest incident!" said a second.

"What an old fudge! you won't give her up, I hope Charles," said a third.

"I sincerely hope you will, my Lord," said Captain Ireby.

"D... me what a Janus face, Charles, one half crying, t'other laughing," resumed incorrigible.

"By God," said Lord Charles, "I am so struck, and so surprised, but now I think of it, it was a d—d impertinent intrusion "

"Cut his throat, Charles, and I'll be your second, and if he should kill you, d—n me, I'll cuckold him for you."

As there may be some readers, who are not in habits of interlarding their most common conversation with oaths, or hearing others do it, we beg such to believe, nothing but a regard to our own character, could induce us to give the above verbatim conversation; but if we were not to make our men of fashion, talk like men of fashion, we should be suspected of writing of what we did not know; and as we have paid a tolerable price for our acquaintance with the superior set, it would be very hard, not to be allowed the credit of it; therefore, however simple, vague, unmeaning, and immoral, the conversation of Lord Dash and his friends, it was taken down by a short-hand writer, and exactly in the order now written.

"*You,*" with a sneer, replied a gentleman with a very red nose.

"*Me,* what d'ye mean by that," answered incorrigible.

"You are a pretty fellow to make a cuckold," answered red nose.

"D—n me, I'll bet five hundred, I have more married women on my list than any man in company," replied incorrigible.

Done, done, done, from all.

"What's the bet?" asked Lord Dash, who had been in a reverie.

"'Tis about Lord Castle Howel," said Captain Ireby who had also been a little absent.

Incorrigible would lay five hundred of that too, done said red nose.

"Done, I say it was not about Lord Castle Howel."

Umpire, Umpire.

"Well then," said red nose, "was it not about cuckolds?"

The umpire gave the bet to red nose, against incorrigible, for certainly it did allude to Lord Castle Howel, and incorrigible, as was *usual,* paid; for few young men had more money, and fewer knew less how to put it to a proper use.

A loud laugh, partly at the expense of incorrigible, and partly at the expense of Lord Castle Howel, concluded the conversation, and Captain Ireby begged to speak to Lord Charles alone.

Captain Ireby was one of those few officers, who without seduction intrigued, without inebriety was a jolly fellow, without swearing was lively and pleasant, and without betting knew how to sustain an argument; he was on good terms with Duke Dash, and better with the Duke's master, which gave him consequence with every body; he talked with such effect to Lord Charles, and being convinced *himself,* had as he thought so effectually convinced *him,* of the propriety of Lord Castle Howel's conduct, and of the justice of his demands, that he extorted from his Lordship the parole of honour the Earl demanded, and carried it to him.

But the parole of honour of a soldier, and that of a man of gallantry, are two of the most different things in nature; in as much as the one cannot be broke without an indelible stigma, whereas the other is seldom thought of after it is given; and Lord Charles returned to England, more bent than ever on obtaining the Countess, if it was only for the notoriety of the thing.

Lord Castle Howel's affection for his wife rendered the hope it might be possible for her to clear herself from every other imputation on her character, both flattering and probable; he returned post to London, and arrived full of these hopes, at the very instant Mrs. Morley and Lady Margaret had settled that Ellen was guilty of every despicable vice; and the spinsters debating whether they should or should not set out for the north, which, as Lady Gertrude thought extremely proper, had been hitherto opposed by Lady Frances, but Lady Gertrude's maid, having heard from another Lady's maid, who heard it from her Lord's valet, who had it from Lord Claverton's valet, that something was on the tapis in that quarter, about Lady Castle Howel, which would surprise some people, she changed her opinion, and thought it better to stay; in consequence of which Lady Frances found just then, it was very ridiculous to live in town when every body was in the country, and insisted on going.

Lord Castle Howel's arrival, however, a little staggered the decisions of one party, and postponed the disputes of the other.

Doctor Macshean, it is true, was prevented by certain considerations from complying with Lord Claverton's wishes, at the time he acquainted him with them; but now, Lord Castle Howel's arrival would probably be soon known, and if a meeting should take place, by any other means than his, doubts might arise prejudicial to the candour of his conduct; he therefore took an early opportunity of communicating Lord Claverton's sentiments to the Earl, who in the eager desire of clearing his wife's honour, instantly paid him a visit; here he first heard of Lady Meredith's death, and having forgiven the penitent Claverton, returned home, in a state of mind not to be described.

That Lord Claverton should, from the time he first saw Ellen, be in love with her, was *not* extraordinary, but that he should, with increasing inclination, nourish hope and passion together, without the observation or suspicion of Ellen, or her friends, for so long a time, *was* extraordinary.

Macshean had always been in Lord Claverton's confidence, the Earl recollected that, and thus, all that gentleman's policy could not keep his footing in Lord Castle Howel's family; for one observation leading to another, his Lordship could not fathom the motives, that prevented a man's becoming the friend and advocate of a woman, whom had reason to believe innocent and injured.

Mr. Macshean was first treated with coldness, and then ordered not to be let in.

Lady Margaret interfered, it would not do; she resented with still less effect; and as the Doctor must not visit her, she spent most of her evenings in Conduit-street with him.

Meanwhile the Earl and his two aunts were indefatigable in their inquires after the lost Countess, as well as in paying every respect to her character; the whole family, and all the domestics, wore mourning for Lady Meredith, and Lord Castle Howel wrote himself letters to Sir Arthur and Mr. Meredith, to exonerate Ellen from every imputation on her character, and condole with them on the death of Lady Meredith.

These letters had nearly been as fatal to Sir Arthur as the contrary one from Lady Margaret was to his wife; it was now he most lamented her loss, – he insisted on having her chair and work table set by him, where he would comment whole hours on the Earl's letter, and hold discourse with the absent dead.

The good news however had lost the talisman; Mr. and Miss Merediths raised a monument in their hearts to the memory of their good parent, which was yet washed with tears; the domestics were most of them old, they had lost their beloved mistress, and her death was a warning to them. Their old master was in a state bordering on second childhood, and the voice of cheerfulness was no longer heard in the family.

Lord Castle Howel's anxiety did not contribute to restore his health, which received a great shock in his illness at Ostend, and all endeavours to discover the Countess being fruitless, the Ladies prepared to leave London, and wait the event at home, when an accident gave some distant hope.

Lady Frances was resolved to cut a figure at her return, and having ordered a new chariot, was saying to Godfal, she wished he could send it down cased; he persuaded her not to think of it, and mentioned as an instance of risk, that tho' he had made a coach for Mr. Frazer, and sent it down to Scotland, under the care of Philip, Lady Castle Howel's former footman, who he recommended to Mr. Frazer, on account of his sobriety, yet that the coach, by some accident was broke, and some woman he had let ride in it thrown out and hurt; "so you see, Madam," said he, "send it by whom you will, there is always such a confederacy among servants, you can't answer for them out of your sight."

Lady Frances, carried this anecdote home; my Lord instantly caught it, and on inquiry, finding Philip actually left town with the coach on the day of the Countess's elopement, he got Mr. Frazer's address and wrote to him, requesting, if he had such a servant, now, he would send him to England to Natly Abbey; or if not, that he would take the trouble of inquiring after his present residence.

Natly Abbey, the seat of Ladies Gertrude and Frances, lay a very few miles out of the great north road, and as the Earl resolved to go in person to Edinburgh, if he did not hear satisfactory accounts of Philip, he was easily persuaded to escort his aunts home.

He visited Lord Claverton before he left town, and in charity to his distressed mind promised to write the result of his journey.

If there is one situation more interesting than another, to a fond husband, it surely must be that in which the Earl found Ellen; he embraced her, wept, hugged his boy, attempted to speak, and gave Winifred all the gold in his pocket; his excess of tenderness affected Ellen, she felt she also had been faulty, when therefore he repeated over and over, *forgive* but *forgive,* she replied with sweetness,

"We will forgive each other my Lord, I have been wrong, but not *so* wrong as *you* – your offences are enormous."

"I confess my angel, I confess it"

"But you are likely I see to repeat them."

"Oh never, never; how can you suppose such a thing?"

"Because," throwing her enchanting arms round his neck,

"your indulgence has been your greatest fault, it was the foundation of mine."

In the mutual endearment of love, honour, and esteem, the day broke, before Lord Castle Howel could prevail on himself to leave his beloved wife and child.

Natly Abbey was the bequest of a maternal uncle, to the Ladies, Gertrude and Frances Howel; the abbey was perhaps, one of the finest examples of ancient architecture in the kingdom; and was the residence of all the Natlys, from the time it was wrested from the Roman see by Henry VIII. The last possessor, Sir Francis Natly left it to the Ladies Howel, with the express stipulation, that they and their heirs kept the abbey in repair; but keeping it in repair did not, as the Ladies chose to understand it, imply living in it; they built an elegant modern house for their own residence, but kept their farmer, and most of the domestics in the abbey; where indeed all the labour of the family was done.

As the Ladies had insuperable objections to living in the gothic apartments of the abbey, their family pride did not object to the display of its antiquity; a door from the great court opened to the lawn, and a covered way led from one house to the other, over which was a long gallery, where they saw and entertained large parties; the end of this gallery led through a double baize door to a very small lobby, through which was a passage, by a very large heavy door, covered with a quantity of nails and plates of iron into the passage or gallery, that went quite round the old quadrangle.

Lord Castle Howel had sent the instant they arrived to Durham, to enquire for letters, and his messenger not being returned, he could not resolve to go to bed, tho' the Ladies had retired to theirs, curiosity tempted him, as he was walking up and down the gallery, having heard much of the ancient building which he understood joined the house, to open one door and then another; his candle which he carried having gone out, he returned, but not being able to find the inner door, and recollecting he had seen a light, returned, and softly rapped at Ellen's chamber, but Winifred in her fright did not hear that, tho' the rustling of the silks still buzzed in her ear.

The Earl retired, by the same way he entered, after begging his Lady to enjoin the nurse and maid secrecy, that he might have the pleasure of agreeably surprising his aunts, who since his return had been her warm friends.

It was in vain Ellen courted sleep after her Lord's departure, the confessions of Lord Claverton astonished, and Lord Charles Dash filled her with contempt; she felt no one pang of regret, for the loss of her *fashionable* friends, should she never more behold them; she had not yet heard of Lady Meredith's death; she rejoiced in the justice done her character, and never felt more gratitude and esteem for her Lord; all her anxieties were at an end, she had nothing to look forward to but happiness, yet spite of all, a melancholy, for which she could not account pervaded her senses.

She sighed, and wept, yet wondered what ailed her, and Mrs. Gordon, who rose early to relieve Winifred, found the latter fast asleep by the fire, and Ellen bathed in tears. Mrs. Gordon knew the theory of medical practice, from long habit of conversing with her husband; she roused Winifred, and angrily charged her with keeping her mistress awake. There was now no talking to Win, the moment Mrs. Gordon opened her lips, she recollected the quarrel at her house.

"As to me, Mistress Gordon," said she affecting great dignity, "I don't mind no such low poties as you, more as the tirt under my feet, for Cot knows you bent worth it, poor ignorant pribble prabbles silly body, and as to my Laty, yon will soon know whether she is kept, or whether –"

"Winifred," said Ellen in an angry tone.

"Well, well, I don't care, you are angry with me for such a witch as that, but I know this, I had rather be at Code Gwyn than any where, for all my Lort, and Cot knows he is no more fit to hold a candle to Mr. Evelyn, than, –"

Ellen hurt at the impropriety, not to say injustice of Winifred's behaviour, sternly ordered her to leave the room. The girl, like all other over indulged servants, loved to give her tongue liberty, but she wanted not respect, and abounded in affection for her mistress, whose anger grieved and frightened her. She went away muttering spiteful invectives against mischief making low poties; but, instead of going to bed, began making inquires after Lord Castle Howel in the kitchen, now filled with servants.

"Oh!" said Mrs. Spackman, "you mean my Lady's heir."

"No, No, foolish woman," answered Winifred, "I mean no such thing as any poty's heir, I mean an old man, Cot help him, Lord Castle Howel."

"Well," answered Dame Spackman, "my Lord to be sure is not young, but he is good, and that is better, he is at the new abbey with my Ladies, – the quality very seldom come here."

"No matter where they co, Mrs. Spackman, for the coot they do!"

"Oh, don't say so, Mrs. Winifred!" replied the Dame, looking fearfully round at the other servants.

"Tifel take me, if I would not say so if I was tying; ah, Mrs. Spackman, you poor woman's knoes nothing about the world; I have peen, Cot help me, where lorts, and tukes, tukesses, and princes, and player people, and kings have peen, and lort knoes, they are no great things; and as to laties, as Cot shall save and help me, they are satan's own nursery maids; there was that great ugly four beer barrel, Lady Gertrude Howel."

"Who?" cried Dame Spackman, with fear and trembling.

Winifred proceeded, "and that dryed shotten herring, Lady Frances, tivel take me if they are not enough to preed an infection among all coot natured souls."

The kitchen was in a moment in an uproar; for tho' the aforesaid Ladies had not the good fortune to be extremely *beloved* among their tenants and domestics, they were what some people prefer, very much *feared*.

"What are you talking of?" said one.

"The woman's mad!" said another.

"To abuse two of the ten virgins!" said a little crooked woman, who occasionally sewed for the housekeeper.

"Ten!" cried Winifred, "are there ten of them? Lort of his mercy save us, if there are ten such ould cats as that prowling about, the world will soon pe at an end, and the sooner the petter, please Cot."

"Hold your blasphemous tongue," answered the crooked woman, advancing, who had wit enough to know, that taking the part of the Ladies against such open abuse, was at least a safe conduct.

"What's the matter with you, little humpy?" answered our amazon, and taking her in her arms, very coolly carried her back to her seat, with an air so good humoured and inoffensive, as set all present in a roar of laughter, except the crooked Lady herself, whose tattling, malevolent disposition, Dame Spackman knew too well, not to fear the consequence of the history she would certainly give to the housekeeper, from whom it would travel, in a direct line, to the Ladies, "of a woman she had taken in, who so openly abused them," she begged Winifred to go with her, and the crooked lady, at the same instant, made her exit at the opposite door.

What a treasure to Hogarth, had he been living, to see the face of Winifred Griffiths, when Dame Spackman told her, she was under the roof of the very ladies she had been so much abusing.

"Then Lort be coot unto me," said she, falling on her knees, "poor miserable sinners as we are; my poor tear Lady, and her tear sweet peautiful papy, is fallen into the claws of satan at last, she hat petter be tied in the red sea with faro and all his hosts."

A servant told Dame Spackman to go to her lady directly.

"There!" said she in a fright, "I shall lose my place."

Winifred continued on her knees in earnest prayer, for the deliverance of her poor tear Laty and the innocent papy.

The crooked Lady had made all possible speed, but as she had often been the fountain of intelligence to Mrs. Marmalade, without receiving a reward nearly adequate, as she thought to her services, it occurred to her that such an important champion as she had just been might have access to the ladies themselves, to whom she could better magnify her zeal, than to the housekeeper who would be very likely to arrogate the principal merit to herself; accordingly having tapped at the door of the breakfast room, and being bid to enter, she gave a detail that absolutely petrified the two spinsters; a visitor of their servant dare to abuse them, in their own house! "order Dame Spackman in." – And enter Dame Spackman.

It had not been above three or four times in her life, this good creature was honoured with the speech of her high born ladies, her humble courtesy indeed had dropped a thousand times as they passed, and even to the sacred place, that held, and the carriage that *drew* them; she fed their poultry, fattened the pork, made all the butter and cheese, was an excellent and honest servant, and they knew it; but what of that? what was she paid and kept for?

The poor woman trembled, her knees knocked together, and her tongue cleaved to the roof of her mouth; when both Ladies, without any very striking trait of female delicacy, opened on her at once.

How she dared harbour vagabonds who abused them? where the creature was? what she said, and why she did not answer?

Poor Dame Spackman could not open her lips, her confusion was such an unequivocal proof of guilt, that her dismission was resolved on; and Lady Gertrude, who chose to be reckoned a woman of sense and sentiment, was in the middle of a parting exhortation, when she was interrupted by the voice of a woman, loud and voluble, now and then mixed with sobs, and farmer Spackman entered, dragging in Winifred.

The farmer heard of his wife's distress, and tho' a good sort of a man enough, he had no idea of losing such a comfortable place for a silly stranger; the moment therefore he understood his wife's situation, he insisted on Winifred's going before his Ladies, to clear her, but she positively refusing, he dragged her by a force, which, tho' she had conquered Mrs. Gordon, over powered Lord Castle Howel, and set down little Humpy, she could not resist.

Lady Gertrude's harangue ended.

Lady Frances dropped her tea cup.

"Winifred here!" exclaimed both.

"Ay, Cot help me, needs must, for the tifel drives, for Cot knoes"– this girl, we have before observed, however free she talked of Lords and Ladies, had a natural habit of subordination, and therefore, tho' she answered from her feelings, which were not very full of respect for the great personages before whom she was dragged, she could not dare *look* at them, but fixed her eye on the door the further end of the long room, – and her speech was cut short by the entrance of Lord Castle Howel followed by the nurse and his young son.

The Ladies were absorbed in surprise, wonder and joy, at the sight of Winifred; as they could not doubt but she would give them intelligence of the Countess; not more eager to receive than communicate, they both arose, Lady Gertrude to meet Lord Castle Howel, Lady Frances to be nearer Winifred; but tho' no terror was in the look of the latter, she avoided her, and was attracted by the scene before her, would have followed Lady Gertrude, had not farmer Spackman held her by force.

Before Lady Gertrude reached her nephew, he had taken his son from the nurse, and having imprinted a fond paternal kiss on its forehead, presented him to Lady Gertrude, his eyes swimming with sensibility and joy.

"There Madam," said he in a voice which his feelings, almost deprived of articulation, "there is *your* heir and *mine.*"

"Oh Cot almighty safe the tear, tear papy, from the ould cats, pray Cot, let me co you tam tivel, let me co to safe the tear papy, I'll tear you eyes out you old pelzepub;" and it was not for want of will she was not so good as her word, but the farmer, who began to think she was mad, kept her back by mere force; the poor girl seeing, as she thought, her Lady's misfortune before her eyes, without power to prevent it, tore her cap off, and her short black hair out by handfuls, and at length fell into strong hysterics and was carried out.

The explanations that succeeded this extraordinary scene, were so entirely gratifying to the wishes of the old spinsters, so interesting to Lord Castle Howel, and so happy for all, it is impossible to do justice to the sensations they excited. Lord Castle Howel invited his aunts to visit the Countess, who he had prepared to receive them, but Lady Gertrude whispering her hysterics, they told him they would follow him, and immediately retired; the Earl was rather surprised, and indeed displeased, but returned with his dear son, to the still dearer mother, in whose society his heart felt not the absence of any person or thing; at her request he condescended to go to Winifred, and having reconciled her to the terrible misfortune, of giving him an interest in his own child, took her to Lady Castle Howel, to whom her uncouth attachment still more endeared her.

After an hour and a half had expired, the creaking hinge and loud report of the door, which fell together by a spring, announced the approach of visitors. It had struck Lady Gertrude that they could not pay too much respect to the Countess on this joyful occasion; the servants were all ordered to put on their best liveries to attend the procession, and the two spinsters themselves walked in front, dressed in rich court suits, with lappets, wide hoops and every jewel in their possession.

The Countess, on whom splendour had lost all attraction, smiled at the unnecessary parade, but, as they explained it as a mark of respect she could not be less than grateful; they were profuse in apologies for the past, thanks for the present, and promises for the future; the child was the greatest beauty on earth, the very picture of the Earl their father, and a strong family likeness of all the Castle Howels.

"Now Cot of his coot grace forbid," muttered Winifred.

An event on which their hopes had so long hung, and had at length almost deserted, seemed to operate like enchantment against all the unamiable propensities, which their unsociable lives had given rise to; they who were haughty, formal and reserved, now condescended to chat on the subject of their joy, not only to their domestics, but every body that came to pay their respects, on their arrival into the Country; *they* who were close bargainers, hard mistresses, and severe landladies; whose delight was in hoarding up riches, for whom they had no heir; were now in the other extreme, kind to their domestics, liberal to their dependants, and even profuse in their expenses and rewards. Lord Castle Howel, in the happy medium, that influenced all his actions, excepting only where the Countess was the object, was gentleman like, and energetic in his thanks, to every individual who had been of service to the Countess; he gave the farmer, his dame, two sons, and daughter, ten guineas each, the Ladies doubled it; he presented Winifred with a £100, the Ladies added £200.

"I wonder," said Winifred, as she was displaying her riches to the Countess, "what is become of poor tear Mr. Joseph."

"And I wonder," said Ellen, "whether they have returned Lord Claverton's money."

Lord Castle Howel had done that, and acquainted Lord Claverton of their present happiness, the first day after their meeting.

Mrs. Gordon, from certain recollections, did not care how little was said of her, but Ellen, who remembered only her services and kindness, would introduce her, before Gordon returned she was loaded with presents, and he appointed Doctor and Apothecary to Natly Abbey, with a salary of £100 per annum, one year's advance of which, besides a liberal discharge of all expenses, the Earl insisted on his accepting.

The Ladies besides, appointed him a small convenient house, then vacant at one of the extremities of the park, and he and his wife were sent home in the Earl's carriage, with two out riders, the Doctor to indulge the benevolent joy of his heart, take leave of his patients, pay his debts, and see his few medicines properly packed; his wife to boast of the respect paid her by a Lord and Ladies, display her elegances, among which were the watch and faux montre, formerly given to Ellen by Lord Claverton, top the superior over Mrs. Clover, arrange her furniture and take care of the chintz bed.

There was now one person, who had been of particular assistance to Ellen, and that was the curate of Little Manor, whom the Earl had not yet seen, but he had too lively a sense of the importance of his service, to forget it. He rode over to Little Manor, and found Evelyn in the little garden of a widow, with whom he boarded, reading Seneca; Lord Castle Howel announced himself, and saw the sudden emanation of countenance, which always gushed from Evelyn's heart, when that was affected! He trembled and turned his fine eyes, which at first were fixed, in manly attention on his visitor, to his book, where he saw no character but Lord Castle Howel, the *husband* of *Ellen Meredith*.

The Earl had never seen so interesting a figure; his dark brown hair, waving from the root into graceful curls, parted on his clear brown forehead, and rested on his well turned shoulders; his eye brows were full and finely shaped, tho' perhaps they approached rather nearer each other than the strict line of beauty allows, but this defect, if it may be called one, was particularly becoming to his turn of face; his other features were regular, his mouth and teeth handsome, tho' not small, on his cheeks were a few dark moles, and whenever a smile was visible, the most expressive dimples were seen; he was tall, and though thin, extremely well made.

The externals of a man, we allow to be of small importance, when compared with his internals, but the impression, which some countenances make on the mind, even of man from man, is very strong; such was the effect of Evelyn's on Lord Castle Howel, notwithstanding a kind of sentimental reserve, that rather retreated *from*, than *met* his gratitude and offered friendship.

There was however that spirit of candour, that mixture of benevolence and sense of propriety, in the little Lord Castle Howel said, for he was not a talker, that Evelyn, spite of *certain disgusts,* could not avoid being flattered, and consequently pleased. The Earl bid him fortify his heart before he went to Natly Abbey, which he insisted should be next day.

The tell-tale blood would mount, tho' Evelyn did all he could to repel it.

"*My* Ellen," said the Earl, "shall personally thank you for your assistance, and you shall christen my boy."

No tell-tale blood witnessed Evelyn's bow for this honour, it all retreated into a heart painfully agitated.

"But there are two dangerous virgins, with both of whom you must be in love, as they assuredly will be with you," added the Earl, "and I give my honour, I shall make such report of you, that I shall be afraid of my own Ellen;" had the Earl meant what he said, perhaps his observations on Evelyn might not have been very pleasant, for the name of Ellen never sounded on *his* ear, but his heart sent into his face, a witness of its electricity.

"I will get the better of this extreme sensibility," said Evelyn, when he returned to his garden, after he parted with Lord Castle Howel, "why should I be thus agitated? The dear Ellen is happy, her honour is cleared, she is restored to the rank she adorns, how selfish is it not to rejoice – to her husband, a good man, a man of honour, who loves her, whose title to her is sanctioned by the law of God, and established by those of man; what would my wayward heart be at? Hers is at peace, and can Percival Evelyn wish to disturb the peace of Ellen Meredith? to disgrace his sacred function? to break himself those commandments he delivers from the altar? Oh! no, I will not go to Natly Abbey; and yet – will it not look strange, that I, who have lived with her so many years, dear happy area of a life devoted to her – now meeting her in such a manner, so obliged to her family, – I *must* go."

If Evelyn had not been more solicitous to establish the propriety of visiting Natly Abbey than to adopt the reasons for avoiding it, he might have supposed, which was really the case, that Lord Castle Howel had never heard of him before.

Ellen who had not yet left her room, was to dine for the first time with the family; her husband meaning to surprise her agreeably, said a gentleman was expected, but not whom; and Winifred's prying gossiping turn only saved her from a surprise, which under the scrutinizing eye of Lady Gertrude, would have been very embarrassing.

"As Cot shall safe us, Madam," said she "here is our Mr. Evelyn, poor tear sweet creature, and there's the two ould ca– Laties hugging him apout and so tifelish kind to him.'

"Where?" said Ellen, out of breath.

"To be sure the ould ca– Laties I mean, bent designing upon the tear sweet young man, but sure enough they be ready to defour him."

"Does Mr. Evelyn dine –?"

"Tine, why I believe, Cot forgive me, he is going to lif here."

Ellen sent her away on some trifling pretence, and employed the time till dinner was announced, in fortifying her mind against a meeting, which would be criminal only in the exact degree that it distressed her, and, when her happy Lord appeared, to lead her to the eating room, she had reasoned herself into an apparent composure, which ever after supported the Earl of Castle Howel's *wife,* and even dispensed its effects on *Evelyn.*

The old Ladies were so charmed with Evelyn, as Winifred truly reported, that their eyes were more frequently turned to him than even to the young heir, who was brought by his nurse into the room, and perhaps that dear object in view, might contribute more to the ease of the Countess, than any thing else could; a noble and tender husband, to whom she had such infinite obligations on one hand, a lovely infant on whom they mutually doated on the other, – there was no room for a thought derogatory to the honour of a wife, or injurious to the peace of a husband; Evelyn saw and respected the victory of reason over sense, he prayed for a continuance of their happiness, and resolved to regulate his own conduct by so bright an example.

The Ladies had by Lord Castle Howel's desire, put off their mourning, and Ellen, finding from all her conversation with Evelyn, that he considered him as a stranger, did not once mention Code Gwyn; she retired soon after dinner, and next day met Evelyn, who as Winifred said, was actually pressed into the service of the spinsters, with little agitation on either side.

A stronger attachment than that which grew up between Evelyn and our heroine, could not perhaps be; but their principles were instilled at the same period their mutual passion commenced; no false glossings, no time or circumstance had power over minds, whose natural rectitude and reason were aided by virtuous instruction, supported by a decent regard to religion, and an entire reverence *for*, and confidence *in* God; it was impossible with them to substitute wrong for right, – they felt the one, and avoided the other; Evelyn's attention, his solicitude, his waking thoughts, and nightly dreams were all Ellen's; but it was Ellen's the married woman, the wife of Lord Castle Howel.

Ellen could not help remembering the companion of her youth; she could not help feeling how superior he towered, both in person and understanding, above any young man she knew; but he was *not* her husband, the tender kind husband, who had relieved the distress of her family, and suffered by *her* imprudence; nor was he the father of her charming boy.

From this time, Evelyn became an inmate of Natly Abbey, and he was called to a consultation, how to break the death of Lady Meredith to Ellen, who excessively wondered why, as she constantly wrote to Code Gwyn, the answers were all from her uncle, or one or the other of her aunts; she became more and more anxious, and Mr. Meredith begged Evelyn to let her know, the dear parent to whom she wrote a circumstantial account of all that happened, was no more.

Winifred again saved a vast deal of trouble, for one of Lord Castle Howel's servants, happening to mention the handsome mourning they all had, she lamented she was always out of luck; the man supposed she had the same, or much better than the other ladies maids; not she, God help her! besides, what should she go in mourning for any of the Castle Howel's for? Cot knew, tho' she was forced to hold a candle to the tifel, she should not mourn if they were all in their peaceful craves; for why, when one went, Cot always sent another.

The man laughed: "but this you know was one of the Code Gwyn saints, Lady Meredith was a saint, was she not?"

Winifred turned pale, "I'll tell you fat, Mr. William, if you offer to take my old Laty's name in vain—"

"Who me, Mrs. Winifred? not I, – nobody could be more sorry, when I heard she had given up the ghost."

Winifred ran up to Ellen, who was then writing to Code Gwyn, "her Laty, her dear sweet old Laty."

"What's the matter?" said the Earl, who was looking on a book, but painfully agitated about the means of breaking the subject to his wife.

"Oh, you tear papy!" continued Winifred, "you will never see your plest great grandmamma, please Cot I will co and kneel on her dear crave, even if she cives up her cost[23] in my face."

Ellen looked at the weeping Winifred, then at the Earl, his countenance like Priam's attendant spoke, though his tongue did not.

"And is my dear venerable parent then no more? and did she die without blessing her Ellen? Oh my Mother! my dear Mother! I see your angel face this moment."

"Oh Lort, where?" cried Winifred.

---

[23] I.e. ghost

"Be gone, trifler," answered Ellen, "look down dear saint!"

"Petter not, my Laty, petter not, for what coot could her cost do you? Or what coot could you do her poor cost?" Winifred lost all regret for Lady Meredith in her fears of ghosts, and now, she lost all her fear of ghosts; when Ellen fainted in the arms of Lord Castle Howel, tears and hysterics succeeded.

Lord Castle Howel, entirely ignorant of his sister's *kindness*, or any other circumstances attending Lady Meredith's death, than merely that it had happened, reasoned her into a submission to the divine dispensations of providence, which from her great age was to be expected; but tho' she submitted, she did not cease to lament the loss of a parent, whose whole life was one continued lesson of propriety, meekness and devotion; she did not afflict her husband by dwelling on a subject so painful, but to Winifred, who was the only person there who knew Lady Meredith, she was most eloquent in her praise, continually recollecting and repeating her words and penning down every sentence she remembered.

This was a piece of confidential favour, from which Winifred would have gladly been excused; for though it frequently happened, that the Lady was sitting at one part of the room, and the maid at the other, the latter contrived to lessen the distance every time Lady Meredith was mentioned till she even clung to Ellen's robe.

The mourning of the family was renewed, in compliment to Lady Castle Howel, who was indulged with keeping her own apartment a month, which she did, notwithstanding Mrs. Holt paid several congratulating visits to the family, nor was Caroline Holt among the last to rejoice with Ellen on her happy reunion with her Lord.

The Ladies Gertrude and Frances were very profuse of

complimentary regrets for the loss of the Countess's society, and the Earl's, who would not stir from her, but to confess the truth, they were merely complimentary.

Two new objects had entirely superseded every other in their favour, these were the young heir and Percival Evelyn; the one gratified their pride, revenge and hatred; the other, sensible, elegant, manly and well-bred, having once fixed an interest in their hearts, was perfectly qualified hourly to increase it; seven miles every Sunday they followed the young divine, and listened with a mixture of enthusiasm, and new born devotion, to sermons that would not have disgraced a mitre, – no meal was comfortable without his benediction, they fancied themselves for the first time in their lives, in want of a protection, and could neither walk nor ride without him.

Evelyn's mind was too moral to be deficient in gratitude, the entire kindness of these old maidens veiled their imperfections, if he saw any thing unamiable, either in their manners or disposition, he attributed the one to the recluse life they appeared to have led, the other to their early disappointments; and as they really appeared to adopt his interest, in preference to any other consideration; and as his company seemed the solace of their lives, he readily would have become their resident, as well as domestic chaplain, had not his honour told him, it was not in the fitness of things, at least while the Countess was their visitor; the cure, which was his excuse, was, Lady Frances said, a paltry reason why he should deprive friends who loved him, of his company and society, – and a thought had struck her, which might, by changing *his* situation, give *them* the thing they most desired, which was his constant residence in their parish, and be of advantage to himself.

"Bless me!" thought Gordon, who was present, "sure the auld Lassie has not gotten matrimony into her head with our young Parson."

The spinsters of Natly Abbey, were 'two upright vestal sisters, unsapped by caresses, unbroke in upon by tender salutations,'[24] they had all the natural propensities and prejudices common to virgins past their grand climacteric; that is, they felt the inestimable something was wanting, which sweetens life's dreary close in a conjugal friend, and affectionate children; that calls memory back to the season of love with pleasure, and bids it look forward to an age of comfort with hope, – peevish at the present, regret at the past, and uninterested in the future, they had nothing to live for but themselves; they confided in no attachments but from their dumb favourites; their servants like all others of the human race, had their good qualities, blended with bad ones; and tho' the former might please, they wanted that natural indulgence, which the maternal heart gives to common error, particularly in females; these were general and natural frailties, and these, in a very full extent they had; but the monstrous appetite which now and then disgraces the female character, in the form of an old woman soliciting a young man, is unnatural, and this they had *not*.

Percival Evelyn had a manner peculiar to himself; for the few disinterested civilities the Ladies Gertrude and Frances had hitherto bestowed, they might have received acknowledgements and thanks. But Evelyn's mind felt, and his countenance spoke the language of that mind; a sudden beam from

---

[24] Quoting Laurence Sterne's *A Sentimental Journey Through France and Italy* (1768)

the most expressive eye in the world, the blood mounting over his face, a smile, half sentiment, half gratitude, that played round his mouth, were indications of gratitude, of feeling, they had either not, or not been in humour to understand; and, as in the birth of an infant, to cut off the hope of the object of their avowed hatred, one sentiment united them; so, in this second instance, the only contention of two women, who could not settle the arrangement of two hours, without spiteful bickerings at each other, was only which best loved, and would do *most* for the young Parson.

"I'll get young Evelyn a living," said Lady Gertrude to Gordon.

"He deserves every thing," answered Gordon.

"And I'll get him a wife," said Lady Frances.

What pity thought Gordon, the sweet and bitter of life so constantly mix *together*.

Doctor Runnington, a robust clergyman, who had lately married the rich widow of an orange merchant from Botolph-lane, that rich widow, now Mrs. Runnington, and a pretty fair girl, his daughter by a former wife, dined that day at Natly Abbey.

Mrs. Runnington, who, as she said, had been used to polite life, and detested Natly Parsonage, was in high good humour at the invitation, and dressed herself exceedingly splendid; she wore a quantity of fashionable jewels, not family ones indeed, her "dear pa" never let a fardin go out of his hands without interest; and as to her dear dead dove, he never minded nothing but turtle in large, and punch in small quantities, so that all these here dimonts was her own taste.

The Ladies admired every thing in and about Mrs. Runnington; Doctor Runnington talked of stocks, he wished he had not dabbled in the four; as the three and a halfes were getting up.

If it was natural for Mrs. Runnington to talk of *dimonts*, of which she had but very lately been in possession, so it was natural for the Doctor to boast of money, of which it was still *later* that he had known the comfort.

He wanted to buy a snug estate with a house on it; she insisted, if he did, it should be in the neighbourhood of London, somewhere about Vauxhall or South Lambeth, and she appealed to Evelyn, with –

"Pray young man, don't you think that there a mighty pleasant spot? and then one sees such a deal of genteel company."

Evelyn had stared at Mrs. Runnington till his eyes ached, he withdrew them in disgust, – and by accident fixed them on a little fair girl, with very sweet blue eyes, fair skin, auburn hair out of powder, rather pleasant than beautiful countenance, dressed in plain white muslin, and blushing alternately *for* her father and *at* his wife, – till she met Evelyn's eye, and then the blush was so much deeper, that he immediately addressed Gordon, to prevent her being embarrassed.

"You have a pretty singer, Miss Runnington," said Lady Frances, "will you try if the instrument is in tune?"

"Do, Jenny," said the Doctor.

The young Lady blushed still deeper, she hesitated.

"Why, Miss," said her polite Mother-in-law,[25] "what signifies your knowing these things, if you won't do um? my pa never bestowed a fardin on my education, but what o' that, one can't have one's cake and eat it too; he gave me a good round sum when I married Mr. Lime, and indeed, when a

---

[25] I.e., Stepmother

woman comes to be married, and have sarvants to look ater, what signifies humstruming."

Miss Runnington, who had made half a motion to rise, sat down.

"Why don't you play, Jenny?" said the father, who was anxious to show his daughter, of whom he was very fond, to advantage.

Evelyn who saw the confusion of the young Lady, and felt an involuntary dislike of the old one, crossed the room to lead her to the instrument, and extremely pitied her agitation, when he found her hand trembling in his; she went through a lesson of Pleyel's, and sung very prettily; and, to the visible mortification of Mrs. Runnington, received the praise and thanks of the company.

"Very pretty, indeed, Jenny," said her delighted father, and kissed her cheek.

Mrs. Runnington, with that narrowness of heart that looks askance on the tenderness of a husband to an offspring not her own, was displeased; she wondered Mr. Runnington was not ashamed to be slavering such a great girl; for her part, she thort it very ridiculous, and indeed any woman was a fool that married a man with children, because why, if he had his will every fardin would go to um; how'dever her pa had taught her a trick worth two of that, – for safe bind, safe find, and a woman wou'd be a fool indeed, who see'd *folks* fonder of other folks children than herself, if she did not take care of number one."

At the conclusion of this delicate speech Mr. Gordon and Evelyn hurried out of the room, and Miss Runnington turned to the window to hide her tears, Gordon and Evelyn just then passed, they stopped and invited her to join them.

Miss Runnington had the head ache.

Lady Gertrude begged she would try the air.

The Doctor looked at his wife, and having received an assenting nod, bid Jenny go, who glad of a release went to the lawn, where she was joined by the gentlemen; confusion at the recollection of a scene so humiliating, and perhaps on some other account to which they were strangers, so agitated her, that happening to step on a loose stone on the gravel, she stumbled, and but for the support of Evelyn would have fallen. She had turned on her foot which occasioned her to limp, Gordon was with great philosophy walking on, in that case, what could a young gentleman do but urge the necessity of her accepting his offered arm? and what could a young Lady do but acquiesce? The lameness went off, but there had been something in the whole scene, so interesting on the part of the young Lady, that Evelyn's heart glowed with kindness towards her, and they were turning back, arm in arm, when Ellen walking up and down her dressing room, in the same position with her Lord, saw them.

Had Ellen seen a spectre, it could not have more astonished or confounded her, – she coloured, turned pale, rubbed her eyes, it was no vision, – but Percival Evelyn with a young female companion leaning on his arm; fortunately Lord Castle Howel was reading some letters and did not observe her change of countenance; she pleaded a sudden head ache, and said she would lye down, he attended her with his usual kindness, and then at her desire left her.

The moment she was alone, a flood of tears relieved her, she gave them way and sobbed as if her heart was breaking.

Winifred, who was sitting by her bed, undrew the curtains. "As Cot shall pless me, my Laty is crying, Cot pless my tear ould Laty, and rest her sole in the peaceful crave, put if you take on so, you will tie too, name o Cot."

"Oh my dear grandmamma," cried Ellen, half deceiving herself, and willing to attribute the tears she was *now* shedding to the cause for which she had lately shed so many.

"Well, Madam, put shure and shure, enuff is enuff, you call so often opon my poor tear old Laty's name, who is now in Apram's posom, that plese Cot, the tivel may one day or another come in her likeness."

"Oh! that I could see her once more," sobbed Ellen.

"Pray Cot forbid," answered Winifred, getting quite close to the bed.

"What are you afraid of?" asked Ellen, angrily, "my grandmamma is an angel."

"Well then so much the petter, and I am shure I have heard her say often and often, with her own dear plest tongue, equals are always pest company; and plese Cot I like to keep my distance from my petters, plese Cot deliver me from angels and costs, for ever and ever amen, pray Cot, for Cot knoes this worlt is pad enuff for me, and all deceitfulness, and falseheartedness, is pad as costs incarnal: put Cot help us poor sinners, we don't know what is pest, for if any person, or if our own reverent at home, had taken his affadavy, that Mr. Evelyn would do such a thing, I should have said, Cot forcive me, it was false."

Ellen was all ear – but Winifred having made her speech, took her work and sat down.

After a few moments silence, in which she had vainly endeavoured to suppress her desire to know what Evelyn had done, Winifred continued.

"Ah lort, it toes not signify, true lof is petter as cold, poor tear Mr. Joseph for that; but as to Mr. Evelyn, for him to co marry anyone else, when Miss Ellen Meredith was alive, and just as her poor tear old Laty was tead."

"Bless me, Winifred," answered Ellen, almost breathless, "what are you talking of? Ellen Meredith is *not* alive, but is Evelyn going to marry? yet why should he not, did not I marry?"

"Why to be shure you did, Matam, more's the pity say I, but then you see, Matam, you married a Lort, and there is some sense in that, tho' Cot knows not much; and if Mr. Evelyn had married a Laty, if it was only one of the auld ca – Laty's of the Abbey, – but to co and marry auld Parson Runnington's daughter, because our Laty and Earl joins to pye the living, and so sell his sole and poty for ungodly mammon, 'tis what I never thought was in Mr. Evelyn."

Every word Winifred uttered, gave Ellen's heart a pang, "where," said she with affected ease, "did you pick up all this stuff?"

"Oh! Cot knows, I tid not pick it up at all, little crumpy, who knoes all the news in the parish, because in teet, Cot forcive me, I believe she makes half herself, heard from the Doctor's ugly wife, as it was all agreed, for as she don't like Natly, and I don't know who does, for matter o' that, Cot pless the place, my Lort and Laty Gertrude has agreed to pye the living, and Miss, a carratty ugly witch, Cot forcive me, is to have it a marriage portion, and the ould ones co to Lonnon, and Mr. Evelyn marries and lifs here."

"Very well," said Ellen, out of breath, "and when was all this settled?"

"Oh, Lort knows, the crooked billet only told Dame Spackman and me to day, Cot help us! I am sure I cried my eyes out, and I told Dame Spackman of Mr. Evelyn's false heartedness."

"You did!" cried Ellen, much alarmed.

"Yes, and I told her, I thought Mr. Evelyn should know petter, for, says I, if plese Cot to take my Lort, and the young may co, but the ould must, and to be sure he is ould, poor tear gentleman, and so he is you know, for I am shure, tho' Mr. William spends a full hour every morning at his head, his poor tear air is as cray as a padger, and so says I."

A thousand daggers struck to Ellen's heart as Winifred went on, – she reproached herself for her servant's folly, and felt the indignity offered her Lord the more keenly, as the sensation of the last moments were, tho' concealed, aggravation originating only with herself; in a transport of passion she never before felt, she upbraided Winifred for her ingratitude to so good a master, and solemnly declared, if ever she named Percival again, or took a single liberty with Lord Castle Howel, or any of his family, she should that moment be turned out of the house.

Winifred was astonished at her violence, and had recourse to her old advocates, tears, but the Countess, with inflamed eyes, and flushed cheek, commanded her instantly to leave the room, and joined her Lord in the other.

"Do you mean, my Lord, we shall live always at Natly Abbey?"

The hurried manner in which this question was asked, the angry glow still on her cheeks, and an unusual elevation of voice, astonished the Earl, he had no doubt but his aunts, in some of their whims, had offended her, and the very idea provoked him.

"Live here my angel! what do you mean? live at Natly!

surely Ellen you know the business of my life is to make *you* happy; if you are weary of this visit, we will immediately set off, to Castle Howel if you please, but I confess, I wish to show my recovered, and dearer bride in the radiance of virtue and triumph of innocence, among people who so little knew her, but it shall be as *you* please; say my love, has any thing happened to disconcert you? has my aunts? – but surely they could not offend you."

Ellen's heart condemned her, the old Ladies actually appeared to have changed their nature to oblige her, how little, therefore, did they merit this return; Lord Castle Howel had promised to stay at Natly, till Christmas, he had entered in a county hunt, and being advised to take exercise, promised to join the chase whenever the hounds were out, – the Ladies, who delighted with the nursery avocations, depended on having the little Lord continued so long under their care, would be excessively angry, – and her Lord perhaps disappointed; add to all this, general directions were given to have the town house painted, outside and in, where it had not been done prior to her marriage; a removal would disarrange all parties, and her eager wish to go to London, perhaps, render her liable to suspicions, of a returning propensity to the follies she abhorred; yet there were reasons to counterbalance these, and a thousand more of equal strength, – Winifred's imprudent loquacity, which had already, she doubted not, exposed her to the gossip of the servants; and Evelyn's approaching nuptials; the last was a spectacle she felt she could not witness; against the effects of the former, she was resolved to take the surest precaution, by instantly revealing that part of her story, to Lord Castle Howel, and condemning, in the severest terms, the folly of her servant.

The ingenuity of her manner, and the frankness of her acknowledgements, charmed Lord Castle Howel and as he considered her wish to remove, to be in consequence of Winifred's prate, thanked her for the confidence she reposed in him, and assured her *his* was unbounded in *her*.

But tho' the extreme delicacy of her mind was properly alarmed both for his honour, and her own, he hinted, a sudden removal at so critical a period was the only thing that could give a face of probability to any conclusions that might be drawn from Winifred's foolish communications; he therefore advised the assigning proper reasons for shortening their residence at Natly, but by no means to leave it, on such a trifling occasion.

Ellen could not avow the real objection, and a feigned one she was not in the habit of inventing; she retired to her room, and Lord Castle Howel rode out.

Chapter VI

It was not from the remotest symptom of jealousy, or want of entire confidence in his wife, that Lord Castle Howel's mind recurred to the history of her early passion. No, ever partial to all her actions and sentiments, it enhanced the value of the sacrifice she had made; he married her in the opinion that the native innocence, and peace of her mind, had not been invaded by any secret attachment; relying on her innate principles, and fully resolved to gratify his own wishes, by every indulgence of hers, he hoped, a sentiment originating in the most lively gratitude, and friendship, would imperceptibly become that kind of love which after all, is the husband's *best treasure.*

But now, he saw her in a different light, saw her, young, loving and beloved, sacrificing her first passion to a sense of duty; the wonder he expressed, when he first heard the person who rendered her such eminent service, and in all probability saved her life, had not been to visit her; changed into respect, into admiration, "even then," said he, exultingly, "friendless, deserted, and at the point of death, my glorious Ellen preserved not only the honour of the wife, but a nice respect to an absent injurious husband; and the young man, but I read his soul in his countenance, – poor youth! – Ah! he *may* marry, but the heart devoted to Ellen Meredith will not easily replace her image."

Lord Castle Howel stopped in his ride next morning at Doctor Runnington's, his aunts had told him their plan, and called on him for *his* half of the sum they agreed to pay for the next presentation of Natly living, – but *he* had not yet seen the Lady they selected for their favourite, – and he greatly suspected, Evelyn was not a man to marry for pecuniary advantage, or mere convenience.

"Bless my soul," said Mrs. Runnington, "who is that there gentleman riding up at the avenue?"

"'Tis Lord Castle Howel," said Evelyn, who with Mr. Gordon had at Lady Frances's desire, called to know how the Runningtons got home.

The reader will understand this was a piece of politeness, Lady Frances expected Evelyn would have offered, without a prompter, for as to the necessity of the thing, that was out of the question, as Mrs. Runnington's new coach was never out of sight of Natly Abbey, till it stopped at the parsonage, and every being it carried might be plainly seen to alight.

But Lady Frances thought it proper; and Evelyn talked Gordon to accompany him.

Doctor Runnington was a well looking Hibernian, of obscure family, who had however interest to procure him a college education, where the son of Sir James Sibley, an Irish baronet, who possessed of a lucrative place under government, also was; Runnington was young Sibley's bosom friend, and almost constantly lived at his father's house; Miss Sibley was young, and as her brother's friend, even at that early period, depended on making his fortune by marriage, he fixed on her as the first step of the ladder to his future promotion. An elopement took place, and the young pair winged their flight, to England. Sir James, though he did not entirely cast off his daughter, till he had provided for her husband, was nevertheless so hurt at the connexion, with a very low, not to say disreputable family, that he forbid her ever returning to Ireland; he procured by his interest the living of Natly, and there Mrs. Runnington lived and died.

The Doctor drank, hunted and intrigued, he lived in every respect beyond his income, despised the amiable creature, by whose interest he might have been in affluence, and by that means, as Sir James took care to have constant accounts of his conduct, deprived himself of all future advantages; that he could not allow *this* or afford *that* was always accounted for, by reminding his wife that her great family had never given her a shilling.

Mrs. Runnington had one daughter by this marriage, with whose help, and for whose sake she supported a broken spirited, insipid existence eighteen years, during the five last of which she bore a gradual decline, with no one uneasy sensation, but the idea of leaving her beloved Jane.

Miss Runnington was a sweet tempered, obliging, modest young creature; and as her mother's family had uniformly declined concerning themselves about *her,* or her child, she very prudently avoided mentioning them or their power to provide for the darling of her soul, and as she well knew her husband had nothing to give, or leave, she gave every lesson, and example of economy to her daughter; her own education had been fashionable, and elegant, and happily at a period when fine works were an employment that did not disgrace young Ladies of the first distinction, – Mr. Runnington's *own* expenses were things that could not be retrenched, he was particularly nice in all his apparel, but it was not his fault that Dryden's couplet was not verified at Natly Parsonage,

While abroad so prodigal the dolt is,

Poor spouse at home as ragged as a colt is.[26]

---

[26] John Dryden's *Prologue and Epilogue on the Occasion of a Representation for Dryden's Benefit* (1700).

The Ladies Howel had always a great veneration for high blood, they understood Mrs. Runnington was of a good family, and condescended to notice her; she, poor woman, was too broken spirited to be very tenacious, and so humbled by constant insults at home, she easily accommodated herself to the caprice and humours of those she met abroad; little Jane would obey Lady Gertrude, and to the infinite displeasure of their Ladyships' women, both mother and daughter now and then came in for a cast off gown; and by degrees, tho' it was a matter known only to the Ladies of the Abbey, and their women, and through them to all the parish, all the fine work, lace mending, &c. &c. was done at the parsonage by Mrs. Runnington and her daughter; the money earned by this means being an entire secret from her husband, enabled the fond mother to procure implements for drawing and music, having borrowed an old spinet at the Abbey, and every leisure moment, becoming a holiday, were passed in instructions which from a mother so dear, in declining health, were sure to make an indelible impression on a mind so amiable as Miss Runnington's.

At Harrowgate, where Parson Runnington as often went, during the season, as his pocket would permit, two years before his wife's death, he boarded in the same house with Mr. and Mrs. Lime; the former an unwieldy citizen of London, who went to Harrowgate for health, being exceeding willing to travel any where, or do any thing to preserve his footing in a world, where he had plenty of the best things in it; good eating, drinking and money; the latter quite tired of having, as a body might say, a husband, and no husband; for what with Mr. Lime's clubs abroad, and sickness at home, nobody could want a companion more than Mrs. Lime.

Mr. Runnington was the man in the world to suit Mr. and Mrs. Lime, he catered for the former, and became the confidante of the latter, and when they returned to London, they gave him a pressing invitation to visit them in Botolph-lane, which he promised, and as soon as he could get a curate, who would trust him, which was no easy matter, he performed his promise.

From this time to that, when Mrs. Lime became a doleful widow, Mr. Runnington had two very desirable events in view, that of burying his wife, and his friend; and as Mrs. Lime was certainly not the sort of woman for a man to place very great dependence on, he trembled, least the latter should precede the former, an event, that to his extreme regret, actually took place; he had now but one card to play with the widow, which was, in a moment, when her heart was unguarded by grief for her dead husband, or melted by tenderness for a living lover, to get a bond he had ready prepared, signed by *her,* forfeiting half of her fortune if she married without his consent.

Mrs. Runnington most provokingly lived till her husband was heartily sick of acting the lover, and her rival as heartily sick of waiting for a second husband; the Lady was on the point of paying forfeit in favour of a Highland Officer, who she got acquainted with at Sadler's Wells, and the gentleman on the point of taking it, when death stepped in and bound them to their former obligations.

The Parson and his Bride came down to Natly in great state, within three months after the death of his former wife; the city dame expected the affluence and finery she carried into the country would create respect; but her pride, ignorance and ostentation, compared with the humility, gentleness, and unassuming worth, of the good creature whose place she now filled, rendered her an object of contempt to the superior, and of hatred to the inferior of the parishioners. She paid the debts indeed, but with loud murmurings, her pa's money, and her dove's wealth, should go for such a purpose; she gave Jane a profusion of cloaths, but took care to assure her they were such as she, from her own right, could not pretend to. Jane was extremely beloved, every knee bended, every head was uncovered, as she passed through the church yard; while, between her unamiable character, and strange way of dressing, her mother-in-law excited only a stare of surprise, or a smile of ridicule.

Mrs. Runnington's violent passion for her husband, was much in its wane; his for her began, as it was like to end, in interest, – she was heartily tired of the country, and he of the constraint, his function imposed on his inclinations; he was fond of his daughter and proud of her little attainments, these however, received from a mother so superior to *herself,* were not likely to conciliate the affections of his wife; and as Lady Gertrude's proposal of purchasing the next presentation of the living, and taking Mr. Runnington's resignation as a marriage portion for Jane, was highly convenient and acceptable to him, it was no less so to her, as by that means, she got rid of the country and of a daughter-in-law[27] she both envied and hated together.

The gentleman, in whose gift the living of Natly was, had, notwithstanding a long minority, became insolvent and obliged to leave his country; of him the purchase was easy, and every other part of the business being settled, it was time to inform the person principally concerned, of what was in agitation, as a prelude to which, the invitation was sent to the

---

[27] I.e., stepdaughter

parsonage, and for which purpose, Evelyn was desired to pay the morning visit.

Mrs. Runnington had been finding fault with every thing and every body. A servant girl who having lived some years in the family was attached to Jane, answered word for word, till she was turned out of doors, and all the rest of the country servants immediately gave warning; bursting with rage and mortified pride, she sat swelling undetermined where next to vent her ill humour, when unfortunately Jane came in sight; this was one who *would* not answer, and who *could* not leave her; she therefore began a string of accusations against her deceased mother, who she proved to have been very idle and extravagant by the number of debts she left, which could not have happened, if like *her* she had paid her way.

Jane could bear any thing, but reflections on her mother, and that she could *not* bear, her answer, tho' in the very essence of mildness, was high treason, and Mrs. Runnington was in the very act of insisting, that either *she* or *Miss* should quit the house, when Evelyn and Gordon entered.

Mr. Runnington endeavoured to conceal the quarrel, but Jane's pale cheeks, and his wife's red ones, were evidence of disturbances that could *not* be concealed.

The gentlemen apologized and would have withdrawn, but the business in treaty was of equal importance to the man and wife, and that consideration alone calmed the latter.

Jane raised her eyes to Evelyn, with a look so piteous it went to his heart, she arose and went out at a door that led to the church yard, – "Tis Lord Castle Howel's" said Evelyn, and took the opportunity, while Mrs. Runnington was running to the glass to adjust her head, and her husband fetching his wig to receive the Earl, to follow Jane.

Ellen, Countess of Castle Howel

He found her in agony of tears kneeling on an humble grave, neatly covered with turf, where no stone had yet been erected, to tell the passing stranger, that "there lay the remains of Mary Runnington;" his heart melted at the sight, he raised her with affection, soothed and consoled her, while she eased her own full bosom, by a recital of her grievance, and while she secured a share in his, by the sad claim of unmerited distress.

Lord Castle Howel, who had no knowledge of the occurrences of the morning, saw with great pleasure, Evelyn walking within sight of the windows with Jane, his arm encircling her waist, and her face often raised in earnest attention to his, – he talked of the time of Mr. Runnington's resignation of the living, and Evelyn's marriage, as things of course to Gordon, who tho' perfectly well acquainted with the intended arrangement of the living, was totally ignorant of the matrimonial treaty, – the Earl made a short stay, and Evelyn soon after joined Gordon in his walk home.

Evelyn told him the incidents of the morning, as he had heard them from Jane, with a thousand encomiums on her, and pity of her situation; Gordon listened to one and joined in the other, without being able to decide, whether Evelyn spoke as lover or friend, and they were in the dining parlour at Natly Abbey, before he could satisfy himself; but the Countess dined below for the first time since she heard of Lady Meredith's death. Evelyn's change of countenance, convinced him the wedding was by no means near; after dinner however the Ladies, instead of retiring, opened the budget, and the bill meeting the warm support of Lord and Lady Castle Howel, only waited the assent of Evelyn.

Never was surprise equal to his. The living was worth four hundred pounds a year, two thousand pounds was paid for the presentation by friends, whose partiality to him was all that in his own opinion impeached their judgement, but his heart recoiled from the proposed marriage; and as to *think* and to *say* were the established tenets, where Percival Evelyn and Ellen Meredith received their early impression, he declined the offers of his friends in toto.

"I thought so," said Gordon.

Ellen cast down her intelligent eyes.

Lord Castle Howel mildly asked his objection.

"You see, sir," said Lady Gertrude, "the price we are willing to pay for your society."

"It is wholly yours Madam, without any price at all."

"I am sure Jane Runnington is very handsome," said Lady Frances, "her complexion is as fine as Lady Daub's, and quite natural."

"And don't *you* think her very amiable, Mr. Gordon?' joined Lady Gertrude.

"She has a bad mother-in-law," answered he dryly.

"But she was very amiable, when she had a *good* mother, sir."

The sir, carried a treble R, and meant more than any simple sir ever did mean before or since, it was quite a sir-r-r.

The Earl apprehending, from the countenance of Evelyn, that the Ladies would mar their own purpose, requested he would walk round the lawn with him; Gordon not being of the party, was left to the terrific frowns of the two spinsters, who threw out so many witticisms, about meddlers, busy bodies and envious people, that it was impossible to mistake their import or direction; he would not have been able to keep the field, had he not been encouraged, by a transient and cordial glance from the eye he most admired on earth.

The Ladies entered into the history of the Runningtons, spoke of Jane's many excellences, the principle in their opinion of which were, her good blood, and skill in darning, and mending lace; while Ellen actually dropped tears at anecdotes, which casually dropped in the course of the story, of the entire love and friendship, which death only could break, between the mother and daughter; these were matters that did not at all strike the quality spinsters, as of consequence to dwell on, and they related them only as leaders to the grand merit of Jane Runnington, namely, her neatness, industry, obedience and economy, and before the last word was out of Lady Gertrude's mouth, "as I live," exclaimed her sister, "here waddles the fat citizen, and her odious spouse; what a sweet walk, to the parsonage sister, when it is Evelyn's!"

Lady Gertrude nodded, and the nurse just then bringing in her boy, Ellen received him with her usual fondness, but although his new hat and feather was put on in a peculiarly becoming style, in order to be carried out with papa and mamma, she took it off, and arranged his toys on a table before her to see the wonderful creature, whom any body could think worthy of Percival Evelyn.

Mrs. Runnington apologized for the liberty she took of presenting Lady Frances with a beautiful artificial bouquet, she had received from her French milliner's out of Cheapside, and happening to cast her eyes on Ellen, made a profound courtsey, very sorry she had not got two; the company and the present were both graciously received, and the Parson and wife being seated, Lady Gertrude bid Jane take a chair.

"Ay, do Jenny," said her father.

"Bless me, Mr. Runnington," cried the bride, "when will

you leave off that vulgar appellation, I vow I am in a sweat, least you should some day, bawl out Jen, Jen Runnington."

The Parson had sense enough to blush, the Ladies looked at each other, Mr. Gordon played with his sleeve button, Jane glanced a kind of beseeching look at the lovely Countess, who sat self collected, like the genius of elegance; while the weak woman bridled, shewed her large white teeth, and fancying she had said a smart thing, at the expense of her husband and his daughter, looked round with a kind of triumph, – Ellen touched the bell, "place that young Lady's chair by me," – the servant obeyed, and the delighted Jane sat down, blushing and trembling, without knowing well why, for Ellen's voice and manner was all kindness, – the young Lord made advances in his way to Jane's friendship, and in a few minutes stretched his little arms after her, – Ellen was all observance of the pretty Jane, and before the gentlemen returned from their walk, thought Evelyn could not be happier than in such a wife.

Meanwhile the Earl had by the most friendly arguments, obviated all the objections Evelyn *could* make to an establishment so every way eligible; driven to his last excuse, he had friends, he said, who he must consult, without whose approbation he would not accept a diadem; on that then we rest, answered the Earl, taking his reluctant hand.

Ellen's heart, with her boy in her arms, and her Lord by her side, was invulnerable, she beckoned Evelyn to her, and introduced Jane as *her* friend, and then arm in arm with her husband, retired, followed by her nurse and lovely boy.

The Earl passionately embraced her, he perceived the delicacy of her conduct, he knelt and even wept at her feet, but the subject was not for words.

Nor could Lord Castle Howel be more struck at her manner

than Evelyn, the truth is, compassion for the gentle girl which pleaded so strongly in the bosom of Ellen, was not allayed by any observation, on her person or mind, that could raise one jealous emotion; and Evelyn's visible reluctance, to the arrangement of the two families, was a certain, and tho' blameable, a welcome proof, that in marrying, he did not absolutely follow the bias of his heart; so that her pride soothed, her judgement satisfied, and the latent remains of her former love amply flattered, she no longer thought on the event with dread, if Evelyn must marry she had the weakness, and a great one we own it was, to be pleased that his wife would be her equal in very few points, her superior in none, darning and mending fine lace excepted.

Evelyn on his part felt abashed and confounded, when spoke to with accents of kindness, on measures of advantage to himself only, by a nobleman of Lord Castle Howel's rank, who condescended to combat all his feigned objections, while the real one would have filled him with well founded resentment, since it originated in an improper attachment to the wife of his noble friend; he blushed at his own littleness, when standing before the honourable adviser, and resolved to die a martyr to his guilty feelings, rather than injure him even in thought.

"My friend, my beloved protector," said he, "knows my heart, if he bids me marry, it will be right to do it."

But what are the resolves of a mind long and ardently devoted to one woman, when its pursuits are directed to another? He entered the drawing room with Lord Castle Howel, met Ellen's look, and secretly vowed never to part with the dear hope of being one day to her what she ever was to him, all on earth he desired to live for. Jane returned the boy to his fond mother, she pressed him to her bosom, Lord Castle Howel hung over her, enamoured, all the delighted father in his looks. It was then Ellen beckoned Evelyn, then she introduced her *friend* to him, and having put Jane's pretty white hand in his, withdrew, – and was then he retracted his vow, and in a hurried tone and manner, told the Ladies he had considered, and – *and* he stammered he had one friend whom he must consult.

"That's well thought," said Parson Runnington, and took out a letter, which he began to read with an audible voice, without the smallest regard to his daughter's delicacy, who was present, till Lady Frances desired she would carry her compliments to Lady Castle Howel, and beg the child might not be kept too late out of the nursery.

"Ay, do Jenny," quoth the Parson, "and shut the door after you, and –"

"My stars! Mr. Runnington," interrupted the Bride, "you are always saying one foolish thing or another –"

"And, you are always finding fault, Mrs. Runnington, "which, I assure you, is not becoming," replied the Bridegroom with spirit.

"I should not have thought –" and the lightening flashed from the Bride's eyes on her inflamed cheeks.

"We will hear the letter, if you please," interrupted Lady Frances, – Mr. Runnington read.

"Sir James Sibley received the account of a proposal of marriage for the daughter of Jane Runnington, once Sibley, and the establishment proposed by the friends of one party; Sir James can make no objection to a contract he does not understand, between a man he does not know, and a child he never saw, but if the young people think it worth their while to ask advice in person, in any presence but that of Patrick Runnington or the woman he has made his second wife, Sir James Sibley will give it to the best of his ability."

"An impudent, ignorant, quality binding fellow," cried Mrs. Runnington in a rage, "I warrant the woman has money enough to buy his whole generation."

"And as to Patrick Runnington," said the Parson with affected dignity, "he is not ambitious of the honour, and though I thought it right, Mr. Evelyn should know what a ridiculous relation he is like to have –"

Gordon and Evelyn, happening at that instant to look first at Mrs. Runnington, and at each other, laughed out.

"Yes," continued the Parson, "'tis very droll, but I don't see why we should put off our matters to please old Sibley."

The Ladies, with their usual veneration for family honour could not agree with him; there was something so hauteur, so out of the way, and so like their own style in the letter, that it carried a certain weight, and the Earl giving the sanction of his opinion to theirs, with the further information, that Col. Sibley, only son of Sir James, had been lately killed in India, and that therefore if Evelyn should happen to please Sir James, he –

"'Tis impossible he should do otherways," interrupted Lady Gertrude.

"My dear Madam," said Evelyn who had no great goût to any part of the business, "you are partial."

"Not at all," answered Lady Frances, "and I have a great mind to chaperone little Jane to Ireland, and take Gordon, not you, but your wife, – you must not leave the child."

"What do you say, Lady Gertrude?"

Lady Gertrude saw no objection, Lord Castle Howel approved the scheme, which he said was very considerate on the part of Lady Frances, as the young Lady was forbid the protection of her natural friends.

When old Ladies take certain affairs into their heads, again and again we say, it is astonishing with what avidity they pursue them; the living was bought; the marriage settled; and a journey to Ireland fixed, before Evelyn had once discoursed on the subject with his intended Bride; tho' not before Jane's eyes had a thousand times invited him so to do.

"You may as well go to Ireland," said Gordon, "for you *must* be married."

There was no longer an excuse, for Mr. Meredith's letter arrived, giving his warm approbation of the measure, and lamenting he could not leave his father to congratulate Evelyn personally, on the acquisition of such generous friends. In a few days all was ready; Mr. and Mrs. Runnington set out for London, Lady Frances, Miss Jane, Mr. Gordon and Mr. Evelyn in the post coach, Lady Frances's man and woman in a chaise, and a couple of outriders for Holyhead, – the spinsters parted with great reluctance; they talked a vast deal of the dangerous passage, and Ellen bid Evelyn adieu, as she resolved for the last time; Gordon and his wife kissed, and parted in good spirits and good humour; the placidity of Jane's looks seemed to say, *I am safe,* when Evelyn handed her into the carriage; Lord Castle Howel accompanied them the first stage, and then returned, to peace and happiness in the arms of his Ellen.

VOLUME IV

Chapter I

Ellen having reconciled her mind to the marriage of Evelyn, and he being now removed, with his destined wife, to a distance, entire tranquillity took possession of her bosom. Lady Margaret, who we have not mentioned a long while, being returned from a visit she had been paying Mrs. Morley, wrote, that the house in Grosvenor-Street was ready for their reception, they had informed Lady Gertrude they should return to London, for one month, before they retired entirely to Castle Howel, which the Countess wished to be at Christmas, preparations were making for their departure, and as the old Lady having lost her sister and Evelyn, could not exist without her nursery, she accepted the invitation to accompany them.

Winifred, to her great joy, was ordered to pack up, and the day fixed for their departure.

Lord Castle Howel having rode out early, to join the hunt, Ellen devoted the morning to letter writing, and was sealing the last, when she was disturbed by the shrieks of the female servants, she rang her bell violently, as, seized with a presentiment for which she could not account, she was unable to stir.

Winifred entered with her eyes wilder and her cheeks paler than ever, she could only articulate "my Lord." Ellen flew down stairs, and the first object that struck her sight was Philip, covered with blood and dust; the honest fellow ran out of the house the moment he saw her, she followed, and met, on the steps the servants carrying the disfigured body of her still bleeding Lord.

Her sensations were not to be described; an ashy paleness took possession of her vivid countenance, but the recollection of duty and affection gave her fortitude; she followed the body till it was laid on a bed, without speaking, and then, Gordon being come, watched the examination of his hurt in silent terror.

A favourite horse, on which he rode, had taken fright on the top of a hill, and having left the reins negligently on his neck while he was speaking to Dean Holt, who was of his party, the beast ran furiously down the hill, and threw the Earl headlong on a rough brake of stones, his foot was yet entangled in the stirrup, and the animal grown more vicious by the stoppage, was plunging and kicking when the Edinburgh stage passed; two outside passengers jumped down, one of them was the faithful Philip, who, having been with his master on a tour to the Highlands, had not received the Earl's letter in time to attend him before, and who was now going to Natly Abbey.

Philip knew the horse the moment he got near, and having seized the bridle, wanted resolution to look at the unfortunate rider; a large posse of horsemen soon came up, and Philip was just in time to receive the last breath of the best of masters.

Expresses were sent to all the surgeons in the vicinity from the spot where the fatal accident happened, but as he died in the instant they removed him, it was in vain to wait their arrival; Gordon, however, with the ardent hope inspired by grateful friendship, examined the body, but finding many wounds of a description that would each have been instant death, he gave up the hopeless melancholy task, and stood with his arms folded, and tears trickling down his cheeks.

"What! is he gone, Sir? quite, quite gone? and shall I never see him more? never hear him speak? can this be, Mr. Gordon?" The calm but ghastly look which accompanied these questions, roused Gordon, who did not before perceive Ellen was present.

"My God, Madam," said he "why do you witness a scene like this?" and he attempted to lead her away, she resisted, but nature, exhausted by the force which her anxiety to attend her husband put on her spirits, gave way; and she was carried to her apartment apparently as lifeless as himself.

Lady Gertrude retired to the nursery, and there, in the moment of her nephew's dissolution it was, she only could find comfort; this Lady's attachment to the Earl, as the head of the Castle Howel family, was as strong as such attachments generally are; had his Lordship died in London, or any other place but Natly, she would have put on mourning; but excepting in the circumstance of his dying without an heir, it would have passed in the mass of natural events, without being commemorated by a tear of regret; death so near home, was, however a terrific thing, in the natural way it would have been more so – for if the insatiable glutton had swallowed Earl Castle Howel, what might not she, who was so much older, expect; she, however, was as much affected as it was in her nature to be, and directed every kind of attention to be paid the Countess; but the important nursery business engrossed her personal attendance, excepting only a few minutes she occasionally spared for the delirious widow.

Gordon sat unwearied, watching every turn in her disorder

on one side of her bed, and Winifred on the other, the latter entirely cured for the present of her loquacity, and fear of ghosts.

God has, in his wisdom and mercy to his creatures, implanted in our natures that kind of resignation to his will, that the separations he ordains seldom operate fatally; whereas madness, suicide, and desperation, are frequently the consequences of separations which are the result of mortal wisdom. Ellen's fever abated, her senses returned, and the sight of her child, who Mr. Gordon insisted should be brought to her, though Lady Gertrude trembled with apprehension least he should get the fever, helped to recall her affections to a world where she had yet much to lose – and a multitude of letters, which came both by post and express, lay unopened till she should be permitted to peruse them. In the mean while Lady Gertrude also received letters, by no means agreeable, which induced her to send express to London for her man of business.

This was a process commenced at law against the two spinsters, and Ellen, Countess Dowager of Castle Howel, for a combination to pass a surreptitious heir on the world as a son of the late Earl, to the injury and exclusion of Walter Howel, of Moor Bank, Esq. in consequence of which the whole of the Castle Howel estates were, by order of the Chancellor, put into receivers hands till the matter was decided. Other letters informed Lady Gertrude, from her niece, Lady Margaret Howel, that she having some time since given her hand to Doctor Macshean, a Physician of great eminence, had removed from Grosvenor-Street; she particularized, with great minuteness, the locks she had sealed, and in whose presence, and hinted, how sorry she was, for the Countess's sake, to find her brother's affairs were greatly involved. "I believe, niece," muttered Lady Gertrude, "*you* can best explain who has involved them."

As soon as Ellen was able to sit up, her letters were laid before her – one with the family arms claimed the preference; it was an exact copy of that Lady Gertrude received from the now Lady Margaret Macshean, with the bare alterations of name and title; the rest contained a cloud of demands from all sorts of tradesmen, by which it appeared that Lord Castle Howel, who for the sole purpose of paying his father's debts, an act of filial piety to which he was not bound, had, the first year of succeeding to the estate, been his own steward, in order to settle the annual expense, had, since that year, never paid a single tradesman, except indeed a few partial payments to some of the necessitous, whose circumstances had rendered very pressing.

It was not till urged and re-urged by Mr. Gordon and Lady Gertrude, Ellen would give a thought to her worldly affairs; one circumstance however did more towards it than all their rhetoric.

The body of the Earl was embalmed; it was intended by the Countess's directions, to be removed in great state to Westminster Abbey, where there was a family vault; Lady Gertrude had the delicacy to forbear hinting at the expense, though from the increasing demands on her nephew's effects, she knew there would be no assets; the night before it was to be sent off, her Ladyship received certain intelligence that an arrest was actually to be sent to meet the corpse, and that if it was not on the road, that arrest would come to Natly Abbey; Lady Gertrude's pride, as well as humanity, was shocked, she sent for Gordon, who undertook to break and explain the matter to the Countess.

To law and all its blessings as well as curses Ellen was yet happily a stranger. She could form no conception how Lord Castle Howel, who, if ever there lived a just man was surely one, could have run in debt; nor what rhetoric could justify a violation of the dead, but the idea that violation should be offered the sacred remains of the best of men, threw her into hysterics, she was prevailed on to consent to its private interment in the vault belonging to Natly Abbey, and not six hours after, the arrest actually arrived.

This shock over, she had yet another to sustain, in the account of the chancery suit, began by the Howels of Moor Bank, against her son's right. The expense and tedious progress of the law, where so much was at stake, must, in the present circumstances, rest on the two great aunts of the young heir; no doubt could be entertained of their attachment to a cause so near to their hearts, and yet Mr. Gordon took the liberty of suggesting, it would be as well if his mother had something in her own power to contribute in defence of her only son.

This was a plea indeed! it opened every wound in her widowed heart, it drew forth all the mother's fondness, all her sense of right, her fear of wrong – she pressed the smiling infant to her heart, called on her dear Lord to protect his injured boy; bathed his face with tears, and gave herself up to a sorrow more poignant than she had yet felt. On the first agonizing surprise, she wept for the loss of her husband, her protector, her friend; the guardian of her youth, the mentor of her maturer years; the alleviator of pain, and the companion who tempered excess of pleasure with the precepts of wisdom – the rock of her confidence was gone, and she felt herself equally unable to support his loss, or be her own directress.

When she was informed he died insolvent, that she was a Countess without dower, or fortune, there was nothing terrible in that; no deprivation that wounded her; Code Gwyn was open to her, hers, there she knew she would be a welcome guest, and there she resolved to go. Lady Gertrude might, perhaps, offer an asylum at Natly Abbey, but there she resolved not to stay.

Lord Castle Howel then was lamented for himself; little did the fond mother foresee, that she whose heart had never known guile, in the smallest instance, would be accused of fraud; or that the innocent child, on whom his noble father doated, would be cheated of his birth-right.

No worldly wisdom had yet found its way into the heart of Ellen; the difficulties into which her ignorance of and inattention to that single point had involved her, were recent proofs, how little qualified she was to take an active part, in a world, where ignorance may be a misfortune, but where innocence is a cardinal sin.

But what is the lesson, the science, the practice, maternal love will not learn? what will it not brave? where will it not insinuate? what does it fear? and what will it not suffer? "It would be as well if the mother had something in *her* power, to contribute to the defence of her son," repeated Gordon, as the violence of her grief subsided into a settled melancholy.

"Ah, Mr. Gordon," said Ellen mournfully, "what have I but tears and prayers?

"And those, be assured, dear Lady, will avail much; but our reliance on God must not render us careless to the means he puts in our own power, you must not desert yourself."

"Ah! Sir."

"Nor must you abandon your child."

"Oh, never, never."

"You do abandon him in the most cruel sense in not asserting your own right."

"My sweet boy," and again she folded him to her heart, "but what can I do?"

Gordon said, he was sure she was wronged. "Ask yourself, could so good, so fond a husband, live in peace, and know the wife he adored would be totally destitute at his death?

You, I know, think little of this. The old women of this abbey have whims, but no souls, when they come to see you dependent on them, even for bread, they will show an old friend with a new face; their money must fly for the child, and if they abandon –"

"God will protect my Arthur," said the distracted mother.

"God forbid I should doubt that, but," continued Gordon, "you also must protect him, you must look spiritedly into your affairs, you must detect imposition, and punish fraud, you must be bold in righteousness, you will then cement your friends, and confound your enemies; if you are wanting in your own cause, those will desert you, and these conquer."

Gordon's colour rose as he spoke, the honest warmth of his heart pervaded his whole frame; he took the child in his arms, and bending one knee to the ground, held it up, and, in an agitated voice, called on the honoured shade of its deceased father to witness he devoted his life and his faculties to the support, protection, and comfort of the widowed Countess and her infant child.

Ellen caught the enthusiastic ardour of her friend; she threw herself on her knees, one hand upraised, the other extended to the child, her fine eyes turned with little visible but the white, a hectic colour animating her pale cheek; she ejaculated, but her ardour subdued her power, she spoke inwardly and fainted away.

Winifred was always near; and Gordon had the pleasure to see her soon recover. "Presently, Sir, presently I will see you," and she pointed to the door. The child was laying on the sofa. "Take him, Sir, take your charge with you."

Gordon obeyed and left her.

Winifred was also dismissed, and the Countess knelt before the only being who could assist her. Sad hearts, they say, make warm devotees; and with as great truth they also say, the essence of cheerfulness is in the true spirit of religion.

Mr. Gordon was again summoned, and found her, from whatever cause, calm and resigned

She felt, she said, all his kindness, and recurred to his argument about her Lord; she knew he thought she would be in affluence, all his personals were settled on her.

Gordon said, Lady Gertrude's man of business was to meet an eminent counsel at Natly Abbey on the morrow, he advised examining what papers the Earl had left there before them. Ellen wished not to be present, but Gordon again reminded her of the absolute necessity of her affairs; still she wished to be spared that one trial: Gordon, without answering, proceeded with the letters. One from Miss Holt, most sympathizing and affectionate, she put into her bosom. There was one with a ducal coronet. "Duke Dash had the honour to offer compliments of condolence to the Countess Dowager of Castle Howel, begged to have leave to pay early devoirs to her in behalf of his son, late Lord Charles Dash, now Marquis of Squandervelt."

Gordon looked earnestly in Ellen's face, all was cold contempt and indifference. "I advise," said he, "all such letters as are not incumbent on yourself to answer, may be put together, for Lady Gertrude's gentleman to do it in the proper way."

"Surely, Sir, that letter does not require an answer?" and she was on the point of committing it to the flames.

"I don't know that,'" answered Gordon, eagerly rescuing the polite scroll, "our young heir's title may come before the Lords, and however insignificant he may be elsewhere, every Peer tells for one in their own house. Another coronet: ah! my old friend, are you here?" He read,

Lord Claverton never regretted his confinement and ill health so much as at that moment, as it deprived him of the honour of personally assuring the Countess Dowager of Castle Howel, how much he was devoted to her service. He could not express his indignation, to find there existed beings, capable of wronging the innocent child of a noble father; nor his grief, that such beings were leagued against the peace and honour of the most charming of women; he offered nothing to *her*, but he entreated she would permit him to be one of Lord Castle Howel's first friends, and that *his* attorney might be allowed to commune with, and go hand in hand in every step towards establishing his undoubted right. "Bravo," cried Gordon, "this is a friend in need," and away he capered with the letter to Lady Gertrude.

Ellen could not but be pleased, and while Gordon was absent she went on opening the letters; a card, in a French envelope, from Mrs. Morley, was put aside, for Lady Gertrude's gentleman.

From Lady Daub, ditto.

And so on.

Not so the welcome packet from Code Gwyn, yet it was not such an one as she expected, it wanted not sympathy, tenderness, or condolence, the letters were not short, but something they certainly did want that went to Ellen's heart.

"Lord help us," said Gordon, re-entering, "if this old friend of mine comes to Natly, he will rival Evelyn; the old dame is already half in love with him."

Gordon looked earnestly in Ellen's face as he said this, no blush arose, no symptom of latent passion, all was settled, pale, widowed grief; the miniature of Lord Castle Howel hung from her neck, she was then holding it in her hand, her eyes fixed, and the tears distilling from them drop by drop on the picture.

Gordon felt a pang of self-reproach, and retired in inward confusion.

Lady Gertrude's man of business kept his appointment, and presently after him arrived a gay chaise and four, out of which skipped a spruce, well dressed, well booted, and well powdered person, who desired the porter would announce Serjeant Pennings.

The Serjeant was shewn in, bowed to Lady Gertrude, was overjoyed to see his very good friend Mr. Process, warmed his hands, pulled up his boots, and asked Lady Gertrude to allow him the honour of setting his watch by her Ladyship's.

"Sat up with my Lord Judge last night; dry business at the assize – good deal to do in Criminal Court – nothing at all at Nisi Prius – Serjeant Clagget made a good thing of a notorious sheep-stealer, brought him off through thick and thin."

Mr. Process sat very impatiently waiting the end of an harangue Mr. Serjeant Penning intended should be introductory, and was just in the second hem, preparatory to an harangue for the same purpose, when a servant threw open the door, and Mr. Gordon led in the widowed Countess.

The beauty and grace of our heroine might have appeared more dazzling, but never so captivating as at this moment. The gentlemen of the law forgot their courts; but what is that, they forgot themselves. We are aware our readers will be incredulous, but the fact may be proved. Two gentlemen, eminent in the law, forgot their own importance one minute, while they were gazing on a beautiful woman! but this was too rare a thing to last. They were hardly seated before Mr. Process made *his* introductory harangue.

Mr. Process was neither young nor handsome, but as he chose to think himself so, it was the same thing to him. [He] was, as he was pleased to insinuate, a great favourite with the ladies, and might marry to great advantage if he pleased, but he did not please; his family was like no other body's family in this world, for they were faultless; his house was a pattern for all other houses, it was all his own taste; his chariot was the finest of all possible chariots, it was made by the first man, from the first model of the age; his business was in the first line, and conducted in the first style, for he did every thing himself.

Mr. Serjeant Pennings took occasion to look very arch at some of Mr. Process's periods; and Mr. Process was careful he should only look; for, though the Serjeant was quite ready to pop in a short sentence, every time Mr. Process breathed, the latter recovered his wind with such rapidity, the thing was impossible.

"I thought, Madam, these gentlemen were come to talk of law," said Ellen, with dignity.

Mr. Process recollected himself, and the Serjeant took out his papers; Ellen drew nearer the table, and Gordon stirred the fire.

"Hem! the ladies wish, Mr. Serjeant, to have your opinion, on the case I sent you, by the York mail."

"I want principally to know, how long it may be kept in the Courts before it is finally determined; for, as to the event, of that I am certain," said Lady Gertrude.

"May be so, Madam, I wish it may with all my heart, but nothing certain."

"How, Sir," said Ellen, "not certain! When the birth of the child is so easy proved, the hour, the minute he was born."

"Nothing to the point. Remember a cause where a midwife sued an unmarried lady for the expenses of lying-in; defendant denied; sued plaintiff for *Scan. Mag.* and jury gave verdict against midwife a thousand pound damages for injuring defendant's character – in that case we had nurses, maids, and gossips, to prove, yet lost the cause. Remember another case, where we claimed as heir, and could not prove, by a single witness, where, when, how, or, indeed, whither we were ever born at all, and there we got our cause."

"Good God!" exclaimed Ellen, "how oft have I heard my dear Lord expatiate on the wisdom, the policy, and the equity of English Laws."

"So they are, Madam," returned the ready Serjeant, "so they are; very wise, vastly politic, and strictly just."

"Bless me, Sir," answered Ellen, "were you not just saying –?"

"Nothing about the laws, dear Madam," rejoined the Serjeant, "I was only speaking of the practice of the Courts."

Mr. Process laughed out, "Very, very good."

"This may be very amusing to you, gentlemen," said Lady Gertrude, "but we are engaged in a serious business."

"Why, then, Ladies, seriously," replied the Serjeant, "on

your answers being put in, which Mr. Process and I will take care shall be in proper time, a Writ of Enquiry will probably be issued, we evade that, and – "

"Why so, Sir," interrupted Ellen, "Why should we evade inquiry?"

"Give me leave, Madam, give me leave."

Mr. Process arose, and whispering to the Countess, begged she would not interrupt the Serjeant, who was one of the first men; *he* always employed him.

Ellen and Lady Gertrude looked at each other, they sighed responsively.

The Serjeant went on. "And get a trial in Court of King's Bench, 'To prove competency of witnesses' then we go back to Equity, ten to one they send us back again to Court of King's Bench; at last get a decree or lose decree, no matter which, just talking for argument sake – then we go to the house of Peers; ten to one again but they send us back to one of the Courts below."

Gordon groaned, and insinuating his hand under his wig, scratched his head.

"I see," said Lady Gertrude, "we shall never understand these gentlemen, be so good as only to tell us; how long this matter may be deciding."

Mr. Serjeant rang for his servant, and standing up, assured her Ladyship he had a strong sense of the high honour conferred on him, by her commands, and should be always proud and happy to obey her; but as to the time it would take, to determine a chancery suit, where 20,000 a year was at stake, no man in existence knew: begged she would be *perfectly easy* in his attention to the business, and was the ladies most devoted and obedient humble servant.

Mr. Process, when out of his egotism, was a conversable

man; he explained the measures taken and to be taken, but the glorious uncertainty of the law left the dispute as much in the womb of time with him, as with the Serjeant; he however warmly recommended it to the Countess to go to London, confessed he thought there was some treachery in the business of the late Earl, and offered his assistance to find it out. Ellen thanked him, and both ladies, ill and out of spirits, retired to their several chambers, leaving Process, who was to set off early, to supper and be entertained by the Doctor.

When Mr. Gordon attended Ellen next day, she reminded him he had not thought of the papers, while the lawyers were there.

It did not much matter, he said, he would not trust either of them with a broken gallipot; he had a friend somewhere in London, who did not indeed ride circuits, but he should make bold to recommend her affairs to him, except, indeed, Lord Claverton's attorney.

Ellen cared not who, if he did her son justice.

Mr. Gordon then, in the presence of Lady Gertrude, and the curate, who officiated for parson Runnington, opened the Earl's cabinet, but there was not a single voucher, nor even his banker's account; on a few letters were written descriptions of different plants he had happened to see, and some figures, but no other papers. A patent key, belonging as Ellen thought, to his writing table in town, was carefully tied to a ribbon, in a drawer with some rings and other jewels, but nothing was found of importance to the grand inquiry.

Mr. Gordon still urging the Countess to go to London, and Lady Margaret's letters hinting something should be done about the house, where she, at her own expense, had put the servants into mourning, she at last agreed to fix the time. But now a difficulty occurred not easily got over – Ellen could not leave her child; Lady Gertrude could not let him go.

To the fondness of the mother was opposed the welfare of the child; it was born at Natly, that therefore was its native air; he had never a day's illness; his nurse, a wholesome country woman, who had not had the small pox, would not go to London, the milk therefore must be changed, and the child's life endangered.

Ellen would then stay with her child, but Gordon so effectually pleaded the service she might be of to herself and him, she at length consented to leave her darling in Lady Gertrude's care, and proceed to London.

On the evening previous to their departure, the Countess told Mr. Gordon, the letters she received from Code Gwyn were so unsatisfactory, and her desire to see her aged grandfather so great, she was resolved to pay them a short visit before she went to London, "And oh!" said she passionately, "that I could carry my boy with me and leave him there."

Mr. Gordon thought she was wrong; he reminded her of the near approach of Term,[28] and as to the child, confessed, in his opinion, he could be no where so well as at Natly, where its infant attractions were cementing the love of those only on whom it was to depend.

"Well," Ellen said, "whatever happened to her she would not be put off seeing her dear grandfather; if he died without giving her his blessing she should never forgive herself, or those who prevented her; so if Gordon would escort her, well; if not she would go by herself, and as soon as the duty her

---

[28] Courts worked on a system of four terms throughout each year, when judges heard cases.

heart yearned to pay at Code Gwyn was over, she would go to London and do all he wished.

Gordon with much murmuring, acceded, and Philip being reinstated into his Lady's service, was directed to take proper measures for the Welch journey; but, as Gordon justly observed, it could answer no end to acquaint Lady Gertrude with their route, as the short stay intended at Code Gwyn would only retard their arrival in London three or four days, and the law suit before her had already began so to operate on her Ladyship's feelings, in respect to money matters, that the smallest expense appeared enormous, and the servants-hall already echoed with murmurs on account of a change in their diet.

To save a carriage Winifred rode in the chaise with her Lady and Gordon, Philip was the single outrider and thus Ellen, who had left her native home a blooming bride, with a show of equipage and attendance, that attracted all eyes as she passed, was now returning a dowerless widow, unattended and overwhelmed with distress, within the short space of eighteen months.

They left Natly Abbey so early that Ellen bathed the face of her sleeping boy, with fond reluctant tears, without his awaking; and Lady Gertrude, whose fretfulness increased with her resolution to sell her last acre, to exclude the man she hated from the Castle Howel estate, having gone to bed indisposed was not disturbed.

Often did the weeping mother form a resolution to depart, and as often return for one look more; and, "Oh," cried she, leaning on Gordon, "if this anguish should be a presentiment, like that I felt on the fatal morning when I lost my Lord; ah! why do I leave my child? What is the world to me without him? What are titles and estates, have I not already, at *my* early period of life, found their inefficiency? Would," added she, lowering her voice, "would the gates of this mansion open to receive the widow and the fatherless without some interest of their own? Oh! no. Why should I not, then, carry my infant to that home, where poverty and distress, with no other than sorrow, are received with open arms!"

Gordon's heart also failed, he could not answer.

"Will not my aunts, dear good-hearted creatures, will not they be as careful of my child, as my Lord can be of his?"

Winifred did not dare to speak, but groaned at every sentence.

"Will not my grandfather doat on him? will not my uncle instil into his young mind a love of every virtue? My uncle, Sir, is a good and a learned man."

"If I am killed I must speak," interrupted Winifred. "Fat signifies talking, I tare for to say Mister Gordon knoes fat our Reverent is. Mr. Evelyn for that – did not he larn him his very letters, and all the outlandish reading, and who is a more petter and a more finer man as Mr. Evelyn? More's the pity, I say; and Cot's pity, he should be thrown away on such rubbish as the Runningtons, but Cot is always above the tivel, and he knows best."

Ellen was not displeased at Winifred's interruption; Evelyn she considered as married, or under engagements equal to it, but if she had not, her mind was entirely absorbed in her situation and too constantly recollecting the goodness of her honoured husband, whose memory it was her delight to cherish, to admit one thought of any other, even of Evelyn. It is true, when she mentioned Mr Meredith as the teacher of her child, his former care of Evelyn very naturally recured to her memory, and no mother, in any station, need wish to see her son arrive to be more than Evelyn now was; but it was the mother, not the lover, whom this thought gratified. "Yes, Sir," said she, looking earnestly at Gordon, "My uncle was the friendly tutor of Mr. Evelyn."

"I know it all, my dear Madam," answered Gordon, struggling with his feelings, "but your son is not, must not be an object of benevolence; he is the just and lawful heir to his father's honours and estate, to rob him of these, or, which is the same thing in effect, to suffer others to do it, is to injure him, and disgrace yourself and the respectable family so justly dear to you. Come, Madam, show your regard to the memory of the dead, by sacrificing the fondness of the mother to the interest of the friend; no friend to this dear child would wish his removal hence, nor any friend to you or him, but would hasten your presence where only he can be essentially benefited.

Again Ellen kissed the closed eyelids of her son; again she pressed his rosy lips, and then, urged by Gordon, threw herself into the chaise and soon lost sight of Natly Abbey.

As they took the cross road to North Wales, and travelled with all possible expedition, they came in sight of Castle Howel about noon on the third day; the windows were all shut, the hatchment up, no living soul to be seen in or near the grounds, where every thing accorded with the melancholy insignia of death; the terrace, where Lord Castle Howel often had accompanied her, explaining his botanical garden under it, an old grey horse he had formerly rode, quietly grazing in the park, with the entire stillness of the day, not a breath of air stirring, were objects of such melancholy note, as drew floods of tears from her eyes. Gordon was admiring the ancient castle, its situation and grounds, without knowing whose it was, till happening to see Phillip's horse with its reins loose, and the rider with his handkerchief at his eyes, and the hatchment at the same moment, he turned and beheld Ellen sunk on the bosom of her servant, shedding torrents of silent tears and seeming literally to enjoy grief.

The servant, who besides his mourning, was well known at Castle Howel, and the arms on the carriage soon informed the peasants who were passing; the men, having uncovered in respect, drew their hats over their eyes; the women's tears accompanied their courtesies, as they crowded to the doors; even the children stopped their play, and those who did not catch the melting mood from their parents, stood quite still, every muscle of their jocund faces contracted in a dismal stare.

Ellen's emotions grew so violent, Mr. Gordon let down the spring curtains, and endeavoured to turn her ideas to the happy meeting with her family. Understanding they were now within six miles of her native home, he directed Philip to go on, and the painful objects out of sight, she really began to anticipate the joyful reception she knew her family would give her.

Code Gwyn steeple appeared in sight, and amidst a clump of trees the white chimneys of the parsonage.

"My Cot!" exclaimed Winifred, "there's our tear little church; Cot pless us! talk of your Westmuster and your Pawl's, did you ever see such a church as that, Mr. Gordon?"

"And there's my uncle's house," said Ellen, a faint smile dimpling on her cheek.

"My Cot! fat are the people all at," cried Winifred, seeing the doors stand open, the houses to all appearance without inhabitants; and a great number of people crowding up the road towards Code Gwyn.

"Ah!" said Ellen, "my grandfather is dead, here is Philip returning, see how terrified he looks!"

Philip rode up to the carriage; to the rapid questions of the

Countess and her servant he could give no answer; he stammered and pointed to the crowd, who, now surrounding something they could not distinguish were slowly returning.

Winifred jumped out, and ran towards the people; Ellen would have followed had she not been forcibly withheld by Gordon, who ordered the carriage to stop, that the crowd might pass; a kind of procession advanced in the following order.

First an indiscriminate number of men, women, and children, all devoutly praying the plagues of Egypt might be multiplied on the head of one Squire Morgan.

The harper of Code Gwyn, blind and lame, led by a grandson of the coachman's.

Miss Catherine Meredith with a huge folio under each arm, and two bare-headed and barefooted girls with as many more as they could stand under.

Miss Mary Meredith, with the ebony inkstand Lady Margaret presented her, attended by a maid with bundles.

Mrs. Griffiths, breathing with great difficulty, and walking between two old female servants.

Sir Arthur Meredith, in his wheel-chair, carefully drawn by numbers of hearty-looking young men, who shouldered each other for the honour, supported on one side by the Reverend Mr. Edward Meredith, on the other by Miss Agnes; his fine eyes dimmed more by sorrow than age, but his countenance still noble, open and exhilarating.

Close behind hobbled old Griffiths; the procession was closed with all the domestics of Code Gwyn house, and was followed by a second indiscriminate mixture of all ages and sex.

"Cot Almighty pless my soul," cried Winifred, pushing

through the crowd, and taking her aunt's arm from the woman on whom she was leaning, and passing it forcibly through her own, "Fat, in the name of Cot is the matter fith you all; are you mat, or have you lost your senses? Aunt Griffiths, are you turned fool in your old age, to let them drag my poor tear owld master apout like a raree show? Cot pless him for ever and ever, amen, pray Cot."

"Winifred! my dear child," cried Mrs Griffiths, throwing her arms round her, "have I lived to see you, where is your dear blessed mistress? Oh, my poor Lady broke her heart about her!"

The name of Winifred was no sooner heard than crowds gathered round: Catherine dropped her books, Mary her ink stand, and even Mr. Meredith and Agnes left their father's side, who, soon as he understood the cause, wept like a child; but the air was too keen, and the good old man too little used to it, for Mr. Meredith to be easy at a long stoppage; he just turned his head to the chaise, where Ellen sat – lost in astonishment, with a look that spoke a thousand welcomes, and hastened towards the parsonage; the Miss Merediths, however, followed by Mrs. Griffiths, partly hobbling and partly dragged by Winifred, met Ellen, who no longer withheld by Gordon, sprang into their arms, and amid their heartfelt gratulations, the strange procession she had seen no longer occupied her thoughts.

Gordon being applied to for orders from the postillions, bid them stop at a clean looking inn, distinguished by a wooden sign, where all that remained of a lion, formerly red, was a splash of faded paint, very little brighter than the ground of the decayed sign post, where the exciseman sat at the door, smoking his pipe and explaining, in few words, the procession which moved still in sight, having not yet reached the Rectory.

"The old man you see there," said the exciseman, "in his wheel-chair, is the Israelite, in whom there is no guile; every body respects, pities, and blames him; he has been such a fool as to mortgage his estate to one of the most avaricious ill principled fellows in existence, son to one of his own menial servants, a pauper of this very parish; that miserable palsy-headed old creature you see picking sticks is his own aunt; this is the second time he has given notice of a foreclosure of the mortgage; it was once stopped, and, as every body thought, cleared, by that lady's husband," pointing after Ellen.

"You know her then?"

"Know her! God bless her sweet face, I walked down to Castle Howel on purpose to see her set off for London, when she married; she looked, as she always did, more than mortal, but, like the face of Charles Stuart, through all her liveliness I foretold a tale of sorrow in hers, didn't I, Landlord?"

"And so," joined Gordon, seeing an audience would soon gather, as the wheel-chair and the Countess entered the Rectory, "the mortgage was not paid?"

"So Morgan says," answered the exciseman, significantly.

"He say, he be d—d," cried a drunken shoe-maker, "I'd sooner trust that old man and even the hinds of the family, with every bit of leather I have in the world, than I would him with a pair of shoes."

"But," rejoined Gordon, "if it had been paid, to be sure there would be vouchers."

"I don't know that," answered orator Gauge, "for the old Earl, and no better man never breathed, thought every body like himself; he never run in debt here, though they say he did in London, but you could not displease him more than by talking of business; I dare say he never took a receipt in his life; however, so far circumstances prove for the Squire, if the mortgage had been paid, the deeds would of course be given up."

"And they are not?"

"No, no, old Mammon has them safe enough in his iron press."

Gordon thanked his intelligencer and walked on slowly towards the Rectory, moralizing on what he had heard.

But however distressing to human nature in general, and to the particular feelings of those concerned, were the circumstances he had witnessed at Natly, and heard of since his arrival at Code Gwyn, it was fully compensated by the scene which presented itself on his entrance into the great parlour at the Rectory.

The aged arms of the venerable Baronet were fondly growing round the lovely Countess, on whose cheek, pressed to her beloved parent's, the tears of both in mingled joy and grief were blended; joy, at a meeting so unhoped by Sir Arthur, so desired by Ellen – and grief, not for fortune gone, or mansion lost, but for her, who so long had cheered and delighted, whose voice was harmony, whose look was peace, and whose beatified spirit was now in eternity.

The Miss Merediths were in a group, contemplating the graceful form of their admired niece, but observing, with concern, her pale and languid countenance. And Mr. Meredith recollecting that Winifred said a gentleman, a dear good friend of her Lady, was with them, apologized to Mr. Gordon for his inattention, and bid him welcome in his usual placid sincere manner.

It would indeed have been very difficult for the nicest

observer to discover a trait of misfortune in the family, except in the face and dress of Ellen herself.

Sir Arthur's last home was entirely forgot while he held the white hand, and contemplated the face of his charming grand daughter; his daughters regarded no inconvenience but *his;* his son had that equanimity of mind that every place was easy to *him,* where his exertions contributed to the happiness of others; and, as to Ellen, she had lately been inured to such successive reverses both of fortune and habitation, she felt no inconvenience from a change, that considering her long absence, and the death of Lady Meredith, rather perhaps relieved than oppressed her mind. Not so poor Winifred – the large kitchen at the Rectory would barely afford sitting room for the domestics of Code Gwyn, though none of them were retained who were able to get their living elsewhere; and so many old men and women, all infirm, and some almost helpless, grieving both for themselves and their master, were a very uncomfortable society for one, who had, in virtue of her office, reigned paramount among smart footmen and dressy waiting women.

"Pless me," cried she, impatiently, "my plack hapit will pe spoiled, I hope we are not all to live together in this creasy hole."

Mrs. Griffiths bid her hold her tongue, which as she did not seem inclined to do, old Griffiths actually held his cane over her head. But times were everyway altered with Winifred, who, with poor tear Mr. Joseph in her head, a valuable wardrobe, and £300 in her possession, was subject to all the caprices a sudden acquisition of wealth is sure to create in weak minds, and much as she had longed to see Code Gwyn, not having any of the nice ligaments that twine round the soul of sensibility, and cement the bonds of love and friendship in her disposition, she in one hour more longed to leave it; "she should not think of Mr. Griffiths taking liberties with her; she was no papy, to be peat, Cot pless her; and if she had known how she would be used she would not have persuaded her Laty to leave the Abbey, to come to such a place as Code Gwyn."

"Such a place as Code Gwyn!" Mrs. Griffiths ejaculated.

"No," Winifred recalled her words, she meant the Rectory, "for as to Code Gwyn house, she had seen the palace, and a poor thing Cot knows it was to see; and the mansion-house, and petlam, and Cot knows none of them was comparable to Code Gwyn. But for a parcel of servants to be crammed into a hole, no pigger, as poor tear Mr. Joseph used to say, than the hole at Galgutter, especially for servants that have seen the world, and scraped a little fortune together, besides spoiling their cloaths, it was too pad!"

Winifred, a fortune! come that was too much. But Winifred no sooner convinced her uncle she really had in her own possession £300 besides valuables, than he gave her his word he would leave her a matter of £80 he had saved, on two provisos – the first, that Sir Arthur did not want it; second that she outlived her aunt; and as the old man thereafter never threatened her with his cane, or addressed her, without preceding Winifred with Mrs. or Miss, and as all the rest of the servants had an extraordinary veneration for £300 Winifred condescended to pin up the skirt of her black habit, and entertain them with stories, consisting of truths exaggerated, and truths mutilated, of what she had seen in London, which, considering they *were truths* at all, was great merit in a traveller.

In the parlour the social party had drawn round the fire, and Mr. Meredith having repeated the facts related by the exciseman, with the addition, that as although he was self convinced Lord Castle Howel had paid a great part of the mortgage, if not the whole, he had no proof to produce, and even if he had, the confused state of his Lordship's own affairs at his death, would have been equally embarrassing to his father; that therefore recollecting how often they had regretted not suffering Mr. Morgan to pay himself out of their own property, instead of incurring obligations which they had paid too dearly for –

Ellen interrupted him, "My dear Sir, *too* dearly?"

"Yes, Ellen," answered he, "when your youth, beauty, and innocence, was consigned to a family who insulted *us* by their false accusation of *you*; who accelerated the death of a woman every way their superior; and who, after all, fancied they made the amende honorable in acknowledging your honour, and their own credulity; we did indeed pay too dear for a mere temporary relief; I therefore resolved to make the matter as easy to my father and sisters as possible, and though we might have staid two months longer at Code Gwyn, face the worst at once; Sir Arthur did not bear the removal so well as I hoped, and indeed expected, but providence sent our dear Ellen in the moment we wanted a comforter, and you see, Sir," said the excellent son, taking his father's hand, over which he affectionately bowed, "every deprivation from God has its fellow comfort, I have found it so in every case but *one.*"

Ellen's heart informed her of the *one* he alluded to, she wiped her eyes, and softly asked Agnes what her uncle meant, by accelerating the death of her grandmother.

Agnes fetched Lady Margaret's letter, it had not yet been read through, nor quite unfolded in the exact manner in which Lady Meredith had laid it down, when death-struck by the three first lines, it had remained, and was now put into the hands of the Countess.

No words can express the anguish of Ellen's heart while reading the cruel letter, and informed of the direful effect it had on the good woman to whom it was addressed; nor the indignation the portrait drawn of herself, and the vile insinuation respecting her servant, raised in her mind; she unfolded the infamous scrawl, and, having gone near through it, started, rubbed her eyes, "sure," cried she, "my tears, though they may prevent my seeing, cannot make words, my brain I hope is not turned; read, Sir," and she handed it to Gordon, "I beseech you read that passage."

Gordon read, "and to prove to you still further how unworthy she is of the honour my brother was weak enough to confer on her, I this day, by his order, paid Mr. Morgan the last thousand pounds, and the deeds will be delivered as soon as the shameless conduct of his wife suffers him to return to his family."

Astonishment tied every tongue; at length silence was broke by Gordon. "This," said he, "is indeed a discovery."

Mr. Meredith took the letter, he turned pale, and laid it down; his sainted mother full in his mental view, "I cannot go through it."

"Let me," said Mary, eagerly.

"Read aloud, my child," said the old Baronet, who was grown a little deaf.

Mary read the paragraph, it was verbatim from the letter, and no illusion of the senses.

Mr. Meredith seeing his father's eyes illumined, as in happier days they used to be with pleasure, prudently reminded him of what he had before observed to Ellen, and Mr.

Gordon, that as the money was actually borrowed, whether Morgan or the Castle Howels, or their creditors, were mortgagees, did not matter to them.

"Not matter! son," said Sir Arthur, the spirit of his gallant ancestors lighting in his visage, and pervading his whole frame, "not matter!" said the impassioned old chief, and he actually stood erect, "does it not matter to punish the murderess of your mother, the defamer of her darling, the *unwomanly* insulter of *woman?* Does it not matter to defeat fraudulent avarice to pay debts where they are justly due, to render unto Caesar the things that *are* Caesar's? Oh, blessed spirit," taking off his hat, which, since his deafness he constantly wore, "if heaven can be more than heaven *now* in this instant thou art among us."

The sudden exertion of an old man, who had not been able to stand on his feet many years, his animated countenance, grey hairs, and elevated voice seemed more than mortal; they all arose, as if by inspiration, and raised their eyes to meet the spirit he invoked, but the strong agitation soon overpowered Sir Arthur, he sunk into the arms of his son, weak and out of breath; Ellen knelt and embraced his knees. "Not matter!" repeated he as soon as he could speak.

Mr. Meredith recanted: "Yes, he saw the advantages of the letter in its full extent."

"It is worth a million to us at this juncture," said Gordon.

"Ah, it will ferret them," said the exalting Baronet.

They now entered into consultations on the situation of Ellen and her child.

Sir Arthur interrupted them, hoped he should see his Ellen's boy before he died.

Catherine doubted not he would be a valorous knight.

·

Agnes talked of the advantage of his long minority.

"Oh, what a sweet letter this will make," cried Mary," but I have lost my ebony ink stand."

"No," answered Catherine, "here are the broken remains."

Mary began to lament – "It was the prettiest thing–"

"Why you would not keep any thing belonging to that sorceress, whose baneful dew has been sprinkled over our family."

Mr. Meredith smiled at Gordon, "we are *too* happy," said he, "to be rational, you and I, Sir, will, if you please, retire to my study."

"Aye, do," said Agnes, "and I'll set the maids to knitting."

Catherine would look after her books – Mary began her letter, "and I," said Ellen, "will take my old seat on the gouty stool, and tell my dear grandfather all that has happened to me since I parted from him." If there are but few young women in the bloom of health, and pride of beauty, who can conceive the exquisite pleasure of thus entertaining an old honoured relation, there are many respectable old people who can conceive the delight of being so entertained; but in this instance it was mutual.

Chapter II

An early happy supper concluded the adventures of the day, and Ellen, having prayed for her dear boy, retired to the first unbroken rest she had long experienced.

Gordon and Meredith were kindred souls, they perfectly understood each other; and the latter having made all the requisite communications, they agreed, that after one day's rest it was absolutely necessary the Countess should go to London, and make use of all her interest on behalf of her son, as well as to discover the fraudulent management of the Earl's fortune; Gordon was lawyer enough to know she had a right to go to the town house, which being a leasehold one, was not in the Castle Howel entail.

The day, and the only one time would now permit Ellen to pass at Code Gwyn, appeared a very short one to all but Winifred, who was persuaded by David to go and see the little garden at Code Gwyn, and who, when there, could not help peeping in at the old house.

Winifred must, when agitated, either cry or scold, and indeed very often both. Her stomach ached, she said, to think David should, in the first place, be such a fool as to marry the Castle Howel still-room maid, and in the next, that he should take such pains with Mr. Evelyn's garden, who, to be sure, by this time, was as pad as married to parson Runnington's carotty daughter, and never, no, never, would see Code Gwyn again; and at the same time have so little regard for a fellow servant, as to let her holly hogs and her polly hauncheses die;

now that, and she looked dismally round the silent house, she thought very hard, and, peeping into her aunt Griffith's room, very cruel, so cruel, that after another mournful look around, she began to cry in a most piteous manner.

David had thought very little on Winifred, and less of her holly hogs and polly haunchesses, but his eye followed hers, and though he had no aunt Griffiths's room to look into, he began to feel his *neglect* on some *other* cause was really affecting; it was hard, it was cruel, he confessed it, and David's tears began to flow as rapidly as his fellow servant's.

"It signifies nothing locking the gate now," said David, looking wistfully over the green hedge.

"No to be sure, 'tis coot enough I hope for old Morgan."

David not only took out the key but kicked the wicket.

"To use me so cruel," cried Winifred as they turned from the garden.

"I am sure, Mrs. Winifred," answered David, sobbing, with his head turned quite round, "if I had thought of it."

"Thought," retorted Winifred, "that's worser as any thing, as poor tear Mr. Joseph used to say, the sin of ungrateful is as worse as witchcraft."

"Stop, let me shut the field gate after us," said David, drawing the back of his hand across his eyes.

"Tivel take the gate, let us leave them all open, coot enough for old Morgans."

David agreed to Winifred's proposition respecting the fields; but as all the neighbours' cattle would certainly get in, he could not find it in his heart to leave Mr. Evelyn's garden open.

"No," said David, "it may be choaked with weeds, but the cattle shan't turn it up," and as soon as he got rid of Winifred, who took care to place stones against all the gates that the cattle might have free egress, David ran back to lock the wicket.

In the course of Mr. Gordon's conversation with Meredith, Evelyn was not forgot; and as he was the confident of his most secret thoughts at Natly, Meredith was sorry to understand there was more compliance with opinion of others, than inclination of his own, in the proposed match; as, however, from Gordon's opinion and description of the young lady, he could not but think her amiable, and the living a great acquisition, he trusted he would be happy, "as happy as a heart can be under the privation of the first object of its attachment." Meredith sighed, he had never before conversed on the subject, with any person in whom he could properly confide the secret history of his own feelings – Evelyn was a part of those feelings, to him it was neither safe nor proper to repose a secret in which he was deeply interested; Meredith's disposition was kindness itself, but inaccessible to friendship, in the common acceptation of that term; he was obliging to every body, intimate with very few, but here was thrown, by accident, in his way, the approved and disinterested friend of the two most dear to him in the world; two, whose hearts were formed to join, but whom fate had for ever separated; and the secret so long hid in the inmost recess of his heart, must some time be revealed, and to Evelyn, who then so proper to entrust as his chosen friend and probable neighbour?

"The young man," said Mr. Meredith, speaking of Evelyn, "is very dear to me."

"So I perceive," answered Gordon.

"I loved his mother more than a reasonable being ought to love the created."

That might easily be, Gordon thought, and smiling significantly, added, he suspected as much.

Meredith assured him he was mistaken.

Gordon smiled again.

"I see," said Meredith, more solemnly, "you adopt a common error, I am not Evelyn's father, I am not so happy."

Gordon, who had set it down for matter of fact in his own mind, looked surprised, and perhaps rather curious.

Mr. Meredith wanted not inducements but invitations to open his heart, those invitations, however, Gordon was too polite to give, and there for that time it ended.

Philip was punctual to his hour with the horses, and Ellen took the same leave of her grandfather, who was in a tranquil sleep, she had of her son; she looked at him, and turning to Gordon and Meredith, "Mark the ways of the righteous man, his end is peace."[29] "That is not quite right, I believe," said she, drying her eyes, "but I have often heard you, uncle, say something like it."

Sir Arthur had vehemently pressed his son to accompany the Countess. It was, he said, unseemly so young a widow should go into a barbarous world, to encounter injury, and perhaps suffer insult, without one natural friend to protect her. The ladies were of the same opinion, and indeed Mr. Gordon, tho' he wanted no encouragement to exert his utmost, thought the measure a proper one; but as there was no time to be lost, and as a curate must be got, to do the church duty in his absence, in whose Christian care Meredith must leave not only his parishioners, but his father, he promised to follow, and in the mean time put, at parting a sealed paper in Gordon's hand, which he recommended to his leisure hour.

---

[29] A misquote of Psalm 37.

The journey directly from Code Gwyn to London was not an hundred miles more than from Natly to Code Gwyn. As they passed Castle Howel, on which Ellen cast a tearful eye, Philip rode up, and taking off his hat,

"We shall return here victorious, Madam, I know we shall."

Ellen rewarded his officious zeal with a half smile through her tears.

"Fiddle faddle, Mr. Philip," cried Winifred, who had been silent half sulky and half sorry, "fat signifies victory, fen there is nothing to fin; for my part if please Cot take my owld master, Cot pless his ansum face, pray Cot, and my uncle and aunt Griffiths, and the owld harper; and two or three more of the owld fograms,[30] I should not care if I never see it again, now that Satan incarnal have cot Code Gwyn house; for to be sure we life like pigs in a stye at the Rectory, not so much as a dressing room now in the hole house."

Nothing ran in Winifred's head but the change at Code Gwyn, and as on the road there she was too full of home to see Castle Howel, so, on leaving it, her mind still dwelt as intently on the same object, though discontent and disappointment were annexed to every recollection.

Gordon was so anxious to get to their journey's end, he would scarce allow the time for rest, and by ten o'clock the fifth evening the chaise stopped in Grosvenor-Street; Philip had rode on, and the single servant left in the house (Lady Margaret had taken some with her and discharged the rest) appeared without light.

Philip stormed, there were no candles but kitchen ones the girl knew of. The difference of her reception in that house to

---

[30] I.e., old fogies

what she had been used to, stopped Ellen's breath. Winifred, always at home, ran into the next house, and returned in an instant with two wax lights, and lighted her Lady up, while Philip discharged the horses, and then ran to Dr. Macshean's, to acquaint Lady Margaret of their arrival, not doubting but she would instantly fly to receive the Countess. He begged to know if there was any message. The servant went up stairs, Philip waited with impatience in the passage; he rang the servants' bell, up came another footman. "Do see if there is a message for me, my Lady don't know where I am."

The man ran up stairs: Philip again rang, at last the Lady's woman, whom Philip well knew, brought her Lady's compliments, she would have the honour to see the Countess in a day or two. Humph, quoth Philip, and returned in as much haste as he went.

"What became of the cook?" said Philip.

"Gone to live with Lady Margaret."

"And the kitchen maid?"

"Turned away."

"And Betty, the upper housemaid?"

"Turned away."

"The porter?"

"Set up a public house."

"James?"

"Gone with Lady Margaret."

"Tom?"

"Turned away."

"So what between Lady Margaret, and turned away, my Lady is come to an empty house; I think somebody's turn will be served next. And pray who are you, my bucks?" to two men who sat in the kitchen.

"We are in possession of the goods, for the creditors," answered one of them.

"Oh, ho! then the murder's out; the old rat has undermined the house, and now 'tis tumbling, she's off, is she?"

The men knew nothing of family affairs, they did their duty and no more.

"That's right my bucks, but, come, who has the key of the plate? My Lady's cloth must be laid; to save you a vast deal of trouble, Mrs. Maid of all work, I have ordered the supper from the tavern, give me the keys."

One of the men, who did not like Philip's looks under his affected gaiety, said, he had the keys, but he did not know whether he had a right to –

"Well said, my buck, but do you know there is such a thing as might as well as right, and so, d'ye see, if you have got the keys and won't deliver, I shall make bold to take them, that's all my buck."

The men consulted a moment, and gave the keys.

Philip ran up stairs as alert as if nothing had happened, and found the Countess standing in an agony of grief before Lord Castle Howel's picture, from whence all Gordon's entreaties could not remove her.

Supper, he told her, in the usual way, was on table, and Gordon presenting his hand, she mechanically walked into a small eating parlour, which Philip had contrived to light up, and place every thing exactly in the order she had been used to see it.

Thus immediately at home, the dreary change that affected her at entrance wore off, and she became tolerably composed.

Gordon took an early leave, meaning to lay at an hotel, but Philip's information of the guests in the house changed his intention, and he returned to a chamber the attentive servant directed to be prepared for him; who, having inquired if his Lady had any further commands, received a sweet dismission from her own lips, with charge to take care of himself, and under pretence of going to bed, sallied out to find some of the stragglers who had been turned away; he returned with Betty the upper house maid, who also promised to see to the cooking, and Tom, with which acquisition he went to take what he much wanted, rest.

It was not in the morning possible, or indeed needful to conceal from Ellen the situation of her affairs. Mr. Gordon fortunately met his friend, a Scotch solicitor, as well as English lawyer of fair reputation. They went first to Lord Castle Howel's banker, and examined the books; all the cash was drawn out, except four hundred pounds, before his Lordship's death.

The accounts were exceedingly clear, and the vouchers produced, with this extraordinary circumstance, that, except two thousand pounds taken by the Earl himself, previous to his journey, and a few loose £20 and £30, payable to ingenious people, all the drafts were payable to Lady Margaret Howel or bearer. This circumstance, added to that in her letter, was so striking, Mr. Traverse advised a consultation before a single step was taken; and Gordon having mentioned Lord Claverton, Mr. Traverse proposed waiting on him directly; "we cannot have too many friends," said he.

Lord Claverton was not in town; a circumstance that, far from disconcerting Ellen, pleased her. The painful hours she had passed in the house where she now was recurred with all their causes and consequences, and she considered that to be on terms of intimacy with a man, for whom her character had so recently suffered, however convenient his friendship would be neither delicate with regard to her then situation, nor respectful to the memory of her Lord.

Gordon, who pursued with avidity every hope of advantage to her affairs, without giving himself time to reflect, could not obviate Lady Castle Howel's difficulties, though they would not have struck him; he therefore said he would wait on Lord Claverton at Richmond, and accept as much of his service as would strengthen their cause, and not expose the Countess to the false conclusions of the ignorant, or the wilful misrepresentations of the malevolent.

A violent rap at the door announced visitors. "Not at home," were the orders, except to the Macsheans; but Philip ventured to disobey them in favour of Lady Mappleton and her daughter, the amiable Caroline.

In proportion to the injuries her Ladyship knew the Countess had sustained, and her present distressed situation, was her kindness, and that of her amiable daughter; after welcoming her to town, she entered with warmth into her affairs, and one of her daughters having married a young counsellor of shining abilities, promised to interest him in the business, and wrote a card, requesting to see Mr. More immediately.

Lady Mappleton was too good a parent not to be immediately obeyed; and Mr. Gordon had the pleasure to see their consultation aided by a volunteer of great sense and knowledge of the law, who approved of Mr Traverse's motion respecting a consultation and named the gentleman whose advice he thought of most consequence. The ladies stayed with Ellen the whole day, in momentary expectation of a visit from Lady Margaret, who, at a quarter past five, made her appearance, with Mrs. Morley.

The respectability of Ellen's companions struck them into visible confusion; Lady Margaret complained of ill health, and her looks confirmed the complaint: Ellen, with her long black robes flowing round, and looks of dignified sorrow, did not appear the forlorn, distressed, and friendless widow they expected; not a complaint escaped her, not a single retrospect; she spoke with calm fortitude of her present embarrassments, and with marked contempt of the futile attempts to injure her son; this was a business which also seemed to affect Lady Margaret; and Lady Mappleton conceived it, she said, to be a family concern – "You, cousin Margaret, was extremely attentive to your brother's domestic concerns even since your marriage and his death."

Lady Margaret trembled, she took out her smelling bottle, and Mrs. Morley declared, it was the cruellest thing in the world to mention the Earl before her dear friend, whose spirits were so weak she could not bear the subject.

"It is a subject, nevertheless, Madam, on which she must make up her mind to bear a great deal." Lady Mappleton's severe look added poignancy to this speech. Mrs. Morley, who felt for neither one or the other of the parties, threw a wonderful stare into her countenance.

"I was saying," continued Lady Mappleton, "the right of our young relation is a family concern, and ought to unite us in one cause, as far as my mite may be of service I –"

Lady Margaret's tremor wore off, *she* would be very happy, *but* the *Doctor* had an insuperable aversion to law suits.

"Odious law suits!" Mrs. Morley declared they were the very horridest things in nature; Mr. Morley had been involved in a chancery suit ten years, and though he knew the justice of his cause, it gave him a regular fever every sitting, and she believed in her conscience would be his death at last; it had cost she did not know how many thousand pounds.

From the account of Mr. Serjeant Pennings, Ellen's dread of the chancery suit was a continual load on her mind.

Miss Holt saw Ellen's soul in her countenance at Mrs. Morley's history of the chancery business; she turned to Lady Margaret, and was excessively sorry to hear of the Doctor's *singular* dislike to law, as it was very probable he would find himself *obliged* to attend to some business of his own, in that way, quite as troublesome as the claims on his nephew's estate.

Lady Margaret did not understand Miss Holt, but, whatever might be the Doctor's concerns, she believed he would be able to manage them without "a family subscription."

"Or a church brief," added Mrs. Morley, who was by this time thoroughly piqued at the cool return to all her advances towards a renewal of former friendship; for, as Mrs. Morley saw Ellen had lost none of her beauty, and had now reason to suppose she would not, as Lady Margaret foretold, be consigned to her original obscurity, with a poor undone family, who could not help themselves, much less her; she thought it not impossible but she might be again for a short season the fashion, and that, in consequence, it would be the thing to be her intimate. But Ellen, without intending it, had, from mere indifference, said more than a volume of words, and as no medium could be admitted between rejected intimacy and open enmity, Mrs. Morley, not being able to attain the former, adopted the latter.

Cards were now left by Lady Autumn, Lady Daub, and Miss Pendergrast, and presently a thunder was heard.

Lady Margaret and Mrs. Morley's carriages being at the

door, His Grace of Dash alighted without ceremony, and as the four footmen belonging to those ladies and two of Lady Mappleton's were in the hall, Philip could not deny his Lady; accordingly, just as Mrs. Morley had been delivered of her church brief, the Duke of Dash was announced. Ellen, who did not intend to let any body in but Lady Margaret, was a little confused, but soon resumed her presence of mind.

The Duke paid her a thousand unmeaning compliments, on her improved looks, and took occasion to be profuse in the same way to every lady present, by turns; made large offers of service and friendship, which he begged the Countess would command, and then took his leave without mentioning his son, the most noble the Marquis of Sqandervelt; as Lady Margaret and her friend arose at the same time, he handed them to their carriage.

At the consultation it was agreed, that as the establishing the right and title of the young heir was the most important business, every other should give way to it. Here was every probability that unfair transactions, with respect to the Earl's personals, would come out, on a close investigation, but as the Countess's credit in asserting the rights of her son would appear so infinitely weakened by a division of the family, which must be the consequence of a law-suit now with Lady Margaret, they advised disposing of what assets the Earl had left, and putting them into such a train of payment as they would allow, and let all his sister's accounts stand over for the present. A woman who could act in the manner Lady Margaret appeared, and perhaps would be proved to have done, might be a very dangerous enemy. In consequence of this advice, Lady Castle Howel moved in to lodgings in Pall Mall, and the furniture &c. in Grosvenor-Street were advertised to be sold.

Lord Claverton received Mr. Gordon with great civility, but neither his name nor person seemed to strike his Lordship with recollection of any former acquaintance.

He entered with great avowed interest into the cause of Lord Castle Howel's son, which by this time began to be much talked of, and, as he promised, ordered his attorney to aid every step proper to be taken both with money and advice.

Lord Claverton was, at this time, far advanced in a settled consumption, but as his disorder was slow in its progress, as no expense or physical skill were spared, and as he was too desirous of life to neglect the minutest precaution recommended by the faculty, except the voyage to Lisbon, which, as they saw his was a lost case, they forbore to urge, it was attended with all those flattering hopes peculiar to the various turns of the disorder.

Ellen, the dear, the injured Ellen, a widow, her character no longer impeached, in narrow if not absolute dependant circumstances, her family reduced, her son persecuted – was again the idol of his thoughts. Her circumstances would reconcile her to his ill health, her gratitude to his constant attachment, and her society, pure and virtuous as he knew it to be, would help to calm that perturbed state of mind, which, notwithstanding his now regular life, often banished peace from his heart, and rest from his eyelids; all his large fortune should be devoted to her and hers, and he was self assured, with her every blessing would be his. But this dear and enchanting plan, an improvement on that which had been predominate on his mind from the instant he saw her, must be managed with caution and delicacy; Mr. Meredith was expected, and to him it should be first opened. He dismissed Gordon with the strongest professions of regard, and begged to see him as often as he could make it convenient, and added he would not intrude on the Countess till her uncle's arrival.

"Do you think, my Lady," said Gordon, attentively looking himself in the glass, "that four and twenty years would make such an alteration as would prevent your knowing or recollecting me, after a tete-a-tete of two hours?"

"Not except you were changed by something more than time."

"Lord Claverton, then Captain Claverton, and I, were sworn brothers in adventure; about that time my Nancy was sent from Scotland to a relation who kept a boarding school, to be out of my way; I soon followed her; and Captain Claverton being then desperately in love with a young girl, for her fortune, which was very large, at the same school, we met in our peregrinations round the sanctum sanctorum, where our treasures were kept, under lock and key, and at last received them out of a window; we had got licences, by contrivance, he gave me my Nancy, and I returned the favour to him."

"Indeed!" replied the Countess, "I never heard Lord Claverton had been married."

"We were pursued," continued Gordon, "Nancy and I not having much fortune got off, but the heiress was recovered, and she wrote us, that dreading the violence of her father's temper, she had prevailed on the governess to conceal the whole affair, which she was the readier to do as her own interest was at stake. The Captain was obliged to decamp soon after, without beat of drum, and the girl wrote to tell Nancy she had reason to fear she was pregnant; we went to the Highlands, and whether she wrote, or whether she died, or what became of her, we never heard afterward; nor probably ever should have thought of enquiring, had we not been honoured with knowing Lady Castle Howel."

"Poor thing!" answered the Countess, "She is most likely dead."

Letters were brought in from Natly, and opened with trembling eagerness by Ellen. It was a mere nursery journal, the child quite well, and, to Lady Gertrude's infinite delight, said Ma every time he saw her.

A large packet for Gordon was directed by the same hand. "News from Ireland I suppose," said he.

Ellen's colour rose, and she felt now, for the first time since Evelyn's absence, an unaccountable something swelling in her bosom, so exquisitely painful, it robbed her of all presence of mind, and she burst into tears.

Gordon, without appearing to observe it, took his letters, and walked out of the room.

"Good God!" said Ellen, "is my poor heart never to be at rest? What is the news from Ireland to me?" She took out Lord Castle Howel's picture from her bosom as a shield from the error of her own thoughts, it excited a fresh gush of tears, but did not expel the Irish news from her mind.

Mr. Meredith entered, he brought the welcome intelligence that Sir Arthur was well, and perfectly reconciled to the Rectory. Winifred cast up her eyes in astonishment, and Ellen tried to look happy, but her impatience for the Irish news got the better of every thing; she sent for Gordon, who, it was likely would immediately tell Mr. Meredith if he had heard from Evelyn.

She was again disappointed, as Gordon and Meredith withdrew together as soon as the first salutations were over. She forgot Lady Mappleton's carriage was to fetch her to dine, it had waited half an hour when Philip reminded her; she entered it with the same absence of mind, her eyes fixed without seeing passing objects; one object, however, there was in the world, whose power over her faculties was invincible – Percival Evelyn running by the carriage, out of breath, and unable to make the coachman hear, soon attracted her eyes, she pulled the check, he jumped into the carriage.

"Forgive me, Ellen," said he, in the uttermost agitation, "I know not what I am doing, I just wrote a line to Gordon and was waiting to see him but I saw you; and thought of nothing else." He had seized a hand that had no power to resist the thousand kisses he imprinted on it; her tongue refused its office, the whole world but Percival Evelyn was forgotten, when the carriage stopped at Lady Mappleton's door and Lord Squandervelt stood on the step ready to hand her out; all the world was then remembered, and the strange appearance of a gentleman in Lady Mappleton's coach struck her with such confusion, she had no power to make an excuse or to take leave of Evelyn, who alighted and stood pale as death on the step, watching for a look, while the happy Squandervelt was uttering a rhapsody of compliments, and even presumed to press her hand to his lips, without her hearing the one or perceiving the other; the turn of the stair, however, as the door was open for another carriage to draw up, presented Evelyn still on the step, despair and anguish on his brow, but he was lifted to immortality by the smile which created a thousand dimples, and a motion of the hand he had just pressed to his lips.

"My dear Ellen, you are so annoyed with lawyers and overwhelmed with business, you will be fit to be made Lady Chancellor," said Caroline, as she kindly met her at the drawing room door, "that, I suppose, was one of the tribe."

"No my dear," answered Ellen, with her usual incorrigible

frankness, "it was –" She had got so far, when she recollected the difficulty of explaining who it was, and on what occasion he had got into the carriage.

"It was who, my dear?" joined Lady Mappleton, and as she waited with some apparent curiosity for the reply, Ellen stammered and blushed, but could not get from her conscious lips the name of Evelyn.

"It was the curate of Little Manor, Madam?"

"Who? my dear."

"A friend of my uncle's, the curate of Little Manor."

Lord Squandervelt measured her from head to foot with his eyes, "If this woman," said he softly to an officer who stood leaning over Caroline's chair, "was not so divinely handsome, there would be no bearing her. The curate of Little Manor! So she kept a party of fashion waiting, while she was entertaining a little dirty curate, and actually stopped me in the current of air on the d——d stair-case, while she was kissing her hand to him."

Lady Mappleton thought the occurrence so odd herself, she the readier penetrated his Lordship's sentiments, though she did not hear what he was saying.

Lord Squandervelt heard it was Lord Claverton's intention to offer his hand to the charming widow; we will not take on us to say the Marquis was in love, because that is a sort of passion minds of his class are not often biased by, but certain it is, her person pleased, and her conversation amused him; and there are those among people in possession of means to give and receive the most exquisite delight, who say, to be pleased and amused is the only business of life. Well then, with an object in view, capable of both, how could Lord Squandervelt suffer another to supersede him? He was alarmed, and fancying himself unhappy, prevailed on the Duke, who having now no other son to perpetuate the noble house of Dash, could refuse him nothing, to visit Lady Mappleton, and make a friend of her, previous to his opening his honourable trenches in due form before the Countess.

If the Marquis of Squandervelt, one of the handsomest men of the day, was uneasy about Lord Viscount Claverton, what reason had not his Lordship, who was a much older man, and in ill health, to be afraid of the Marquis; each of these noble enamoratos kept a strict watch over the other. If the Marquis had the advantage of Lady Mappleton's friendship, the Viscount secured one of still greater importance, for being now in town, he had instant notice through Mr. Joseph, whose visits were renewed in Grosvenor-Street, of the arrival of Mr. Meredith, to whom he immediately sent, and who, in company with Mr. Gordon, actually dined with him that day.

Chapter III

Lord Claverton, the reader must have observed was a perfect master of human propensities; he well knew Meredith's affection for the Countess, and had long reason to understand family pride had great weight in the Code Gwyn arrangements; their niece, the flower of their race, was accused of a crime, of which her accusers knew her to be innocent, and which was set on foot to gratify disappointed ambition and private malice, at an expense the fortunes of the Howels of Moor Bank could not support, and must fall to nothing; but it was not his business to make the simple parson acquainted with the little there was to fear, no; it was rather his cue to exaggerate the danger, that so his great friendship might be of more value and importance, and the secret passion he had so long nourished, was too accordant to Mr. Meredith's own feelings to be condemned.

He supposed it not impossible Ellen might accept a fortune and title, the one superior the other nearly equal to Lord Castle Howel's; and, moreover, be it remembered, that the confessions Lord Claverton had made in his penitent fits were to Lord Castle Howel, a man who never betrayed confidence, even if his own interest depended on it being revealed; and to Doctor Macshean, who only considered confidence as sacred, as it did or did not coincide with his own private views; in this instance he had no interest in telling the world what he had long known himself, he was therefore secret.

Mr. Meredith's arrival reminded Gordon of a sealed paper he received from him at parting, and which lay in his trunk yet unopened; ashamed to own he had not had time, or curiosity, to break the seal of a paper committed to him with such solemnity, he rose from table earlier than strict politeness would warrant, on pretence of business, and hastened to the Countess's lodgings, where he had a small room appropriated to business. No sooner had he drawn his chair, and ordered candles, than he perceived another packet, which had also been strangely neglected.

"*News from Ireland, I suppose,*" said Gordon, when he saw Lady Gertrude's large packet, and he was in the act of breaking the seal, when Ellen's emotion put a stop to that act, and obliged him to go out of the room to conceal his own.

"*News from Ireland,*" repeated he to himself, and throwing the packet on the table walked up and down the room assigning his own reasons for Ellen's tears, and sincerely regretting he had at that time any correspondents in Ireland. He looked towards the table, "I told him he must be married, and by this time it is over," thought Gordon and made a motion to take up the packet, but his heart failed. Mr. Meredith's arrival was announced, and he left it on the table – they returned together, and still he had not curiosity or inclination to see *the news from Ireland.*

Well, thought Gordon, I might as well have opened the old Lady's letter, perhaps it required an answer; before I open Meredith's deposit I will see *what news from Ireland* – he broke the seal, the envelope was from Lady Gertrude, it just contained·

"Dear Sir,

I can make nothing at all of the enclosed from my sister, I suppose Lady Castle Howel has her head full enough of her own business, and so indeed have we all, which is the reason I send the enclosed to you: I can't think my sister right in her conjectures, she never had much solidity, and less penetration; I never can think Evelyn was the kind of man to run mad – there is indeed, I am told, a madness in the Sibley family, and I always thought Runnington himself acted like a lunatic; one does not indeed know, who, or what, the Evelyns may have been, he was always vastly shy about his family, but if it should be as Frances conjectures, we have sunk our own and our nephew's money to a fine purpose, in buying a living for a mad man: I protest to you, Sir, I am bewildered, and shall wait your opinion with great impatience.

I have the honour to be, &c."

"What is all this?" cried Gordon, impatiently opening Lady Frances's letter to her sister.

"My dear Lady Gertrude,

"Your letter with the black seal excessively shocked me, I was dressing to go to the Castle, the Lord Lieutenant is vastly polite to English ladies, and Sir James Sibley, I assure, you, a great beau, he really reminds me of a certain person you and I have reason to remember: Well, I thought as we had a large party, it would be vastly shocking to break it up, particularly as Sir James depended much on *my* going, tho' upon my honour I was extremely sorry for our poor nephew, and once I was really going to shed tears, but you know what a horrid redness they always leave on my eyes; and, besides, I was quite dressed. Well, but what I have to tell is a vast deal more terrible, than what you tell me – not about the ball, for we were vastly comfortable and happy there, but Evelyn, poor fellow, has actually lost his senses; and this morning eloped God knows where. To be sure, as Sir James Sibley says, it was vastly ridiculous in us to lay out so much money and take such trouble about a young man who was quite a stranger to us. I really thought him excessively agreeable at Natly Abbey; but then, as Sir James says, that was because one had no earthly being to kill the ennui with. Well, sister, you have no Idea what a charming place Dublin is. Evelyn, poor fellow, was affected from the time we left Natly; to be sure he was very attentive, but so dull, and little Jane cried excessively, and would have it Evelyn did not like her, but that, as I said, was impossible, when her father had agreed to resign the living to him, and he was to be so well settled. We had a very tedious passage, which, indeed Sir James Sibley says, is often dangerous, Jane was very sick, and Evelyn amused himself with leaning on the rail of the vessel, once I obliged him to look up, and his face was actually bathed with tears; this I thought odd at the time, but since I know he was mad, you know it is easy accounted for.

Well, Sir James Sibley had our letter, and waited in an elegant carriage – Evelyn complained of indisposition, and I thought Sir James rather tiresome, but that was because I was not acquainted with him; he asked so many questions about Evelyn's family, and told so many anecdotes of his, which I find is a very ancient one, that I saw Evelyn was excessively tired, and Jane greatly offended Sir James by crying.

Well, next morning Evelyn was ill, and Jane wished to attend him, but Sir James would not suffer it, and you know I am frightened to death at a fever; however I sent to enquire, and he wrote me several little billets, to beg I would think of returning, or permitting him to go by himself, as he had not his health in Ireland, and little Jane was in a vast hurry to have matters settled; but really Sir James was so polite, and made so many parties, and so many engagements, I had not a moment to spare.

When your letter came, you may be sure I was vastly unhappy, and I told Gibson of it, and left it with her, she says she only hinted it to Evelyn, and he ran raving mad directly; he gave her a guinea for the sight of the letter, ran up and down the house, packed and unpacked his things, and at last went out without them, and we have not heard of him since. Sir James blesses his stars, and indeed I think it was fortunate he was not married to Jane, for, poor little thing, he might have done her a mischief. I fancy Sir James will give her a husband of his own choosing; he is a prodigious sensible man; and I believe, if I pleased, would be my humble servant, but as I tell him it must be a very extraordinary thing indeed that would make me change my condition.

I am, dear Lady Gertrude,
Your affectionate sister,
F. H.

This long letter rendered the reader almost as mad as the writer supposed Evelyn; but there was another enclosure, signed J. Runnington, which began

"Oh, my dear Lady Gertrude!

I may write to you though I must not speak to Lady Frances. Mr. Evelyn is not mad, but I am nearly so. Sir James Sibley, for he has not once called me child, has a very hard heart, and a cross look, but that you know my poor Mamma always said; he does not like Mr. Evelyn, and you will easily believe Mr.

Evelyn does not like him. My papa has not always acted well, but he is my father, and it is grievous to me to hear him constantly abused, and his relations pointed out to me among the very dirty ugly people we daily see in the streets; but all that is not so bad as a secret I have to tell you – Mr. Evelyn is gone, and God bless him, he loves Jane Runnington as a sister, and will always be her friend, but his heart was long gone, and I know who has it, I am sure Mr. Evelyn will be happy, for never was there a being who more deserved to be so; I am vexed he had not been inducted into the living, for now, I suppose, my papa won't resign: I think sometimes Lady Frances is a greater favourite here than ever I shall be, and if she should stay, and dear Lady Gertrude would let little Jane be her companion and handmaid, it would make me happy, and Lord Castle Howel would love me, I am sure I should love him, and I should then hear all about Mr. Evelyn and the beautiful Lady Castle Howel; I might have said the good, for she is both good and beautiful: God bless her and all who love her, and all whom she loves.

> Dear Madam, don't answer this for I shall get anger.
> From your very humble and sincere friend,
> J. R.

Gordon now began to comprehend the letters, and while he was considering on what step Evelyn would probably take, the door opened and in came the supposed maniac in propria personae.

What either said at the precise moment of meeting is of little consequence; Evelyn had a number of questions to ask; Gordon was exactly in the same predicament, and when two friends meet, who each fancy they have a vast deal more to hear than to communicate, much confusion and little rationality may be expected.

"So you are not married?" pointing to the letters, was Gordon's first address, after they were seated.

"I hear Lady Castle Howel is left in very indifferent circumstances?" was the pertinent answer.

"Indifferent! worse than indifferent," replied Gordon, "they begin the sale of the goods tomorrow, the horses went to the hammer yesterday, and though they were very fine creatures, did not fetch what was due to the livery man – the carriages were sold too today, Doctor Macshean, I find, bought the coach."

"I never regretted my poverty but once before," sighed Evelyn.

"And you had never more reason," answered Gordon, "for no living will you get now at Natly."

"But I may be curate to my friend, my beloved protector, and he will receive me with open arms, the Countess I am sure will rather go back to Code Gwyn than any where, and—"

"Fine castle building," interrupted Gordon, "the family are all turned out of Code Gwyn, Mr. Meredith cannot afford to pay a curate, and there is no room for the Countess."

Evelyn was confounded, "Impossible!"

"Very true, though – now the best thing in my opinion for you to do, is to return to your station at Natly, I can see with half an eye." We hope the reader will not cavil at the phrase, it was not only Mr. Gordon's, but as we presume of true Caledonian growth, as it came to the author, in the official letter of a council eminent for learning and abilities! "I can see with half an eye, that old painted Jezebel will marry the Irishman, but as her sister has rather more sense, and won't probably fall in the way of an Irishman, you will easily make your peace with her."

"No," Evelyn said, the gratitude he could not help feeling for the particular and unsolicited friendship the family had shown him, had absolutely blinded his eyes and sealed his understanding; but though he could not see their absurdities, he could not, on impartial retrospect, but despise his own, for standing neuter in his own cause, and suffering two women, who substituted whim and caprice for friendship and generosity, to lay out his future life just as it pleased them, when, as it had proved, a *new* whim or caprice would whistle him down the wind.

"Come, come," answered Gordon, "this is resentment and mortified pride, a vapour of disappointed vanity; but Natly living is a good substantial thing, will stand wind and weather, long after the old damsels are dust, and, peradventure a certain young Countess might be a fixture at the Abbey."

"Upon my honour you mistake," replied Evelyn, "I have no disappointed vanity in my heart, nor any of the hopes you imply, from the possibility of the Countess becoming as you call it, a fixture at the Abbey; you little know me, if you believe, I could form one plan dependant on the Countess's future acquisitions, and still less do you know me if you think I could be so selfish as to wish her to accept the fond but humble heart that adores her, in my present situation. No Sir, I have at this instant no wish, with respect to Lady Castle Howel, but to serve her; no ambition but to deserve the name of her friend; while *she* is single, and I am so, which on my part, will always be the case, hope may, perhaps, play round my heart, but it shall not have entrance there – that I love her, you know; that she has grown into my very soul, with its vital stream I feel; and I think, I trust,—" the colour mantled over Evelyn's face, as he *thought* he *trusted* he was not quite indifferent to her. "I left my curacy at Little Manor abruptly, but Dean Holt has not, I know, withdrawn his good opinion of me; I certainly have, as you say, been building castles in the air respecting Code Gwyn – but my trust is in the master I serve.

"Oh," replied Gordon, shaking his head, "all this is mere young man's wisdom, you think more of the mistress than the master; however, Meredith will be glad to see you, truant as you are – we will return to Lord Claverton's, where –"

Evelyn again coloured. Lord Claverton, that man was born for my destruction! Is he on terms here? Is Mr. Meredith dining with him? A being he despised, who –

"Young man's wisdom again!" interrupted Gordon, "pretty talking of despising a rich Viscount, who has three Boroughs, and several fine livings in his own gift."

"If he had the world in his gift, *I* would not go to his house. Oh! I never knew one minute's pain till he gave it me; and now, in her forlorn and distressed state, if Ellen should–"

"I shall never see you a Bishop," said Gordon, gravely.

"You will always see me an honest man," returned Evelyn.

"Will you go to Lord Claverton's?" asked Gordon.

A stern No, was the answer.

"Will you stay here till I return?"

Another stern No.

"As much as to say," said Gordon, "I am not to go."

"By no means," answered Evelyn, "I will stay to see my friend, but if you have business, go."

Gordon took him at his word, and hastened to inform Meredith of his arrival; it was easy to perceive, during the time he stayed at Lord Claverton's, what his hopes were, and although Gordon would, with great cheerfulness, share his little all with Evelyn and Ellen, yet as neither that, nor any thing Evelyn could do, with, or without the Merediths, would amount to a decent support; and as he saw, though Ellen talked and thought with indifference and contempt, of the agremens of an exalted state, she had nevertheless been so used to enjoy them, a return, or rather entrance into common life, would be attended with inconvenience, neither the delicacy of her constitution, injured as it had been, or frame of mind could sustain; and as in such a case as her marrying a curate, when such splendid offers were making, she must not only forfeit the respectable friends, who now countenanced her, but incur their blame, and involve Evelyn in debt and difficulties his whole life would not discharge, he considered it as the wisest and best proof of friendship to concert measures with Meredith to separate them immediately; and when, after Meredith had promised to be at his niece's to receive Lord Claverton's visit next morning, they left his Lordship, Gordon took him into the first coffee house to tell him of Evelyn's arrival, and communicate to him his opinions and conclusions.

To his surprise he found Meredith extremely cold in the business.

He told Gordon frankly, that Evelyn would and should succeed to his living; that as to the elegancies Ellen had lately been used to, if she was in ease and happiness it would essentially contribute to her health; if instead of going to rest at one or two, and rising at eleven or twelve, she should be obliged to retire at ten and rise at eight or nine; if instead of never walking on foot, she should never step into a coach, will she not be in better health and better spirits, and have a chance of living much longer? If instead of being tied to a debilitated man of fashion like Lord Claverton, or a dissipated one like the Marquis of Squandervelt, she should vow to honour and obey the companion, friend and love of all her happy days, will she not act politically with respect to her own happiness, honourable to the young man, and with proper regard to the eternal law of doing as she would be done by? "In this scale," added Mr. Meredith, "so evidently preponderating to the side of Evelyn, I have not put the pleasure I know she will feel in smoothing the pillow of our venerable parent; in reciprocal acts of affection with her family; and the many little kindnesses, I call them so, rather than charities, our power being so contracted, she will, notwithstanding, have it in her power to extend to the distressed; perhaps the amusements of the town, acquaintance with the great, and the adulation of sunshine friends, may be set in the opposite scale; but how intrinsically valuable are those, how futile, and at certain periods, disgusting, are these."

Gordon had one little sneaking corner in his heart where the ardent desire raged to see Ellen again fill the rank and fashion for which he thought her born; but as every other part of fashion for it was open to reason, good sense, and friendship, and as this was a family business in which he had no real right to interfere, he said not one word in opposition to Mr. Meredith, but walked cheerfully to Pall Mall with him.

Gordon had no sooner left the room than Winifred entered, but not the little sturdy, discontented, ill-dressed Winifred Evelyn had hitherto seen. From her first attendance on Ellen finery was so much her delight she was sure, when she called herself dressed, to be loaded with all the colours of the rainbow. The woman of whom the Countess had the upper part of the house, was a French milliner, who soon understood

Winifred had three hundred pounds, and as, notwithstanding she had one of the best houses in Pall Mall, elegantly furnished, she was, from being a very fine Lady, often in the predicament of having bills become due she was not provided with money to pay; she had made Winifred very smart, and borrowed two out of her three hundred pounds.

Winifred, with her hair well dressed and powdered, a black silk trained gown, muslin flounced coat, and correspondent linen, then came swimming into the room, and Evelyn with his natural politeness bowed.

"The Lort save us, Mr. Evelyn!" He caught her joyfully in his arms, and, we confess we are at a loss for an apology for his vulgarity, almost smothered her with kisses.

"Pless my sole, Mr. Evelyn, I am sure nopoty would think you was a parson, see how you have rumpled all the powder out of my hair, and I am coing to a party at Lord Claverton's."

Evelyn thought every body talked of Lord Claverton.

"Well, but Mr. Evelyn, have you prought me a fever? Pray where is your prite? I suppose *we* shall visit her; but, dear me, we visit none but the quality, quite different sort of people than used to come to our house in my Lord's time, quite soper quizzies, as Mr. Joseph calls them. Lort pe praist we are comed from Natly, such a tull treary place; and then, Lort help us, we went to Code Gwyn; but such hups and downs in this world – there's old Morgan, pilzeebub will certainly put his cloven foot on all his sins and iniquities, he has turned my owld master out of Code Gwyn, uncle Griffiths, and all; and there, to be sure, I had not so much as a hole to dress in by myself at the Rectory, though the Reverent made bed rooms of the great hay-loft, Cot knows where he must cram the tithes at harvest, ah Lort knows nothing looks as it did put your little carten, for all my holly hogs and polly haunches are tead and cone, what we must all come to, Mr. Evelyn, our poor Lort, you know, proke his neck, and the tear papy is cheated out of his pirth right, and my Laty and I, Cot help us, if she don't marry Lort Claverton –"

Winifred might have run on a long summer's day, if she had not unfortunately mentioned Lord Claverton, a lapse that reminded Evelyn of her breach of promise to him, and of the many difficulties in which her babbling had involved Ellen.

He therefore, in no very soft tone, told her it was his opinion, the best thing that could happen to her Lady was to get rid of *her,* and before she could get so far the better of her anger and astonishment as to answer, he proceeded to upbraid her with her duplicity, and demanded a locket, the only valuable thing he ever was master of, which had been given him by Mr. Meredith, with solemn charge to preserve; and which having taken out two locks of hair which was in it, and replaced them with one of his own, he had given to Winifred for Ellen, but which she was prevailed on by Mr. Joseph to say nothing about, but consign it to his care.

Winifred's conscience had always upbraided her with this breach of trust; and guilt confounded, said, when she come from Lord Claverton's she would give it him.

Lord Claverton again! Evelyn was in a rage, and had not Mr. Joseph happened to call at that instant, in a coach, to take her to the party, we will not answer for the consequences.

The meeting between Mr. Meredith and his eleve was the true feast of reason and flow of souls, they supped together with a cordiality that made the meal a banquet, and parted before Lady Castle Howel's return.

The curate of Little Manor attracted more than the Marquis,

and Lady Mappleton; Mrs. Holt, who was come to visit her Ladyship, had only arrived an hour, advanced in the most friendly manner to our heroine, and after the usual compliments, asked if it was Mr. Evelyn, of whom she was speaking? And on being answered in the affirmative, spoke of him in such terms as partly reconciled Lady Mappleton to the *curate,* but rather increased Lord Squandervelt's spleen, who, in consequence, instead of making the most of an opportunity Ellen's time of mourning would not with propriety allow at her own house, if she had been inclined, he was barely civil to her; whether she perceived his mighty spleen or not we will not pretend to say, but if she did, her mind was taken up by an humbler subject.

In course of the evening Lady Mappleton took occasion to ask Ellen if there were any thing or things in the Grosvenor-Street house she particularly valued, as she intended to be at the sale? No, Ellen answered, the creditor had, of his own motion, sent all her books, which as Lord Castle Howel chose them, were of most value to her.

It was near two before the party separated; and Ellen was not up when Gordon proposed going once more to Grosvenor-Street, to try the key Ellen thought belonged to the writing table, but which, on trial, did not appertain to it, nor was that piece of furniture locked.

Every drawer had been carefully sealed by Lady Margaret, who had not taken any further notice of Lady Castle Howel than to send her a formal invitation to dinner, which she declined accepting.

Gordon, Meredith and Evelyn walked to Grosvenor-street, where also they met Lady Margaret and the Doctor, seeing as the latter *said,* if there were any particular thing Lady

Margaret would like, – but as *appeared* from the avidity of the former in searching every drawer, rapping her knuckles against every partition, and trying all the locks, on the same search with themselves.

The truth is, among a parcel of spare keys, in one of the Earl's private drawers, Lady Margaret had met with the fellow to the one tied to the ribbon, which so puzzled Gordon; the curious construction of the wards, and form of the key altogether, persuaded him it belonged to a lock of consequence, which he *hoped,* and her Ladyship *feared* to discover; but after the strictest scrutiny the search was concluded, to the disappointment of one party, and satisfaction of the other.

All the world crowded to the auction, and as his Grace of Dash, and the Marquiss Squandervelt were there, for the express purpose of buying up every article that had been the Countess's; as Lord Claverton, it was well known, would attend for the same purpose; and as Lady Mappleton, and a large party of friends were also expected to bid high for the beautiful furniture of the Countess's suit of apartments, these at least were expected to fetch a great price.

When Lord Claverton entered, Meredith made way and procured him a seat, but such was Evelyn's antipathy or jealousy, or whatever the reader please, he immediately left the party, and found himself by Mrs. Holt, who most affectionately accosted, and introduced him to Lady Mappleton.

"That is a prodigious fine young man," said Duke Dash, looking through his glasses, and speaking to Caroline Holt, "who is he?"

Lord Squandervelt was near enough to hear Mrs. Holt's introduction, and to his extreme mortification, saw that the curate of Little Manor, dressed and powdered as smart as a clerical Adonis could dress and powder, had the personal advantage even of himself; and that tho' a curate, and a country one, he had a confidence in himself, that while the crimson glow of modesty animated his countenance, gave an unspeakable grace to the compliments he was paying a knot of Ladies, whose eyes, if eyes are to be credited, said as Duke Dash did, "that he was a prodigious fine young fellow," so much indeed was he the object of general observation, that Lord Claverton saw and immediately recollected him.

Certain natural antipathies have been variously explained, by different casuists and philosophers; there was but one way of accounting for that, which in this instance equally reigned in the bosom of the peer and the curate.

Had a basilisk struck the eye of his Lordship, it could not have had a more baneful effect; weak and enervated as he was, his pallid looks were lightened, in the hope of obtaining the woman he really loved; the rival of his first impression stood before him, towering in elegance of person and improved manners, above all compeers, in the full bloom of perfect manhood, health and vivacity; destitute only of the one thing, which his declining health and low spirits, told him, in a language his soul understood, amounted to nothing; he complained of excessive heat, and instantly every body was in motion to give a sick Lord air.

The auction began, and was proceeding in a very flourishing way, when a fresh coloured old man, with a brown wig in small curls without powder, a brown surtout buttoned close, an India handkerchief tied loose round his neck, brown silk stockings and square toed shoes, who Mr. Meredith felt his blood rise at, and who Lord Claverton and Evelyn both recognized to be Squire Morgan, begged to know whether Mr. Auctioneer could put up a couple of articles, to oblige him, as he wanted to go out of town, which was in the catalogue for tomorrow.

Mr. Auctioneer, who was a very polite and accommodating person, could not stir a step, in so important a measure, without taking the sense of the company.

What articles were they? the company must know that, before they could decide.

One was an iron chest in the library.

A loud laugh; "Oh, pray let the gentleman have the iron chest."

"Ay ay, pray do," said a silversmith, who waited to bid for the plate, "if any man in England can fill it, it is Mr. Morgan."

"Ah! what old mammon," cried a young foxhunter," are you there?"

Another loud laugh, which Squire Morgan bore with great philosophy.

The second article was the porter's chair, which truth to say, was a very comfortable one, high backed; semicircular, stuffed with down, and covered with fine Spanish leather.

Another laugh, and the company, to whom he again appealed with wonderful deference, agreeing, Mr. Auctioneer promised to put up the iron chest and arm chair, as soon as the room they were now about were sold.

Mr. Morgan, with many and many a low bow, returned thanks to the company, his bows were as usual very judiciously varied, and adapted to the different rank of the company, from Duke Dash to the silversmith, and he retired with a joy he could not conceal, to contemplate his intended purchase.

"Damme, we'll work the old boy up with his iron chest,"

said the fox hunter, winking at the Marquis, who returned the wink, and as this agreement was made in hearing of every body present, it occasioned much observation, some laugh, and a good deal of curiosity.

When the lot was called, the porters declared it was too heavy to move, and all who chose to concern themselves in the business, went to the library to look at it.

The chest was one made for Lord Castle Howel, by his own particular directions, and from a drawing of his own; it was square, and so indented and painted on the outside, as to look like a parcel of folio volumes but as excepting that, it had nothing extraordinary, and the silversmith declaring, that to his knowledge, the squire never read a book in his life, but the London directory, it was not supposed he would bid very high; the young blades were however resolved to try.

Mr. Auctioneer begged the company would do him the honour to name a beginning.

Mr. Morgan offered two guineas.

"Two guineas, old mammon, D—e I'll give ten," said the foxhunter.

"Pounds or guineas?" asked Morgan, with a tremor on his voice and a very low bow.

"No matter," said the Marquis, "I'll give twenty."

"Pounds or guineas?" with a lower bow, and additional tremor on his voice.

"Now d—me Marquis that's not the go, to bid against me, come d—me I'll go twenty five."

"Thirty," said the Marquis.

Morgan loosened his silk handkerchief for air, and kept edging in towards the table, *but* as he did not speak, it was the general opinion, the knowing ones were taken in.

After a pause, when the Auctioneer had declared again and again, that was the third and last time, the bow and the question were repeated, "did your Lordship mean pounds or guineas?"

"D-me, there's life in the game yet," cried the overjoyed foxhunter, "Thirty five pounds, mind, not guineas."

"Forty for the Marquis," said the Auctioneer, obsequiously regarding his look.

"Forty-five."

"Fifty."

"Fifty-five."

Morgan had now wedged himself into a position fronting the Auctioneer, next to the table, when in his extreme agitation he threw down his hat, and turned the hind part of his wig front, and while the two jesters were out bidding each other, with sham eagerness and the room in peals of laughter, the head of poor Morgan was in perpetual motion, for the foxhunter being on one side of him, and the Marquis on the other, anxious to watch the motion of each party, turned his head from the foxhunter to the Auctioneer, from him to the Marquis, &c. his lips every moment severing to speak, but closing at each bidding which with his heat, and situation, were such provocatives, the Marquis could contain no longer, and the foxhunter catching the laugh, the Auctioneer, who, tho' he was so very obsequious, and joined in the laugh, saw his precious time wasted in a joke, took the opportunity to knock down the iron chest, at fifty-six, to Mr. Morgan.

"I advise you Mr. Auctioneer," said the foxhunter, with affected gravity, "to knock the chest to pieces, before you let it go out of the house, for I'll be crucified if old mammon would pay so dear for iron."

"Depend on it," joined the Marquis, "it has a secret lining of bank notes."

Morgan bowed to the ground, "my Lord," said he, readjusting his silk handkerchief, "I am a very private obscure man, but I have my whims as well as my betters, – and humbly hope, as iron chests are an article of furniture, seldom wanted by those of your Lordship's description, and never by those of *yours,"* bowing to the foxhunter, "I may be permitted to buy *one* dear bargain in my life time, while my superiors have the privilege of purchasing so many every day."

The laugh being now turned, and the sale going on, he retired with renewed spirit, and was followed by some of the idlers, among whom was Evelyn, to the library.

If the chest had been, as Lord Squandervelt said, lined with bank notes, it could not have been more the object of Mr. Morgan's anxious attention; he received the key with hurried eagerness and opened it, eagerly exploring every corner, then shut it down, and calling the porters, was on the point of turning the key, – yet one more look he could not help bestowing on the inside.

Evelyn, who had been moralizing on the whole transaction, kept his eye constantly on him; he knew the rapacity of his disposition; had heard from Meredith of Lady Margaret's letter, and tho' he had himself, in company with Gordon, examined that identical chest, before the auction, he could not help thinking there was something very extraordinary in a man, who would make fifty excuses rather than change a shilling, giving fifty-six pounds for an iron chest not intrinsically worth ten.

Morgan opened the chest once more, he looked round, – the few people in the room were looking at some fine prints, except Evelyn, who pretended to be reading; impelled by that providence which over rules all our actions, he reached his right arm into the chest, he felt about with his fingers, and instantly the cover which was exceeding weighty, fell down and crushed the bones of his arm in a miserable manner.

The unfortunate man fell down with extreme anguish, and twisted the already disabled limb in the fall, in such a manner as also to put the shoulder quite out.

Evelyn ran to sustain the fainting body, he opened the chest to liberate the arm, but what was his astonishment, to perceive in the bottom of the chest a square small *lid*, which closed as he put up the cover; he gave a cry of joy, and sent in for Meredith. By this time the accident had reached the auction room, and the crowd surrounded the fainting Morgan, Meredith came in, Evelyn locking the chest, charged him to be careful of it, and then lifted Morgan to a sofa.

A surgeon, besides Mr. Macshean was present, they cut his sleeves and shook their heads, a chair was ordered to convey him home, – Evelyn finding it was with difficulty they could keep life in him, sat at his back, chafed his temples and supported him in his arms.

"Where am I going?" said he, as they were lifting him into a chair.

"Home, sir," answered Evelyn, in a voice of tenderness and sympathy, "you are hurt and had better be with your family."

Morgan looked in Evelyn's face, he started, tears of anguish burst from his eyes, – "I have no family."

"Who are *you?* are you not the boy? the boy that Meredith –?"

"Yes, sir, I am the boy that owes his *all* to Mr. Meredith."

Morgan again fainted and did not revive till laid on the bed, at a lodging he had in Suffolk-street. Evelyn had the charity to stay with him till he recovered, which was not till the exquisite pain occasioned by the surgeons examining his arm had roused him to a sense of torture.

The first object that met his eyes was Evelyn, still in the charitable act of supporting him, – he gazed on his face, – "Yes," said he, with a deep groan, "I see it is so." Immediate amputation was necessary; "will it save my life? cut me to pieces so you do that, let me live a little while, but a little, for reparation, for repentance!"

The surgeons told him, much depended on himself.

"Will *you* stay?" to Evelyn, who promised he would.

The operation was performed, and the composing draught being swallowed, Evelyn thought himself so far absolved from his promise, as to have a quarter of an hour to take one glance at Ellen.

While Evelyn was supporting Morgan at the auction, Meredith asked Gordon, if he had read the paper he gave him.

Gordon really blushed to say he had not.

"Then you are deprived of the gratification I feel in an observation, which confirms my favourite thesis."

"And pray what is that?"

"That there is no such thing as natural instinct, except when aided by memory."

"I deny that," said Gordon.

"Excis homo," answered Meredith, "Percival Evelyn would have been just as attentive, and felt just as much for the poorest beggar, as he is now feeling for the only relation I know of he has in the world; that miserable old man's only child was Evelyn's mother, and if I have any skill in the cast of the countenance, he now remembers how often I have told him his duty; but that is not any more than Evelyn's compassion instinct; one is the sting of conscience, the other the dictates of humanity."

"I must go and read the paper directly," said Gordon.

"I shall keep these objects in my eye" answered Meredith, and they parted different ways, without thinking on the iron chest.

Gordon eagerly opened the sealed parcel, the first paper that dropped, was a receipt, signed James and Elizabeth Thompson, for nursing of master Horatio; then several letters full of tender enquires, and charges from a mother to the nurse of her child, signed E. C. "where have I seen this hand?" said Gordon to himself, – then the paper wrote by Mr. Meredith, giving an account, which the reader has already seen in vol. I. of his passion for Morgan's daughter, and her elopement, – "my health from this period," he wrote, "became injured, and my mind deranged, my dreams and waking thoughts were full of Elizabeth; I saw her in deep waters; on the top of precipices; surrounded by wild beasts; exposed to want; in short there was no evil, real or imaginary, but what I saw her environed with, – her death, when I heard it, was at first some relief. Dear woman had she known my heart, and confided in my friendship, what evils might she not have escaped; the vague and indirect accounts that reached us, left all uncertain but the event itself, – I went to her obdurate father, as soon as he arrived at his manor, I besought him to ease my heart by the particulars of her release. Gloomy and reserved, he insisted on my leaving him, said she was to his great joy *dead,* and had it no more in her power to disgrace him; disgrace him! alas! could Elizabeth disgrace her father; was she not formed, were not the purity of heart designed to honour her heavenly father! – my mind continued to be harassed, my thoughts never wandered from her grave, and after near three years suffering under a nervous fever, I at length thought if I could see the grave, which thus haunted my imagination, I should be easy, – I got from his servant the direction, and set off on my melancholy pilgrimage, the end of which I reached, my eagerness increasing as I drew near the spot, which held her dear remains.

He had placed a white marble urn on a black slab, and I saw that, near the ostentatious monument, lay the remains of Elizabeth Morgan, – but where said I, and looked wildly round.

"What are you looking for, sir?" said a very poor but neat woman, with a jug of skim milk in one hand, and a beautiful boy in the other.

"The place, the very place," answered I wildly, "where Elizabeth Morgan was buried."

"Ah, sir," replied the woman wiping her eyes, "you now stand, as near as I can recollect, on the very spot, she is a saint I dare say, but as to her father–"

"Name him not," I answered, "be gone," and in bitter regrets, I threw myself on the ground.

"If you loved the mother so well," said the woman, "you will bestow your charity on her child."

Her child! Ah Gordon, it was indeed the child of my Elizabeth, he looked in my face, he came instantly to me.

"We are starving, sir," said the woman, "and I have brought him to his parish, else, God knows, I would not part with him, I must leave him in the work-house, they have promised to receive him, they will make his hard hearted grandfather maintain him, I cannot."

Gordon, you are a good man, you are married to the woman

you love, but to know what I felt at this instant, you must have loved the soul of Elizabeth.

The woman directed me to the house where she died; I sat on the chair, I slept on the bed that was hers.

She had gone to some man who kept a public house at Chelsea, formerly a soldier, he took lodgings for her, and himself and his wife attended her, during her lying in; for Gordon, she was pregnant when she left her father's house; the child was put to nurse, and handsomely paid for, never was a fonder mother, "nothing," said the poor woman, "was too good for me or my family, while the dear Lady lived; but her health declining, and change of air being ordered, she was attended to Highgate, by the Publican and a maid, who were never more heard of at Chelsea," nor did the nurse know of her death, till two months after it happened, when she traced her to Highgate, and was directed from thence to Mr. Morgan's; "but, oh sir," continued she, "I no sooner produced the dear child, than he spurned me out of his doors, called me cheat, and after all, when I offered to prove I was no cheat, he swore he would put the little innocent son of his only daughter to a parish, and as soon as he could walk, apprentice him to a chimney sweeper; I told him he should not do that, and took the poor child home again" – but it seemed the poor people did not prosper according to their desert, the man who was a gardener lost the use of his limbs for one whole winter, and having a family of their own, the woman walked to Highgate, and told her piteous tale to the parish officer, who promised he would make old Morgan pay for the child, without apprenticing him to a chimney-sweeper.

I need not tell *you* I paid the woman, and took the child; she had got a toy, she said, with glass on one side, and she believed gold on the other, which in all her poverty she would not part with, because his mamma gave it the child to play with, the last time she saw him, and which by accident, was wrapped up in his cloaths, when she brought him home, this she would send me, and she was as good as her word.

From that hour to this, I have never dreamed of my Elizabeth, but I have seen her happy, and I became insensibly so myself; I put my little charge to board, with a decent woman, till he was old enough to come under my own instruction.

I found all the mother in his disposition, amiable, affectionate, and docile; his apprehension quick, his memory retentive, and his application beyond any thing I had met. With such dispositions, and such talents to improve; I could not answer it to my conscience, not at least, to let Elizabeth's father know the treasure within his reach; I knew his immense riches, and though all his father-in-law's estates were settled to return to *his* family, if Elizabeth died unmarried, yet thousands remained to do him honour in such an heir, had he been wise enough and just enough to adopt him; twice I made unsuccessful efforts in favour of my young friend, and each time was spurned from his house; nothing could convince *him* that I acted from a virtuous regard for his daughter; that I made a journey to London to shed my tributary tear on her grave; that I would adopt her illegitimate offspring by another man; he perhaps examined his *own* heart, and found no such sentiment *there* as those which actuated mine, and thence doubted any such existed. Enraged and basely suspicious, he charged me with being the ruin of his daughter, and the father of her child; ignominious was the title he gave him, and bitter were the oaths he swore never to leave him a shilling, or forgive me, whom, notwithstanding the solemn asseveration, my regard for Evelyn induced me to make, he looked on as his daughter's seducer; and he has kept his word, it is me he pursues more than our estate, and his revenge is more insatiate than even his avarice. The whole matter is a secret to my family, and young Evelyn; I want courage *now* to tell him *whose* he is, but if I die before him, it is fit he should know: Who his father is is an impenetrable secret, but time may develop even that, and it is to lend him every assistance on that head I repose this confidence in you; for, as to the unnatural father of his mother, I do not now even wish he may adopt him; I should be sorry to see Percival Evelyn, a name I gave him, blush for his progenitor."

Gordon read the packet with a mixture of wonder and attention, and before he had laid it down Mr. Meredith came in to receive Lord Claverton, and Evelyn to pay his respects to the Countess.

Always particularly *neat* in his person, there was little more to be added to the habit of a clergyman, that little, however, was not wanting. His hair had been deranged by the accident of Morgan, as well as sitting behind to support him, both on the bed and sofa, but now fresh dressed, elegant and graceful, before Lord Claverton was well seated, or Ellen in the drawing room, Mr. Evelyn was announced.

There is something particularly interesting to all invalids, in the voluntary attentions of the young, the gay, and the healthy. Morgan was robust and corpulent, he had no claims on Mr. Evelyn's friendship or esteem but, judging from his transactions with a family, to whom the latter was bound in duty and affection, the precise contrary – yet, with humanity and strength that astonished all the lookers on, among whom was Lord Claverton, he lifted Morgan, while fainting with agony, supported and attended him home, with a tenderness and compassion in his manner, that pleased even a man who had ever disliked him; Lord Claverton was often as helpless from weakness, as the unfortunate Morgan from the dreadful accident he met, and he could not help thinking the assistance of such a man preferable to the attendance of even Macshean. Thus, then, with a newborn complacency, as soon as Evelyn's bow was made, and they were seated, his Lordship enquired after Morgan.

Evelyn shook his head, and then recollecting the small aperture in the chest, asked if it had been examined.

Meredith answered, there was nothing in the chest, but was not a little astonished at what Evelyn told him. They sent to Mr. More and Lady Margaret, to request their presence, and went to Grosvenor-Street, leaving Lord Claverton in Pall Mall.

Ellen had been apprized of one male visitor, and her heart forewarned her of another; she spent some little time longer than usual at her toilet, and descended with a grace and manner all her own. Gordon not being present when Meredith went out, stepped into the drawing-room for his hat, and discovered Lord Claverton on his knees before the Countess.

His Lordship's looks testified chagrin and disappointment. "I have been endeavouring, Sir," said he, addressing Gordon, "to soften marble; I have been entreating this Lady to give herself a protector, her son a father, and me the only woman I ever loved; can you suggest nothing to strengthen my plea? You have influence, Sir, you shall never regret your politeness. Come, Mr Gordon, say something for me."

The only woman he ever loved! thought Gordon, how can people forget themselves so?

Ellen arose – "When I tell you, my Lord, not only my judgment but my inclination is averse to your proposal, it is not polite to press me; I could not give Lord Castle Howel's son a father, who entertained, in *his* life time an improper sentiment for his wife; but, independent of that, for I see, my Lord, you are going to plead, that whatever were your sentiments, you did not offend me with them, I confess I cannot command my esteem, it is not in that light disposed to Lord Claverton."

"But might not time, assiduity –?"

Ellen begged she might not be urged, she was obliged to Lord Claverton for his kindness to her son, but she could be no more than obliged.

Gordon thought it a pity she should not accept Lord Claverton; and the instant he saw Evelyn, he would have thought it pity if she had.

Lord Claverton was visibly affected; he regretted he had not waited, till time and the attention he resolved to pay the family, should have made him the friend in her heart he saw she wanted. He left compliments for Mr. Meredith, with request to see him, and took his leave.

"God bless me," said Gordon, turning from the door, up to the glass, "I should have known Lord Claverton any where, do not you think it very odd he should not recollect me?"

"Upon my word, except you are very much altered," answered Ellen.

"Altered, not at all," interrupted Gordon, "I am exactly the same, except I then wore my own red hair, and have now a brown wig; and except having had the small pox.

And except being twenty years older."

"Well," said Ellen laughing, "I do not upon the whole think it so very wonderful, his Lordship does not recollect you."

"And, on the whole, Madam," replied Gordon, "I am very glad to see you laugh, though it is at myself, 'tis a good sign."

"Why, to tell you the truth,", said Ellen, "my bosom's Lord sits lighter on his throne than I have long felt him."

Lady Mappleton was announced. "Bless me, my dear," said her Ladyship, "what a shocking accident that poor old man had today, I declare he frightened us away from the auction, but I have bought you a world of things, because I thought you would like to take them from me, rather than from that poor poor pallid looking mortal, Lord Claverton. Duke Dash and his son have also been great purchasers for you."

"For me! Madam," answered the Countess.

"Yes, for you; come, my dear, you must not be a prude, you must be in present Marchioness of Squandervelt, and in future Duchess of Dash; it will be a great alliance; the Duke really talks nobly, and it will be the pride of my heart to see you the envy of those who now affect to pity you."

Lady Mappleton then showed a letter she received that morning from the Duke, and not suspecting it possible a woman in embarrassed circumstances, who would not literally have a shilling, and whose son was obliged to his father's relations for supporting his claim to title and fortune, would, or could refuse such splendid offers.

Ellen, however, convinced her the thing could be, and also told her, the recent offer of Lord Claverton.

Lady Mappleton did not wonder at her rejection of *him,* but the Marquis, one of the handsomest men of the age, she could not comprehend it; she hoped this Phoenix, as Mrs. Holt called him, this curate, had not got into her head – "You blush, upon my honour, my dear Countess, the world will think it exceeding silly if he has."

"The world is, on all occasions, too good to me," replied Ellen, "but though I do not allow its infallibility in all points, I confess it would censure with reason, if I were to marry this curate, and give so obscure a man a paternal authority over the Earl of Castle Howel's son."

"Very prudent, my dear Ellen," said Lady Mappleton, kissing her cheek, "charmingly expressed, I thank you for the family: I confess when I saw your indifference to the first match in England, I really *did fear* the curate, for he certainly is a very fine young man, and his humanity to the old man when he met his accident charmed us all; but a poor parson for Lady Castle Howel! a curate! –"

"And yet, Madam," replied Ellen, "this poor parson, this curate, was the first, and will be the last choice of my heart."

"Ah! my dear," returned Lady Mappleton, shaking her head, "after such an acknowledgment, what confidence can one place in your promise?"

"The utmost," answered Ellen, "It is a promise witnessed by my own conscience, registered in the respect I owe my Lord's memory, and sealed with my last kiss on the lips of my dear boy; his father raised me to his rank, and his mother will not dishonour her son; but neither will she dishonour herself by giving her hand to the first man in the world, while her heart and all its faculties are devoted to the humble object of her first esteem."

Lady Mappleton was struck, but she affected to treat the matter lightly. "All this is very fine, my dear, but it will not support your rank."

"I did not promise to do that," replied the Countess, "*I* only promised not to dishonour it."

The subject had brought rosy strangers into Ellen's cheeks,

she looked remarkably lovely, fit, as Lady Mappleton told her, to grace a diadem. When Mr. More, Meredith, Gordon and Evelyn entered, her Ladyship was a sedulous observer, and she could not help allowing, if Ellen kept her promise she would act with more fortitude than in the same case, she could do herself.

Mr. More having paid his respects, and it being the first time Evelyn had seen Ellen in public, Mr. Meredith introduced him, he spoke low, trembled, touched her hand, and retired to a seat.

"I could not have thought," whispered Lady Mappleton, "that young man could look so much like a fool."

A servant brought a message from Mr. Morgan, he was awake and wished to see Mr. Evelyn.

"I will not go," said he, with resolution, "the man is incorrigible, on the brink of eternity, his thoughts are employed on fraud."

Mr. More said it was too true, and informed the ladies, that on their arrival in Grosvenor-Street, to re-examine the iron chest, they found Morgan had sent for it away; hardly expected to live the day out, yet he resolved to devote *that* day to his former practices; he added they immediately went to his lodging, where his people, acting no doubt by his orders, denied any such thing had been brought there.

"Oh, what an error!" cried Evelyn, passionately, "to let it go out of sight."

Meredith and Gordon excused themselves on their ignorance of what Evelyn had discovered, they thought they had examined every part of it.

Another messenger came from Morgan, to request to see Mr. Meredith, who instantly attended him.

Mr. More gave Ellen hopes a speedy end would be put to the suit against her son; he had seen Serjeant Pennings and Mr. Process.

"Oh, for heaven's sake," said Ellen, "don't name those gentlemen, I can hope for no decision where they are concerned; if you have no better comfort –"

Mr. More laughed. "These gentlemen," he answered, "will do your cause ample justice; the Serjeant chooses to be a wit out of court, but he is a man of sense at the bar; Mr. Process is a man of gallantry out of his office, but a very sound lawyer in it; and you'll find, they have lost no advantage it was possible to take. I foresee we shall very soon go in grand parade to put the heir in possession."

Ellen, in maternal transport, threw herself into Mr. More's arms and burst into tears – she knew he would not say so much if he had not reason to hope the best.

Evelyn measured the happy Mr. More with his eyes.

"Come, come," said the good-humoured Counsellor, "I beg you will not be fond of me, remember, I am another's property, my madcap will be jealous; when is your dinner to be served?"

Evelyn begged to have the honour of being known to Mr. More, and was then modestly taking his leave.

"My dear," said Lady Mappleton, "are you provided for so many? Mr. Evelyn and I expect to dine with you."

Lady Castle Howel politely bowed to both, and the grateful Evelyn was then re-seated next to Lady Mappleton, and took the bottom of the table at dinner.

Chapter IV

Mr. Meredith returned before they rose from table, "here is some mystery," said he, "that wretched man knows nothing of the chest, it is with great difficulty he speaks, he denies it, and the servants all say, no such thing was brought there."

The moment dinner was over Evelyn disappeared.

Meredith informed them he had prayed by Morgan, on whom the composing medicines had failed to operate, he was in extreme torture, and the Physician was apprehensive of a fever. The messenger came for Meredith a second time, and having commissioned Gordon to go about on business for him, he obeyed the sick man's summons.

The ladies were again left alone, and Lady Castle Howel's prospect of her son's cause put her in such spirits, she proposed paying some visits, and calling on Lady Margaret Macshean, which she had not done since her Lord's death.

Lady Mappleton agreed, but their astonishment is not to be expressed at finding the knocker muffled.

"What can be the matter?" said the Countess, "they were both at the auction, I heard, today."

"Yes," answered Lady Mappleton, "and vastly delicate it was in them *to be* there. I hope cousin Margaret is not in the straw."[31]

The door opened – to the servant's enquiry if Lady Margaret was at home, the footman stammered, in answer,

---

[31] I.e., pregnant

that she was ill; the ladies were ordering their cards, but the servant again stammered, he supposed *they* might go in.

"Bless me," said Lady Mappleton, "what's the matter? no iron chest affair here, I hope."

"Yes it is, Madam," answered the man.

"Is what?" asked Lady Mappleton, following him to the Doctor's room.

He threw open a door and discovered Lord Viscount Claverton, Doctor Archibald Macshean, and the Reverend Percival Evelyn seated round a table, with several small and some large parcels of writings, tied together, two small account books, and some loose papers, which they were examining; near them stood a large open iron chest.

The moment Evelyn saw our heroine he ran to her, and taking her hand, "Ellen, my dearest Ellen," said he, "we have discovered your grandfather's house and estate is his own; your fortune too is recovered, your enemies defeated, and Oh!" added he passionately, "long may the Countess of Castle Howel enjoy and adorn her high rank, while her humble friends are praying, that the best of women may be the happiest."

"I hope you are not mad, Sir," cried Lady Mappleton.

"These, at least," said Lord Claverton, "are not illusions," presenting a parcel, consisting of twenty bank notes, of a thousand pounds each, in an envelope, addressed to the Countess, in Lord Castle Howel's hand.

"And that, Madam," faltered Mr. Macshean, "is not all; Lady Margaret has acted very culpably; it appears by these accounts, that she has not always paid the bills for which she gave vouchers, and that there remains a large balance now in her hands."

"Which," interrupted Lord Claverton, "I pledge myself to see paid."

"And here, Madam," said Evelyn, kneeling, "let me present to you the receipts for the mortgage of your honoured grandfather's estate," and laying them on her lap, he hid his face, arose, and retired.

Ellen had sat in silent wonder, indignation, and astonishment; but as if one sentiment animated hers, and her congenial heart, she now burst into tears and hysteric sobs; the Doctor gave her some drops, and when she was composed Lord Claverton took her hand.

"You must not withdraw it," said he, "for here I resign the lover, and here I swear to be a true and disinterested friend; that," pointing to Evelyn, "is a noble fellow, if any man deserves you from personal and mental merit it is him. Will you Madam," added his Lordship, "accept me for your friend, not in the common acceptation of the term, but a bosom, a confidential friend?"

Ellen bowed gratefully.

"But you must speak, Madam," continued his Lordship, "your voice is music to my ears and harmony to my soul."

"Have a care, my Lord," said Lady Mappleton, "all that sounds much more like love than friendship."

"I have made my resolution, Madam," replied his Lordship.

"And I, my Lord," answered Ellen, gracefully courtesying, "accept it as an honour I am proud of."

If Doctor Macshean did not share his wife's guilt, it was plain he did her shame, for his pale cheeks and quivering lips were visible to the company.

Lord Claverton recommended it to Ellen to send for her lawyer, to take minutes and inventories, and in the mean while told them, by what means the important discovery was made.

Mr. Morgan's extreme eagerness to purchase the iron chest,

very naturally alarmed Lady Margaret, who had quite as many inducements to seek after any concealed papers of Lord Castle Howel's as Mr. Morgan could possibly have.

To explain these inducements it is necessary to retrace the regular and uniform line of conduct, that Lady had many years adopted. Her mother's fortune, twenty thousand pounds, had been, as usual, settled on the younger children, all of whom, five in number, lived to be of age, and received their respective shares, although her Ladyship was the only one now surviving. The small pittance of four thousand pounds to an Earl's daughter, brought up in the most expensive style, was such a trifle, added to a very plain person, as entirely precluded all hope of settlement by marriage equal to her rank, and, from the death of her father, she had resolved to remove this objection, as far as depended on fortune, but it was not till her brother's death she formed the resolution of absolutely linking the money she had from time to time placed in the funds, and lent out, merely for the sake of the interest, instead of paying the tradesmen.

The late Lord Castle Howel was supposed to be very careless and inattentive to money matters, and so he certainly was, as far as was consistent with his principle of honour; he saw that managing and paying bills was the hobby horse of his sister, and he knew, from the above state of her situation, she had many secret mortifications, which he allowed for in her temper, and endeavoured to alleviate, by the most brotherly affection and indulgence. What bills Lady Margaret did pay, she took care to have a handsome discount for, and for those she did not she was accountable, as she constantly signed a book, acknowledging the receipt of the different sums, and what bills they were to pay, his Lordship then gave her drafts, and in entire confidence of her integrity never troubled himself about her vouchers; all the bills being ordered to be carried to her, it was not possible she could be detected; as, when they became troublesome, she immediately paid.

On the death of her brother, as she had a duplicate to his writing table key, she got possession of all the others, and having in vain searched every part of his library and private drawers for the book he kept against her, and finding it was not at his banker's, nor with him in the country, she at once proposed to enlarge her already genteel fortune, by leaving the tradesmen's accounts open, and appropriating to her own use upwards of nine thousand pounds, she had of her brother's, in the funds, and other securities.

Mr. Morgan went express to London the instant he heard of Lord Castle Howel's death; the last thousand pounds paid him was in the Earl's absence, and the deeds being not yet assigned, he hoped, his eye still on Code Gwyn, he might, on repayment of the money, yet have a chance to seize an estate that most provokingly lay between him and all his other purchases; he had already the lands all round, to the amount of twelve thousand pound a year, but this house fronted Code Gwyn vale, whose present owner he despised, and for whose heir he felt both revenge and hatred; well as he loved money he would rather give double the value than not have it, what an acquisition would it then be to get it at half.

These were Morgan's inducements to pay Lady Margaret a visit of condolence; but if the reader has at all entered into his character, they will form some idea of his feelings when he understood she was ignorant of a secret of which he was master; and by which means he had it in his power to defraud

Lord Castle Howel's heir of the whole sum his Lordship had paid on account of his mortgage on the Code Gwyn estate.

The late Earl, besides his botanical taste, had something of a mechanical genius, and had an iron repository for his papers made on a very peculiar construction, of his own invention, which so pleased him, that, Morgan happening to attend his appointment the day it was brought home, he showed and explained it to him.

It had a false bottom, which, by indenting a part in the visible one, forced up a small square, and shewed the lock, and at the same instant, by the same spring, the lid was let down, unless fastened back by a small bolt, made on the inside for that purpose: – "And here," said the Earl "am I hoarding a dower for my Ellen from the sale of my timber, and here, Master Morgan, will I deposit for her your mortgage; in that book I keep my sister's account and in that my own."

Morgan could scarce respire; all these were now as good as in his own possession; he saw it was not Lady Margaret's interest or intention to make discoveries, and reveal them. The coach-maker came in with a long bill, and was answered by Lady Margaret with as long a face, that her brother's affairs were in the utmost disorder.

Now it had so happened, this very bill which was for the new carriages and harness for the year, and for the wedding, had actually been presented, in the presence of Morgan, by her Ladyship to her brother, who had instantly given a draft for payment, at least so Mr. Morgan *believed,* but *his memory* was *very bad,* he *might* be *mistaken.* Lady Margaret did not often colour, she turned pale, but a few sentences settled a right understanding between the parties, and Lady Margaret having also a *bad memory,* no wonder *she forgot* the thousand pounds paid on her brother's account to Mr. Morgan.

Morgan remained perdue in town, to seize his prey; and Lady Margaret being too guilty to be free from suspicion, took the alarm, when she saw with what eagerness he bid for the chest; she then recollected how particular the Earl had been about the making it, and resolved not to lose sight of Morgan or the chest, till she was satisfied; not that she suspected the treasure it contained, but as she knew, if her accounts got into Morgan's hands, he would not fail to make her pay very dear for them. His accident put it in her power to get possession of it herself, by the help of her spouse, to whom she imparted, if not her *guilt,* her *suspicions;* he, for reasons he had not assigned, hastened to Lord Claverton's, and sent the chairmen, both his countrymen, for the chest, in Mr. Morgan's name, and in the confusion, though a cart was still waiting at the door to take it away, as it had been paid for when knocked down, it was delivered to them.

The moment Evelyn heard the chest was not at Morgan's, nor at Grosvenor Street, he hastened, more and more convinced of its importance, to Bow-Street, and having promised a handsome reward, was, by the ingenious retainers of the public office, conducted to Lord Claverton's, where the chairmen pointed out, as the persons who conveyed the chest from the auction.

The men had been well paid, and as they supposed, the business being transacted by their Lord's particular friend, had his sanction, would render no account either to Evelyn or the officers of justice.

Evelyn who suspected Lord Claverton's designs on Ellen, concluded he had some end to answer by getting the chest into his possession; perhaps to claim a merit, he was resolved no rival should have, of putting her in possession of her right, – he insisted on seeing his Lordship, who tho' not risen from table, immediately admitted him.

Lord Claverton's surprise, when Evelyn, with well mannered firmness, demanded the chest, was too natural to be assumed; he rung for the chairmen, who at his command gave up their employer, and the place where they deposited their ponderous burthen.

Lord Claverton sent for a hack; and ordered his servant to give a single knock at Doctor Macshean's door; as soon as it opened, he rushed in, and led the way to the Doctor's private apartment, where they found Lady Margaret and her cara sposo on their knees, with a wax taper, exploring the inside of the iron chest, impatient to discover what they had nevertheless sent for the maker to do for them.

Lady Margaret was seized with convulsions, the moment she saw the unwelcome visitors, and while the Doctor attended her, by the help of the maker, who now arrived, the lid being by him bolted up, they saw the important lock, and the Doctor, with affected readiness, produced a key which opened the repository of so much treasure, and information.

Mr. More, Mr. Traverse, Mr. Process and Serjeant Penning now arrived, the latter so transformed, it was not till he had made some half dozen speeches, Ellen could believe it was him; his hair, of which he had no small quantity, being all crammed under a rye wig,[32] of immoderate size, which was drawn in front so near his brows, as to cock up and expose

---

[32] These wigs were treated with a paste made from rye flour then heated to make them bigger. They were popular with barristers and clergy.

part of the great bundle of hair behind; he had a black gown, a band, a pair of stiff top'd gloves with open fingers; and looked so unlike the Serjeant Penning she saw at Natly that when she did find out it was the same, important as the business was, she could not help laughing.

"Very well, my Lady, vastly well," said the serjeant, "they *may* laugh that win, we always allow that in our courts."

Mr. Process, who with Mr. Traverse, was taking inventories and minutes, laid them down, to wish a certain pretty widow of his acquaintance could find a false bottom to her husband's iron chest, he would marry her tomorrow.

Traverse took off his spectacles, and laid down his minutes, to hear what matter of mighty import his brother in the profession had to say; but returned both his pen and glasses with a contemptuous paoh! – paoh! Widows and false bottoms – Mr. More declared himself too happy to attend to business.

Lady Mappleton invited the whole party to eat cold meat with her, and they accepted the invitation, all but Dr. Macshean, whose pale cheeks and unsteady limbs, witnessed an inward perturbation, but whether on the account of the refund, or his Lady's fits, we will not presume to determine.

They found Duke Dash and his son, with Caroline, waiting to see Lady Mappleton.

Lord Claverton, on the credit of the newly entered into compact, between him and Ellen, assumed a right to hand her out of her carriage, placed his seat next hers, and engrossed to himself all the polite attentions of so much importance to fine women from fine men.

Duke Dash looked grave, and Lord Squandervelt watched Ellen's eyes, which were oftener fixed on Lord Claverton than anyone else, and never on him, till he swore to Caroline she looked quite ugly; nay, he believed she absolutely squinted.

Lord Squandervelt felt the indignity offered him; *him!* who was the dear fellow of one Lady, the fancy one of another, and the agreeable impertinent of a third; who was well made, six feet two high, had bright eyes, fine teeth, a roman nose, and whether he wore his hair cropped or straight, out or in powder, was followed by the men, and admired by the women; and who, moreover, was but just turned of thirty; *him,* to be neglected for a man at least a dozen years older; with jaundice eyes, parchment skin, and no calves to his legs, by a dowerless widow, without family or fortune; the thing was actually incredible! but such an insult merited, and should have, the severest punishment; she should be sensible of what she lost, and he actually flirted with Caroline before her face.

"If the first match in England should pass me to my dear cousin," whispered Ellen to Lady Mappleton, "how I should grieve!"

Caroline Holt was a fine figure; her features were not regularly beautiful, her face however had that kind of harmony and take in it, which when it has once pleased, will not cease to do so; and is perhaps a more lasting attraction than beauty: Lord Squandervelt found his attentions received, with their usual flattering effect; he thought Caroline infinitely agreeable, and wondered he had not found it out before.

The Duke's object was to have his son married, and if to a woman of family, fortune was not the object.

Ellen now was so pleased with the Marquiss, she more than once officiously addressed him, – "yes," thought he, flushed with inherent vanity, "she feels it, but her presumption shall be punished," and he became more attentive to Caroline!

At two the party separated, Lord Claverton insisted he had a right to set his *friend* down, and as he offered Mr. More the same civility, who was her neighbour, Ellen did not object.

Chapter V

The next morning was employed in writing to Natly and Code Gwyn; to the latter sheet after sheet was filled, and still there was matter, just as she was sealing the last, in came Gordon, leading his Nancy.

"Ay," said he, "you may well be surprised, but she will tell you news that will more surprise you. The old girl is married to an Irish giant, who won't let her throw away her money on law suits for her relations; little Jane is run a way to Lady Gertrude, who is called on for half her sister's fortune; and God knows what we shall do with the cursed Howels of Moor-bank."

"Really, Mr. Gordon," said Lady Castle Howel, "you are a most agreeable creature to come upon one with such a flow of good news at once; I am however glad to see Mrs. Gordon, and if I did not think she had given you as much of the sort as you can bear, I have news to tell you."

Gordon turned pale, "why," answered he, "except Lady Gertrude has taken it into her head to fall in love with Parson Runnington, whose wife broke a blood vessel last week, in which case we are all handsomely done for, I can't see how we can be worse off."

"Ah," replied Ellen, with affected gravity "you have more of the infidel than the Christian about you; there, read and tremble;" and she laid on the table the envelope with the bank notes.

Mr. Gordon removed his wig, replaced it, wiped his face; the world was so full of wickedness, and seemed so determined to league against honesty, he protested he was afraid to look at the paper.

Mrs. Gordon hoped things were not so very bad; tho' she was sure Sir James Sebley, who in her opinion was very ugly, tho' Lady Frances liked him, because he was tall, – would never let her do any thing for the young Lord.

"Lady Frances! an old – do, Nancy, describe the wedding, what do you think of Nancy for a bride-maid?" Gordon's courage so entirely failed, he would talk of any thing, rather than look at the papers on the table.

"Be so good," said Ellen, pointing to the envelope.

He removed his wig, again, changed his seat, resumed the old one, complained of heat, at last "I shall never have another happy day I firmly believe," and he took a resolution to see the worst; "what in the name of God is all this," said he staring at the notes and the late Earl's direction.

"The lining of the iron chest, my dear Gordon," answered Ellen, extending her hand to him, and embracing his wife.

Off went the wig, and exposed his short thick red bristles, while he exhibited one of the best Scotch reels, to his own voice, ever danced; Nancy at first joined in the tune, then beat time, and at last kicked the chairs out of their place, and capered about with her husband till the house shook.

In the midst of a scene, at which Ellen stood laughing, Lord Claverton entered, he was on the point of retreating, at a sight so novel and outré, but seeing Ellen, ventured in.

Mrs. Gordon had danced her hat off, and her cap on one side, and Gordon who took a great deal of snuff, and never, in any excess of joy or grief, forgot his nose, having in his violent exercise dispensed the contents of his mull[33] to every part of his face, the good couple cut as grotesque figures as his Lordship had ever seen.

Ellen was explaining, with infinite spirit and good humour, the cause of their extravagant joy, when she observed Lord Claverton's eyes fixed, and saw him change countenance; she looked round, and beheld Mrs. Gordon stop short in the act of setting her cap even, and staring at him; as however he turned to the window without speaking, Mrs. Gordon adjusted her head in silence also; Gordon's former knowledge of his Lordship was an explanation of this embarrassment, and gave rise to some conjectures not altogether to his advantage.

Gordon, who remembered nothing in his own conduct to check his honest joy, continued a thousand extravagances; his wife, from the same motive, recovered her surprise; and Ellen, who now had a fore taste of liberty and independence, was pleased, because they were happy, but Lord Claverton's brow dropped over his hollow eyes; he stood with his arms folded, looking at the window, seeming however not to see any thing.

A noise now was heard, which tho' a few months back it daily saluted the ears of the Countess, was lately become very unusual.

Winifred grown too fine a lady to scold, and too genteel to cry, had nearly got rid of old habits, Mademoiselle thought them so common! and vulgar! She was now, however, as it seemed, in the very last distress, and whined in the loudest key.

"What is the matter with my uncle and Winifred?" said the Countess, distinguishing his voice.

---

[33] A particularly Scottish type of snuffbox made from the tip of an animal horn.

"I insist on knowing where it is; I will keep you in a prison as long as you live, if it is not restored."

"The Lort be coot to me, pray Cot," cried Winifred, rushing into the room in tears, followed by the mild, the peaceable Meredith in an actual passion!

"What is the matter?" cried all, but Lord Claverton, who was still in his reverie.

"Lort help me," sobbed Winifred, "I gave it to Mr. Joseph; I tell you if you cill me I can say no more."

"And was not you ordered to get it from him?" replied Meredith.

"Why he – he lent it to a young laty of his acquaintance, and she – she lent it to a person of her acquaintance, as lives at the sign of the three cowlden balls, and he is con to see for it."

"Ah, thou wretch! ungrateful! perfidious!" said Meredith, stamping with anger.

"What is the matter?" said Ellen, "what has she done?"

Down dropped Winifred on her knees, "pray tear reverent have mercy on your poor old sarvant, ton't tell my Laty, I am sure I should not hurt a hair of her heat, nor Mr. Evelyn's, for all he is so cross to me, put it's all about Lord Claverton, because I said as how a Laty, that is a Laty, ort to marry a Lort, and not a poor poy that nopody owns, and so –"

Lord Claverton now slightly attended.

"And so now he picks a quarrel, apout a foolish locket, as Mr. Joseph, poor tear, says it is not worth a kinney, and offered to pay it hover and hover."

"This creature will make me mad; I tell you it is of the last importance," and Meredith really looked terrible.

"Oh Lort of his cootness safe me, pray Cot," cried Winifred, sideling up to Ellen, "certainly Satan as put his cloven foot on our reverent."

Ellen could not comprehend it, Gordon could, and therefore told Winifred he would go with her to Joseph, for the locket must be found.

Winifred hoped Mister Cordon would call a coach, for no chenteele people falked.

"'Twas a very fine morning," Mrs. Gordon said.

"Yes, Mistress Cordon, it may to fery well for a couple of the kennel, for as Mr. Joseph says –"

Mr. Meredith's *be gone* put what Mr. Joseph said, out of her head, and she left the room with Gordon.

Meredith apologized to Lord Claverton and the Countess, by a brief relation of his Eleve's history, with which the reader is already acquainted, and informed them that Morgan awakened to the feelings of nature, was anxious to leave all *his* fortune to Evelyn. "As the world had done me so much credit," he added, "as to give the young man to *me,* I wish to prove how little I am entitled to the honour, as I really esteem it, of being father to Percival Evelyn; I have found his honest nurse and her husband, – but they have forgot my face as well as his, and as I did not give them my name, they can only identify him by the locket this creature gave to her Mr. Joseph!"

Ellen's infant years had passed in the exchange of kindness with Evelyn, without thinking of inquiring about his parents; as love began to usurp his sway in her young heart, Evelyn's *self* still more engrossed her; but since her acquaintance with the world; and since she had by accident heard the report of the country, her own observation on her uncle's extreme fondness, and Evelyn's implicit duty, had partially confirmed these reports, and it was perhaps no small advantage to him, in her opinion, who had *some* of her family pride, that he was *their* relation.

The history related by Mr. Meredith opened a new source of ideas, – Evelyn would be the rich heir of one of the most wealthy private men in Britain; but this acquisition, far from rendering him more worthy to succeed her late Lord, fixed a stigma on his birth, that all her love for him could not reconcile.

Lord Claverton seemed to hear, and not to hear Evelyn's story; he was attentive for one minute, and absent five.

When Meredith concluded, Ellen became as absent as Lord Claverton, and a message from Morgan who could not bear to be a moment alone, by taking away her uncle, left a dumb trio, who seemed little disposed to be entertained, and less to entertain.

Lady Mappleton and Caroline Holt dropped in, in high spirits and good humour; Lord Squandervelt had aired by their carriage, and excited the attention of the whole ring; they were pleased, and so was Ellen.

Gordon returned with Winifred, without the locket of which Joseph had gone in search.

Mr. Evelyn called to take leave, said he was going to Code Gwyn immediately, he had been indisposed, and had not seen any of his friends that morning.

"My God! sir," said Lady Mappleton having been told by Ellen his relation to Morgan, "would you leave your grandfather in the moment he is making you his heir?"

Evelyn started.

Ellen smiled, and told him she would now be as happy a harbinger to him, as he last night was to her; tho' without the pleasure of having, like him, been an instrument in bringing about the good fortune.

Gordon said he would save her some repetitions, and gave him Meredith's papers, which, when he had read, left only to be told that Morgan's heart was touched, and that he was probably at that moment making a will in his favour.

"And this," said Evelyn, with a melancholy and reproachful look to Ellen, "is your good news; I am found to be the spurious issue of a man who is hateful to *you* and all *yours,* I am not only disgraced in my existence but in the source of it. Ah, Madam, fate had done its worst before."

From the moment Evelyn entered, Lord Claverton had been attentive; he saw the despondency of his look, and considered the discovery just made exactly as he did, rather a misfortune than an acquisition, for Morgan's character was as odious as public; and his Lordship's dislike of Evelyn, having vanished, with his hope of obtaining Ellen, the exact contrary tendency led him to desire to see two people who seemed born for each other, united; he took hold of Evelyn's arm, and drew him to the window, where in the middle of a very friendly harangue, Evelyn earnestly and seriously looking him in the face, Lord Claverton stopped and clapped his hand to his forehead.

Mrs. Gordon, who stood at a little distance, came hastily to them, and laying her hand on Lord Claverton's arm, looked at him and at Evelyn; my Lord turned hastily to the window, and Mrs. Gordon to her seat.

Lady Mappleton, Ellen and Caroline formed a little group, half angry and half laughing at Winifred's distress, who stood crying behind her Mistress's chair; when a servant entered with Joseph's humble duty to his lord, and begged to speak with him.

"This locket I see is not to be found," said Gordon, "Joseph wants Lord Claverton's interference in his favour."

Lord Claverton a little ashamed of a manoeuvre of his servant's, which he was conscious had his sanction, was rather embarrassed; he did not choose however to appear as a party in so vexatious a business in its present state, much less did he wish any thing should transpire, that could lead to his concern in it originally.

The servant waiting for an answer, Ellen begged Lord Claverton would have Joseph in "that we may hear," continued she, "the history of this famous locket," and his Lordship still hesitating, Joseph entered, followed by an elderly woman.

Winifred was in her way, no less ashamed of the part she had acted, than his Lordship, and fearful of the consequences not only to herself, but poor tear Mr. Joseph, as she had received the locket of Mr. Evelyn under solemn promise of persuading Ellen to wear it for his sake, but had been coaxed out of it by Joseph, who told her it would be much more to *her* interest, and *his,* if her mistress never thought of Evelyn or his locket; she set up a loud lamentation as soon as she saw him.

"My Lord," stammered Joseph, "the locket I received from – Mrs. Winifred gave –"

"I cive," interrupted Winifred in a fright.

"That I – I took."

"Took! what, did you steal it?" said Gordon.

"Steal! Mister Cordon; I dare say Mr. Joseph scorns your words," answered Winifred, spitefully.

"Well, well," said Lord Claverton impatiently "whether it was given to you, or you took it is not the present question, all you have to do is to produce it."

"My Lord, I beg leave to differ with you," joined Evelyn, "the locket was mine, I gave it that woman in special confidence to –"

"To give," interrupted Lord Claverton, with affected ease, " to the woman you loved, and she gave it to the man *she* loved, let us get to the point, is it forth coming?"

"My Lord!" stammered Joseph again, "I – I happened to give, to desire a young woman of my acquaintance to – to keep the locket for me, and she being a little distressed, borrowed a little money on it of this gentlewoman, who refuses to deliver it to any body but your Lordship."

"Me!" answered Lord Claverton, still sore with former remembrances, "what can I have to do with it?"

The elderly woman advanced and courtesying, produced a bundle of papers, out of which she took the locket, and said, if that was Lord Claverton she had some private business with him.

Gordon however willing to get possession, begged to look at it in the mean time.

The woman, with some reluctance gave it into his hands, and followed Lord Claverton, who did not motion to leave the room, to the further end of it.

"Winifred," said Lady Mappleton, "it is well for you the lost sheep is found, you and your lover would have certainly finished your amour in a prison."

"Then I am sure, my Laty, our reverent must have gone to Satan with the plessing of Cot, for his ardartness and Christian cruelty, for why, Cot pe coot unto us, if a thing is lost it is lost; sarvant can put pay, Cot is apove the tivel still, and as to the ugly locket –"

"Pray let me see it, such as it is," cried Ellen.

"Mister Cordon, let my Laty see the tivilish locket."

As Gordon was leisurely handing it across to Ellen, his wife snatched it out of his hand.

"Fery well inteed, Mistress Cordon," cried Winifred, "that is your manners now I warrand; fell, fell, ashes to ashes, and tirt to tirt, say I, I suppose you have cot your auld stories and pribbles and prabbles and jealousies, but I tell you fat."

A loud shriek from Mrs. Gordon stopped Winifred, and alarmed the company, "my Lord! Lord Claverton!" said she in a voice that echoed through the house.

Lord Claverton, to whom the stranger was just beginning to open her business, was interrupted by this loud call on his name, and advancing towards Mrs. Gordon, saw the locket in her hand, held at arms length, which she had opened at the back, and displayed his own picture to his view, such as it was 24 years before.

Lord Claverton staggered back, his sight failed him and he fell almost fainting into the arms of Evelyn, who fortunately stood near enough to receive him.

"And was this locket yours, sir?" said Mrs. Gordon, exceedingly agitated, "was it your mother from whom you received it? Oh my dear friend! my sweet Betsey Martin! What have you done with her, my Lord? What have you done with your wife?"

"His wife!" cried Lady Mappleton.

Ellen had heard from Gordon of Lord Claverton's early marriage, and concluded it had been dissolved by death; had she found herself inclined to listen to his offers, it is probable mere conjecture would not have satisfied her; but totally indifferent, whether there existed a being who had or had not a legal, or other claim on him, were matters that never occupied a single thought of hers.

"Yes," continued Mrs. Gordon, crying violently, "you know my Lord she was your wedded lawful wife, and Gordon knows it too, as much and as legally as I am his."

"With us small folks," answered Gordon, "marriage is a thing, so little liable to be forgotten, that I have been astonished, and so I told the Countess, how it could slip his Lordship's memory, which it must certainly have done or he would have recollected me."

"Not perhaps," replied Ellen, smiling, "as you had cut off your red hair, wore a brown wig and had the small pox."

"Hoot, that's perfectly nonsense," answered Gordon, "compared to the change from a fine handsome Captain in the guards, to a sickly Viscount, and yet you see I knew him directly."

Lord Claverton recovering, looked earnestly at Evelyn, "I dare not trust myself with my own ideas, are you sure, sir, that locket was your mother's?"

"Ah! no, my Lord," answered Evelyn, humbled by a question which recurred to his degrading original, "*my* mother was *not* a *wife,* nor was her name Martin, this must be some mistake."

"True," replied Lord Claverton, "I did not think of that, but, however it came into your hands, this locket certainly did belong to a young woman to whom I was married before I first left England, and whom I heard from an old servant, Joe's father, died, with her infant in child-bed, – the fellow could have no interest in deceiving me, yet from a circumstance that struck me, and I saw it had the same effect on my old acquaintance Mrs. Gordon –"

"Oh!" interrupted Mrs. Gordon, "he looked exactly like her as he was speaking to you at the window; but is she indeed dead my Lord? were you not ashamed of your first choice, when you became a Lord, and so have hid her some where? for God's sake tell me."

"I can tell you no more than I have already done; I received certain intelligence from the servant who used to carry my letters to her, she was dead; the fellow's son is now my servant, and he himself would have attended me to the West Indies, had he not met with a widow woman who –"

"I, my Lord," said the elderly woman, "am that widow, – I was imprudent enough to love Jack Wilks so well, as to buy his discharge, – and ruin myself and a family of children by doing so. I saw your lady safely delivered of a son, and put him myself to a nurse in my neighbourhood; the poor young creature was in a deep decline, she told me her heart was broken."

"Oh! my Lord," said the Countess in a reproachful accent.

"She was the sweetest girl," joined Mrs. Gordon.

"Poor Betsy," said Lord Claverton, in a very low voice.

Lady Mappleton begged the stranger would proceed.

Evelyn, who found he had a heart too big for his bosom, too proud for his birth, and too accessible to sympathy for his peace, by degrees reached the Countess, and resting his forehead on his hand, at the back of her chair, gave way to emotions for which he could not immediately account, and which he found it impossible to restrain.

"Yes," continued the stranger, "the last words she spoke to me were, "my heart is broke;" my own was at that time little better, my husband was spending my substance on bad women, and profligate companions, God help me! I did not know which way to turn; my creditors were pressing, Jack minded nothing, I dreaded every day he would be arrested, Madam grew worse and worse, the Doctors advised her to change the air; a pretty girl, a niece of my own attended her, and my husband, under pretence of escaping the bailiffs and that his Captain would expect to hear from him about his Lady, went with her to Highgate."

"To Highgate!" said Ellen, her soul in her eyes, "to Highgate, did you say?"

"Pray proceed," said Lord Claverton, not attending to Ellen's eager question.

"There," continued the woman, "the Lady died; and there my faithless husband, and abandoned niece, robbed her of every article of value they could carry off. I was so fearful of his being arrested, that I did not dare to send any body to enquire after him when he missed coming home, as usual on the Sunday, but as I could not be easy I walked there, and knowing the poor Lady had many valuables with her, concluded, after such a wicked robbery, I should hear no more of him."

"Oh! the cootness of cootness, fat a son of darkness, and witchcraft, and fornication, and idolatry fas poor tear Mr. Joseph's father. Oh! if I had sarved my poor tear Laty so, and her sweet tear papy, I could not sleep in my ped for fear of Satan; Lort preserve his poor sarvants and forgive their iniquities, amen, amen, pray Cot."

This half reproach, and half prayer of Winifred's, was too much for Joseph's modesty, – he moved in a retrograde motion towards the door.

"Wait, sir," said Lord Claverton.

The stranger went on.

"I returned home heavy enough, God knows; I had five children, and had reason to be sure, the instant it was known my husband was gone, my goods would be seized, so I thought I would keep my poor little ones a bed to lye on, out of what their honest father worked for, and by help of my friends moved away in the night."

"What became of my child?" asked Lord Claverton, "and how came this trinket to escape the vile plunderers?"

"My Lord, the child, the finest little fellow, methinks I see him now" – by accident the woman's eyes were fixed opposite where Evelyn sat, and near where Winifred stood.

"Cot of his cootness and marcy forbid," cried the latter, giving a spring to a distance, "because to be sure it must be a cost or an apparition, for there's nothing there put Mr. Percival Evelyn, crying like a papy, and to be sure poor tear, he has cause, for if he is ever so rich, he can be nothing put a pastard, as Mr. Joseph says."

"Leave the room," said the Countess, her face and neck in a glow.

"Tear my Laty, let me hear the old gentlewoman's story, I am sure –"

"This instant go," and Ellen's fine form shook with anger.

Evelyn arose in a sudden start of resentment, but his mind was in a state of mortification; why should I be angry thought he at a truth, which if not spoke *to* will be sure to be spoke *of* me.

Winifred had neither sense, or delicacy, enough to be conscious of any fault, in what she had said, and protested, when she got out of the room, that witch Mistress Cordon, was always making mischief.

Lord Claverton rose himself, and flung the door after Winifred, "you were speaking of my child," said he.

"I can only say, my Lord – he was a lovely boy, but as to the locket –"

"Ay now," said Lady Mappleton, eagerly.

Ellen *did not*, *could not* speak, but she looked.

"I knew it, the minute I saw it," said Mrs. Gordon, "I remember your giving it Mrs. Claverton, dear creature! she always wore it round her neck; Mr. Gordon, you – bless me, where is Mr. Gordon?" he had slipped out unobserved.

"My husband, my Lord," continued the stranger.

"Prithee woman," interrupted Lord Claverton, "no more of thy husband, the villain wrote me word, my wife and child were dead, doubtless fearing he should be detected; but if he is above ground –"

"That my Lord," resumed the woman, "he is not; I have little more to say, but it is all about him. My first husband's brother was a pawnbroker; a year after Jack Wilks left me he pitied the children, and took us all to his house, and when he died, left the business to my son and me; soon after his death Wilks came like a beggar, in a dying state to my door; poor fellow! he was very handsome when I bought him out of the guards, and I could not help pitying him. I took him in, but my son was angry, so I thought as I had plenty, thank God, to live on, and my children provided for, I'd e'en give up the trade and take poor Jack into the country; my son agreed to pay my share of the property, and as we were taking stock, my husband, who was then very ill, poor man! sitting by, saw this locket, which had been pledged by a girl of the town, a year before; he took it up and opened the back by a spring we had not seen, and there was your Lordship's picture. Poor Jack fainted away, and never held up his head after – I wanted him to ease his conscience, and confess all his sins."

"Oh! God!" cried Lord Claverton, "he certainly destroyed my child." The ladies shuddered, Mrs. Gordon wept; the woman continued,

"But he would not, he said, for he knew he should be hanged; all he begged with his dying breath, was, that whoever came for the locket might be stopped, and obliged to account to you, how it was come by, and he desired if it was not redeemed within the time I would carry it to your Lordship, with these papers, which he had found among the poor lady's cloaths."

Lord Claverton trembled so violently, he tore the first letter in two; it was a letter of his own, on the corner of which, and on a few more of the same signature, she had left the impression of a death's head in black wax.

"Oh!" sighed he, "more eloquent than speech."

These and some letters from Mrs. Gordon made the first parcel, except two papers which had dropped from the rest; one was a letter begun to Captain Claverton, near the time of her labour; the other also begun to Mrs. Gordon, a few days before her death; these half finished posthumous addresses, were too affecting to be audibly read – that to the husband struck a dagger to his heart – that to the friend, left a remembrance of the writer sweetly painful. Lord Claverton handed his to Lady Mappleton, over whose shoulder both Ellen and Evelyn read it, while he gave way to a gush of sorrow and self reproach.

THE LETTER

"I address you, my once loved Claverton, perhaps for the last time; my miseries are drawing to a close. My child, the legal offspring of wedded love, deserted by an unfeeling father, may have nothing of parental relics, when it sees the light, but a breathless mother – Oh! Claverton, let me speak to your soul.

If my infant lives, it is, from its birth, heir to great wealth – alas! and so is its unhappy mother, yet she is now wretched, deserted, and poor. If I could have born the journey, my intent was to go to Gordon's, who are the only witnesses, besides Jack, that I am not the victim of shame as well as folly, but I could not; and, abandoned by you, it would have been equally difficult for me to prove my marriage, or reconcile my papa to it; his severity is dreadful, I could not bear it – your man pretends he is ignorant of your station, and I am really so; how to end – say?"

The ladies wept.

"Amiable unfortunate," said Evelyn.

Mrs Gordon would read her fragment herself, and Lord Claverton, as well as the rest, drew near her as her voice was rendered nearly inarticulate by her feelings – almost blinded with tears, she read,

"The longings of my soul have been to find a home with my dear Nancy and her Billy but it will not be.

Oh! Nancy, 'tis but a span since we lived together in peace and amity, health and innocence spread a bloom in our countenance, but 'the cruel spoiler came!' Were you to see me *now*! –

A good man talked to me of love, alas! he little thought the worm of corruption had already began to gnaw my vitals, and that the form he admired was fading into dust!

I have wrote to you, my Nancy, but you have not received my letters, if you had, your poor Betsy's eyes would not be closed by strangers, they shut in darkness, but will open in everlasting light.

I hope I shall have strength to finish this letter.

I have a son, Nancy, your Willy must take him if my papa

will not; I am not *sure*, but believe, from the hour of my death, he has a certain fortune – if his fath –"

"Barbarous father!" exclaimed Lord Claverton, "I see, ladies, your indignation; I ought, indeed to be an outcast, but this I beg to say; culpable, cruel as I was, in the first instance, in leaving my wife, she *was* my *lawful wife*, had not that villain imposed on me, I should have enquired strictly after her and the child; and what, perhaps, may a little extenuate my conduct, I did not, upon my honour, know she was pregnant when I left her. I was very wild and dissipated, and got into some scrapes, which, if my relations had not assisted me to avoid, I should have found very troublesome, I knew if I told her I was going abroad, she would wish to accompany me; it was a wild boyish attachment, and not proof against the inconvenience to which she, who had nothing but her watch, and a few jewels, would expose me; and the governess, afraid, I believe of her own character, assured me I had nothing to hope from her father, who was a city miser. I had no intention to deny or evade the marriage, but when I heard it was dissolved by death, I thought it could answer no purpose to make it public. I did not recollect Gordon, notwithstanding his name, but I knew Nancy the moment I saw her, and should have taken an opportunity to renew my acquaintance, though not, perhaps, in the presence of *all* this company."

Lady Mappleton acknowledged, though the story was in many parts a pitiable one, yet, that Lord Claverton, considering his youth at the time, was not so very blameable, as, she confessed, she at first thought him. That with respect to the locket, as it appeared to her to be most probable the child actually did die, as well as the mother, though to conceal his theft, the man had mis-stated the time; it might have been sold, and so come into the possession of Miss Morgan.

Evelyn's eyes were involuntarily averted at hearing his mother called Miss. A small parcel of papers had dropped at Lord Claverton's feet, which Evelyn saw, and from a natural impulse of politeness stooped for it.

On presenting it to Lord Claverton, he saw the hand writing – he started – all his blood rushed into his face; again and again he looked at the writing, at Lord Claverton, at Ellen.

"What have you got there?" said the tremulous voice of one, whose attention was riveted to every motion of Percival Evelyn.

"Good God! what is this?" said he to the woman, "did *you* bring those papers?"

She answered in the affirmative.

"And did your husband get them from Lord Claverton's wife?"

"From *Captain* Claverton's wife, so he said on his death bed."

"What is it, Percival? Why do you tremble so? How nervous you are!" said Ellen, in a soothing accent.

"Tremble indeed," replied he, "if ever I saw Mr. Meredith's hand, it is in the address of those letters to Miss Elizabeth Morgan."

"How! What is that?" cried Lord Claverton.

The fact was exactly so. There were several letters and pieces of poetry, from the pen of Mr. Meredith; and in that moment the writer and Gordon entered.

Many artists have exercised their genius, and exerted their skill, to paint a good man in the hour of tribulation, of danger, and of death; but the triumph of art would be to trace from the countenance of Mr. Meredith the fervent gratitude of devout Christian – the gratified zeal of sincere friendship – the corrected joy of parental solicitude – and the modest triumph of benevolence – that so we might see portrayed the countenance of a good man in the hour of prosperity.

"Lord Claverton," said the good divine, "you have heard of your wife's death, 'of the early blast that destroyed the loveliest flower of modest nature!' and I will not doubt your regret; but are you disposed, my Lord, to receive her child? To *pay* him the debt of gratitude, and of tenderness, due to his beatified mother?"

"Oh! Mr. Meredith, can you, can you doubt it? Tell me where he is, my only child is an orphan, while his father's riches accumulate, while –"

"No, my Lord," interrupted Meredith, tears stealing down his cheeks, "he has not been an orphan, he had a friend who felt that dearer affection for him than riches can purchase, or power command; son of my care and of my love, dearest Percival, once more let me embrace thee, before the name I gave thee, when denied to *share* the smallest part of that immense wealth that may in a few hours be wholly thine, be resigned; before you, my Lord, bestow your blessing – which if not bestowed in thankful rapture, you will not deserve to bless my mental son, Percival Evelyn, your Horatio Claverton.

"Oh! that was his name, sure enough," cried the woman. "Please your Lordship I was his godmother, and now I look at him, I remember his eyes to this hour. Oh! he was a fine creature!"

The embrace of Mr. Meredith and his eleve left the former unable to speak, and Lord Claverton's surprise was only exceeded by his pleasure. Evelyn gracefully bent his knee, and the honest woman who nursed him was introduced, she immediately knew Mrs. Wilks, who also recognised her, and the change of name, from Martin to Morgan, like all other mysteries, when explained, became no mystery at all. Every body wondered they could be so stupid as not to find it out, except Gordon, who declared he had found it out the instant the old Lady mentioned Highgate air; nay, he found it in his feelings the first hour he saw Evelyn.

Lady Mappleton thought of Ellen's promise, not to marry the *curate*, and Caroline kissed her hand, as cold, and her cheek as pale, as if the grizzle glutton had already seized on the most charming morsel in creation; but they were suddenly animated with the deepest glow, when Lord Claverton begged to introduce to her *his son, Horatio Claverton*. Evelyn again knelt, he took the hand at liberty, pressed it to his lips, to his heart, "*Now, my own Ellen*," said he, "*now —*"

Ellen, though silent, certainly understood, and, understanding, did not disapprove the expressive *now*.

Mr. Meredith showed a will just executed by Morgan, making Horatio heir to all his fortune; he lamented, he added, it was not in his power to leave you the Morgan estate, but we shall rejoice him when we present to him his father-in-law's legitimate heir.

As Morgan was now to be grandfather to a Viscount, it was proper every body should be sorry for his accident, and anxious about his recovery, which was at present very doubtful.

"As Cot shall safe me," cried Winifred, entering to her Lady, who, it was not possible for her to suppose was angry, as she had herself already quite forgot both that and the cause, "I believe all the world is con mad, and to be sure every poty reposes on poor me, Cot help me; if I had a man to stand py me and manage my bisness, and, Cot knows that is pad enough, for men are satan's walking sticks, Mr. Joseph for that, civing my cifts to a pad young woman."

"What's the matter now, Mrs. Winifred?" asked Caroline.

"Why, the matter, Miss," answered Winifred, "is pad enough, Cot knows, for here hat I lent my new plack spotted scarf, cut out by Mademoiselle, to Mrs. Gibson, Lady Margaret's woman; and here's the owld deceitful cheating Lady Margaret, as owes me two shillings and eight-pence, as she stopped for postage of my aunt Griffiths's letters, is con away with that poor shabby Doctor, as never cived a sarvant a fever at his wedding, who – but they are cone to Scotland, and taken Mrs. Gibson and my new scarf with them."

"I am very glad they are gone," said Ellen.

Lady Mappleton thought it was as well.

Mrs. Gordon was glad too they were away, but she wondered they would go to Scotland! for she was perfectly sure, such people would not be noticed there.

"Hoot," Gordon was sure their money would make them noticed any where.

"Yes," and Winifred dared to say Mrs. Gibson would show away in her black spotted scarf.

Lord Claverton looked at his watch, he observed it had been a long happy morning.

"Yes", replied Lady Mappleton, "and we will make it a long day, you must all dine with me and tomorrow –"

Evelyn looked tenderly at Ellen: "Tomorrow, what shall we do tomorrow?"

"You shall make it as happy as today," replied Lord Claverton, "happier," politely bowing to the ladies, "it cannot be," and taking his son's arm, "Come, my *son*," emphatically, "you must order your things *home* to dress," and his Lordship, who was an elegant figure himself, *looked* like the elder brother, but *felt* like the father of the more elegant Evelyn.

We will not pay our readers' judgment or their sentiment so ill a compliment as to suppose we need say, what congratulations passed in a family so endeared to each other as the Merediths. Or that Ellen took care to make Lady Gertrude a sharer in her happiness, as far as regarded the recovery of her fortune; more would at that period have been indelicate. Neither can we enter into a particular account of Evelyn's passionate entreaties to Ellen, to bless him with her hand, nor her evasions and delays, because no such thing happened on either side; they mutually agreed that while Ellen wore her first mourning and Morgan's life was in danger, a marriage festival would be improper, but as soon as these impediments were removed, the news papers announced the marriage of the Honourable and Reverend Horatio Claverton, son and heir to Lord Viscount Claverton, and to the immense fortune of the late Walter and present John Morgan, Esqrs. to the beautiful Countess Dowager of Castle Howel; and that, after the ceremony, the young couple set out, with a grand retinue, on a visit to Lady Gertrude Howel, at Natly Abbey. Lord Squandervelt, enraged at the triumph of Lord Claverton and the Curate of Little Manor, and resolved to avoid the good things his witty friends would sport on the occasion, led Caroline Holt to the altar, on the same day, and set out also with a grand retinue for Dash Castle, where he lived with the amiable Marchioness, on the happy terms men of his high notions generally do live with their wives; that is to say, he was the obsequious admirer of every other woman, was the life of every company abroad, died with ennui at home, kept a mistress, and despised the Marchioness.

In the mean time, the Howels of Moor Bank no sooner heard Lady Castle Howel was independent, and able to support her son's right, than they dropped the law suit.

Little Jane lives with Lady Gertrude; where Captain Meredith is also resident; and the young Lord is left in his native air, on which, as her pride and hope was wrapped up in him, Lady Gertrude laid the utmost stress, to induce his mother to let him remain with her, at least for some time, which the Countess consented to, on condition that Gordon became residentiary governor and Doctor. Sir James Sibley and his bride came to England to receive her fortune and visit her relations; to whom, as no part of them wanted Lady Frances's assistance, he was very obsequious.

The Merediths stayed at the Rectory till Code Gwyn had undergone a complete repair, when Horatio and Ellen attended the house-warming, and the whole parish, rich as well as poor, commemorated the return of Sir Arthur and his family to the place of their nativity.

Miss Catherine and Mr. Meredith are still spinster and bachelor, and live with their aged parent; Miss Agnes married a banker of Chester, and Miss Mary gave her hand to Mr. Serjeant Pennings, who, happening to see her at an assize ball with his client, and thinking the Claverton interest worth cultivating, fell in love.

The Lieutenant is a post Captain, but neither is or ever will be a rich man, except in a match, which is likely to take place, he should adopt the policy of Sir James Sibley, in the management of his fortune, which, as well as Lady Frances's, will centre in little Jane.

Mrs. Griffiths is deaf and lame, but still housekeeper, as her brother, with almost total deprivation of sight, is butler at

Code Gwyn: David has an annuity for his past and present care of the little garden.

Mrs. Dean Holt, after being married fifteen years without children, has lately blessed her good spouse with a son and heir; and as Dr. Ferguson was the accoucheur, he no longer talks of the adventure at Little Manor.

Winifred Griffiths on finding Mr. Evelyn would be a Lord, felt her old friendship for him revive to that ardent degree, that she actually, as *she said*, refused a very good settlement from Lord Claverton, with Mr. Joseph, merely because he had prevented her giving her mistress Mr. Evelyn's locket, tho' the truth was, that Winifred could never reconcile the giving the said locket to the pad young woman; and as Joseph, notwithstanding his Lord had no further employment for his talents in intrigue, was so used to attend him, and pay court even to his aches and pains, well knew, if he continued in his place till my Lord died, he should have an annuity, besides the usual perquisites to a valet on the death of a rich and great man, he was at no uncommon pains to remove her jealousy; they, however, still continue to flirt and quarrel by turns, and when each are rich enough to ape their betters, may at last possibly agree to wrangle out the evening of their lives together.

Philip preferred continuing gentleman out of livery to the Countess, to a good place in the customs, offered by Lord Claverton.

In short, as in duty bound, the author leaves all parties who have preferred her favourites, rich, happy and respectable.

Lady Margaret and her caro sposa she has banished *to*, and not *from* Scotland, where the Doctor unfortunately for himself, happening to speak rather free, though true, of the great man we have before mentioned as the rushlight of the next age; the said great man, in the depth of his wisdom, discovered the Doctor had carried a ring fence he was making round a new purchased estate, full the fortieth part of an inch beyond his absolute right; which encroachment as the great man could not in his zeal for justice pass it over, being carried into a court of law, where the accuser was judge, or, what is better, *made judges*, it became more than adequate for all the sins even Lady Margaret could commit.

To the courts of law then we leave the Doctor, and her Ladyship, where all strict justice would perhaps impel us to carry John Morgan, Esq. and his one arm; but, with respect both to him and Lord Claverton, the author violates all rule of novel writing, for the Viscount, though in very ill health is still alive; and Morgan, returned to the corner of his own mansion, intent only on repairing the injury he did a grandson, who is the pride of his age, by the only means, that, according to the tenets of the creed in which he had lived, and in which he will probably die, all injuries are to be repaired, namely money; and is at this time denying himself the common necessaries of life, in order to make his rich heir still richer.

Horatio and Ellen are ornaments of the age, so sensible, affluent, liberal, and handsome; the polite world is astonished it could neglect the one or defame the other. Ellen's parties are as brilliant and as numerous, though not exactly in the former set; her taste, her dress, as much the rage as ever. Mrs. Morley and her sort, think their time and attention vastly well bestowed, if, after watching her eyes half an hour at any public place, they obtain a nod or a courtesy – she speaks not but to be approved, nor is seen but to be admired; her virtue is the theme of conversation, and as to faults, it is impossible a woman so rich and beautiful should have any.

Horatio perseveres in the sacred function to which he was educated, he already wears lawn sleeves, and preaches before the strangest character ever heard of, A good wife, a tender mother, a sincere friend, a queen, and a Christian! indeed it is astonishing with what rapidity Horatio Claverton, who wants nothing, attains every thing.

Sensible men admire, dissipated ones respect, and those of his diocese and all his particular friends love him.

The few readers who have had patience to accompany the author thus far, will be apt to exclaim, "Aye! those are the monsters we meet at the end of all LANE's collections, men without error! and women without faults!"

LADIES AND GENTLEMEN,

The truth is, notwithstanding all that has been said to the contrary, the Honourable and Right Reverend Bishop Claverton and the Countess of Castle Howel are quite as subject to the common frailties of human nature as the reader, or even the writer of this delightful history, but as they are among the most noble, the most affluent and most admired pairs, in the most flourishing kingdom of the most enlightened world, it would be very rude to pry into secrets at parting we have hitherto so carefully avoided, particularly such secrets as never have, nor ever will be exposed, when concealed, as in the present instance, by the impenetrable veil of

IMMENSE RICHES.

FINIS

ABOUT HONNO

Honno Welsh Women's Press was set up in 1986 by a group of women who felt strongly that women in Wales needed wider opportunities to see their writing in print and to become involved in the publishing process. Our aim is to develop the writing talents of women in Wales, give them new and exciting opportunities to see their work published and often to give them their first 'break' as a writer.

Honno is registered as a community co-operative. Any profit that Honno makes is invested in the publishing programme. Women from Wales and around the world have expressed their support for Honno. Each supporter has a vote at the Annual General Meeting. For more information and to buy our publications, please visit our website www.honno.co.uk or email us on post@honno.co.uk.

Honno
D41, Hugh Owen Building,
Aberystwyth University,
Aberystwyth,
Ceredigion,
SY23 3DY.

We are very grateful for the support of all
our Honno Friends.